Praise for Melinda Viergever Inman
and *Refuge*

"Dear reader, do you want to expand your world view and color outside the lines boldly, where it is safe to do so within the comfort of an intriguing fictional story? Venture into the dark side that begs for redemption, and Find it? You decide! Jump in and explore, you won't be disappointed!"

—Susan Lloyd, Goodreads reviewer and Biblical counselor

"This is a very powerful book showing the power of sin to destroy a perfect world and tear apart a family; Cain's physical power over his brother and Satan's intense anger and hatred for humankind. As a reader, seeing the brokenness of Adam and then his son, Cain, over their own personal sins really hit home when I think about how blasé I sometimes am about my own attitude toward God. The discussion questions are not to be overlooked, either."

—Kristin Beck, Goodreads Compulsive Reader, Literature Major

"I read this as I was editing the first pass. I could NOT put it down to go to bed, preferring to lose the sleep! I just had to see what happened next! I love the way it is so compelling that the reader hardly realizes the positive spiritual impact the book is having! Thanks, Melinda, for following the dream God put in your heart to write!"

—Jacqueline Garrett (Freelance Editor) on Goodreads:

"*Refuge* is a very powerful novel with themes that can't help but hit home with all of us. Not only is this a story of sin and the ramification of our actions, it is also a love story. We see how Cain's act affected not only himself, but also the people he loved most.

Throughout the story, I found myself questioning several things I had never really thought about before. A story like this that can keep my attention is difficult to find. I hope others get as much from the story as I did. A job well done, Melinda."

—Jessica Higgins, writer

"Refuge is not only historically enlightening but a fascinating and poignant depiction of human nature. Real struggles with guilt, lust, anger, frustration, jealousy and insecurity are depicted with honest, raw and truly captivating candor. The characters are diverse, the setting is engrossing; the story feels very real.

The author includes some fantastic information and questions in the back of the book demonstrating the impressive breadth of her historical research: ranging from nomadic mythology to the ancient Israelite church. Cover to cover, a great read."

—Erin Chesney Holcomb, Classical Literature Instructor

"Refuge captured my attention at the onset. Within the first few pages, I was hooked. Totally recommend this book! Even though the setting is unfamiliar compared with today (immediately outside the Garden of Eden with Adam and Eve), Melinda's rich and engaging development of the setting and the characters drew me in. The people and the relationships are believable, and I could relate to them as though they were people I know now, faults and strengths. I think what was most evident to me throughout the entire story is how God so deeply loves each and every one of us no matter what we have done or where we are in our journey. He yearns for our fulfillment through Him as we were designed to be, and desires for us to receive His forgiveness and healing, to become who He created us to be. That message is strong. I also enjoyed the straight-up recognition of Satan as the leader of the fallen angels, prowling around like a roaring lion, seeking someone to devour (1 Peter 5:8). What the adversary can and cannot do is addressed in various situations, and the study guide helps readers understand and apply this important knowledge of spiritual warfare, a reality of life whether we like it or not. An appropriate ending for the time being, but the ending left me wanting more..."

—Kelli Flanagan, Editor

To my husband, Tim, whose passionate support
strengthens me in all of life's endeavors.
To my children, by birth and by marriage,
and to my grandchildren—
all of you shape, teach, and inspire me.

Jen & Luisa —
Thank you for all you've done to help me market this book! your design work, your eye for fashion, your oversight, your long hours! I am truly grateful!
Linda

Refuge

by Melinda Viergever Inman

Visit the website at
www.melindainman.com

ISBN 978-1-938467-88-2

Refuge is a work of fiction. The characters are both actual and fictitious. With the exception of verified historical events and persons, all incidents, descriptions, dialogue and opinions expressed are the products of the author's imagination and are not to be construed as real.

Published by

K köehlerbooks™

210 60th Street
Virginia Beach, VA 23451
212-574-7939
www.koehlerbooks.com

A Biblical Story of Good and Evil

REFUGE

A LILITH & CAIN NOVEL

Melinda Viergever Inman

VIRGINIA BEACH
CAPE CHARLES

CHAPTER 1

CAIN BROKE INTO A RUN when he left the circle of firelight, loping along the side of the river. The half-moon was just rising, so its light enabled him to avoid most obstacles, but occasionally a branch whipped across his face, giving him a strong slap. He needed that. He was angry at God.

Why couldn't he have a wife? Could only his father have one? Could only his parents marry? If this was the case, it didn't seem fair.

By the fire his father had told that story again, the one about God giving him their mother. Father always recounted a tale on the evening of the sixth day, a verbal chronicle of their time in Eden. Tonight he had related this account. Why this one?

Listening to the story, discontent had nearly crushed Cain. He longed for the type of love a man and a woman shared. Gazing into the eyes of his sister Lilith, sitting across the fire, he had realized he was dissatisfied with his life. He wanted a wife of his own. He didn't know how he'd ever get one though. Apparently, only his parents could marry.

He couldn't take it anymore. Frustrated and angry, Cain had jumped up from the bonfire, running off, surprising his parents and siblings. Now he lowered his head and ran harder. The situation discouraged him.

After he had covered a great distance, he slowed to catch his breath. The pounding of running feet sounded far behind him. When Cain had jumped up from the fireside and stormed off, Abel had been holding a pile of small sleeping siblings. Though Abel had glanced up quickly, kind concern on his face, he wouldn't rise and disturb the slumbering little ones. Cain realized Lilith must be the one chasing him.

Cain peered into the distance. The moonlight illuminated Lilith; she was running fast. He considered racing on ahead. He didn't want to talk to her. Frustrated with the state of his life, he couldn't articulate his feelings. But then he remembered her eyes by the firelight and waited for her instead.

Lilith fell. She must have tripped over something in the dark. Concerned, Cain took a step toward her. Her head reappeared.

"Cain," she called. "Wait! I'm sorry."

Sorry? Sorry for what? He waited.

She raced up to him, winded as she bent to rub her shin. "Will you forgive me?"

"What have you done?"

"I shouldn't have teased you about your beard."

That evening he had scraped the stubble from his face with one of his sharpened stone cutting tools, and Lilith had noticed, gesturing to him from across the fire.

"I wasn't mad at you," he said.

Noticing a trickle of dark blood running down Lilith's leg, Cain grasped her hand and led her toward the river. Silently, he bent to wash the wound. Caring for her and all his younger brothers and sisters was a habit. Kneeling on the earth, he bathed and inspected the injury as well as he could by the moonlight. Without speaking, Lilith watched his ministrations.

"Then what's wrong?" She broke the silence.

"I can't talk about it."

"Yes, you can. You tell me everything."

"I can't tell you about this."

"Why not?"

"It's too confusing," he said.

****

Waiting for Cain to say more, Lilith stood quietly. From long experience she had learned if she gave him time, he would unburden himself. Maybe that was why they got along so well—she knew when to be quiet. Getting him to divulge his heart required patience. He never liked to reveal his fears, worries, or insecurities. But he revealed them to her.

Motionless, she studied the top of his head, black in the moonlight. He finished tending her leg. He looked up at her but didn't rise. When he spoke, it was from his position on the ground. Barely above a whisper, his voice sounded unsteady.

"I want a wife."

It was as if he had punched her in the chest, the impact swift and sudden. *A wife!*

Lilith recalled the way their father gazed upon their mother and how their parents kissed. They murmured together in the night. If it was even possible for Cain to marry, she didn't want him to have a wife. But her heart clutched—longing and despair filled his whispered confession. Even in the dark, she detected it in his eyes. She hated to see him in pain.

Lilith couldn't speak. The thought of Cain marrying struck terror into her heart.

"I'm frustrated about it." He looked away. "I'm mad at God."

Answering softly, she found her voice. "Maybe God will give you a wife somehow."

Why had she said that? The words had simply burst out; she couldn't seem to help herself—she always encouraged him when he was downcast.

Quickly, he looked back at her. "What do you mean?"

"I don't know." She shrugged, swallowing hard. "Just maybe He intends to give you one."

A confusing mix of despair and hope flitted across Cain's features. He rose, peering into her eyes in the moonlight. For a long while, he studied her face. Then, gently, he caressed her cheek, his thumb lingering as it glided slowly across her skin.

Ever so slightly, he leaned toward her, his breath soft and warm upon her face.

Abruptly, he turned and ran off into the night, leaving her shaken.

She didn't follow him. Stunned, she stared after him before turning toward home. Far away she detected the faint glow from the fire's dying embers. Cain wanted a wife. If God gave him one, everything would change. The hopelessness of the situation hit her hard.

The intimacy would cease—the thrill of his sky-blue eyes, bright and animated when he spoke to her, such a contrast against his dusky skin and jet-black hair. This would end. No longer would he lean close, breathless with some secret to share, confiding in her alone. These would belong to another. Heartbroken, she stumbled back with her head down.

As if they'd been awaiting her return, her father and mother still sat by the burning coals in the clearing. They were alone, everyone else having gone to bed. Mutely, Lilith looked at them, anguish filling her heart; but she didn't want to speak. She couldn't tell them that she wanted Cain for herself, so she headed toward the chamber she shared with her sisters.

Silent and grief-stricken, Lilith stood in the doorway of her room, staring at her parents before entering the quiet dwelling where her sisters slept. She rolled back the woven reed matting from the roof so she could see the stars. She doubted she would sleep.

****

Adam and Eve watched the darkened doorway for a moment after Lilith had disappeared; then they looked at one another.

"I'm glad she came back," Eve said quietly.

"You didn't expect her to return?"

"I wasn't sure. Cain needs a wife."

"What does that have to do with Lilith? Do you think that's what's wrong?"

"Yes. He jumped up as you were recounting our first night together."

"Well, that could have been a coincidence."

"I was watching them both all evening. They kept looking at one another across the fire. Since Lilith was small, they've been able to communicate without even speaking. Their attachment has grown with every year and each decade. I think Cain should marry Lilith. I thought he might simply take her and leave."

"But how can they marry?" Adam turned to stare at her, his face contorted with consternation. "She's not part of his body; they're not one flesh. The Creator made you from my side. That's how I got my wife."

"They will be one flesh when they're united. Remember what it was like? We already knew we were both made from your flesh; but it truly felt like it after we lay together."

"That's worth considering." Adam turned his gaze away, his eyes once more on the embers. "But why would God change His ways with our children?"

"There were no women when He made me from your side. There are women now."

"Yes, but these women are their sisters."

"For our sons, these are the only women there are."

"But I've expected God to make them wives from their own bodies, as He made you from mine." Adam glanced at her. "The fact that the first ten were boys, one after another, seemed to verify this."

"But then the daughters came," she said. "What about them? How are they to get husbands if God doesn't have a different plan for them than He had for us? It won't be so for their children and for their children's children. But this is how it is for them."

"I'm not sure about this."

"Adam, God made their bodies to beget and bear children. At least twenty of them are physically ready to do so. God told us to be fruitful and to fill the earth, and He gave us male *and* female children. Maybe they're to marry each other, and we're all to multiply on the earth. It seems Cain and Lilith might be discovering this. I think it's time."

"I want to hear from Yahweh." Adam's shoulders stiffened.

"Cain may be tired of waiting."

"Do you think they've discussed this?"

"No, not yet." Eve fixed her eyes on him. "But they will. I've been watching them. I think they're realizing how special they've always been to one another."

"I don't know if it's right. I've been praying about this, but Yahweh remains silent. He doesn't act. Why can't things remain as they are?"

"How long did you wait for a wife, Adam?"

"One very long and lonely day." Smiling, he rose and extended his hand. Taking it, she returned his smile.

"Cain is just as mature as you were when the Creator made me," she said. "He can grow a full beard, if he would let it grow. His body looks like yours did then. Think about that."

"I will. Let's pray about it. Now come, lie with me."

****

Cain ran along the river until he reached the cherubim on the far side then he sat on the riverbank to rest. Watching them, he was always astounded by their size and brilliance.

They stood on the opposite bank of the Tigris within the Garden of Eden, guarding the way to The Tree of Life. Silent sentinels, they illuminated everything on the river's far side and cast a soft glow on this bank as well. Nearly three times his height, whenever they beat their broad wings the breeze stirred even on this side of the river. Sitting this close made Cain feel as if he were on the edge of danger—their flaming sword pointed straight at him.

Tonight they stood in a pose of readiness, as if preparing to charge into a fight. Their many eyes seemed to be fixed on something beside him. He turned and stared hard into the night-blackened shadows—nothing was there that he could see. Still, they remained poised in absolute stillness, as if waiting for the word to strike. He'd never seen them like this before. Settling onto the riverbank, he watched, wondering what they saw that he didn't. They remained motionless.

He wished he could ask the cherubim for advice, but their stern eyes made it clear this was not an option. He didn't know what to do. Lilith's words had confused him.

What had she meant? How could God give him a wife? Would He make a wife for him, as He had done for his father? If so, why was God taking so long?

The desire for a wife had been growing in Cain without his awareness. It was only as his father had told the story of holding his mother under the stars for the first time that Cain had realized how strong this desire had become. When combined with his father's words, staring at Lilith across the fire had awakened something that surprised him with its intensity.

"Maybe God will give you a wife," Lilith had said.

Cain didn't pray as much as Abel, but he aimed his silent prayer at Yahweh:

God, why are You doing this to me? I'm a full-grown man. I'm ready for a wife; I need one now! Lilith's words ...

At the thought of her name, Cain's mind wandered from his prayer and lingered on Lilith—the sound of her voice, the gray-hazel tint of her eyes, her honey curls hanging down to her hips, the shape of her body. He tore his mind away; he had battled this when he was a younger man. Several times, he and some of his brothers had sneaked out to the river to watch the girls bathe. Lust for Lilith had nearly consumed him then.

Was it right for him to think this way about his sister?

If they were going to multiply and fill the earth, would they all need to marry and reproduce? Or was his mother to bear all the earth's children? His father had named her "Eve"—the mother of all the living. After one hundred twenty years, she had borne fifty-five offspring. That was a large number of children, but at this rate it would take a long time to fill the earth and subdue it. Vast wilderness still surrounded them on all sides.

As he and all his siblings reached adulthood, their bodies

were clearly designed to beget and bear children too. What did this mean? What were they to do? Were they to marry? How were they to do so? Was there another way? What was it?

Lilith's eyes intruded into his thoughts. He thought about bathing her bleeding leg. He had carried her around since she was a baby. Physical contact was common between the two of them, but touching her leg while talking about wanting a wife had awakened something within him. He desired her. But it was more than simply desire for her body.

He reflected on her expression when he had said that he wanted a wife. Desperation had shown in her eyes; she had inhaled sharply. Why? Was she upset about the idea of him loving another woman, even if God made her for him? Perhaps, Cain considered.

Lilith was everything he thought a woman should be. She was artistic, and she sang beautifully, inventively weaving songs through the air. Intelligent and funny, brave and adventurous, she was always loyal to him. On his carefree adventures, she was usually right beside him, choosing to accompany him in spite of Abel's warnings about getting hurt. It satisfied Cain that she always chose him over Abel.

Once, long ago, he had sat on this very bank with her, studying the cherubim. She had come with him, rather than heeding Abel. Lilith had leaned against him as she stared across the river at the blinding radiance, her chin lifted, jutting toward the two angels in a show of courage.

"You're my favorite brother of all," she had whispered, flicking her eyes toward his for just a moment, a small smile curving her lips at the corners. "I always feel safe when you're near." Her warm arm had stolen around his back to clasp his waist and pull him closer.

His heart had raced, but he had snorted out a laugh. "As if I could fight both cherubim!"

"Still, no one else makes me feel safe. No one."

Grinning, he had reached across her bent knees to caress her far leg, his fingertip tracing whorls around her kneecap. She had leaned nearer, her breath caressing his face before she nestled her head upon his shoulder. In embrace, they had lingered there a long while.

Cain realized he didn't want another woman—he loved Lilith.

What did his love for her mean? How did he love her? His love for Lilith involved passion of some sort—wanting her to know everything about him and having no fear of revealing his true self to her. It demanded that he strive to know her as fully as he knew himself, driving him to be near her and to value her good opinion above all others. It entailed wanting to commit himself to her, to live with her alone for the rest of his life, to take her body as his own, to care for her, to beget children with her. He couldn't hide this from himself any longer.

It was an epiphany: He wanted Lilith to be his wife!

His father and mother loved each other passionately. Cain had witnessed their love his entire life. He saw their affection, often hearing them in the night as he grew up. That was one reason he had built his own sleeping chamber far up the riverbank. He was a man; he didn't want to hear this. It made his sleep restless, his dreams confusing, his thoughts more difficult to control, his discontent more acute.

Having observed mating in the animal world, he had a general idea of what physical unity between a man and a woman entailed. He had seen the physical evidence of his parents' love in the continually growing brood of siblings.

This was how he wanted Lilith. He now realized this. He longed to be her husband, to cherish her, and to make her his own.

Now, what should he do about it?

CHAPTER 2

SATAN PROWLED. DESPISING HIS FORMER angelic comrades who stood watch on the river's other side, he sneered at their ready stance. He could take them both. But he hated even looking at them. They reminded him of his future crushing.

Charred and singed from his blazing fall from Heaven, Satan's ashy spirit drifted nearer to Cain. Encompassing the weak boy-man, Satan's burnt arms and wings spread wide. Even in his reduced state, Satan towered over Cain, menacing as he curled his soiled, unclothed spirit about the man's body, completely enveloping him in black mist.

Formerly, Satan's spirit had blazed glorious, his wings supple and powerful, shining with the glory of heavenly radiance. He had ranked first and had orchestrated the hosts of Heaven in musical praise. Now his wings were damaged, his entire form reduced from what it once was. Now, frayed and scorched, he hovered over the man.

Yet Satan was still powerful, capable of completely eradicating this puny boy of a man, if God allowed it. Satan loved to maim, debase, and ruin what God had made beautiful, provoking the humans to mar their forms and to corrupt their thoughts. Satan lured them to destruction.

Black maw stretched wide, Satan's once melodious voice

screeched a horrific cackle. The stench of degradation rose from within his vile spirit—all unseen, unheard, and undetected by Cain. Satan guffawed as he considered how he would destroy this beautiful man.

Focusing on his prey, Satan watched and listened to Cain. His interactions provided significant insights into his weaknesses. Obsessed with discovering ways to harm him and all the rest, Satan sought to eradicate the humans God had created. He was now God's enemy.

Stalking the loathsome human beings, Satan maintained constant surveillance of one or the other, attempting to discern their thoughts and motives. Their words, actions, scent, flush of cheek, or beat of heart that indicated emotion—combined, these informed him, shaping his strategies. When they spoke their considerations out loud, it was even better.

One by one, day and night, he investigated their similarities and their differences. These, he analyzed. God had designed them intricately. They were not like the animals. The humans had an inner moral guide. Though they all came from one father and one mother, each personality was unique. Because of this, the deformity of a fallen nature that had polluted them all since their parents' first sin affected each one in a different and particular way.

However, there were commonalities. A plethora of corrupt and discontent desires tempered their ability to heed that sense of right and wrong within them—their consciences. Satan and the other fallen angels had learned that this place of inner conflict was the tripping point, the area to nudge and to prod. Here, he sought the weak points. He always found them.

Manipulation, entrapment, and deception were Satan's expertise.

But God constrained him. He could only touch Adam and Eve and their family if God allowed it. And then it always seemed to be for some purpose that Satan couldn't discern. God took every malevolent action of Satan's and twisted it, shaping it for good in the humans' lives. This irked him, filling him with restless agitation. Quelling the snarl of rage that nearly burst out, he tamped down his frustration. But it simmered inside.

One of the humans would defeat him.

One day a seed of the woman, one specific offspring of Adam and Eve, would crush his head and destroy him. God had decreed it. Satan could not discern which one it might be, nor could he comprehend how this crushing would occur. The humans he observed every day called it a mystery; they didn't know either. No one did except God. He knew.

In Satan's mind, the likeliest candidate was Cain—the oldest son. Surely, it was him. Silent and unseen, Satan leaned near Cain, sniffing his reeking pheromones. They told much. Cain appeared hopeful. His cheeks flushed with expectancy; his heart thumped with passion. Satan despised them when they looked like that! Machinating over how to harm him, Satan stewed.

Since Abel's birth, Satan had whispered discouragement to Cain, prodding insecurity's inner bruise and snuffing hope when it flamed. That underpinning warped Cain's view of himself. With those wounds in place, Cain's sinful nature led him into various temptations, but Satan wanted to draw him even further in. Thoughtfully, he studied him.

This boy-man was arrogant; he relied on himself. He would be easy to break. Temptation regarding Lilith might be the trigger to Cain's fall. Satan considered ways to hurt Lilith in the process. And, what about Abel? Unlike Cain or Lilith, Abel adored God and called upon Him for assistance. For this, Satan loathed him.

But his hatred of Cain was zealous. He must destroy Cain. It was imperative. He would seize every opportunity. Bitterly, Satan mulled over these facts. He had to win this battle.

The outcome held eternal implications.

CHAPTER 3

THE NEXT MORNING CAIN WOKE long after the sun had risen, having crept back to his room so late that the nightly mist had begun to fall and the moon to set. Pondering Lilith, he had lingered by the riverbank. Today was the holy day of rest, a chance for their bodies to recover from the week's hard labor of tilling the soil, weeding the crops, and tending the sheep—a day they were to remember Yahweh, the Creator God. But Cain lay considering all he had decided last night.

He could scarcely believe he had finally ascertained what he wanted. Pursuing Lilith would disrupt the flow of life for the entire family as it had existed for the past one hundred twenty years. But this outcome had been building since Lilith was born into the family ninety years ago. It was inevitable.

She had arrived when he was thirty years old. He had just started to grow toward manhood—his body beginning to change, his limbs to grow gangly, his movements to become awkward. He had adored her, carrying her pudgy infant self around, kissing her head with its profusion of honey-colored curls, studying her gray-hazel eyes, which, depending on the lighting, seemed to change color. Though Cain now had twenty-two sisters, Lilith had always been his favorite, the one he adored. And now he would make her his own.

Glad he had insisted that no other brothers share his sleeping chamber, he could be alone with his thoughts without being bothered by chatter and questions. How should he proceed? Since it was the day of rest, he could spend the entire day with Lilith.

That thought propelled him off his sleeping mat.

After tidying his hair and donning his sheepskin garment, he parted the doorway's woven hemp covering and stepped out into the sun. Though he had slept late, most of the family still congregated around the morning meal. He observed Lilith's honey head among them. After stepping into the trees to relieve himself, he jogged toward the gathering.

When he arrived, everyone greeted him except Lilith. Busying herself with the food and the younger children all clamoring to be fed, she kept her eyes on her task, ignoring his presence.

This puzzled Cain. Usually she was the first to greet him each morning. Why was she ignoring him? He decided to speak to her.

As he stepped in her direction, three of the younger boys—Gilam, Jeriel, and Zuriel—cut him off. They planned to travel down the river to explore and to take their ease by the water. They wanted him to accompany them. He listened to their plans but made no promises, telling them he'd think about it.

He looked up and discovered Lilith had vanished.

Trying to be inconspicuous, he scanned the family circle, the familiar faces blurring as he sought her, but she was gone. Then, in the distance, he glimpsed her moving among the fruit trees, traveling downriver from the family compound, walking fast. She was alone.

His younger brothers still clustered about him, urging him to join them in their plans, making suggestions for activities, telling him the locations they wanted to visit downriver.

"I'll meet you," Cain interrupted. "Come later. I'll go first." He took off running toward the water. "Give me a while," he called back to the three boys.

Laughing joyously, they hooted over their success. It would

be a good day! They were to spend it with Cain! Behind him, they chattered. Cain smiled.

As he jogged out of the family gathering area and through the fruit orchard, Lilith raced away ahead of him. He could easily outrun her. Confident of this, as he gained on her, he fixed his mind on what he would say. He couldn't figure out why she ignored him. Why was she running away? Eager to get the answer and to close the gap between them, he ran faster.

Suddenly, she stopped and turned to face him, folding her arms across her chest. As he sprinted up to her, she looked displeased.

"What do you want, Cain?" She frowned; her voice was sharp.

Abruptly, he halted, thoroughly confused. This wasn't what he had expected. Desirous to begin his pursuit of her heart, he was eager for her company; but she pushed him away. *Why?* Breathing heavily, he cocked his head as he considered her.

"Why are you running?" he asked.

"Answer my question first."

"I want to talk to you."

"About what?"

"Umm ..." Cain didn't know what to say.

As he examined her face more closely, her eyes filled with tears. He was mystified. Why was she on the verge of crying? Before he could ask her, she spun and sprinted away. He looked after her for a moment then pursued her.

"Lilith, wait!"

She ran faster.

Lowering his head, Cain raced after her, pulling even and then running alongside. He glanced over, but she wouldn't meet his eyes. Her tears had overflowed and streaked across her cheekbones, blown back by the rush of her running.

Unable to resist, Cain grabbed her. Their momentum spun them around, causing them to lose their balance and to roll across the dust, tangled up together. Lying on her back on the ground, Lilith covered her face with both hands and sobbed.

Cain sat up, giving a cursory glance at his bloodied knee then he focused on her. He couldn't begin to count the number of times he'd comforted her when she was crying. When she removed her hands, her eyes and her nose would be red. She wouldn't want him to see her face.

"Are you hurt?" He stroked her head.

Still weeping, she shrugged away. This meant she was angry. Why? What had he done? He considered all that had occurred last night. Slowly, it dawned on him. She was angry that he wanted a wife. Probably, she also hadn't considered that the wife he might want was her. She was jealous. She loved him too! The knowledge jolted his heart and changed his strategy.

"Lilith, listen to me."

Her crying rose in pitch, and she twisted away.

"Lilith," he said more loudly.

Hands still covering her face, she wept heavy sobs of despair.

Cain grasped her hands, pried them from her face, and peered down into her tear-filled eyes. Ducking her face to her shoulder, she tried to hide her grief. He had comforted this weeping girl so many times before, he knew everything about her grief. She couldn't fool him. He had desired her for so long that he now made an impulsive decision.

He bent over her and kissed her full on the mouth.

Drawing back, he looked into her wet eyes. Astonished, she stared back at him. In her eyes he saw triumphant joy, desire realized, prayers answered, and dreams fulfilled. He smiled.

"Lilith, I want you to be my wife. I want no one else."

She sniffed. "You do?"

"Yes." Gently, he wiped her nose with the corner of his garment. "I didn't understand how much I wanted you until last night. I didn't think I could have you. It wasn't even something I comprehended in any way. That's why I kept waiting for God to do something. But, after what you said, I realized God might intend for us to marry. I've wanted you for decades. Will you be my wife?"

"Can we do this?"

"We will do it. I don't care if we can or not. I love you; I want to be your husband."

"I love you too, Cain. I've always loved you. I couldn't bear the idea of you loving any woman but me."

He chuckled softly—he had been right. Her jealousy was endearing.

"So will you be my wife?"

Seeming to consider all the implications, she solemnly studied his eyes.

"Absolutely," she whispered. "Without a doubt."

Pressing his lips to hers, he lingered this time. Returning his kisses, she grasped his head and held it to hers, obviously as overwhelmed with joy and affection as he.

Then he heard their younger brothers making their way down the river. The boys were singing. Cain made another quick decision. Pulling Lilith up, Cain ran away, taking her with him, traveling perpendicular to the river. Their brothers wouldn't search in this direction. They would continue down the river.

Cain wanted to have Lilith all to himself.

****

Cain and Lilith darted into the woods. Abel knew they hadn't seen him. Back at the family gathering area, he had noticed Cain seeking Lilith. Abel knew their little brothers might end up being disappointed, so he had taken the shortcut through the trees to the downriver location the boys had mentioned, hoping to avert their distress when they couldn't find Cain.

When he had spotted Cain and Lilith embracing in the grass, he had been surprised and puzzled about what to do. Should he speak? Should he circle wide around them? Now that Abel had seen to what purpose Cain had pursued Lilith, it confused and troubled him.

Heading to intercept the little brothers, he would spend the day with them in consolation for the fact that they would not find Cain. These particular younger brothers were partial to their eldest brother, but Abel would make sure their day was fun.

Was Cain and Lilith's behavior appropriate? Abel needed to consider and pray about that. Did Yahweh intend to give them wives? Was this the way He was going to do it? Abel wasn't certain, but he would keep their secret unless it became obvious that it needed to be told.

He would try to do what was best for all of them.

CHAPTER 4

CAIN SPENT THE ENTIRE DAY under one tree with Lilith, talking about their lifetime together. Recounting all the ways they had ever been special to one another, they remembered their history of mutual love. Deep within they had always known this would be the outcome.

Up close to Lilith's face, Cain marveled at the flecks of green in her hazel eyes. Her laughter soothed his soul. Her lips tasted warm. Learning to kiss, they sprawled together in the grass, clenched in each other's arms, experimenting with kissing.

Between kisses, they wondered how becoming husband and wife should progress. No one but their parents had ever done this, but then they had been the only two people on the earth. Therefore, what should be done now? Did those steps still apply?

"Before we lie together, I need to say the lifelong vow to you," Cain said. "Father said that to Mother when he first saw her."

"Can you do that right now? Would that make us man and wife?"

In doubt about that, Cain hesitated. "Hmm. I'm not sure. That's one possibility, but we might need to have Father and Mother's blessing."

"Yes. They had God's blessing."

"But that means we'll have to tell them, and I don't want to."

Emotions churning and foreheads creased, they stared at one another.

"Do you think they'll disapprove?" Lilith asked.

"I'm afraid they will. They'll want us to wait."

Certain of this, they both nodded.

"I don't want to wait," Lilith whispered.

"I *can't* wait," he said.

Cain pulled Lilith more tightly against him. Their kissing had awakened something he had only been vaguely aware of before. They needed to settle this soon; it would be difficult to bridle his passion. Why couldn't they simply pledge to one another now, alone, out in the woods? That would certainly make this easier.

Uncertain, he settled for kissing and professing his love. She responded.

They lost track of the sun's arc. The day became timeless, filled with love and their awe of the other. When darkness descended, they became aware of their surroundings. Hand in hand, they picked their way through the trees at nightfall, returning to the family compound.

Everyone had gone to bed, anticipating tomorrow's return to their usual labors. The fire had burned down to embers. Before they stepped out of the orchard to cross the fireside opening, Cain pulled Lilith into his arms. As he kissed her mouth, he ran his tongue lightly across her upper lip. She laced her fingers through his hair, grasping him near. He yearned for her. He longed to be joined today, this moment. Now.

But he released her. They stared into each other's eyes; then they separated, their fingers trailing down the other's arm, lingering at the fingertips as they parted. Each walked to their individual sleeping chambers. Down the length of the stone wall, they gazed at one another's darkened forms before stepping into the blackness of their own rooms.

****

From inside the parental chamber, Eve observed Cain and

Lilith's parting. Behind her, Adam and little Judith slept, their breathing soft and slow. It was exactly as she had suspected. After seeing Cain pursue Lilith this morning, she had been awaiting their return all day.

She needed to speak to Adam quickly.

****

The next morning, Cain woke and smiled at the heavens, bright where he had rolled back the reed matting. Lilith would be his! He leapt from his bedding, wrapped himself in his sheepskin garment, ducked under the hemp door covering, and jogged down to the family gathering area.

Upon arriving, he gazed at Lilith. She looked back with longing in her eyes, but a crease formed between her brows. Something was wrong. Their father strode toward him.

"Cain, why did you abandon your younger brothers yesterday? You gave them your word. They looked forward to spending the day with you."

"I went up the river as I promised." Cain shifted uncomfortably. This was a half-truth; he wasn't good at lying.

"They never found you. In fact, they spent the day with Abel."

Cain looked around for Abel, who met his eyes evenly from the other side of the clearing. Something was there in Abel's serious eyes. If Abel had spent the day with the younger boys, he might have come up the river and seen them kissing. Had he told their father?

"I want you to take Gilam, Jeriel, and Zuriel to work with you today," Father said. "Make their day a good one. Do the weeding in the field nearest the house."

Cain didn't argue. He had erred. Since he would be near home, he might see Lilith; this thought made him smile. He cuffed the younger boys and drew them to himself, mussing their hair. They grabbed their tools and headed toward the field.

As they left, Cain met Lilith's eyes over the top of the boys' heads and shot her the special smile he saved for her. Squinting her eyes at him affectionately, she smiled in return.

As he turned away, he noticed their mother eyeing them. He beamed in her direction the most innocent smile he could muster. The most subtle of smiles uplifted the bare corners of her mouth, a mere twitch of an acknowledgment of his grin. What did she know or suspect? He needed to be more circumspect. Mother saw everything.

Cain worked hard with the boys, laughing with them, telling them stories, showing them how to do their tasks more efficiently. He wanted to make it up to them—he loved all his siblings. But, surely there was some way he could talk to Abel. His flock grazed right over the hill.

About midmorning, Cain suggested they take a break to eat some fruit with Abel and the boys who worked with him. His three little brothers were more than happy to comply. They raced off, glad to drink, eat, and play while their big brothers rested.

As they came over the hill, Cain saw he already had Abel's attention.

Abel stood among the sheep with the small brothers who helped him; they were all smiling. Patting his young helpers on the back and tousling their hair, he dismissed the boys. They squeezed him tightly about the waist before running off. Then, his smile at their affection fading and his expression growing increasingly somber, Abel walked silently toward Cain.

Keeping their eyes on their little brothers, they sat side by side under one of the trees.

"I saw you and Lilith," Abel said quietly.

"What did you see?"

"The kissing. I heard you ask her to be your wife."

"Did you tell Father?"

"Of course not. You need to do that."

"I can't. He'll tell us to wait. I can't wait, Abel."

"There's nothing wrong with waiting. We don't know if this is right. This is a new way of forming a family. We all need to pray together and ask Yahweh to confirm this."

"Why? I'm absolutely certain. I've loved Lilith her entire life, and she has loved me."

"But how do you know you should take her as your wife?"

"Because I love her!" *How can I explain this?* "It's different, Abel. It's not like my love for any of the rest of you."

"Then talk to Father. He is a husband after all. I'm certain he'll understand."

"No, he won't. He and Mother never had to wait. He doesn't know what it's like. I can't wait any longer."

"Don't be impetuous, Cain," Abel said softly. "You always are."

"Always? I am not! I've loved Lilith for ninety years. This isn't a rash decision."

"You're right—I'm sorry. You're not always impetuous, but you often are. It's true."

"That's not fair."

"You don't usually think before you act—you know this. But this is a serious matter. It involves lifelong commitment and Lilith's heart and future children. You need to consider this carefully, and we all need to get confirmation."

"And what would this 'confirmation' look like—all of you telling us what to do?"

"No, not at all." Abel glanced at him. "God will show us."

"I already know what to do. The Creator has given me love for Lilith. She loves me too. God has spoken. I'm marrying her."

"Please, pray about it first."

"I have prayed about it. It's my life. It's Lilith's life. It's not your life."

"If you're that certain, then you have to talk to Father."

"How do you know that?"

"What do you mean?" Abel now faced him, studying his eyes seriously.

"Father made the promise to Mother before God. He didn't have to consult anyone before he married her. Why do I have to talk to him?"

"It seems as though there needs to be more than that now."

"But we don't know that, do we?" Cain held Abel with his stare.

"It doesn't seem right to simply say those solemn words to her alone, now that there are more people on the earth."

"It seems fine to me."

"Cain, examine your conscience. You know I'm right."

"You're always right. It's disgusting."

"Always?"

"Okay, you're not always right," Cain said, "but you think you are."

"Cain—"

"Mind your own affairs, Abel."

Cain leapt up and gestured to Gilam, Jeriel, and Zuriel. Glaring at Abel over his shoulder, he turned to lope back. Of course, he would talk to their parents. He wasn't being impetuous.

Abel's words irritated him. He didn't need a lecture.

Cain threw himself into weeding the field, instructing, and supervising the little brothers as they worked. He loved the smell of dirt and the satisfaction of cultivating green things—waiting for the first shoots to burst through the topsoil and watching the plants grow because of their hard labor. He loved working the land. It helped ease his worries about his parents and Lilith.

They had the entire field weeded by the time the sun reached its zenith. When Cain stood and straightened his back at the end of the last row, he saw their father watching from the hill.

"Well done, Cain," Father called, clearly pleased. "Come down to eat."

The little boys ran ahead, and Cain walked back with his father. Now would be the time to talk about Lilith, but Cain couldn't bring himself to do it. He dreaded his father's negative response. Instead they discussed the work to be accomplished after lunch.

When they arrived at the gathering place, there lay all his favorite food arrayed on the stone slabs. Obviously, Lilith had supervised the meal preparation. Glancing around, he saw her ordering around the younger girls and knew he was right.

Carrying a newborn lamb, Abel appeared over the hill with the youngsters. He stopped to speak with their father, who took the lamb. The ewe had probably died giving birth. It was lambing season. As Abel stepped up to the spread of food, he looked beaten, as he always did when one of his ewes died leaving a newborn. Cain decided to kick him while he was down.

"Why don't you go first, Abel? Since you're better than all the rest of us."

Cain stared hard at him and saw the blow had struck home—Abel winced and swallowed hard. Several of their younger brothers laughed at his remark, but the rest looked embarrassed. Cain lifted his eyes to Lilith's and met her look of disapproval. *What?* Raising his eyebrows, he gave her his best expression of innocence. Her continued solemnity pricked his conscience; his remark had been uncalled for. He needed to soften the blow.

"I'll go to the end of the line, since I'm the worst," Cain said.

Now everyone laughed. After his unkind remark to Abel, they all agreed with his assessment. Abel was caring and compassionate toward everyone—they all went to him for comfort and advice. Sometimes his advice niggled, as it did today; but he was usually right. Cain shoved that thought away. He wanted to obtain Lilith in his own way.

As Cain walked to the back of the line, he passed his mother toward the end, preparing to help the smaller children. Mother looked at him with kind sympathy and patted his shoulder. From the end of the line, he watched everyone console Abel. Cain dropped his head. He felt guilty. He tended to be mean when he was angry, and it had happened again.

****

Nonchalantly, Lilith made her way toward Cain, talking with one or another sibling as she moved along the line. Occasionally she flicked her eyes in his direction. He looked uneasy. Surely something had happened out in the field to provoke his verbal smack at their kindest brother.

"What was that all about?" Lilith whispered when she reached him.

Facing the river, Cain turned his back toward the rest of the family. "Abel knows. We had a disagreement."

Lilith also turned, so no one could see their faces. She felt apprehensive. "What did he say? Did he tell Father and Mother?"

"He thinks we should pray and wait, but he didn't tell them."

"What did you say?"

"What are you both looking at?" Shielding her eyes, Nissa examined the Tigris. They startled. Neither had seen or heard her coming. Had she overheard their conversation?

"Oh nothing," Lilith said. "Just standing and waiting."

"You've both been very secretive lately. What's going on?"

"We're working on a surprise," Cain said quickly.

"Ooh! What is it?"

"If we told you, it wouldn't be a surprise, would it?" Lilith said.

Nissa raised her eyebrows and looked away. She wouldn't pry now, but Lilith knew she would later. Cain usually intimidated Nissa, so she would attempt to ferret out the secret later. Tonight, after they went to the sleeping chamber they shared with Ariel, Nissa would pounce.

They finally reached the food, picked over by now, but there was still plenty to eat. Lilith reached for the last piece of Cain's favorite fruit and popped it into his mouth. As her fingers left his mouth, he kissed them. Lilith arched her brow at him and turned away, smiling to herself. Taking the food, they sat by the river.

This was the norm. They always ate together. It would draw no attention. Usually others gathered around, but today they went far down the riverbank so they could eat alone. Sitting closely, they leaned into one another, pressing their shoulders together as they ate.

Telling Nissa that they planned a surprise was a good way to gain privacy. She would spread the information around and others would leave them alone.

"So, what did you say to Abel?" Lilith asked.

"I told him that I was going to marry you and he should stay out of it. That is, I'll marry you if you still want me after the way I skewered him."

"Of course I still want you. You're always mean when you're mad."

"I know. It's not a very good quality. Are you sure you want a mean husband?"

"Well, you're hardly ever mean to me."

"Hardly ever?" He smirked.

"You are occasionally. You knocked me in the water the first time I watched you shave."

"I think I was about forty-five. Sparse whiskers had sprouted on my chin. I had no idea that was the norm for boys that age. I compared them with Father's. Mine looked unmanly, so I decided to scrape them off. I sneaked out to the river with one of the sharpened stones. When I bent over the smooth water, there was your little face peering back at me. You had followed me. I knew you wouldn't tell; but when I cut myself, I realized everyone would know. I felt angry, so I knocked you in. I felt horrible for doing that. I remember yanking you out and apologizing."

"It's not an isolated incident. Remember when you grabbed me by the hair and—"

"Yes, yes ... I'm sorry. Even though it was decades ago, it's still upsetting to think of losing my temper with you like that. I try not to be mean to you."

"You try." She regarded him archly. "You aren't always successful."

Lilith glanced behind her. No one was watching. Quickly, she kissed his shoulder, so he'd know she loved him in spite of his occasional fits of temper.

"Now, what about Abel?" she asked.

"He thinks I'm being rash. I'm always impetuous. Pray and wait, pray and wait. It's all he ever says."

"You are always impetuous."

Cain glared at her.

"It's what I like most about you," she said. "You can't hide how you feel. You must act."

****

Cain wanted to grab her up and kiss her when she said that, but they were in full view of the entire family. She liked him exactly the way he was, as flawed as he was, with all his faults. She seemed to like him better than he liked himself.

"If we were alone, I'd kiss you," he said.

"If we were alone, I'd let you. And I'd kiss you back."

"I'm going to sneak you out of your room tonight. Will you come with me?"

"Of course. Where are we going?"

"I just need to kiss you."

Hearing movement, Cain glanced over his shoulder. Father walked around the fireside, gathering everyone back to work. In addition to lambing season, many of the crops were being planted. Others were being harvested. Everyone would be busy day and night. Cain didn't know if he'd be able to steal a moment with Lilith, but he would try.

Making sure their backs were turned toward everyone, he placed his finger on Lilith's lips. Keeping his eyes on the river, he puckered a kiss. She kissed his finger back. Smiling, he rose and jogged off to work. It would be a good afternoon.

Tonight he would sneak out with Lilith.

CHAPTER 5

YAHWEH, THE CREATOR GOD, REIGNED. The time now came for the multitude of angels to gather before His throne to present themselves. All of them were under His authority. They must submit to His edicts; they had to obey His boundaries and specifications.

The elect angels obeyed by nature and love, the infernal angels by force and decree.

With all the other angels, Satan returned to his former domain. Assuming an attitude of nonchalance, he noted the radiance blazing brilliant from God—Father, Son, and Holy Spirit. Yahweh existed triune: three Persons in One God. The familiar angelic worship thundered and echoed through the vault of Heaven.

No longer did Satan offer praise to the One God. Others now led the symphony of adoration. They didn't need him. With bitterness, he realized he was envious. *Jealous!* He was disgusted with himself. He detested the elect angels who sang their praises around God's throne. Satan dropped to one knee before God, but in his heart he remained unbowed.

God the Father pointed at him. "Satan, from where have you come?"

Bowing lower, Satan feigned humility. As always, God

knew exactly where he had been but demanded an accounting. Attempting to maintain the correct tone of deference, Satan replied:

"From roaming about the earth, wandering to and fro, watching the humans."

"Have you considered Cain?"

"Of course, I have." God knew he considered Cain more than the others. Why mention Cain?

"I have given him strength, intelligence, and creativity. Though his heart doesn't yet know how, he longs to worship and please me."

"And constantly fails. He doesn't love You, and he never will."

The mercy and compassion flowing out from God in response to his derisive words practically flattened Satan. Scowling, he picked himself up.

"He has every reason to want to please you." Satan made his voice silken and ingratiating. "His family is happy, even outside the Garden. They are still quite innocent, but let me tempt him and prove his true nature. He will fail then he will no longer seek to worship or please You."

"Because of my great love for Cain, you may test him."

The Father gazed at the Son. Their eyes locked, the Spirit in unity with Them. The intensity of Their love and commitment to Cain and all of Adam's family reverberated, shaking the heavens. Loathing the sensation, Satan braced himself as the sickening wave of love washed through him.

Narrowing his eyes, Satan studied the Godhead carefully. What was going on here?

The last time Yahweh had responded in this way, Satan had been granted permission to test Adam. He had succeeded in tempting the man. Both humans had eaten the forbidden fruit, violating God's command, thus bringing sin and death into the world. They had been cast out of the Garden as a result. But God had not killed them immediately as Satan had hoped. Instead, God had made this ridiculous promise that Satan's head would be crushed by one of the humans.

What did God have in mind now?

"You may not touch Cain or harm his body in any way," God said. "But have you considered my servant Abel? He is a man of faith and will not curse me, even if he faces death."

What?! With eyes still and cold, Satan glowered at the Godhead. How was he being granted what he hoped? How was God a step ahead of him, even suggesting what he most desired?

"Must I spare Abel's life?" Satan tried to appear indifferent.

"No, you need not spare his life. His death is precious in my sight."

The Father once more focused His attention on the Son. The Spirit intertwined with Them in harmony of purpose. Some sort of mysterious delight surged from the Father through the Spirit toward the Son—a burst of holy energy, like a Fatherly embrace that filled the heavens. The love and unity of the Godhead resounded. Satan cringed.

"But," God the Father said, "you may not touch Cain. You may only test him. You are dismissed. Go."

As Satan moved to leave, he turned back. Filled with anticipation, the Son's eyes gleamed victorious as they fixed upon him, as if He had just triumphed in a battle. Confusion clouded Satan's mind—a vile sensation. He wondered: This had been almost too easy. Was there more to this than he knew? Would there be further consequences of his actions?

Having learned the hard way, Satan knew God designed testing to turn the humans toward Him. All of Satan's works of destruction would be warped and twisted, as God orchestrated them for good. From past experience, he knew God's Spirit would pull and tug at Cain's conscience.

But Satan would darken Cain's view, making certain he didn't see it as God intended. He would seek a base of operation in Cain's heart. His plan was to devour.

Though he had tricked the humans into eating the forbidden fruit, none of them had yet tasted death. Now, one would die! A voracious thirst throttled him—a craving for human blood, for human life. Finally, he could slake his lust for destruction. Finally, he could kill! Into his mind burst the exquisite solution for the ruin of both Cain and Abel.

Satan and the other fallen angels would coax and pressure Cain, luring him to open the door to greater sin than his family had ever known, introducing sins previously not even considered, crushing Abel and hurting Lilith in the process. They would foster depravity and violence upon the earth, twisting what God had made to be beautiful, breaking and ruining it.

Satan snorted at the thought.

Throwing back his head, he guffawed. He would enjoy this! Eager to commence, he streaked toward the earth's surface. Cain would not be doing any crushing of his head.

Satan would destroy Cain by using him to kill Abel.

CHAPTER 6

AS JUDITH NURSED TO SLEEP, Adam talked quietly with Eve. The day had been long, but the burden of raising a large family with many conflicting personalities impinged on their sleep this evening. Earlier, Eve had said they needed to talk. Rather than collapsing exhausted onto their pallet tonight, Adam lay propped on his elbow, determined to sort out the day's mysteries.

"What happened between Cain and Abel at the midday meal?" he whispered. "Why did Cain insult Abel?"

"What did you hear?"

"I asked the three boys. They said it was about Cain abandoning them yesterday. Apparently, he and Abel had an argument about it out in the field."

"Who told you that?"

"Zuriel."

"Did he listen in?"

"I didn't ask him. I just assumed he had."

"I don't think that's why they were arguing," Eve said.

"What was it, then?"

"Cain was with Lilith all day yesterday. They came back late last night. That's why Cain abandoned the little boys. I think Abel saw them."

"How do you know?"

"I was watching Abel when you rebuked Cain this morning. He was disturbed about something, and Cain was uncomfortable about it. I didn't get a chance to tell you this earlier—you had gone out before I woke this morning—but last night I saw Cain and Lilith come home."

"And?" Adam looked into her eyes, wondering how she always saw so much.

"And they stood on the far edge of the clearing, kissing before they separated. They were passionate, Adam, like we kiss when we make love."

Stunned, Adam sat up. Everything seemed out of control, and he liked order and predictability.

"How did this happen so quickly?"

"Quickly?" Eve's rising voice roused the sleeping baby. Adam kept his eyes fixed on hers as they waited for the infant to settle down. "Cain has been in love with Lilith since she was born. I've mentioned it to you many times. He must have figured out how he felt about her. We talked about this when Cain ran off a few nights ago and Lilith returned alone. Remember?"

Adam pondered this string of events and observations. He hadn't heeded Eve's words, and now the situation had gone forward.

"What do you think we should do?" he asked.

"Well, you need to talk to Cain. Tomorrow, if possible. For some reason he feels he can't tell you. They're being secretive. He needs your guidance. He probably has no idea what he's supposed to do."

"But I'm still not convinced this is the way."

"I'm sure he knows you feel that way, Adam. That's probably why he hasn't come to you. He thinks you'll say no."

"That's no reason not to come. If he wants to become a husband then he needs to act like a man and tell us."

"You make me so angry when you say that about the boys. They didn't have the advantage you had—you were created in the form of a fully grown man. All you had to do to 'act like a man' was simply to exist. Just by living, you accomplished it."

Adam stared back at her; he never understood what she meant when she said that.

"They're intimidated by you," she added.

"That's no excuse."

Eve sighed. Adam watched her face—she was adjusting her argument.

"I'm afraid he thinks we'll tell them to wait longer," she said, "to continue to pray. I think it's beyond that. You need to tell him to stand before us and pledge himself to Lilith before he lies with her. They may have already done it. You didn't see them kissing."

"I want him to come to me," Adam said. "He needs to reveal his intentions. He needs to talk to us about marrying Lilith. It's the right thing to do."

"He feels insecure about it. I'm sure that's why he took the verbal swing at Abel."

"That doesn't matter. He should do what's right."

"But, Adam—"

"Eve, he needs to come to me. And we do need to pray about it."

****

Eve nodded. Adam's inflexibility and uncertainty showed in the set of his jaw. He really did need to pray or his mind wouldn't be able to embrace the idea. He continued to look seriously into her eyes; she could tell he felt unsettled.

Finally, he turned his back toward her and lay down—she doubted he would sleep. Judith's little mouth released her nursing hold. She was done suckling. Gently, Eve positioned her against the wall and rolled away from Adam.

Discouragement washed over her. She was making no headway. She couldn't make him see the humanity of their son—his confusion, his uncertainty, his fears. There was this rivalry always between them, father and son. Who would end up on top? Who would win?

Why couldn't there be unity?

She knew exactly why. It began the day they ate the forbidden fruit. She would always regret what they had done and the consequences it had brought. She wondered which one of their children would crush the serpent's head and put an end to sin and conflict. Would it be Cain? Would it be Abel? Perhaps another of their offspring? She longed for that day.

****

Silently, Cain lay in the darkness outside Lilith's sleeping chamber. Flattening himself to the ground, he listened to Nissa blathering on and on, trying to pry information out of Lilith. Smothering his laughter at Nissa's tactics, he had to clamp his hand over his mouth. Apparently, she didn't know Lilith as well as he. He could get Lilith to tell him anything.

Finally, Nissa grew silent then she breathed deeply. Cain slid across the ground and reached in under the woven door covering. He knew Lilith slept against the wall with her feet toward the door. Groping around, he grasped her ankle and heard a sharp intake of breath; he hoped he didn't have Nissa by mistake. After tickling Lilith's slender foot, he backed into the darkness.

Out she came. When she emerged, he drew her into his arms and gave her a quick kiss. Then he grabbed her hand and led her up the rocky hill behind the family home. They stole across the moonlit field and into the night-blackened woods.

This felt dangerous. No one knew they were together.

Cain's heart raced from the exhilaration of Lilith's presence and of sneaking out with her. He felt as if he were perched on the edge of a precipice—the euphoria made him jittery.

When they reached the deep darkness of the woods, Lilith yanked on his arm, turning him about. Grasping his face, she warmed his lips with hers. He hadn't been prepared for her to do that! Enticing him, she had caught him off-guard. He responded by kissing her fiercely.

Slipping her garment lower on one shoulder, he nuzzled across it. Her skin felt so soft! Taking her into his arms, he collapsed to the forest floor, holding her close.

"I love you so much," he whispered. "I want you to be mine." He tasted the skin at the base of her throat. She grasped his head, pulling his lips back to hers.

"Lily ... let me ...," he said out of the side of his mouth.

Deeply, longingly, she kissed him again. Clearly, she didn't want to talk. Overwhelmed by desire, a lifetime of yearning propelled each kiss.

Cain gave way; passion triumphed. Giving Lilith hot, eager kisses, he slid her onto the soft leaves that carpeted the ground. Lying over her, he breathed her warm exhalations.

"Lily, I want to commit my life to yours."

"Can we do that now?" she asked between the small kisses she layered upon him.

"I don't care if we can or not. I'm going to. You're so precious to me; I want you to be my wife. I don't want to wait any longer." Cain heard something. He paused. "What was that?"

Drifting in the night, Abel sang the soft crooning melody he always droned to the lambs. His footfalls ambled toward them. Too quickly, he was upon them. Not detecting them in the shadows, he tripped over Cain's legs and stumbled across the clearing, dropping something that thumped upon the earth. A newborn lamb bleated piteously.

As Abel's hands searched about for the tiny, fussing lamb, Cain jumped up. Lilith stood, straightening her garment as she pressed against the tree. Both attempted to compose themselves.

"Cain?" Abel peered at their obscured forms. "Is that you? Lilith?"

"It's us," Cain said quietly.

"What are you doing here?"

Both were speechless.

Cain couldn't tell Abel the truth. A long silence grew and swelled, compounding Cain's embarrassment.

"Well?" Abel asked, an edge to his voice.

More silence.

Abel blindsided Cain with a punch to the chin. His head smashed into the tree where Lilith stood. He saw stars. Rushing him, Abel shoved him hard, scraping his shoulder against the bark. Abel's forearm pressed Cain against the trunk, his momentum pinning him. Leaning into him, their faces nearly touching, Abel's voice rumbled indignant.

"Cain! Lilith!" Abel turned to stare at her, immobilized beside him. "What have you done?!"

Breathing heavily as he looked from one to another, he restrained them with his umbrage. Then Abel shoved away, struggling to control himself. Without saying another word, he gathered the bleating lamb and lurched out of the woods. Stunned into silence, they stared after him.

"Are you hurt?" Lilith whispered.

"I'm fine." Cain pushed away from the tree, rubbing his chin and opening wide his mouth to wiggle his jaw. On the point of his chin, he felt a painful, swelling lump. His raw shoulder ached.

"What should we do?"

"I'm not sure. I don't know where he's going."

"Should we go back to our rooms?"

"Yes, let's go," Cain said. "I don't know what he'll do."

Cain took Lilith's hand. They tiptoed from the woods. Careful not to step on the crops, they picked their way across the field, watching their feet. The night was dark, even in the moonlight.

"We almost did something really stupid," Cain said quietly, ashamed by his lack of control. "I want to make my promise to you so everyone can hear me say it. I want them all to know you're mine. And we need to do that before we lie with each other."

"I know. I lost my mind. I'm sorry."

"It wasn't your fault. It was mine."

"I started it."

"I guess you did, but I was overtaken by my desire for you. I'm sorry."

"At least you wanted to promise yourself to me." Her voice dropped. "I was ready to give myself to you. The passion I feel for you surprises me. I had no idea it would be like this."

Cain pulled her into his arms. Smoothing the hair away from her face, he stared into her eyes, darkened in the moonlight. Out of the corner of his eye, he glimpsed a light moving up the hill. What was that? Horrified, he realized it was a torch, and it was coming toward them.

"Lilith, stand behind me." Shoving her behind his back, Cain faced whoever was coming. He was afraid it was their father.

Now he detected three people in the group with the moving brand of fire. It had to be their father, their mother, and Abel. Fury surged within Cain; hatred burned in his heart. He wanted to hurt Abel. Why did he wake their parents?

The firebrand came closer, and Cain saw that he had been right.

****

Adam held the torch aloft, illuminating the five of them. Awkwardly, they all stared at one another, Lilith peeking out from behind Cain's shoulder. Adam inhaled deeply before speaking, lest his temper get the better of him.

Surprising everyone, Cain beat him to it. Rage came growling up from his chest as he hurled himself at Abel. Bellowing as he flew across the space between them, he had landed three solid blows before any of them could react. Then they all moved at once.

"Cain, stop!" Lilith darted about, trying to grasp Cain.

But he moved too quickly. Straddling Abel now, he hit him repeatedly. Arms up, Abel tried to fend off Cain's blows. But they connected. With each punch, Abel grunted and moaned.

Eve hovered over the group of beloved fighting children, shrilling: "Stop! Stop it! Stop now! Stop, Cain! Stop!"

Dropping the torch, Adam dove for Cain, knocking him off Abel and pinning him to the ground. Cain struggled to get out from under his weight.

"Don't you move, son! Stay right where you are," Adam commanded. Cain quit struggling and closed his eyes, resigned. Adam felt the fight drain from him. "Lilith, pick up the torch. Eve, tend to Abel."

The ruckus had wakened some of the children who slept nearest to the field. They emerged from their sleeping chambers, their frightened, questioning voices drifting up the hill.

"Children!" Adam called. "All of you go back to bed. It's just your mother and me and some of your older siblings having a disagreement. Go back to bed ... now!"

Hearing his tone, they all obeyed immediately, their voices softly questioning and discussing what could possibly be happening.

Abel didn't retaliate. He was bloodied and silent. One of his eyes had already swelled shut, dark blood ran from his now-crooked nose, and his cheekbone had an open gash. They hadn't fought like this since they were much younger. Cain could hit harder now.

"Eve, take Lilith with you," Adam said. "The two of you help Abel down to the fireside. Throw more wood on the embers. Tend to his wounds. Go! I need to talk to Cain. Leave the torch if you can see. I'll talk to you later, Lilith."

Adam looked up at her. Lilith's eyes darted away.

She shoved the torch upright into the field's soft soil and turned to go, glancing once at Cain where he lay pinned, his eyes still closed. Then, one on either side of Abel, Eve and Lilith helped him down the hill. Adam, his weight still leveraged by his legs, looked down at his firstborn son.

"If I get off you, will you stay here to talk with me, or will you run?"

Cain opened his eyes to glare at him. "I'll stay." His voice bit.

Adam gradually eased his weight off Cain, watching him warily. Cain sat up.

"You get your temper from me, boy. I know how you feel."

"No you don't. You can't possibly know how I feel."

"Try me."

"I'm in love with Lilith, and I want to marry her. How long did you wait?"

"One miserable day. You know that."

"Then you don't know how I feel. I've waited for Lilith her

whole life."

"Why didn't you come tell us?"

"I was confused. I didn't think it was possible to have her, so I tried to ignore the attraction. Once I knew I wanted her, I couldn't tell you. I knew you'd make me wait and wait and keep waiting." His voice rose in pitch. "I've been waiting for decades."

"Cain, I didn't know if you children were to marry. And, if you were, I expected God to give you spouses in the same way He gave me your mother. But He never did. Still, I didn't expect this. I need to talk to God about it."

"How long will that take?"

"I don't know. I don't feel peace about this—it's a new idea. I need to think about it."

"I'm going to make Lilith my wife."

"If you want my blessing, you have to give me time."

Cain didn't answer.

Adam watched his son's face as the bitterness took root—Cain's countenance hardened, his jaw set. Sometimes this son of his was difficult to manage, short-tempered, impulsive, often feeling as if he wasn't getting his due.

"Did you lie with Lilith?" Adam asked, watching him carefully.

Cain looked off into the night. "I wanted to, but I didn't. Abel tripped over me. Otherwise, I would have. She wanted me to." He turned to stare hard at Adam, defiance in his gaze.

Mystified, Adam gripped his forehead, momentarily stunned. In his one hundred twenty years of parental experience, he hadn't encountered this before. What should he do? Silently, he begged Yahweh for wisdom then he met Cain's eyes.

"When I first saw your mother I vowed to be her husband. I made that promise in the sight of God and all the nearby creatures, since there were no other people. I wasn't ashamed of it; I wanted all of creation to know. We didn't make love until after I'd pledged myself to her. We weren't animals; we were above the animals. I had named them. God had given us dominion over them. I didn't take her body immediately like the animals were doing all around us. Our union was sacred; I pledged myself to her first. God was our father; He had made both of us. He poured out words of blessing after I made that promise. We had His full approval. That's how you should make your promise to Lilith."

Cain's eyes had softened during this short speech.

"I know," he said. Pausing, he sighed. "I don't know why Abel had to bring you up here. Lilith and I were glad he stopped us. I was going to say the vow to her right there. But it didn't seem right. I didn't want to promise myself to her alone in the dark. It didn't feel like a strong enough pledge. It wasn't how I wanted to do it."

"You're right. Good. You need to pledge yourselves to each other first, for everyone to see; then you can unite your bodies."

"I said I know."

"You did, and you're correct. I can't imagine how difficult this is for you. You and Lilith have ninety years of love between you. Your mother and I had only known and loved each other a little over three days when we first lay together. So I'm implementing a plan to help you."

"What do we have to do?"

"I'll be sleeping in your room with you tonight, and you'll be working by my side tomorrow. I need to talk with you. Lilith will sleep with your mother and work with her. Something you would have always regretted was barely averted tonight. I want you and Lilith to come together with no regrets."

Cain looked up at him, hopeful. "So we can marry?"

"Let me pray about this. I still need some time."

As Adam studied his son, he saw that some of this had made sense to him; but his hard heart was still reflected on his face. Cain wanted what he wanted, and he wanted it now. It would be a trial to get through this. They would all need to pray for God's help.

"Go on to your room. I'll be there shortly. I'm going to talk to Lilith first."

Rising, Cain peered downhill at the fireside. Lilith looked

back up at him, her features betraying her curiosity. As Cain headed into the darkness, he appeared dejected and hopeless—head down, shoulders slumped, his stride devoid of self-assurance.

Adam went down to speak to Lilith. She told him the same story Cain had given. Hearing this relieved Adam. Not only had Cain been entirely truthful, but both Cain and Lilith wanted to declare their love for each other before everyone, celebrate their love openly, and then start their life together.

But they wanted to do it now. Years ago, in fact. They had waited long enough.

Even though Lilith wasn't crafted from Cain's body as Eve had been formed from Adam's, they loved one another as Adam loved Eve and she loved him. That hadn't seemed possible to Adam, but here was the evidence:

It was now clear that God would not create marriage partners for their children. Yahweh had designed their bodies to marry and beget children, precisely so they could do that very thing. Adam had made a mistake. Eve had been correct. He could have averted all this frustration by suggesting this to the children sooner. Hopefully, he could rectify the situation.

****

Looking over Abel's injuries, Adam spoke to him gently, "I'm saddened by your injuries, son. Thank you for coming to get us, even though this was the result."

Abel's troubled eyes met his. "Father, I fear I erred."

"No, son. We needed to know."

Cain had hit Abel hard, but the only thing that appeared broken was his nose. Adam wrenched the nose straight. His quick action brought tears and a grunt of pain, but it was done. Of course, Abel thanked him. The cut on his cheek would heal. Lilith and Eve had tended his wounds well. With fifty-five children in the family, they had a wealth of experience.

Leaving Abel and Lilith by the fire, Adam drew Eve aside.

"You were right, my love," he said quietly. "Once again, I didn't trust your judgment. Will you forgive me?"

"Of course. You forgive me often enough."

"Lilith's story matches Cain's. They're both being completely truthful with us—finally."

"You could have made it easier for them to approach us."

"I know. Another mistake." He sighed. "I'm grieved."

"What are we going to do?"

"They both realize they should do this openly, not like they're ashamed of it. We're going to help them achieve that."

"How?"

"Lilith will be sleeping with you tonight and working with you tomorrow. Talk with her; keep her under your watchful eye. I'll be with Cain."

"Watch her?"

"I want to prevent them from making a mistake," Adam said.

"But is that our place? Is that even possible? They're fully grown."

"I'm afraid for them. I feel a need to protect."

"Husband, I don't think we can guard their every moment."

Adam was thoughtful. "I'm fearful about this violence between the boys. They haven't fought in years. I feel protective of them all right now. I seem to have made everything worse. Let's pray about this."

He leaned in to kiss her. Then he headed toward Cain's room.

****

Silently, Eve watched Adam go before returning to the fire. The rumble of Abel's bass carried softly in the night. Though she couldn't make out his words, she could tell he was comforting Lilith, who sat shamefaced beside him.

"Come with me, daughter." Eve held out her hand.

As they left the fireside, she patted Abel's shoulder. How she loved this son of hers; perhaps he would be the one to crush the serpent. Reaching to squeeze her hand momentarily, he remained where he was, staring into the coals with a contemplative expression.

Pulling Lilith close, Eve turned toward the bedchamber, explaining the arrangement as they picked their way carefully through the darkness. They entered the room and lay next to each other fully clothed. Somehow, little Judith had slept through this.

Lilith faced her and whispered, "Mother, I'm sorry."

"Lily, you were only being human. You don't need to apologize to me. I saw what was happening and tried to help your father to see. I'm sorry I couldn't get through to him. God made us to fall in love, to marry, and to beget children. Keeping your conscience clean before the Creator requires continually bringing your mistakes to Him. Letting your passion for Cain overwhelm you was a human mistake. Confess it to Yahweh; He sees everything anyway."

Lilith looked relieved. "Mother, I love Cain."

"I know you do. You've loved him your whole life. I wondered why it took you both so long to realize it."

"You knew?"

"It was obvious. I'm not that astute."

"I wanted him to lie with me," Lilith said quietly. "It was my fault."

"The love between a man and a woman is a powerful thing. The lovemaking binds you to each other. Of course you wanted to lie with him. Let him make his pledge in front of everyone then you can give yourself to him. Can you wait until then?"

"Yes. Now that I know you and Father understand and will let us marry, I can wait."

"I'm glad, dear. I trust you."

"How long will we have to wait?"

"I don't know. Your father and I will be praying about it. I'll pray for strength for you. Now let's get some sleep. The sun will rise no matter what happens during the night."

CHAPTER 7

SOON AFTER SUNRISE, THE FAMILY gathered for the morning meal. On first sight, Cain and Lilith stepped silently into one another's arms, where they remained. Cain kissed Lilith's forehead repeatedly. Abel had multiple facial injuries, one eye swollen completely shut. Cain's knuckles were bruised and torn. He had a large, purple knot on his chin and a weeping shoulder wound. The children who had awakened in the night had talked with the others. Everyone seemed to know about the night's sleeping arrangements.

This was no secret. Adam knew an announcement needed to be made.

"Everyone, give me your attention."

Standing in the midst of his family, he waited for each to take seats on the logs and stones that surrounded the firepit. Some moved where they could see him. Still embracing, Cain and Lilith remained right where they were.

"Cain and Lilith have made a promise to become husband and wife."

As Adam had expected, this prompted whispering and looks of consternation.

"I'm calling this commitment a 'betrothal.' Lilith is now Cain's betrothed, and he is hers. They now belong one to the other and will soon marry."

Over Lilith's head, Cain gaped at him, triumphant joy shining in his eyes. Smiling broadly, he grabbed Lilith up in his arms and gave her a smacking kiss. A murmur of voices rose up, some jubilant and concurring, others shocked and opposing.

Settling Lilith back onto her feet, Cain frowned at his siblings. Obviously, he hadn't considered their reaction. It was clear he hadn't thought anyone would object. He didn't seem to understand why anyone would judge Lilith and his decision.

Sifting through the ramifications, Adam realized he needed to say more.

"I didn't understand what God had planned. I thought of you as my offspring, not as men and women with the same desires I had, to marry and have a family. I'm afraid it took me too long to realize the miracle of love that could occur between you. I don't know if later generations will wed their own sisters and brothers; but for you, our children, this seems to be the only option."

Again the murmur of discussion arose as debates sprang up within each group.

"There was a disagreement last night. You can see the evidence before you."

Silent now, the children all looked at Cain then at Abel.

"As a result of last night, new arrangements have been made. I'll have Cain with me today, so everyone's work for the day will change. Your mother will watch over Lilith. Pray for them to arrive safely at the day when they proclaim their commitment before us."

****

Slack-jawed, Eve stared at Adam. Why had he added this last information? He should have left it unsaid. Mortified, Lilith hid her face against Cain's neck. Flushed with embarrassment, he turned away from his gawking siblings, seized Lilith's hand, and stormed away.

As Cain and Lilith left, whispering started. Everyone speculated and counterspeculated; discussions were heated, disagreements fierce.

"Cain, stay close," Adam called after them.

The whispering ceased as they all listened to Adam's command. His words sparked curiosity. Eve was amazed. What was Adam doing? Why did he humiliate them like this? He had spoiled this beautiful event by bringing shame into it! Incensed, Eve left the fireside.

****

Cain didn't acknowledge his father's last words. Intent on getting away from the humiliation of prying eyes and curious looks, he strode out of the family circle. Pulling Lilith along, he stalked far up the river then he turned and drew her into his arms again.

"I'm so sorry, Lily. I've ruined this for you. This is something we shouldn't have to be embarrassed about. I shouldn't have come to get you last night. If I hadn't, none of this would have happened. I'm really sorry."

"It was my fault as much as yours. I wanted you so badly."

"You did want me."

"I still do."

He answered her statement with a long kiss then pressed his forehead against hers.

"What did Mother say to you?" he asked.

"She comforted me. For a long while, she's urged Father to accept our love—she recognized it even before we did. She trusts us to commit to one another before we come together. We talked about the strength of passion between a man and a woman. She understands."

Of course. Mother saw everything, and she always understood. Cain wished their father was as understanding. Lilith pulled back to look at him.

"What did Father say?"

"He made this arrangement today so we can talk, but apparently we need to be watched over. At least that's what he just said to everyone." Annoyed, Cain stared into the distance, biting his lower lip; then he looked back at her. "He wants them to pray for us. Last night, I told him we'd realized our error, but in light of what he just said, I don't think he trusts us."

"Did he say anything to you in your room?"

"He urged me to listen to my conscience, to guard myself, and to do what's right for you. My conscience bothered me when I sneaked you out, but I did it anyway."

"I wanted you to get me." She shrugged. "What else did he say?"

"He apologized for not realizing how much I love you. He couldn't discern that God wanted us to marry. He expected God to provide us with spouses in the same way he got Mother. Now he's ruined the joy of it. I feel like a chastised child. It's humiliating."

"We've been embarrassed in front of our siblings many times," Lilith said softly. "The important thing is that we can be married."

****

Trying to encourage Cain, Lilith beamed up at him, but his eyes remained dark. This awkwardly worded announcement clearly bothered him. His brow was tense and furrowed.

"The knot on your chin is a little more significant than you let on last night." She kissed it.

"It's nothing. We've hit each other before."

"You broke Abel's nose. Father had to set it."

"It felt good to break his nose, except I nearly broke my knuckles doing it." Cain flexed and twisted his hands, studying his bruised and battered joints.

"Last night by the fire, Abel told me he brought Mother and Father because it seemed best for us. He loves us and didn't want us to make a mistake."

"Well, he shouldn't have done it. Because he did, they had to find out in the middle of the night, catching us in the dark."

"His intentions weren't evil."

"But he's always so smug."

"No. Not really. He's usually kind, but you always react to him."

"I have to. It's what I've been doing since he was born."

"Would you have talked to them if Abel hadn't?"

"Of course. Why would you ask that? I almost did yesterday morning. I was working up—"

Their father's voice interrupted, calling Cain to work with him. With an irritated expression, Cain looked down the river and gave a cursory wave. He turned back toward Lilith.

"Well, at least we don't have to be sneaky anymore. I can kiss you all I want."

So he did. Then he turned and jogged up the riverside. Lilith watched him go, hopeful that he would let go of his anger. He usually did—eventually.

****

Though Abel's brothers and sisters tried to pry information out of him, he disclosed nothing. He ate his morning meal and left quickly. He needed to discover if any lambs had been born in the night. He would search for the pregnant sheep, making certain they were all accounted for. He needed to determine if any needed assistance with their deliveries.

Taking a group of the oldest brothers with him, he hoped to cut down on speculation by removing them from the discussion. This upcoming marriage should be cast in the best light. Father had discerned that this was God's plan. It was now right for them to move forward. For their sake, Abel was relieved—he loved them. Their union would change everything.

Joda and Yonas—the brothers closest to his heart after Cain, posed questions. Abel responded with positive comments about Cain and Lilith's relationship. Concerning the fight, Abel deflected their curiosity by reminding them that this wasn't his first conflict with Cain. This was all too true. With that to ponder, he suggested they separate to look for the missing sheep. He needed time alone to think.

Now that the correct order for becoming married had been discussed and clarified, Abel didn't feel there was any need for this additional restriction or the public embarrassment. As he considered his actions last night, he realized he should have stayed and talked to them rather than running to get their parents. They were all adults. He shouldn't have hit Cain—he was grieved that he had. He had jumped to negative conclusions. He hadn't treated them with dignity.

Abel set out on his own to escape the questions of curious brothers and sisters and to tend to his sheep. As he walked through the hills and gullies looking for missing ewes, he cried out to Yahweh, asking for forgiveness for his misjudgment and his hasty action. He hadn't treated them like he would have wanted to be treated in the same situation. He would apologize to Cain, but he didn't know if Cain would listen. With a heavy heart, Abel went about his work.

****

As Lilith assisted her mother all morning, opinions about her upcoming marriage were divided among the siblings. Some of the speculations were almost humorous, but none came near the truth. Lilith was relieved. Without comment or defense, she let the mistaken theories swirl around her. With raised eyebrows, she often met Mother's eyes to gape in amazement. She avoided responding entirely until Nissa sidled up to her.

"So, this is the surprise you two were working on?"

"Yes."

"Why didn't you tell me?"

"Then it wouldn't have been a surprise, would it?" Lilith repeated her earlier words.

"But you could have told me. I wouldn't have told anyone

else."

"It was between Cain and me." She glanced at Mother, who gave her a reassuring smile.

"How did you decide to get married? What happened? Did he ask you?"

"Yes. He asked me."

"When?"

"On the day of rest, when we went for a long walk. That's why he didn't go with the little brothers up the river."

"What did he say?" Nissa asked.

"That he had loved me all my life, but he had just realized he wanted me for his wife. Before this week, he hadn't thought it was possible."

"Did he kiss you then?"

"Of course."

"Did you like it?"

Nissa giggled. She was clearly curious. Lilith knew she was jealous too. There was one particular brother whom Nissa hoped would want to marry and kiss her.

"Absolutely." Lilith grinned at Nissa, who blushed.

"What's all this about keeping you safe until you say your vows?"

"I can't talk about it."

"Can't or won't?"

"Won't."

"Come on! Why not?" Nissa wheedled.

"It's between Cain and me."

Lilith knew this made Nissa feel shut out, but that's the way it was. Cain was her world. If the earth had been filled with people, he still would have been more important than anyone else. She wouldn't talk about this; it embarrassed him. She looked at Mother, who squinted her eyes affectionately, smiling assurance as she cared for little Judith.

Clearly displeased, Nissa flounced away, but Lilith knew Nissa would spread her words. That would cut down on the speculation and eliminate at least half of the theories.

****

Cain resented his father. The rage he felt toward Abel could barely be contained. What must everyone think? Agitated as he was, he had to make himself not care.

Father had arranged for them to work alone. Together, they seeded one of the freshly turned fields. Walking silently down the rows, side by side, each used a long stick to poke a hole. They dropped in a seed then scraped the dirt back over it with their feet.

Breaking the silence, Cain glanced at his father. "You don't have to watch us like this."

"When you sneaked Lilith out of her room last night, what were your intentions?"

"I only wanted to kiss her."

"What altered what you wanted?"

"She grabbed me and surprised me by ..." He stopped. He didn't want to reveal the details.

"Do you think you could be surprised like that again?"

Cain answered slowly, "Yes."

"That's why I want to protect you."

"Can't Lilith and I try to protect each other?"

"I don't know. Can you?"

Cain considered this. His desire for Lilith simmered under the surface all the time; she filled his dreams. Perhaps they did need to be protected. Still, it humiliated him.

He changed the subject. "When can Lilith and I be married?"

"I thought perhaps the day after the coming day of rest."

Mentally, Cain ticked off the days. "In six days?"

"Yes, I think we can pull it together. The day you wed will be a holy day in the life of our family. We're too busy now with the lambing and the planting and harvesting, so we can make it part of the celebration at the end of the week. First, we'll have the yearly offering and sacrifice. After the day of rest, we'll rejoice over your wedding the following day. That gives us time to finish the work and prepare. How does that sound?"

"Six days."

Struck by the fact that the impossible was going to happen in only a few days, Cain stood amazed. God had heard his pleas and had answered his prayer—Lilith would be his.

He toyed with the idea of asking if they could marry immediately. As he considered the passion he and Lilith felt for each other, it seemed he should ask. Marrying right away would be a relief, but he decided against it. Resigned to the fact that his request would probably be refused, he focused on what had been granted. He could marry Lilith in six days!

Cain grinned at his father. His father smiled back, reaching to grip his shoulder.

Clearly, Father had arranged for them to work alone so they could be reconciled. Cain was still embarrassed about the announcement, but he felt kindness toward his father. Maybe he did understand him after all. Maybe Cain had misjudged him. Cain stepped over the row and hugged his father tightly. Father hugged him back.

"I'm sorry I didn't see your heart's desire sooner," Father said as they embraced. "I don't know how I missed it—your affections and temperament have always been so open. This oversight makes me all the more aware of my flawed and broken nature."

Stepping away, Cain studied his father. Cain didn't want to hear a long lecture about the effect his father's sin had produced since he had eaten the forbidden fruit. Whenever Father erred or made a mistake in judgment, they usually had to endure a long spiel about sin. It was too gloomy for Cain to consider today—he could be married! There were other topics he wanted to discuss. But he felt awkward asking. Embarrassed to make eye contact, Cain looked down.

"Since I'm going to become a husband, can I ask you some questions?"

"Certainly, son."

Both turned back toward their individual rows. They worked while they talked.

"Last night you told me that you didn't lie with Mother until three days after you'd made your vow. After Lilith and I say our pledge, do we have to wait three days?"

"No." Wearing a wry expression, Father chuckled. "With your mother and me it was all new. No one else existed. We didn't know what we were doing. It took us that long to figure it out."

Cain raised his eyebrows. "Three days?"

Laughing, his father nodded. Cain looked into his father's eyes, sharing the laugh. He didn't think it would have taken him three days. He knew it wouldn't have. As he thought about it, he grew sober. No. Three days were out of the question.

Cain asked his father some specific questions about what was involved in the physical union of a husband and wife, things he had always wondered about. His father gave him thoughtful answers, which prompted more questions.

Then Cain walked along silently, planting his row. He wanted to do what was right for Lilith, because he loved her. He didn't want to leave something undone that should be done. But neither did he want to be burdened with unnecessary stipulations.

"Can't I make the vow to Lilith in private, like you and Mother did?"

"We were the only people in the world, but we didn't do this secretly. It's difficult to explain the relationship we had with the animals in the Garden; there was more camaraderie, more friendliness and comprehension. It was like promising ourselves in front of God and our family."

"But if I promised myself to Lilith before only God, I would mean it. No one else would have to be there for my pledge to be sincere."

Father looked at him. "You said last night that you wanted the pledge to be strong."

Cain nodded. Yes, that was what he wanted.

"When you make a promise in front of others, it makes it stronger. Those watching then know of your commitment and love for each other. They are witnesses to your vow."

"But did God say to do it that way?" Cain asked.

"After I vowed to your mother, God blessed our union. Since then, He hasn't said anymore about this. We have to discern what He would want by listening to our consciences and remembering His words. Other than your mother and me, no one else has married yet."

"Then why can't we do whatever we want?"

"Your mother was made from my own flesh and bones. But even though that is so, after we lay together our attachment was even stronger—we truly felt as though we were one flesh then. Yahweh designed it this way, so this unity is significant. The fact that marriage will make you and Lilith one body is important. We need to move forward with care. Since you're the first, your actions lay the groundwork for your siblings."

It was always this way. As the firstborn, everything had to be tried out for the first time on him. Because no one had ever done this before, it had taken decades for him to discover he wanted Lilith as his wife. If they had discerned sooner that this was how it should be, he might have realized he loved Lilith a long time ago.

Everyone was learning, and his life was the experiment. Most lessons seemed to take place at his expense. It wasn't fair, but there was nothing he could do about it. Lowering his head, he got back to work, attempting to focus on the good rather than the resentment.

CHAPTER 8

WHEN THEY CAME IN FROM the fields to eat the midday meal, there stood Lilith, waiting for Cain with his food already prepared and heaped on the woven platter. All he had to do was follow her down the riverbank to sit and eat. A pleasant surprise.

Cain told her what their father had said. Well, some of it. He didn't tell her the many questions he had asked about what happens when a man lies with his wife.

Everybody left them alone, respecting their desire for privacy; but everyone watched them carefully, their eyes always upon them. They were all curious. Their long absences of the past few days now made sense to all their siblings. But no one spoke to them.

Cain washed his hands then devoured the food Lilith had prepared—all his favorites. Side by side, they leaned against each other, their backs pressed to a tree that grew by the river. Their feet hung in the shallows while they ate and talked.

"How do you feel about saying the vow in front of everyone?" Cain asked.

"I'd rather be alone with you. It seems private to me. But it makes sense when you consider that Father and Mother were in front of everyone, given their relationship with the animals then. What do you think?"

"I want to say it right now, take you to my room, and make you mine."

"Let's go!" She acted as though she were going to get up.

Then Lilith studied his face, her eyes flitting from one of his eyes to the other. Clearly, he didn't look playful. Her face grew serious. She leaned against his shoulder again.

"Father says I need to listen to my conscience and do what's right for you," he said. "Saying the vow in front of everyone makes the pledge stronger because everyone knows of our commitment. But I'm committed to you, even if no one else knows or sees it."

"So what do you think we should do?"

Cain sighed. "Part of me thinks we should say it in front of everyone. I want to please our parents and do what's required, but it's difficult to wait. And I really just want to be alone with you when I say it because of what it means. It's sacred."

****

Cain's eyes had a faraway aspect, as if he were engaged in some inner struggle. Given the good news they had just received, he was more somber than Lilith had expected. But then he turned toward her with an amused gleam in his eye.

"Father told me that he didn't lie with Mother until three days after he vowed to her."

"Really? Do we have to wait three days?"

"No." Cain chuckled and leaned in to kiss her forehead. "I asked the same question. He said it took them that long to figure out what to do."

"What?!" Lilith giggled. "I don't think it would have taken us that long."

"That's exactly what I thought! I know it wouldn't have." He smiled with her at this funny insight into their parents' early married life.

"I'm glad we don't have to wait three days. I want to give myself to you as soon as possible."

"And I want you to." He grinned at her and then grew serious again. "Can you wait six days to marry me?"

"I'd rather we did it today. But I can wait, so we can make it a celebration, especially if you think it's right. Six days until you're mine and I'm yours!"

Jumping up, she did an impromptu dance in the knee-high river water, bending to fling water on him each time she circled by. After she had danced by several times, he waded toward her. Taking her in his arms, he twirled her around, both of them laughing. She stopped dancing, cupped his face in her hands, and kissed his mouth.

"These six days will be the longest days of my life," she said.

"And mine as well. How will we wait?"

"By realizing that our hopes will be fulfilled. We *will* have each other. We've waited decades. What are a few days?"

"Nothing at all," he said.

****

But the days dragged by.

Though they were filled with busy activity—lambs born, seeds sown, crops gathered, and food prepared, the days lingered. It didn't help that the days stretched into the nights, when both of them tossed and turned upon their beds, sleep evading them, longing consuming them, impatience possessing them.

Their parents watched them with understanding eyes, their siblings with curiosity.

Their brothers and sisters had never witnessed anyone in love other than their own parents. They had never seen new, unsatisfied, impatient love, filled with desire, consumed with passion, obsessed with the other. Sometimes it was highly entertaining. At other times it brought the older ones to tears, because many of them realized they yearned for this too.

****

Two days after their betrothal, following a night of little sleep—what sleep there was having been consumed with sweaty, lustful dreams—Cain still slept. Bringing in the commotion of the morning's talking, arguing, eating, and laughter, the woven hemp fabric lifted from his doorway. He awakened. Eyes still closed, he heard someone lean into his room.

"Father's looking for you." Abel's bass rumbled low. "I thought you'd like to know."

The curtain fell shut. Cain's eyes snapped open. It was bright in the room, the sun already full in the sky. Quickly, he rolled to his feet, grabbed the small clay water jar from the corner, and dumped the water on his head. Hurriedly, he straightened his wet hair, applying the wooden comb Abel had made when they were boys. He wrapped his garment and rubbed the stubble on his chin, but had no time to do anything about it. The point of his chin still felt tender.

Those were the first words Abel had spoken to him since that night. The mere sound of his voice annoyed Cain. Abel was one to reconcile quickly; his voice had been sad—he should have apologized already. It goaded Cain that he hadn't.

Feeling the jolting thuds of determined footsteps nearing, Cain started for the doorway. His father ducked inside.

"Father, I was on my way out."

"God's blessing on you, Cain. Did you sleep well?"

"It's impossible to sleep. I toss and turn all night and dream things I'm ashamed to admit."

"I know how that is, son. I still remember some of the dreams I had." His father gave him an understanding look and a pat on the back.

"I'm sorry I'm late this morning. I just woke. I know we have a lot to do today."

"We do. We need to harvest that field upstream, as we spoke about yesterday. I'm sending Akiva, Hesed, Azriel, and a group of the younger boys with you, including Koren. Abel will be nearby with the sheep, if you need him. I'll only be with you for part of the day."

This would be the first time Cain would work away from his father's eyes since the escapade in the woods three nights ago. They had engaged in many long conversations. Father had slept in his own bed last night. Cain realized he had regained his father's trust.

The brothers he had assigned to work with him came next after Abel in birth order and would be the most help. It would also be a benefit to have Koren. He was young—barely fifty, his beard thin and his muscles long and lean—but he was strong and hardworking. Their father obviously knew Cain was worn-out from lack of sleep. He was glad Father had chosen these.

"Thank you, Father. Do I have time to eat?"

"No, the others are waiting outside. I've brought you something."

From his side, Father brought forward a small traveling basket and handed it to him. Cain didn't know if his mother or one of his sisters had prepared the food today, but it was ready to go. He would eat as they walked to the field.

Stepping out behind his father, he found his brothers waiting. They looked annoyed that he hadn't been ready earlier. When they noticed his expression, they quieted their grumbling. He was certain he looked haggard and unpleasant.

Silently, they all headed up the river toward the field. As they walked, Cain peered inside the soft-woven basket. All the foods inside were his favorites, and the bread was still warm.

This was Lilith's doing.

As he thought of her preparing his morning meal, his heart filled with contentment. She would be a good wife. When he had been tardy in the past, he had usually received cold bread and a few pieces of leftover fruit, unless Lilith had anything to do with it. Obviously, she had prepared it today. He smiled.

The others glanced at him and relaxed, clearly deciding it might not be such unpleasant work today after all. Their change of expression amused Cain. They began to chat with each other, to shove one another, and to joke as they marched quickly toward the harvest.

"How's your sleep been, Cain?" Akiva smiled widely. "Dreaming of Lilith?"

"Terrible!" Cain belied his words by grinning. "I can't sleep for thinking of her. When I finally do sleep, I dream of her all night. I'm miserable."

"Well, you're smiling, but you look really bad!"

"Thanks!" Cain reached into the basket and grabbed the warm bread, musing on the slender, graceful hands that had prepared it for him.

Hesed raised an eyebrow, looking at him inquisitively. "So, you ever going to tell us what you and Abel fought about that night? He won't tell us anything."

"No."

"I have a theory." Azriel pinned him with curious eyes. "You were out with Lilith in the woods doing things you shouldn't have been doing, weren't you?"

"Couldn't be," Hesed said. "What would Abel have to do with it?"

They all looked at Cain for some kind of confirmation.

"Not saying," he said, his mouth full of bread.

"Come on, Cain," Azriel said. "Give us something. We need to know how this works. We all want to get married too."

Akiva nodded vigorously.

"Still not saying."

Eventually, they gave up. Cain smiled. The younger brothers had all been listening intently to this exchange, not understanding much of what was said, but curious nevertheless.

Arriving at the field, they examined the waiting grain. They would cut the stalks and spread them out to dry on the spacious stone slab nearby. Later they would thresh the grain by flailing the stalks to loosen the kernels and by walking the oxen back and forth across the stone slab. Then they would sweep up the seeds to store in baskets—their grain until the next harvest.

The work involved much bending and straightening, cuts on hands and arms from the sharpened stone knives, and scratches from the ripened stalks. When the sun reached its zenith and beat down on their bent backs and shoulders, they all headed toward the compound to rest and take some refreshment. As they walked, they stretched their backs and examined their lacerated, itchy, and irritated arms.

Cain loved harvesting. He enjoyed everything about tending the fields, planting the crops, and bringing in the food. Joy and satisfaction swelled in his heart when he did this work. He had spent many days with his father as a small boy learning how to cultivate the land. It was what he was made to do. He especially loved throwing himself into the hard task of working the land now.

Work made the waiting easier.

CHAPTER 9

WHEN THEY ARRIVED FOR THE midday meal, Cain scanned the area searching for Lilith. She bustled up with his food, as she had each day since their betrothal—it seemed she had already assumed her role as his helper. He liked the idea.

First, she offered him a drink from a small jug of water. He could taste the sap from the bdellium tree. Concerned for his health, she must have added it. The sap from this tree healed wounds, settled stomachs, and rejuvenated the body during sickness or duress. Their parents had overlooked it in the Garden, not mindful of its restorative properties. Later, when Mother had used its sap to seal one of their first water-carrying vessels, they had accidentally discovered these benefits. Cain was glad Lilith had added it; he was definitely under duress.

Filled with gratitude, he leaned down and kissed her gently on the lips, then once more simply to taste her breath. Peals of high-pitched giggling sounded all around. They looked down and discovered an audience of small, interested siblings. Cain kissed Lilith again, just for them.

They all squealed and ran off together, chattering, laughing, and squealing some more. Cain smiled down at Lilith. Soon, he hoped, they would be the parents of a brood of children. The idea of having their own children filled his heart with happiness. Balancing the tray of food, he pulled her close and kissed her forehead.

"Thank you," he said. "It's a blessing to have my food ready. I'm hungry and tired. I'm not sleeping at night. Are you?"

"Hardly at all. I dream of you all night."

"And I of you. Sometimes things I shouldn't be dreaming."

"The same for me." She stood on her toes to kiss his mouth.

They turned to stroll toward the shady trees along the river, but Abel's voice stopped them.

"Cain, can I talk with you?" he asked quietly.

At the mere sound of Abel's voice, rage surged within Cain. Remembrance of Abel's actions burst to the fore of his mind. Never before had he been this angry with Abel. Poised to walk away with his arm about Lilith, Cain kept his back turned. He couldn't look at him.

"There are some things I'd like to say to you about that night." Abel sounded sad.

"What?" Cain still didn't turn.

"I'd like to speak privately."

"Thanks to you, the only time I get to see Lilith is under the watchful eye of the entire family. I don't want to sacrifice my time with her for you. So, no, I won't talk to you."

Without a glance back, Cain took a step, attempting to take Lilith with him.

****

Slipping out of Cain's grasp, Lilith stood her ground, torn between her two brothers. A scowl and a question on his face, Cain glanced back at her but kept walking. Shoulders stiffening, he picked up the pace. She stared at his departing back.

Then Lilith looked into Abel's grieved eyes, both darkened with bruises. Normally, Abel's eyes radiated kindness, their soft brown warmth drawing you in. Simply being near Abel always made her happy. He truly cared for each of them, often seeking them out for conversation, remembering their concerns and cares. But now, the weight of conflict showed in his eyes.

She had to do something. Cain had gone too far.

She looked around. Everyone watched this exchange, questions and opinions already forming, their conclusions showing plainly on their faces. Sympathetically, she patted Abel's shoulder then she trotted after Cain.

When she caught him, she wrapped her arms about his waist, keeping pace with his crisp steps. Once away from the family, Cain stopped. He looked down on her with piercing eyes.

"Why did you stay with him?"

"Cain, he's my brother too. You should speak to him."

"Why?"

"He's truly sorry."

"So what? That doesn't change anything. He betrayed us."

"Just talk to him. Promise me."

Cain bristled. "Are you on my side or his?"

"There is no side."

"Yes, there is, Lilith."

"I'm on the side of brothers getting along."

"You're supposed to be on my side. You always are."

"Not when you're wrong."

Cain's jaw dropped and his eyes narrowed. "So, you think I'm wrong?"

"Yes. You should listen to him."

"He's been talking to you when I'm not around, hasn't he?" Narrowing his eyes, he regarded her suspiciously. "You've never taken his side before. You've always been on my side in any disagreement. What happened? He's trying to come between us, isn't he?"

"It's not like that. Look at his face. He's grieved."

"Sure he is. Yeah, I'll talk to him. There might be more than merely talking."

"Cain, stop it!"

"He started this dialogue with you the night we were in the woods, while you both sat by the fire. That's when you first started to sympathize with him, when he turned you to his way of thinking, isn't it?"

"No. Of course not. Stop it right now."

Lilith had experienced his black moods before, especially when there had been some conflict with Abel or their father. Convinced they were against him, Cain's thoughts grew dark and insecure. Uncertain of their love and loyalty, he entrenched, positive they plotted ways to hurt him. Usually, she agreed with his grousing. She loved him despite it, but his suspicion now marred this happy week of marriage preparation.

This wouldn't be borne! Indignant, she turned to march away. Cain seized her arm, gripping it tightly. He jerked her back to face him.

"Where are you going?" His blue eyes flamed hot, smoldering with rage.

"I'm not going to listen to you talk like this." She attempted to pull away.

He clutched her arm more firmly, not letting her move. It hurt. His eyes bore into hers.

"Cain! Let go!"

Lilith wrenched her arm free, slapped her hands onto his chest, and shoved hard, glaring back at him. Then she stormed far down the riverbank and plopped down to examine her arm. Red marks rose up on her skin; they would leave a bruise.

Cain didn't follow her.

Displaying an attitude of indifference, Lilith remained where she was. She refused to even look in his direction. Inside, she seethed. After a long while, she heard him coming.

Incensed, she kept her face turned away.

****

Silently, Cain stared down at Lilith. She wouldn't look at him. He bit his lip.

His conscience bothered him—he felt guilty for hurting her. This disagreement shouldn't come between them. He didn't want to anger her, but he couldn't forgive Abel. He wanted to be reconciled to her, but he couldn't promise to resolve the conflict.

Abel was a traitor. But Cain decided he could at least concede to talk with him.

"Lily, I'm sorry I hurt you. I shouldn't have grabbed you or spoken like that. I'll talk to him."

Peering up at him, she studied his face. Submitting to her inspection, he met her eyes.

She always said his emotions shone on his face as clear as day. So he knew she'd detect his shame at the way he'd treated her, his rage at Abel's betrayal, his certainty that talking with Abel would do no good, his bitterness, his unwillingness to yield. His jealousy. His remorse.

Examination complete, Lilith looked back at the river, absentmindedly stroking the hair on his calf. It tickled. With her fingertip, she whorled a pattern. Mind elsewhere, she traced down his leg and gripped his ankle. Then she looked back up at him.

"You're forgiven," she said. "Thank you. At least you can talk."

"I'll try."

"Cain, I love you more than I love Abel. I love you more than our parents, more than any of our brothers and sisters. I'm always on your side. I want you to talk to Abel because I am on your side. It isn't good for brothers to disagree."

"I'll talk, but I can't agree. It hurt me that he did that."

"I know. Me too. But he's truly sorry."

"We'll see."

"Yes."

Lilith turned and kissed his thigh, right behind the knee. The warmth of her lips jolted him. He dropped down beside her. She stroked his back, slipping her hand inside his sleeve opening to lightly caress his skin. He always liked it when she tickled his back.

Gently lifting her arm, Cain pressed his lips to each fading mark left by his fingers, one by one. Leaning against him, she kissed his shoulder.

"I'm truly sorry," he whispered.

"I know." She gazed into his eyes. "You always are; I always forgive you." She sighed. "I probably love you more than I should."

"Is that possible? Should there be a limit on love?"

"I don't know. I'd do anything for you—break rules, disappoint people, hurt others, abandon people I love, leave my home. That might be too much love."

He leaned his forehead against hers. "I love you that way too."

Loudly, their father called to Cain that they were heading back to the fields. Waving back, he gave their father his attention then he turned back to Lilith.

"I'll talk to Abel because I love you," he said.

"Because I love you, I want you to talk to him. It's the right thing to do."

****

Jumping up, Cain returned to work. Lilith stayed by the river, considering this conflict between her brothers and hoping it could be resolved. She evaluated Cain's reaction to her insistence that he talk to Abel. He had felt betrayed and jealous—*jealous!* As if she could ever love anyone as she loved him! Sometimes he was so easily wounded. She shook her head.

Despite his temper and insecurities, she adored him—actually, because of these flaws. She understood him; she *knew* him. Anything he asked, she would do.

Was her love for him out of balance? Her parents had modeled love, often saying hard things to one another when necessary. When Cain turned surly, Lilith had been shocked that she'd been able to walk away from him. It was a first. Insisting he talk to Abel was right—her passion for him had obviously grown. Now she wanted what was best for Cain, dark moods and bitterness aside, and that meant reconciling with Abel.

****

In the harvest field, Cain labored with Father and the oldest brothers. They would stack this grain with what they had

harvested in the morning, drying the entire harvest on the flat
stone area where they threshed. Grasping the grain firmly, Cain
severed the stalk. Attempting to get all the work finished, he and
his brothers worked with frenzied energy.

Suddenly, everyone stood still. Straightening, Cain looked
around. Abel stood behind him wearing an expression of abject
brokenness.

Cain hadn't looked at Abel since he'd pummeled him.
Humble, apologetic face aside, Abel's injuries appeared worse
than his own.

"Cain, can we talk?" Abel asked him quietly.

Cain looked at their father. He waved them both off, pointing
to the shady trees along the far edge of the field. They would
have privacy there. Silently, they walked toward the trees. Cain's
heart felt as hard as a stone. When they arrived in the shade, he
leaned against one of the trees, crossed his arms over his chest,
and fixed his eyes on Abel.

"Why are you trying to turn Lilith against me?" Cain asked.

"Turn Lilith?"

"Yes. What have you been saying to her?"

"Only that I'm sorry for what happened that night."

"There has to be more. She's never taken your side before."

"How has she taken my side?"

"She insisted I talk to you. She says I should reconcile with
you."

"That doesn't sound like she's taking anyone's side. She
simply wants us to get along."

"That's exactly what she said. Did you tell her to say that?"

"No! Of course not."

"I don't believe you."

"Why would she listen to me? She's always favored you; she
wants to be your wife. I think she knows it's the right thing to do."

"There's no way to reconcile. You betrayed Lilith and me,
embarrassing us in front of the entire family. You're a traitor."

"That's what I want to talk to you about."

"So, talk."

****

Abel shot up a prayer, begging Yahweh to give him strength—Cain never made apologies easy. He glared in disdain with his arms folded across his chest—face hard, eyes cold, battering you with angry words while you tried to humble yourself. It had always been like this. It had never been easy to reconcile with Cain. Yet, Abel loved him, so he always made peace.

"Cain, the night I came upon you and Lilith, I shouldn't have gone to our parents ..."

Here Cain snorted, curling his lip into a sneer. Abel didn't allow himself to lose heart.

"... and I shouldn't have jumped to the conclusion that you had made love with Lilith when you didn't answer me immediately. I'm sorry I hit you."

Drumming his fingers and tapping his foot, Cain looked away, as if he wanted him to hurry up and say what he had to say so he could get back to work. Lilith had told Abel that they would have made love if he hadn't stumbled upon them. Cain seemed not to remember this fact of the evening. Nevertheless, Abel knew he had handled it wrongly.

He continued, "I didn't treat you the way I would have wanted to be treated. I believed the worst of you."

Cain whipped his head around to stare at Abel, his gaze piercing. "You think so?"

"Yes. I should have talked with you and Lilith. I brought our parents into it too quickly. I was wrong."

"Are you done?"

"Yes, I think that's all I have to say. I'm sorry I wronged you. Can you forgive me?"

"No."

Head held high, Cain strutted out into the glaring afternoon sun, back to the field, leaving Abel staring after him. He had been afraid it would go this way. The only hope Abel could see was for God to turn Cain's heart. Head down as he staggered back toward his sheep, Abel sent up a fervent prayer pleading for Yahweh's mercy on them all and for healing for Cain's heart. Once more, he begged forgiveness for the way he had wounded Cain and Lilith with his hasty action.

****

When Cain returned to the field, everyone stopped working and looked at him expectantly. When Adam saw his face, he knew all their hopes had been dashed.

"What?" Cain asked, clearly irritated.

"Did you talk? Did you work out your differences?" Adam asked.

"He talked. I listened. No. We're still at odds."

Cain grabbed the sharp rock he'd been using, checked the bindings, and proceeded to hack off handfuls of grain again. He seemed to expend all his frustration on the grain, working hard and fast, fueled by angry energy.

Watching Cain's hardhearted response to Abel, Adam considered again all the consequences of eating the forbidden fruit. Cain seemed to have learned or inherited from Eve and from him all their best qualities and all their worst—all the things that sprang from their sinful natures.

Cain was brilliant and hardworking, innovative and compassionate, insightful and thoughtful, as well as a good listener; he had an ironic sense of humor. He loved with all his heart and soul and body, thoroughly, passionately, totally; but, he also hated the same way. He could be paranoid and insecure if he felt anyone was against him. Cain's temper was like Adam's, and he outshone his mother in the area of bitterness.

Adam sent up a silent prayer to Yahweh, a prayer for peace and love in his family, a prayer for strength for Abel and compassion and healing for Cain.

God was their only hope.

CHAPTER 10

OUT IN THE RIPENED GRAIN, Satan listened to two of his chief princes—Samyaza and Azazel. Together they had stood in Eden—glorious angels then, watching the first man and woman and designing ways to tempt them. Together they had rebelled against God. Together they had fallen. Burnt, blackened, and maimed now, they were united in their hatred of the humans.

Now they snickered as they studied Cain working alongside his brothers.

"This is progressing exactly as we planned," Samyaza stated.

"One hundred twenty years of watching and plotting are yielding more effective results," Azazel added. "Their sinful natures make them easy to manipulate."

Samyaza snorted. "Indeed. When we distract them from thoughts of God, they believe they are strong and capable, right in their man-made viewpoints, and entitled to hold them."

"They swell up with their own arrogance and self-sufficiency."

"And then they fall."

"It always works," the three said together, eyeing one another. Satan nodded.

"Pride and bitterness fuel the sin-poison within them," Samyaza sneered. "They think they're the measure of all things. Once we've stifled their consciences, no need to forgive or extend mercy impels them. Simply examine the specimen before us."

Here they all looked at Cain. He worked with angry energy, fuming within. It was too comical! The three fallen angels guffawed with derisive laughter.

"Look at him." Azazel snickered. "They all do that when we've cornered them. He's a little god, an idol of his own making, worshiping himself, meting out proclamations and vendettas, thinking he's hurting the ones he spurns and belittles. Yes, he's wounding Abel. I'm glad."

"But, in reality, he hurts himself far more."

"He has no idea he endangers his eternal soul. The humans comprehend next to nothing."

"Idiotic dirt creatures!" Satan scoffed. "We coerce and tempt them into our likeness, even though they're made in the image of God."

"You're right!" Samyaza nodded. "They're becoming like us!"

Satan fixed his gaze upon Cain. Hatred filled the entirety of his spirit. "Just as I planned, we're destroying the work of God's hands. Driven by their deformed sinful natures and their mindless reactions, the humans mar the likeness of God within them."

"In this state, none of them will be qualified or capable of crushing you."

Satan agreed. This was his goal. Their efforts pleased him.

He sneered wide and menacing. "Once I've used them up, I intend to kill them all."

CHAPTER 11

IT HAD BEEN A DIFFICULT day of work with the grain—bending and straightening, stooping and gathering, cutting of hands and scratching of arms. Small bits of the stalks caught under their garments, irritating their skin. But, when Adam trudged with his sons back to the family compound, the day's work satisfied him. It was now time to celebrate and give thanks to God.

The harvest season was Adam's favorite time of year. Tomorrow they would ready their gifts for each other, their offerings for the Creator, and their hearts to praise Him. As their slow and heavy steps brought them in from the various fields, Adam sensed the burden lifting from his weary sons. In spite of their fatigue, each face was happy, each ready to rejoice.

All were jubilant except Cain and Abel. They were preoccupied with the conflict—one face embittered, one face grieved, and he, their father, worried and heartsore.

All of them rounded the river bend to the secluded area where the male family members bathed. Stripping off their leather garments, they leapt into the river, hooting, laughing, and splashing. But, on one end of the group, Adam bathed near Abel, consoling him as they washed. On the other end, far down the river, Cain stood alone.

****

Unable to watch his father comforting Abel, Cain turned his back. He was the one who had been embarrassed in front of the entire family, not Abel.

Wading around the bend to the private place where he bathed, he distanced himself from the noise. He needed to think. He'd never felt this angry before. His head throbbed.

To enjoy the coming holy days, he needed to shake off this resentment he felt toward Abel. He would turn his mind toward his upcoming marriage—he would think about Lilith.

Moving against the current, he waded out into waist-deep water and scrubbed all the chaff and salty sweat from his skin, using handfuls of sand he scooped from the bottom. Then he immersed himself and massaged his scalp, enjoying the sensation of the water on his tired body. The crispness of the river cooled his emotions.

He surfaced. Keeping his head barely above the water, he let the river wash over him. Gently, the light sound of female laughter drifted to his ears. *Who is that?*

Following the sweep of the river as it curved, he waded upstream toward the sound. The long, green grasses grew in the shallows here. On the other side of the thick grasses, women's soft voices lilted and laughed. Perhaps his sisters bathed there. He was about to turn away when Lilith's voice uttered his name—it floated to him lightly across the surface of the water.

He paused. If she was bathing, he should turn and go downstream. But then, his thoughts captured him. Irresistibly, he was pulled toward her voice. Perhaps he could glimpse her body again. Desire coursed through him; his heart throbbed in his chest.

The memories of all the times he had hidden and watched her when he was younger—a guilty, sinful pleasure—snared him. He hadn't done it often, but often enough. That was how he knew what Lilith's body looked like under her garment. He remembered how hiding and looking at her body made him feel.

Moving carefully into the cool shade of the bulrushes and other tall grasses, he edged close enough to hear Lilith and his sisters talking about ... him. Motionless, he strained to hear more.

"... but it's difficult to wait," Lilith said.

"What do you think it will be like?" Nissa asked quietly.

"I don't know. But if it's like kissing him, it will be beyond what I've ever dreamt or imagined—much more intense. Just kissing him has been ... there's no way to describe it."

Hidden in the thick grasses, he still couldn't see them. Again his conscience nudged him, but he shoved away the guilt. Gliding silently, he edged closer and caught a glimpse of the back of Lilith's head and her bare shoulder. Surprising him, she stood up in the water—her back to him, and all of her beautiful shape was revealed.

Water ran off her wet body, glistening in the setting sun. She was lovely!

"Mother said it hurt the first time," Ariel said.

"Surely that would be temporary, wouldn't it?"

"It won't matter," Lilith said. "It will be worth it. I'll be Cain's. It will make me truly his."

Turning to look at Nissa, Lilith's entire right breast was displayed. Cain quit breathing. He wanted to wade through the tall grass, grab her, and take her. The temptation nearly overpowered him. He was already naked; it would be a delightful thing to accomplish.

"I hope, well ... Akiva decides to marry me," Ariel said. "I want ... Oh! Look at the sun! Mother will need us."

They all stood, and Nissa and Ariel waded toward the shore. Without even a ripple, Cain slid away. He felt dirty inside for having looked on her unseen, but the thrill of seeing her body overpowered his disgust with himself. Shoving aside the condemnatory thoughts that filled his mind, he tried to move quietly.

"Cain!" hissed a whisper across the water.

Startled, he turned. Lilith frowned at him through the thick bank of bulrushes between them.

"Lilith, come on," Nissa said loudly from the shore. "We have so much work to do. The sun is near setting."

Lilith looked toward her. "Go ahead. I'll follow. I want to get one of the flowers from the lily pads. Cain likes them. I'll be right there."

She turned back and fixed her eyes on his as she slipped toward the cluster of lily pads. Only her head and shoulders showed above the surface. She glanced over her shoulder then back at him. A thick wall of various tall grasses separated them.

"What are you doing here?" she whispered.

Biting his lip, he dropped his head. Shame's warmth tickled his cheekbones. Keeping his eyes on the river, he couldn't look at her. She awaited his reply.

"Lily, I'm sorry. I was watching you. I was washing downstream, and I heard your voice. I shouldn't have looked at you, but I couldn't resist."

"So, did looking make it more difficult to wait, or easier?"

He lifted his eyes to hers. "Much more difficult."

"Finding you watching me makes it more difficult for me. I want you too, you know."

"I'm really sorry, Lily. I shouldn't have done it."

"Leave. Then I'll get out of the water. There's no need to make this more of a trial than it already is. I know I couldn't look at your naked body right now and be able to bear waiting."

Her eyes gleamed. He hadn't thought how this might affect her; he had been selfish.

But, having her catch him like this, while it was embarrassing, was also tantalizing. He felt himself blush. Then she sang to him, very softly, in low tones, captivating him with her words, her voice, and her eyes as she gazed at him through the bulrushes.

"I will be Cain's, and he will be mine.
I will delight in the strength of his arms
Holding my body against his.
I will cherish his kisses.

He will be like sweet perfume to me,
Resting between my breasts.
He is like a palm tree, laden with dates.
I will sit in his shade and eat the fruit.
It will be sweet to my taste.
I am my beloved's, and he is mine."

The song's promises would soon be fulfilled; the union of their bodies was nearly upon them.

"Lilith, I want to make love to you right now." He groaned and looked away before turning his gaze back to her.

Talking, loud splashing, and laughter announced several of their brothers heading their way. Lilith gestured a kiss toward Cain and disappeared among the tall grasses. He ducked under the water, swimming rapidly back down the Tigris. The four-day wait might kill him. He felt as if he would never get to have her. He hoped the river water cooled his face.

Surfacing, he smoothed back his hair, wiped his eyes, and watched Akiva and Azriel wade in his direction. Akiva had something pressing on his mind—Cain had seen the look before.

"What do you think?" Akiva asked as they neared. "How should I pursue Ariel?"

"First, speak to Father then you can avoid any conflict."

"That's what this is all about?"

"Yes …," Cain answered slowly. "If I'd spoken to Father first, the conflict probably would have been avoided. Father will explain what you're to do and how."

"Can't you resolve it with Abel?"

"No."

"Too bad," Azriel interjected.

Cain shrugged then returned his attention to Akiva, not wanting to discuss Abel. He had just cleared his mind of him. He thought about Akiva and Ariel. Yes, he had seen this coming. Ariel was two years older than Lilith and slept in the same room with Nissa and her. Because Ariel was usually near Lilith, Cain had seen Akiva's attentiveness to her throughout the years.

"Does Ariel know?" he asked Akiva.

"I'm sure she does, but I haven't spoken to her yet."

"Speak to Father first. Do it soon."

"I'm glad you brought this issue forward."

"I didn't do it on purpose," Cain said. "It just happened. I didn't even know it was a possibility until recently."

"Neither did I. You're always first. Firstborn bears the brunt."

"Unfortunately." Cain smirked.

Discussing strategy, they waded back. Before donning their sheepskin garments, they beat them against the rocks along the bank, removing the dirt and chaff. When the men and boys had dressed, they strolled home for what they knew would be a joyous meal. The happiness of the holy days was uplifting. There would be special food to eat and time to sit around the fire and talk. All had gifts to finish.

Cain needed to complete a delicate leather bracelet for Lilith. He had plaited it intricately; it would barely slide over her hand to fit her wrist closely, so she could always leave it on. Proud of the design, he felt certain she'd like it.

As they came into the clearing, the children, girls, and women hurried toward them, greeting them with joyful words and hugs. Lilith welcomed Cain home as though she hadn't seen him since the midday meal, not as if she'd just caught him looking at her naked in the river.

"Cain, I've missed you."

She entwined her arms about his waist. She wore the lily from the river in her hair.

His cheeks grew hot again with the shame of what he'd done. Arching one eyebrow, she cocked her head in reply. Grasping her about the waist, Cain laughed out loud. He swept her up into the air, gazing up at her, twirling her until he was sure they both felt sick. He felt giddy with love and desire. Again the small siblings chattered, laughed, and shrieked.

"He picked her up!"

"They're in looooove!"

"Cain, spin me around too. Spin me!"

"Kiss her, Cain! Kiss her!"

"That's how you get married."

After the family meal, they piled the fire high with wood. All gathered around to sing songs, tell stories, and laugh together. All except Abel, Cain noticed, who sat alone, quietly, on the opposite side of the fire. Cain didn't look at him again.

Rosy by the firelight, Lilith leaned on Cain; he kissed her frequently. Much had changed since the last time they had sat around the fire together. It was good to be alive, good to have their wedding day nearly upon them, good to love each other so thoroughly and completely, to be tantalized with the other, surprised by one another, even though they had loved for decades.

When they left the dying embers, he strolled with Lilith to her sleeping chamber, pausing to allow Nissa and Ariel to enter before drawing Lilith aside. Then he lingered with her. Singing softly of his longing, he held her close against his body, kissing her. With racing heart, he nuzzled the smooth skin of her neck, whispering his undying love.

Then he walked to his own room. There was no way he would be able to sleep.

Gazing up at the stars, he sat outside for a long while, the cold stones against his back. He wished the waiting were over. He felt frantic to have Lilith. The waiting was torturous.

CHAPTER 12

HAVING PRODDED AND PROVOKED CAIN and Lilith's passions, Satan now whispered a suggestion to Adam and Eve, chortling at his craftiness. He framed the thought using their own voices, their own pronouns, as if it originated within them.

We should let Lilith and Cain spend the day together. That will reestablish trust, soothe Cain's anger, and, hopefully, soften his bitterness toward Abel.

In their bed, Adam and Eve rolled toward one another, both animated about an idea that had simultaneously occurred to them. They whispered together. It seemed like the perfect solution. They smiled. Pride in their parenting skills showed on their faces. Completely unaware, they had grabbed up Satan's scheme, walking right into his trap. Feeling magnanimous, forgiving, and wise, they remained completely oblivious.

Satisfaction swelled within Satan. He was so good at this!

****

The day of preparation started well. Lilith kissed Cain on the mouth. Shocked and surprised, he blinked, heart thudding. Under the covering of leather, he lay naked.

"God's blessing on you, beloved," Lilith said softly.

"What are you doing here?" Cain whispered, his eyes darting.

"Mother and Father have given me permission to spend the day with you. We've regained their trust. They're right outside, allowing me to awaken you."

It was a gift! An answer to prayers! Cain grabbed Lilith and pulled her to his chest, squeezing her tightly. She squealed with laughter. On the other side of the hemp door covering, their parents chuckled at their joyous sounds.

"Your beard is growing in beautifully." Lilith kissed his chin. "I like your stubbly whiskers, but I assume you want to shave. Should we do that first?"

He nodded. "Step outside, and I'll dress."

After she disappeared through the woven door covering, he sprang from the grass matting and hastily donned his garment, not wanting to waste a single moment. Hair still tousled, he hurried outside. Father, Mother, and Lilith stood waiting. Throwing his arms around them, he hugged all three together, kissed his mother's cheek, and thanked his parents profusely. Then he grabbed Lilith by the hand and raced with her toward the river.

The water slowed as it rounded the bend, forming a smooth surface near the bank. He always peered into the water here to scrape off his whiskers. This was where he had thrown in Lilith when she first watched him shave. He had bathed here last night before he heard the girls.

Edging out over the riverbank, they lay flat, studying their reflections in the water.

"Ugh," Cain said. "Look at my hair."

Leaning over, he plunged his head into the river. The cold water bit. Under the water, the sound of Lilith's laughter echoed. Water streamed off his head when he lifted it.

"Well, that was thorough." She giggled. With her fingers, she straightened his wet hair. "Your hair looks even blacker when it's wet. I love your hair—it's dramatic, like you."

He grinned at her—she made him happy in every way.

The Tigris settled and smoothed again, reflecting the two of them. Cain had tucked into his belt the sharp stone he used for shaving. He now pulled it out, studied his mirrored reflection, and scraped the stone slowly across his face, removing the stubble.

"Let me try," Lilith said.

He propped himself on his elbows. To get the angle right, she reclined between his arms, her legs sticking off to the side. Intently, she focused on his face, pressing the sharp edge against his cheek. He inhaled sharply; she had cut him.

"I'm so sorry!" she said. "You're bleeding! I wasn't sure how much pressure to use."

He looked down at her. "It's alright."

"Tiny droplets," she whispered, running her finger along the cut. She studied her finger then licked off his blood.

How he wanted her! He didn't know why this aroused him, but it did. He lowered his mouth to hers, parting her lips. The shaving came to a halt. He kissed her thoroughly. Then Cain pulled back, and they looked into each other's eyes. *Resist her,* he told himself.

"Continue." He raised himself onto his elbows again.

Taking a deep breath, she drew the stone across his cheek, cutting only whiskers. Gingerly, she shaved along his jawline then down his neck, slowly scraping over the lump that vibrated when he talked. She paused, pressing her lips to the spot; he spoke her name as she did. She giggled. Laughing softly, he bent to kiss the top of her head. She smiled. Then she steadied her hand to shave his chin and upper lip.

"This part is more difficult," he said. "I often cut myself."

"Do you want to do it?"

"No, I trust you. Even if you cut me, it's fine."

✳✳✳✳

Because Lilith had seen Cain's face her whole life, she was more familiar with it than she was with her own. Hardly ever did she pause to look at her own reflection. But now, she was up close to him. She hadn't had the leisure to study his face like this before.

It would be a pleasure to be his wife. She would enjoy having this intimate knowledge of every aspect of his body. Every whisker, every scar, every part of him was beloved. She couldn't wait to see the rest of his body this closely.

She realized he was looking down at her.

"What's wrong?" she asked.

"You weren't shaving. You were just stroking my face. Your eyes weren't focused."

"I was daydreaming about examining your entire body this closely."

His blue eyes softened as he sighed a contented sound. She wondered if they could make it three days. Gazing at him, she considered yielding right then. It would be blissful. But she decided to wait—she saw it in his eyes too. They were agreed. They would publicly proclaim their love, make the vow, and then possess each other, in that order.

Softly, Cain caressed her lips with his. It was a kiss of desiring everything right now, but making the choice to wait. His fingers burrowed into her hair, clutching her to himself. Her heart overflowed with love.

At this moment, someone crashed through the riverbank shrubs.

Out of the corner of her eye, Lilith caught a glimpse of Abel. Obviously, he had not expected anyone to be here. Carrying a clay vessel, he sang a melancholy tune as he headed toward the river. Abruptly, he halted before he tripped over them.

Neither of them moved; they continued to hold each other.

"What are you doing?" Abel asked.

"Go away, Abel," Cain muttered, his eyes still fixed on hers.

"Are you supposed to be alone?"

Lilith felt the fire of rage stoke within Cain. His breathing quickened, and his eyes grew dark and menacing. With a sneer, he snapped his head around, glaring up at Abel.

"Mother and Father know exactly where we are and exactly

what we're doing."

Abel looked to her for confirmation.

"Why are you looking at her?" Cain asked. "Don't you believe me? Leave!"

"Go, Abel," Lilith whispered.

Keeping her eyes on Cain's face, Lilith tried to keep hold of their beautiful moment. She felt it fleeing. Cain turned toward her and pressed his lips to hers again, heedless of Abel. After kissing her, Cain glanced over his shoulder. Abel hadn't moved.

"Go!" Cain's yell whopped across the surface of the river.

As Abel walked away, Cain gritted his teeth. The muscles in his jaw clenched.

"Judgmental pest!" He inhaled long and slow. "I'm not going to let him ruin this day too. I did talk to him yesterday, like I said I would. I didn't forgive him."

Nodding, she looked at him. The moment was gone.

Carefully she finished shaving Cain, but more from duty than desire. She nicked him and immediately pulled his chin to her mouth to lick off the blood. When she did this, his eyes grew large and he grabbed her, kissing her eagerly. His reaction had surprised her each time. There was some underlying passion that she didn't understand. Then, laughing, he splashed water on his face, sprinkling them both.

"When are you going to let your beard grow?" she asked.

He shrugged.

"After today, don't shave again. I bet your beard will grow in as thickly as Father's."

"I'll be all stubbly on our wedding day."

"I don't care. I like to kiss your face either way. I'll take the stone so you're not tempted." She tucked it into her belt; she loved his stubble. His face would be striking with a beard.

"I won't be tempted. I'll do whatever you want."

"Now we'd better get up, or I won't be able to resist you any longer."

Grinning at her, he complied, helping her up. "What shall we do next?"

"Let's go gather some of your favorite fruit, so we'll have it for our wedding day."

Linking hands, they headed for the orchard. Lilith's heart swelled with happiness.

****

Confused, Abel left the way he had come. Needing some time to think, he hiked north along the river. Did his parents really know what Cain and Lilith were doing and where they were? This posed a dilemma. Should he trust them, or should he inform their parents?

He didn't want to repeat his earlier mistake.

Praying about what to do, Abel walked until the sun neared its zenith. He offered up his emotions to God. Cain and Lilith's ardent affection had shaken him each time he had stumbled upon them. He had witnessed romantic love in a way he'd never seen before—up close and in the throes of passion. Would he ever love anyone like that?

Eventually, he concluded it would be best to return to the fireside with the rest of the family. If they were looking for Cain and Lilith, he would know where to take them; if they were unconcerned, he would say nothing. He chose to believe the best. He would trust them.

When Abel arrived, Mother appeared so harried and overwrought with her preparations for the meal and tomorrow's feast that he lifted the baby right out of her arms. After kissing Mother's cheek, he carried Judith to the shade and settled in. He couldn't resist placing nearly constant kisses upon the infant's small head with its soft halo of curls—babies were so precious.

Being a holy day, the children ate first. Spying him in the shade, one by one they headed toward him, each carrying their individual basket of food. Soon, small eating siblings surrounded him. How he loved them! The youngest clustered at his knees, prattling away in their sweet, high-pitched voices. Their childlike words caused him to smile.

Hearing laughter and loud greetings, Abel glanced up. Cain and Lilith had arrived. They smoothed back one another's hair, caressed each other's arms, touched the other's face, and finished one another's sentences. It was almost as if they were one body already.

Abel kept his eyes focused on Cain, hoping to communicate his brotherly love with a smile, since Cain wouldn't listen to him. He was grieved that he'd been suspicious and was glad he'd said nothing to their parents. Seeming to sense his gaze, Cain turned.

Cain's cold expression eradicated Abel, wiping him from any consideration, as if he were of no consequence in any way—a nonentity. He felt as if he'd been struck by a physical blow. Jolted by the hatred in Cain's eyes, Abel felt heartsore.

This rift saddened him. Cain was his closest friend. Looking down at the little ones, Abel noticed they had all grown still. They stared at him with round, solemn eyes, as if they sensed his mood. This wouldn't do.

"Let's go see the newborn lambs." He smiled gently at them.

The toddling ones jumped about joyously. Judith gurgled a baby laugh, catching the improved mood of the others. Hoisting her up into his arms, he took comfort in her unabashed affection. It helped salve the ache in his heart. He hated conflict.

****

Cain saw the dejection in Abel's eyes and was glad he'd hurt him. He was probably the only one who had detected that Abel was downcast. Abel never drew attention to himself, and the others didn't know him as thoroughly. Irritated by his mere presence, Cain muttered as he watched him depart with the small children. Abel's proximity destroyed the day.

After eating their food, Cain drew Lilith apart, not wanting to waste any more of this precious day. Enough of it had been spent on Abel—the pest! Cain shook off his foul mood.

"I have to finish your gift," he said. "I need to work on it in my room."

"Take me with you. I won't look."

"Yes, you will. You always do."

"You're probably right. My gift for you is all done. What should I do?"

"Sleep."

She nodded. He knew she hadn't been sleeping. Before hurrying off, he kissed her forehead.

While he finished the bracelet, he considered her reaction. He wanted to see her respond naturally and openly. He decided to ask her if she'd like to exchange gifts privately. He left to search for Father to explain his plans. Finally, he detected his father's voice in the parental bedroom. Announcing himself, he pulled back the doorway covering.

Facedown, his father lay stretched out on the floor.

Embarrassed, Cain realized he'd interrupted his prayers. Father was preparing for the day of sacrifice and thanksgiving tomorrow. Cain had neglected his own preparations.

"I'm sorry, Father." He started to back out.

"It's fine, son." His father sat up. "What do you need?"

"I'm going to ask Lilith to take a walk up the Tigris. We'll take some food and eat together. I want to exchange our gifts tonight, so we can do it privately. We'll be back by bedtime. I wanted you to know."

"Are you prepared for tomorrow?"

"As prepared as I can be under the circumstances."

"Are you certain?"

"Yes." Cain knew he sounded testy. He didn't want to answer any more questions; he wanted to get away from here and give Lilith her gift.

"Alright," Father said. "I'll see you tonight."

As Cain walked away, he heard Father praying again.

"Yahweh, make Yourself real to Cain. Change his heart. Save him from ...."

Cain walked faster. He didn't want to hear this. He knew his father prayed for all his children, but Cain's heart hardened. Why would his father pray for him in particular? He shrugged and tried to clear his head. He didn't want to think about this.

Quietly, he slid into Lilith's room and gazed down upon her, asleep on her mat. Her breathing was soft, her curls spread out around her on the pillow. A trace of perspiration beaded upon her upper lip. She was so beautiful! He squatted to kiss her ear.

"Lilith," he said softly, "wake up, dearest."

She stirred, opened her eyes, and stared up at him, disoriented.

"Oh!" She stretched. "I was dreaming about you."

"Good dreams I hope. You're beautiful when you sleep, Lily. You always have been." He kissed her again. "Do you want to open your gift alone with me? We can eat in the woods. I already spoke to Father."

"Yes! I had hoped you'd want to do that!"

Laughing for joy, Lilith vaulted from her floor mat and raced out to get all they would need. Following her out, Cain smiled broadly; their hearts were in sync. He couldn't wait to see what she thought of his gift, since she wouldn't have to guard her reaction.

Anticipation and excitement washed over Cain as he watched her run.

CHAPTER 13

CAIN HURRIED TOWARD THE FOOD storage cave. Sooner than expected, Lilith burst out, carrying a soft-woven basket. Lacing his fingers through hers, he raced with her up the river.

The beauty of this day astounded him. Soon they would never be separated. He would have long periods of uninterrupted union with Lilith, with no boundaries, no need to stop at any point, ability to know and love each other completely. His entire self had yearned for her for most of his life. Exuberant with their freedom to be together, they ran along the water.

"How far do you want to go?" he asked.

"Wherever you want."

He had in mind a tranquil grassy spot far up the river. Long ago, they had discovered it while exploring. A small stream ran through the meadow, bubbling and gurgling over a rocky bottom. It fed into the Tigris. They had enjoyed wading in its shallow depth. An abundance of flowers flourished in the patch of sunlight. It was as if the Creator had planted it all for them.

Cain could run faster than Lilith; but she had endurance, so he slowed his pace to run side by side. In a hurry to see the other's reaction, they covered much ground before they spoke.

"We can walk," he said, his words choppy with heavy breathing, "when you get tired."

"You mean, when *you* get tired."

"Oh, I won't get tired before you do."

"Yes, you will. You always do."

"No, I don't!" He laughed. It was exactly the opposite.

Eventually her pace slowed, and she walked first. He didn't say *I told you so*. She smiled at him for not saying it.

"Are we almost there?" she asked.

"Almost. It's right around this bend, back in the woods."

"Oh! Is it that tiny meadow we found that one time?"

"Yes."

Lilith began to skip and dance. "I was hoping we were going there!"

Twirling, she threw her arms wide. Laughing, he scooped her up, carrying her for the rest of the way. Tickling his ear with her breath, she smothered his face with kisses. Leaving the river, he followed the small stream until the little meadow opened before them. There he put her down.

The grass was bright green in the afternoon sunlight; the heads of the flowers all bobbed gently in the warm, heavy air. Butterflies fluttered and bees bumbled from flower to flower. A circle of sunshine filled the middle, where no trees grew, leaving an open space. In awe, they walked reverently into the shaft of light and sat cross-legged, facing each other.

Silently, they stared into one another's eyes, neither speaking.

"It's exquisite." Her voice held a sacred hush.

"But not as breathtaking as you."

Softly, she smiled. "Food or gifts first?"

"Gifts. Open yours first, Lily."

From his waistband, Cain pulled out the small package wrapped in soft leather. He handed it to her and sat back, uncertain what she'd think. Pulling his knees to his chest, he clutched them.

Both of them were artists. They created things with their hands. Sometimes they were critical of each other's work. Other times, when they revealed their efforts, they found they had miraculously produced pieces that were similar in appearance. They designed in wood, leather, clay, and rocks. Currently, they were experimenting with spinning sheep's wool into fibers. They had dyed these with colors produced by various plants when boiled. Lilith's gift was a leather project.

Cain had funneled all his love for Lilith into this delicately plaited bracelet. He had rubbed the leather with oil until it was black and shiny. Carefully, he had sliced the hide into strips of exactly the same width, weaving them into an intricate pattern with numerous strands twisted and overlaid. The bracelet was delicate, but it was about three fingers wide. It was made to slip over Lilith's hand with no fastening.

As she opened it, he held his breath. The wrapping fell to the ground between her crossed legs, and her face told him everything he needed to know.

"Oh, Cain!" she said softly, her voice tinged with awe. "It's the most exquisite thing you've ever made. It's perfect, so balanced and intricate."

She looked at him in amazement then dove across the space between them, knocking him to the ground. Laughing with joy, she kissed his face repeatedly then pulled him upright again. He wouldn't have gotten this reaction in front of the entire family. The long run had been worth it!

"Put it on me." She held out her wrist.

"It has to ease on very carefully. I made it so you never have to take it off."

She looked at him seriously and nodded.

"Scrunch your fingers, pull in your thumb, and make your hand as narrow as possible."

She scrunched.

With meticulous care, he eased the leather bracelet over her fingers, across her palm, and over the critical juncture of her thumb. Just when they feared it wouldn't fit, the bracelet slowly slid over her thumb joint and onto her wrist. Admiring it, she flourished her hand.

"It's so beautiful! The leather is almost as black as your hair.

I love it!"

"It took a lot of hand holding to get the exact measurement."

"I wondered what you were doing. I thought you just enjoyed studying my fingers."

"It had to be perfect."

"It's amazing! Thank you, thank you, thank you!"

In her exuberance, she knocked him down again. This time he flipped her over, resting on his elbows as he kissed her repeatedly. Then he stopped. He could have lost himself. Soberly, he pulled them both up to sit on the ground.

"Now your gift," she said.

****

From inside the basket of food, Lilith withdrew a package also wrapped in a small square of soft leather. Now she was the uncertain one. Shyly, she handed it to him, crossed her arms over her chest, and chewed on her thumb. After seeing what he had made, she was afraid her gift to him was inadequate.

"You're going to laugh." She hoped to stave off any disappointment he might feel.

"Have I ever laughed at any of your gifts?"

She thought about it carefully. "No. No, you haven't."

Her gifts to him were all sitting in a row back in his room. At least the ones that weren't perishable were there. Some had been edible.

When he opened the wrapping, he would know they had made the same thing again. She had braided him a leather bracelet as well, but his was thick and manly looking—the weaving sturdy, the leather honey-golden. He pulled the wrapping away.

Beaming at her, Cain looked up. She quit chewing her thumb. He peered back down at the weaving, pulling it close to his face to examine it, turning it, smelling the leather.

"I know what oil you used," he said. "Good choice!"

"I made yours so you could wear it around your ankle or your wrist."

"Is that why you grabbed my ankle the other day by the river?"

She laughed. "Yes, I had to test the length to make certain it would fit both places. I already knew the size of your wrist."

"Where should I wear it today? Put it on me."

Lilith crawled across to him and decided to put it on his ankle. He bent his leg, pulling his knee to his chest. Their heads bowed together, black- and honey-colored hair touching as they concentrated on the fastening. She found the sight lovely. She wrapped it, showing him how she had designed it to secure the extra length of leather when he moved it to his wrist.

He smiled at her, his gaze sincere. "I'm not saying this because you said the same thing to me, but this really is the most beautiful leatherwork you've ever done. It's perfect. It's exactly what I hoped you would give me. I can think of you every time I see it, no matter where I am."

"Do you really like it?"

"I love it! But I'm not going to knock you over like you did me. Come here."

He held out his arms, and she threw herself at him, knocking him onto the ground as she had previously. The sunlight accentuated his sky-blue eyes. They were filled with love as he looked up at her. Wrapping his arms about her waist, he held her against his chest.

"With the sunlit leaves behind you," he said, "your eyes look almost green."

She stared at him solemnly then laid her head down on his chest, listening to his heart. Pounding so strongly, it soothed her. As he breathed, his lungs filled and emptied—such an intimate sound, life itself. Inhaling his fragrance, she touched her tongue to his skin, tasting the salty bite of his flesh. Lying peacefully, she breathed at the same time as he, imagining she had melded with him, the two of them like one person already. The unity of their breathing and the beating of their hearts so near each other made their oneness feel as if it were already a fact.

"In three more days you'll take me into your room," she said softly, "and we'll become one person. Just like this. But better."

Cain sighed softly, murmuring in agreement. Clearly he was also caught in the beauty of the moment. Scooting up, she kissed behind his ear where he smelled the best. Then she moved her lips slowly down his neck. His steady heartbeat against her cheek thrummed reassuring and warm. Nuzzling into the base of his neck, she stroked her fingertips across his bare shoulder. He bent to kiss the top of her head.

"Lily, I adore you."

"And I you, Cain," she whispered back to him. "I love you with all my heart."

****

The warm memory of Lilith's bare breast as she stood in the Tigris, her wet body glistening in the setting sun, filled Cain's thoughts. His heartbeat accelerated, but he squelched the quiet voice of his conscience. The desire to see and touch and taste her bare skin rushed through his body. It was too much.

She was wrapped in his arms. They were alone.

Slowly and carefully, Cain rolled the two of them over. Keeping his eyes fixed on hers to assess her reaction, he untied her garment and opened only the top. He had to see her breast again. Steadily, she gazed back at him, her eyes never leaving his. She was willing. Cain kissed her softly on the lips then looked down at her body.

She was captivating! Lightly, he caressed her exposed skin then bent to kiss her. *So soft!* The delicate scent and taste of her warm flesh enticed him, seizing him with the urgent need to have her. His heart lurched. He could no longer resist. He didn't want to anymore. He drew off his garment and made love to her in the meadow.

When their act of passion was complete, he lay between her breasts, breathing in the fragrance of her skin, holding her tightly in his arms. Against her warm body, he spoke his vow:

"Lilith, you are now bone of my bones and flesh of my flesh.

You are my wife, and I am your husband. We are one flesh."

"Does that mean we're married?" she murmured into his hair. "I mean, after all that Father and Mother said."

"I don't know. I love you. I'm committed to you for all my life. I should have said it before."

"I want to say the vow back to you. I know Mother didn't, but I want to."

Cain planted his chin between her breasts so he could look up into her face—she was so incredibly lovely, and she was now entirely his.

"Say the vow," he whispered.

Lilith repeated the words, her eyes fastened on his. "Cain, I am now bone of your bones and flesh of your flesh. You are my husband, and I am your wife. We are one flesh."

And they were. They would say the words again before all their family in three days, but they meant them now. They didn't know if they were secretly married, or if they had just destroyed everything. They didn't care. They made love again.

****

After a long while, they reluctantly sat up, deciding to eat before heading back. Again, Lilith had prepared Cain's favorites, as she had since their betrothal. To surprise him, she had included a few hemp leaves and flowers. To ease their suffering when they were ill, Mother used this, some other herbs, and bdellium for medicine. Cain liked hemp; it made colors brighter, everything more intense. Sometimes they ate it for fun on the holy day of rest when they had no work to do, lying in the grass and laughing together as they watched the beautiful vibrant sky.

Still naked, they fed each other; then they drank from the little stream that ran through the meadow. Afterward, each re-wrapped the other in their leather garments, binding and tying the fastenings. Lilith treasured each moment, storing them all up to savor later. She felt more profoundly attached to Cain than she had ever imagined possible.

As they sat on the ground, he combed his fingers through her hair, smoothing all the tangles and pulling out the bits of grass. He braided it down her back, using the soft leather gift wrapping to secure the braid's end. Then he tucked a small flower behind her ear and kissed her.

Tidying his appearance, she combed her fingers through his hair where it had gotten mussed. Cain tucked into his belt the leather she had wrapped his present in, storing away his own keepsake, he said. He kept whispering that he loved her.

Their conversation drifted toward what they hoped their lives would be as man and wife. Praising one another's gift, they debated their art. They discussed what they liked best about the other's body, having a more intimate knowledge now; they pondered whether making love was as they had imagined, both proclaiming the actual act better than the imagining. They projected how many children they would have. They discussed which of their siblings would wed.

They avoided the topic of Abel.

As they talked, they ended up lying side by side in the grass. Lilith rested her head on Cain's outstretched arm. Feeling the warmth of his pulse against her neck, the pounding of his heartbeat relaxed her. Gazing up at the sky, they snuggled comfortably together, their breathing slowing, their words slurring. All was blissful.

****

Disoriented, Cain jerked awake and opened his eyes. It was dark, and Lilith lay curled in front of him, curved to fit his body. In his sleep, he had cradled her within the circle of his arms. It was some time in the middle of the night. The nearly full moon was still up.

He didn't remember falling asleep. The last thing he recollected was some sort of speculation about their siblings and the gentle sound of Lilith's voice. At least they had their clothes on, though they were drenched by the mist that watered the earth every evening.

Lying still, evoking the exquisite memory of making love to Lilith, Cain recalled each detail, the warmth of her body as he made his vow to her, the look on her face when she stated her commitment to him. His father had said they shouldn't do this, but they had anyway. He couldn't detect any damage done.

But some nameless dread, a disquieting fear, rose in his heart. Shoving it away, he focused on the need to get Lilith home. He kissed the top of her head then he blew softly into her ear. She swiped at him as she would an insect, burying her face against his arm.

"Lilith," he whispered. "Lily, wake up."

Making no headway, he picked her up and carried her in his arms like a small child. Trying not to trip over things in the faint moonlight, he began the long walk home. This seemed to lull Lilith into a deeper sleep. She lay heavily against his chest, her saliva wetting his shoulder. Recalling that the same effect had resulted when she was young, he chuckled softly.

The moon's light reflected off the water, so he followed the river's course easily, even when he had to dodge trees and shrubs along the bank. It was a long walk, especially when carrying a young woman; but his arms were strong from tilling the soil, and he didn't want to wake her. Like him, she had hardly slept since their betrothal. Cradled against him like this, he knew the sound of his beating heart and the motion of his body kept her relaxed and sleeping.

Before he had awakened in the meadow, he had actually slept better than he had in a very long time. He knew it was because she had been in his arms. He felt refreshed.

As he walked, he wondered what he would tell their father. The best course of action seemed to be some version of the truth. He wouldn't tell him that they had made love or that they had vowed to each other secretly, only that they had fallen asleep while lying in the grass.

Though the misty fog lay thick, he located landmarks indicating home. But, gradually, he detected an unusual sound that puzzled him. He heard it, and then it fell silent. Was it someone crying? It was. He tried not to breathe so he could hear. It was someone crying and pleading with someone else. Talking. More crying. Silence. What was going on?

He didn't want to call out; so, silently, he walked on.

It sounded like Abel's voice, muffled, as if his face were covered by his hands. Cain thought he heard his name and Lilith's. There was weeping. He realized Abel was praying, probably pressed to the ground like their father prayed when he was alone. Had he prayed all night? The sacrifices were to be offered in the morning. Cain wasn't certain how long until sunrise.

Was Abel praying for him? Cain's heart hardened at the thought. Abel must consider him to be particularly evil if he was out here praying for him all night. He wanted to go over, kick Abel, and tell him to keep his prayers to himself. Walking on as quickly as he could, Cain put the sound far behind him, trying not to think about Abel anymore. This infuriated him.

Eventually, he arrived at home. He slid into Lilith's room and silently laid her down. After pulling the leather covering over her, he bent to kiss her head softly before slipping out. As he left, he caressed her cheek. On the next pallet, Ariel sighed and turned in her sleep.

Then Cain went to his parents' doorway and whispered for his mother. Mother slept lightly. She came to the doorway, and Cain murmured his explanation. She nodded that she understood, patted his back, pulled him down to kiss his cheek then waved him away. Yawning, she turned to crawl back into bed; she would tell Father. Her trust in him made him feel guilty.

****

Abel couldn't find peace. Recounting each offense, he begged Yahweh to forgive him for his treatment of Cain and Lilith this week. Enumerating each interaction, Abel asked God what he should have said or done differently to gain Cain's forgiveness.

Nothing came to him. He was without peace.

He implored God to pardon him for his wrong assumptions. Abel loved Cain; he couldn't bear this division. He beseeched Yahweh to move Cain's heart to forgive him. An unworthy brother—that's what Abel was.

He hadn't loved them like he would want to be loved. He hadn't treated them as he would want to be treated. Abel judged and evaluated his own behavior, grieved that he had hurt his brother, ruining the most beautiful time of his life, bringing pain into the plans for his marriage.

"Creator God, have mercy," Abel pled. "Yahweh, please forgive me, I beg You; make me more loving, my God; please send the one who will crush the serpent's head; put an end to sin and death, an end to my sin; then I won't continue to hurt the ones I love; please, God, help me; my heart hurts; forgive me, please."

Abel wept over his sin, crushed by how evil he was.

He wanted to come before God with a pure heart, but his brother held an offense against him. He was unworthy to make the sacrifice in the morning. Abel pressed his face into the dust, weeping as if his heart would break.

It was breaking; it was broken.

CHAPTER 14

CAIN OPENED HIS EYES AND stared unseeing at his mud-and-stone walls, remembering what he and Lilith had done yesterday, thinking about her body and what it felt like to make love. He wished she were beside him now, so he could do it again. He didn't see that it had hurt anything and wondered if there was any way he and Lilith could sneak off today to lie together again.

Hailing him from outside, Father's voice intruded into his reverie as he ducked into the room.

"God's blessing on you, Father." Cain sat up.

"Cain, your mother said you came in during the middle of the night—something about falling asleep in a meadow."

"We fell asleep in the grass as we talked, so I carried Lilith home. The moon was still up."

"Are you ready for today?"

"Yes."

Cain had made no preparations, but he knew that freshly gathered fruit, grain, and vegetables were in the storage area. At least there was last time he had checked. He could easily gather some for his offering. Not all of the stored produce would be bruised.

"Is your heart prepared?"

"Of course." Cain squelched his guilt. He was grateful for Lilith; he would thank God for her. He would ignore the rest—it was inconsequential.

"Are you sure, son?"

"I'm fine. A little tired, that's all."

****

Adam assessed his son's eyes. Something wasn't right.

"Did you make love with Lilith in the meadow?"

"No!" Cain snapped, sounding offended.

He wasn't a very good liar; his eyes shifted, and his body always belied the falsehood—he blushed. He didn't realize how guilty he looked when he did it. Adam noted this, glad that his son was so easy to decipher. He considered his tack.

"You know it's best for Lilith to pledge to her openly, before you unite with her body. Your commitment to her will then be a reality in everyone's eyes. It will make her more certain of your love for her. It's the selfless thing to do."

"Lily knows I love her."

Adam eyed Cain, almost certain that he and Lilith had given way to temptation. But he decided against making an accusation. Perhaps they had only been tempted and had stopped, and now Cain felt guilty about it. Adam would let this be between Cain and God.

"What are you offering today?"

"I put some fruit, vegetables, and grain in the storage area." Cain didn't meet his eyes.

"Have you selected the best of the yield?"

"I always do."

Actually, Adam knew Cain had done nothing. He had been completely preoccupied with Lilith yesterday. That had been obvious when Cain had stumbled in on him during prayer. He was afraid Cain thought of this day as simply another hurdle on the way to his wedding day.

It was supposed to be the day when they thanked Yahweh

for all He had given them to keep them alive here outside the Garden. Willingly, they made an offering of the best of all their produce and the firstborn of their animals, showing trust for God's future provision. God had not demanded this. They did it freely, because they loved Him and wanted to thank Him and praise Him.

Adam had started this tradition after they left the Garden, one year after their creation, when Cain was only two months old. An abundance of crops had ripened at that time, Eve had risen from childbearing, and their gratefulness to Yahweh had overflowed. They had offered the best of their crops. The alignment of the stars was now as it had been at creation and at the day of that first offering. This was the holy day to make the yearly observance.

"Cain, it was one hundred twenty years ago that we dedicated you to God on this day. We hoped you would be the one to crush the serpent's head."

"I don't know what that means."

"Neither do we. It's a mystery."

"Then how do you know it will happen?" Cain looked up at him.

"Because we believe Yahweh. He told us it will occur."

"Well, He hasn't spoken to me. I don't know."

Adam looked intently at his son. Though Cain believed in God and worshiped Him, he did not believe Yahweh's promise that He would send one to crush the serpent's head. Cain didn't seem to be presenting his offering because of his love for Yahweh.

Adam hadn't seen him preparing his heart. Cain didn't appear to be in a state of humility and adoration of their God. This year Cain appeared to be simply going through the ritual. As Adam thought about it, he realized it had been this way with Cain for a long while.

Adam hadn't observed him choosing the best from the fields as he had seen Abel taking care to prepare his offering of the firstborn lambs. Perhaps Cain didn't love God passionately, as he should. He knew Abel had spent much time in prayer. He hadn't seen Cain pray. But prayer was a private matter. Who knew?

"I'll see you in the field, son."

Adam ducked back out the doorway. As he walked away, he prayed that God would soften Cain's heart.

****

Cain wanted to speak to Lilith, and he needed to prepare the offering as hastily as possible. It was a good thing his father had mentioned it. He leapt out of bed and threw on his garment. Then he dashed toward the food preparation area, hoping he could accomplish both goals in one location. When he rushed into the storage cave near their parents' room, he found Lilith. She was gathering some fruit for later.

"Lilith!"

He was relieved to see her. It felt as though he'd left part of his body lying somewhere last night. Now that he had found the missing piece, he felt like an entire man again.

"Cain!"

She dropped the basket she cradled and ran into his arms. Holding her face, he smothered it with kisses.

"I didn't know if I'd see you this morning before the offering," she said. "I woke up and didn't feel whole without you by me."

"That's how I felt too," he whispered against her cheek. "I wished you were in my bed so I could make love to you again. I thought about it before I was even fully awake."

"Me too. Mother told me you carried me all the way back."

"I did." He pulled her into his arms. "You drooled on me all the way home."

"That's embarrassing."

"I like your drool."

Various sisters or brothers on errands for their mother kept popping in to get something from the storage cave, then backing out again when they saw them embracing. A group now whispered at the mouth of the cave.

"We're slowing everything down." Lilith glanced at the cave's entrance.

"Yes, I need to gather my offering. I didn't think of it yesterday; I was so glad to be with you. You are what I'm thanking God for today."

She smiled. "And I, you. Remember the fruit we picked yesterday morning. It's on top, nice and fresh. I have to take these things to Mother."

Stooping, she gathered what she had dropped. When she stood, he kissed her farewell. Then he picked up an empty basket and sorted through the baskets of grain and produce, gathering what he needed. Cain found the freshly picked fruit; it was perfect, but the vegetables were sadly picked over. He found a few good pieces. He would position them on top so the bruises and worm holes in the other pieces didn't show.

What was left of the old grain lay scattered in the bottom of one basket. The fresh grain was still out in the sun; he hadn't brought it in. He scooped out a handful of dusty grain and blew lightly across it, sifting off the chaff. After picking out the weevils, he heaped the grain with the fruit. He would grab some of the freshly cut grain to place on top.

He found the clay jug of oil. A small amount remained in the bottom. Sniffing it, he drew back quickly; the oil was rancid. He would pour it onto the produce. He hadn't pressed fresh oil.

His offering was ready.

Leaving the cave, he headed toward the field to build his stone altar near the one Abel would construct. He would offer the produce, the work of his hands. Abel would offer the firstborn of the new lambs, his work. This year, Cain's offering looked sadly shabby. He shrugged it off.

As he climbed the hill toward the field, Abel walked toward him, his head down, evidently returning for something. Orange and green bruises discolored the skin around his eyes now. His face was haggard, his shoulders sagging. Sacrifice day was always hard on Abel.

When they were young, Cain had talked him through it,

holding each tiny sheep still so Abel could slit its throat. He did this early in the morning, before the family arrived. With meticulous care, Abel chose the finest of the new firstborns. Then he butchered their little bodies, presenting the fatty portions— the best of each. In giving Yahweh the first and the finest, he wanted to demonstrate that he loved God and trusted Him for future provision.

But Abel disliked killing the lambs, bereaving the ewes, even though he would train them to suckle the newly orphaned lambs. While slaughtering the little lambs, Abel talked to God about the ram he had killed in the Garden to cover their parents' nakedness. The sight of the blood running out of each small sheep moved Abel. When they were young, he had sniffled as they died, and Cain had laughed at him.

Their mother took the hides of each, along with the ewes and oxen that had died bearing young; this was their year's supply of leather. All year, as they worked over the pelts, each small hide caused Abel to reminisce over the offering. He often wept, because it reminded him of some intimate attachment of faith that he felt toward God.

Over the years, he had nearly worn off Cain's ears talking about this. Cain never understood what he meant. Obviously, Abel had just completed this task. He was preoccupied, staring at the ground. Sheep's blood besmeared his garment. He almost bumped into Cain.

"Cain! I'm sorry! I didn't mean to stumble into you."

"It's nothing." Cain shouldered past him.

Halting him in his progress, Abel placed his hand on his shoulder.

"Cain, I'd like to ask your forgiveness again for all the ways I've wronged you. Can you please find it in your heart to forgive me? I had hoped to help you this week, so we could begin to prepare your new home. I knew you were working hard and couldn't do it alone, but this strife between us kept me from ever bringing it up. I'm so sorry."

Abel's words stabbed at Cain's heart. He hadn't even thought about preparing a home for Lilith! Why did Abel have to be the one to think of this neglected and forgotten task?

"You're only apologizing because it's time for the offering," he shot back at Abel.

"No! I'm grieved, brother. I want to be reconciled; I want to help you. I'm so sorry for all the ways I've hurt and offended you; I've been so wrong."

Cain ignored Abel's words. *How could I have forgotten to build a home for Lilith? I'm an idiot!* Hiding his distress, Cain looked away, feigning indifference.

"Can you please forgive me?" Abel asked him.

"Shut up, Abel. The damage is done."

Cain shoved past him, then remembered something and spun around. "And don't pray for me out in the dark. I don't need your prayers."

Abel's face fell. Cain smirked.

Preoccupied with his neglect of a home for Lilith, Cain walked onto the field to ready his offering, irritated by his stupidity. When he arrived, he saw that Azriel, Akiva, Hesed, and other brothers who worked the fields with him, had gathered the stones he would need to build the altar. They acknowledged his arrival. Nearby, Yonas, Joda, and others who worked with Abel had also assembled the stones he would need. Behind them the family would soon gather.

Though he hadn't done much to prepare, Cain hoped that presenting this offering would gain him favor with God. He began to stack the gathered stones, building the altar on which to offer the produce. He was eager to get this over with so they could all go eat. He would sit with Lilith to discuss their new home.

Abel returned. Cain glanced at him; it looked like he'd been crying. Good.

Turning his back on Abel, Cain focused on finishing his altar so he could arrange the produce before anyone else arrived. Behind him, he heard Abel working.

When the altar was ready, Cain picked up the basket of

produce, positioning the bruised and wormy vegetables on the bottom and covering them with the good pieces. Over these he laid the freshly gathered fruit. Gently he blew on the old grain as he dumped it beside the fruit and vegetables, blowing off more chaff and empty kernels.

The offering had to appear fresh, the best of the produce.

Hesed stepped up beside him with a handful of newly gathered grain. Standing shoulder to shoulder with Cain, blocking their actions from the view of the family, Hesed sprinkled this new grain across the top of the damaged kernels. When he was done, he looked at Cain, one eyebrow cocked. Hesed knew. Cain nodded to him and dumped the stale oil over the top. Its fusty scent drifted toward them. Then both moved back with the family.

His offering prepared, Cain watched Abel position the bodies of the firstborn lambs on his altar. They were big and fat, the best of his flock. With the fatty portions on top, he placed them lovingly onto the altar, as if he were presenting parts of his own self. Then, covering his face with both hands, he stood silently for a moment before also stepping back.

Everyone gathered behind them now. Lilith had worked her way close enough to link her little finger with Cain's. They all waited for their father to offer the prayers and light the offerings. Father stepped up, planted the torch in the dirt, and raised both hands to pray.

As his father's voice droned on, Cain's mind wandered to Lilith's little finger. She had hooked it around his. The skin of her delicate wrist felt soft; her new leather bracelet pressed against his arm. Head bowed, he cast her a surreptitious, sidelong glance; she was gazing at him. Keeping his eyes on the ground, he smiled, knowing she would understand his smile was for her.

Finally, Father quit praying. He now stepped forward to ignite the offerings.

Since Cain was the firstborn, he lit his first. The offering sputtered and smoked. Confident that the fire was catching, his father stepped over to Abel's offering. On first touch, it burst into flame. Cain's offering still smoldered. Everyone looked up, willing it to light. Father pressed the torch to it again. Thick, dark smoke ascended.

Shifting his feet, Cain cleared his throat. Certain they all stared at him, the back of his neck tingled. Old oil ignited as well as fresh, yet still only smoke arose. He cleared his throat again.

"Abel has presented his sacrifice from a clean heart." A quiet melodious voice wafted on the breeze. *Yahweh!* It was a shock to hear the Creator speak. "Abel prepared his offering with a broken and contrite heart, and he has given me his best. I accept his offering."

Cain recognized God's voice—gentle and kind. He had heard it a few times before in his lifetime. In his younger years, he had often felt it in his heart.

Consuming Abel's offering, the fire blazed higher. The aroma of sizzling lamb filled their nostrils. Abel collapsed to the ground, burying his face in the dust.

"I'm unworthy," Abel whispered. "I'm completely flawed in every way."

Cain heard him. He agreed. Abel was unworthy. Why had God accepted his offering? Cain's own offering did nothing more than smoke. No flames leapt up. Shamed, his cheeks tingled now and grew hot.

"I do not accept Cain's offering," God said. "His heart is not clean; he is not broken and contrite; he doesn't give me the best he has to offer."

The feeble smoke puffed out on Cain's offering, leaving it singed.

Anger filled Cain; his throat grew dry as dust. God had rebuked him before his family, humiliating him in front of Lilith, who now grasped his trembling hand, soothingly rubbing her thumb across it as she looked at the ground, embarrassed for him.

Within Cain, hot wrath grew and swelled. He hated Abel! Yet the weight of his guilt—his taking of Lilith, his anger, his arrogance, his lack of forgiveness—bore down on him. He shoved it aside, unable to bear this conflict of emotion. He wanted to hit someone and burst into tears at the same time. He was ashamed of himself, yet mad at God for doing this to him.

Flinging off Lilith's hand, he stormed away.

CHAPTER 15

WHEN CAIN WAS OUT OF his family's sight, he hurtled away, charging down the hillside. Tripping over stones, he stumbled and tore his hands and knees. He descended too rapidly; but rising, he plunged on again. Angry tears streaked his cheeks.

He didn't know how to react. Guilt over his sin engulfed him, yet defiance over that very sin seethed within. Anger at the Creator for shaming him swelled and burned. Lilith and the entire family had seen and heard. But mostly, with every fiber, he hated and resented Abel.

Overcome by emotion, he wept hot tears.

"Cain, why are you filled with anger?" He hadn't expected to hear Yahweh's voice again. "Why are you indignant and your face downcast?" Within his heart the voice continued urging gently, *"Repent. Trust in me. Humble your heart. Call on me! I will help you."*

Impatiently, Cain thrust away the persuasive voice's offer. He could handle this himself; he had been handling it. This was Abel's fault. He had caused it. Abel was to blame—smug and self-righteous with his advice and his perfect offering.

How Cain despised him!

"If you do what is right, won't you be uplifted?" Yahweh

continued His calm urging. "But if you don't do what is right, sin is crouching at your door, lying in wait for you. Sin desires to have you; but, Cain, you must master it."

"*Do what's right?*" God's words offended him. "*Master it?* I was worshiping You! I made an offering! I thanked You! I do the best I can. It's never enough. Why did You humiliate me?"

Cain awaited more words from God. He sensed Yahweh's eye upon him, but nothing more was said. Cain didn't know what to do. Already he strove to do what was right. What sin crouched at the door? Since he couldn't seem to please God, maybe he should go ahead and welcome this sin.

"Come on in," he screamed, arms wide, turning slowly to survey the surrounding forest. "Have at me! Whatever's out there, go ahead, pounce, since I can't do anything right!"

Nothing.

Recalling the quiet urging of the Creator's voice within his heart, Cain squelched its effect. He didn't understand. He could determine nothing. What other act could he perform? What deed would earn God's favor?

****

Lilith wriggled free from their mother's grasp. Following Cain's voice, she tried to locate him in the forest. As he yelled, his words echoed, garbled with rage. There he was, up ahead!

"Cain!" She ran toward him.

Surprising her, Cain swiftly turned away. She slowed her approach and came to a stop, staring at his stiffened back. One shoulder and one knee were bloodied, the skin scraped off. Blood trickled down his leg and his arm. Clearly, he had fallen several times.

"Go away, Lilith." His voice was thick and hard. It hurt her.

"Why?" She choked back a sob.

"I'm embarrassed. I don't want anyone to see me."

"Not even me."

"Especially you."

"But why?"

"Because I love you. I want you to respect me. I've been disgraced. I can't look at your face; I don't want you to see me like this."

"But I don't care. I've seen you chastened before. I'm always on your side."

"Except when I'm wrong."

She didn't know how to answer him. Silently, she stared at his back.

"Leave," he said. "Now."

"I won't."

She stepped around him and seized his face—his eyes shifted away from her gaze. There was bark stuck in his hair from some tree he'd run into. Dirt smudged his face. One of his cheeks had been scraped raw and red. He cast her a quick glance. The agony of rejection tortured his eyes.

She saw it then—he was certain he had lost her. Now he stared at her hopelessly.

"You're sorry you made the vow to me, aren't you?" He jutted his chin toward her, his words telling her what she already knew.

"No! Absolutely not! I'll promise again in two days. I'll pledge right now."

"Why? The Creator rejected me."

"Because I love you. I've always loved you."

Lilith watched tears pool in his bright blue eyes—hot, angry, hopeless tears, tears of frustration and despair. He struggled to turn his face away, but she clutched his head more tightly. She decided to restore him, to soothe his mind, to rebuild his confidence.

"Cain, *I* haven't rejected you."

Wrenching from her grasp, he covered his face and sank to the ground.

She knelt, pried away his hands, and smothered his face with kisses, lingering over the wound on his cheek. Soothing him with her words, she used her thumbs to wipe away his tears. But when he looked at her, something was dead. Some spark was gone.

Regarding him silently, she knelt before him. She didn't know how to fix what she saw in his eyes. For a long while they stared at each other—her eyes pleading, his remote.

Finally, she spoke, "Please, beloved, come back with me. It will be fine."

"I don't want to see anyone."

"Then I'll come away with you. I'll go wherever you want."

"No, there's something I need to do alone."

****

Cain turned his eyes from Lilith's pleading. Looking at the ground, he made fast his resolve. A choice had been made, and he intended to carry it out. He didn't care. His heart felt hard and still and dead. He didn't know how to resist. Enticing him, sin beckoned.

Lilith tried to recapture his gaze, but he refused to meet her eyes. Decision made, his heart grew cold. He felt himself falling into the abyss.

"I'll walk with you back to the river." He gave way entirely.

Going around the altar with his charred and rejected offering, they walked together. Lost in thought, he occupied himself with his options. Lilith tried to draw him out, telling him again how much she loved him, affirming her desire to say their vows before the family, repeating her vow to him again, just for his ears.

Plotting and planning, his mind engaged elsewhere. He gave short answers.

When they arrived at the river, they sat on the edge. Dipping her hands into the water repeatedly, she washed his wounds. He let her. Everything was going to change. That he would provoke the change hurt him. But he had no choice; it couldn't be helped. Hatred had done its work. Leaning into her hand each time it touched him, he turned once to kiss her palm. *Farewell.* He resisted allowing her ministrations to soften his heart.

When she was done, he looked at her. "Go and tell Abel I want to talk to him. Stay there. Eat some food. I don't want any. I'm not hungry."

Lifeless, that's how he felt. His actions seemed irrelevant. All was dead already.

****

Hugging Cain tightly, Lilith kissed him then she leapt up to do his bidding. Maybe there would be reconciliation at last! Talking to Abel would be a good start.

When she approached the family gathering area, she found a bustle of activity. Some were despondent over what had happened. Others were jubilant. Her parents looked worried, though both were occupied with the younger children. When they saw her, they studied her face. Eager to reassure them, she smiled.

Looking for Abel, she scanned the group. On the far side of the clearing, she found him behind a tree. His knees were drawn to his chest, his head bowed. She had expected him to be jubilant that the Creator had spoken well of him, but instead he looked crushed with grief.

His tear-streaked face stared up into hers.

"Cain's waiting by the river where he bathes. I think he wants to reconcile with you."

With hopeful eyes, Abel jumped up. He gripped her arm, giving it a squeeze, then he jogged across the clearing and headed up the river.

Their parents watched him go then looked back at Lilith. Perhaps there would be healing.

****

Anticipation grew in Abel's heart as he raced toward Cain. He was grieved over all that had happened between them this week. He hoped Cain would forgive him.

Cain stood waiting by the Tigris. His eyes appeared flat and dull, but he smiled. Abel observed his wounds and knew he had fallen as he ran.

"Let's go out to the field, Abel."

As they walked together, hope glimmered within Abel. He had missed the camaraderie of his older brother and felt joy just walking with him. Once again, Abel apologized and offered to help Cain build a house for him and Lilith.

Cain remained silent, until they arrived at the field. Then he stepped ahead a few paces and grabbed a large stone. Tossing it up and down, he slowly turned.

"I don't want your apology." His eyes were hate-filled. "And I don't need your help."

Without warning, Cain smashed the rock into Abel's head. It staggered him. Abel wobbled and nearly lost consciousness. Warm blood trickled along his eyebrow.

Stunned, he gaped at Cain. "What are you doing? ... Why?"

"I hate you! Hate you!" With cold fury in his eyes, Cain advanced, his voice low and menacing. "You humiliate me before our parents, before our family."

Cain tossed the rock to his other hand and swung. Abel tried to ward off the blow; it scraped past his raised forearm then grazed his ear.

"Stop it, Cain!" Abel panted as he dodged, arms raised in defense. His head hurt.

"You try to separate me from Lilith. You want to take her from me."

Cain swung the rock upward, hitting Abel under the chin and knocking him backward. His teeth smashed together. He stumbled, trying to catch himself.

"Cain, *don't!*"

"You judge me and condemn me!"

Cain switched hands again and bashed the rock into Abel's temple. Abel fell hard, landing heavily on his side. He didn't understand. He could scarcely draw a breath. Throbbing agony. Blackness closed in. Cain's voice seemed far away.

"You cause God himself to turn against me."

****

Seething with rage, Cain jumped on Abel and bashed his head again. Like a crazed animal, Cain struck him over and over. Hatred drove him. He lost himself in it. Vengeance reddened his vision. Moisture spraying his face sobered Cain's temper.

Blood and fluid from Abel's head covered Cain and splattered the field, flung in all directions by each backstroke of his rage-driven arm. Abel's face was shattered, his forehead cratered, and his hair soaked and matted with blood. One of his eyes was misshapen, the other unseeing. Abel vomited and was convulsing. Horror-struck, Cain dropped the rock and climbed off of his brother, staring at Abel's distorted face.

What have I done?!

Panicked, Cain covered Abel's head wounds with both of his hands, hoping somehow to repair the damage. He began to cry. Smoothing and patting Abel's head, Cain rocked back and forth, shaking uncontrollably.

"It will be alright. It will be alright. It will be alright. It will, it will ...."

But it wasn't. Cain couldn't fix this. The entire side of Abel's head was crushed and his body continued to jerk and stiffen. Foamy vomit seeped out from between his teeth.

Horrified, Cain backed away. Abel's body twitched and then lay still, relaxing as his bodily fluids drained slowly into the dirt. Cain stood immobile, staring at his brother. The back of Cain's neck tingled with the horror of it. The hair raised on his arms.

Abel was dead. He had murdered Abel.

What have I done? My God, what have I done?

He stared at his hands. There was Abel's blood. How had he done this? Seizing his hair, he yanked as hard as he could. He needed to hurt himself. Opening wide his mouth, he keened a long, high-pitched wail that didn't even sound human then he dragged his hands down his face, smearing himself with death.

Cain's knees buckled and hit the ground.

Lilith! What would she think? Killing Abel could never be explained or forgiven. He remembered his parents, his siblings. He would be an outcast—or worse.

Lilith might be back any moment. He had to act fast. Could he keep this gruesome secret from her? He was terrible at lying—he would have to become a different person.

Consumed with shame and terror, he scanned the field. A short distance away, he spotted some freshly turned soil. Frantic, he scurried across. Digging with his bare hands like some animal, he clawed a trench into the earth. Flying dirt mingled with the blood and gore.

When the hole looked long enough, he crawled back and grabbed Abel under the armpits. Abel's lifeless head lolled across his shoulder, revealing what was left of his brain. Blood seeped slowly from his crushed skull. Aghast at what he'd done, Cain dropped him.

Reluctantly, he peered at him again. One of Abel's eyes was destroyed; one dead eye stared back at him, unseeing. It made Cain sick.

Retching repeatedly, Cain wondered how he could have killed his own brother. He was more evil than he had ever imagined. *Am I even human?* He had murdered his closest friend, one of the kindest, humblest people on the earth. The ghastliness of it repulsed it.

Fear of discovery propelled him back into action. He had to finish this. He wiped vomit from his mouth and rose, lugging Abel by his feet so he couldn't see the head wound. He couldn't seem to quit crying and shaking. Sliding first Abel's feet then his upper body into the trench, Cain shoveled the dirt over his body with trembling hands.

Just before he covered Abel's head, Cain lay on the ground beside him. He stroked the matted hair from Abel's face, clearing away the dirt-caked blood. One last time he gazed at his brother, mangled and damaged as he was. Gently, Cain kissed Abel's dead face.

"I'm so sorry," he whispered.

Then he closed Abel's eyelid and scraped dirt over his head.

Using his hands and feet, he covered all the grisly evidence with soft soil. He couldn't see what he was doing. Tears clouded his vision. Through the teary film, he noted that he was covered with dirt-blackened blood.

He surveyed the entire area. There was a slight mound where Abel's body lay buried, but he had done a good job covering the evidence.

Then Cain ran.

CHAPTER 16

ABEL NO LONGER FELT PAIN or anguish. The fear lifted. Detached somehow, Abel observed himself lying on the ground. He was kneeling next to his own battered and bloodied body. He saw his brother running in the distance, covered in blood, crying.

How can this be? How can I be seeing myself?

Suddenly, Abel felt as if he were being yanked backward rapidly—up, away from his body. The grisly scene fell away, fading from his sight.

Everything familiar grew indistinct; Abel spun away from the earth. He soared!

Looking to his right and left, he discovered two powerful, shining angelic beings! They embraced him, transporting him upward at great speed. As they gazed into his eyes, their nostrils flared in fierce expressions of love and compassion.

"Do not be afraid," one angel said gently, yet with reverberating power.

This soothed Abel's heart. Gathering strength, his attention turned toward the place he now journeyed. Before him the sky split open, and he beheld a radiant, shining place. It was lovelier than anything he had ever seen. Bright light illuminated everything his eyes beheld, making each vista sharp and glowing.

There was no shadow. Everything dazzled!

Waiting at the entrance, with arms thrown wide and face beaming, stood the purest, kindest, most truthful being Abel had ever seen. Intuitively, he knew this One somehow, in his heart, which now surged toward the waiting figure. This being's heart was attached to his by some kind of cord that pulled Abel toward him.

Love drew Abel into the kind One's arms, and he embraced Abel tightly to himself.

"Welcome home, my first prophet and martyr—one who died for the sake of righteousness!"

Abel wasn't certain what he had done that was righteous. He had been grieved over his inability to reconcile with his brother and broken over all the mistakes he had made. All the errors and sins of his life flowed through his thoughts. He was flawed.

Then Abel realized he gazed upon Yahweh—this was who had greeted him with arms open wide; this was the kind One who drew Abel to Himself as with a cord of love. He beheld God.

Shaken, he realized God had said he was dead.

"Am I dead?" Abel thought he'd better verify his assumption.

The kind One chuckled softly. "You've only left your body. Your family will think you're dead, but you're more alive than you've ever been."

Abel looked down at himself now. Somehow, he lacked substance. He was spirit, slightly transparent. He touched his head; it felt whole and unharmed, no longer smashed, yet different. He now had a spirit body. He remembered that his physical body lay back on the earth, the blood running out. The one who had taken his life—his own beloved brother—was crying over his body and regretting his actions.

"What about my body?"

"Your body is sleeping. I will awaken it, make it new, and reunite it with your spirit on The Day. Until then your blood has a lesson to teach. It will demonstrate a paradigm of justice until I return to judge mankind. It will teach the lesson that every act requires an accounting. Your blood will cry out for vengeance and justice."

"What about my brother?" Abel asked. "He regrets what he's done. This will destroy him."

"One particular generation will be held accountable for your blood, Abel. I myself will inform them. Justice will be meted out on The Day."

Radiating passionate emotion, Yahweh paused, grasping Abel to Himself again. Love washed through Abel, overpowering him, making his knees weak, and permeating his entire self. Adoration of this God who now held him so intimately filled Abel and overflowed.

The kind and loving One now held Abel at arm's length and gazed into his eyes.

"My own blood will teach another lesson. It will offer a paradigm of mercy. I will lay down my life. My blood will make payment for every act that demands justice. It will ransom all those who humble themselves, repent, and call on me."

"Your blood? The blood of God?"

"Yes," Yahweh said.

Abel paused, mystified by how this could be. Then he remembered Cain.

"Is there any hope for my brother? I love him."

"Your death was his only hope."

Abel was content. Trusting Yahweh unreservedly, he let it go.

God now turned him to behold a magnificent, shining place. Thousands upon thousands of glorious voices sang, praising Yahweh in majestic tones. Elated, Abel glided toward the music. Unexpectedly, he heard a low growl behind him. He turned back.

A deformed and darkened angel strode toward him. It looked somewhat like the cherubim by the river, but was charred and ashen rather than radiant. Enormous and sinister, it glared at him.

Stabbing its bony spirit finger toward his chest, it snarled, "What is he doing here? I had permission to take his life."

Calmly, Yahweh stepped between Abel and the dark angel.

Abel peered around the kind One; no harm could come to him here. The sinister angel cowered now.

"Satan, you have no right to question me," God said.

"But Abel is a rebel like me—a sinner." The ashen angel whined; he groveled. "He deserves the same penalty as I. He should not be here enjoying Your presence."

"There is a provision. I have shrouded my plan from you; it is a mystery. Abel's life is mine."

"That is unfair. How can he be restored to You, but I cannot? You are unjust!"

"You know that is untrue. I am perfectly just. I see all, know all, and have all power to bring about my plans, including my plan for Abel's redemption. You know nothing of this. You are the one in error. Depart!"

Shrieking, the dark angel threw his head back, howling in frustration. Clearly he had been thwarted in some harmful intention. As Abel stood behind Yahweh, he felt relieved to be in this position, very glad the kind and loving One shielded him. The dark being stormed out.

****

Defeat throttled Satan. Constrained more than he had ever surmised, hot wrath detonated his senses. Wide and roaring and furious, he screamed. Once again, God had impeded his purposes. Unable to comprehend God's plans, Satan stood outside them, in the dark—*jealous!* As always, this last emotion sickened him. Banished and ostracized, he could never be restored.

His goal was to exterminate the human family or to bring upon them the same type of eternal punishment he now experienced. But there was Abel in God the Son's arms, taking pleasure in Yahweh's presence, even though Abel was a sinner. What had happened?

Satan hadn't expected this outcome. God had outwitted him.

Obstructed in some manner about which he had no knowledge, Satan was baffled. As the wisest creature made by

Yahweh, his confusion aggravated him, increasing his wrath and his craving for vengeance. Bitter hatred of God boiled within.

Like a flaming inferno, Satan shot to the earth. He would obliterate Cain. It would be a pleasure. That one's heart was in a different condition than Abel's. Cain's heart was hard, so his sinful nature had entrapped him. All Satan had needed to do was nudge, whispering simple suggestions into his mind, posing his ideas as Cain's own thoughts, guiding him step by step into the trap. Once more, Satan had found this effective. Cain had grabbed up his ideas quite quickly. Cain would be eternally damned and join Satan.

Cain did not love and adore Yahweh. Maybe that was the singular issue.

Abel was humble and contrite. He had cried out to God for help whenever Satan had tried this on him. Abel loved God with all his being, in fact, was there now basking in His love. Abel believed God's promise that one of them would crush Satan's head.

Cain did not. Perhaps that was also part of the conundrum— Cain lacked faith.

Satan determined to keep it that way. He would utilize all the forces of darkness and all his powers of cunning against Cain to keep him distant from God and angry at Him. Not only did he have God's permission to test Cain, but Cain himself had invited him in.

****

Cain sprinted far down the river. Somehow, he had to clean himself, to wash away the evidence of his brother's murder. And, he had to learn to lie, and quickly. He was too forthright a person; he always spoke exactly what he felt and thought. How could he hide who he was?

When he reached a location far from the family compound, he jumped into the river fully clothed. This was the only way he could think to wash Abel's blood and vomit from his garment.

He would rub sheep's fat and beeswax into the leather as it dried, so it wouldn't stiffen.

As he scrubbed at the sheepskin, bits of matter worked loose from the wool and floated down the river. Witnessing this made him retch again. His own bile mingled with Abel's bodily fluids and dissipated into the current of the Tigris.

When his garment was clean, Cain untied the drenched sheepskin and spread it out in the sun. Then he ducked under the water, repeatedly using sand to cleanse his body, removing all the blood and bodily fluids that had dried on his skin. Wondering if he'd ever feel clean again, he scrubbed himself raw.

When he left the Tigris to dry his chafed body, he turned his garment over, exposing the other side to the sun. He might have to put it on wet and say he had fallen into the river. All he could do was stand here, naked, and wait for it to dry.

"Where is Abel, your brother?" said the quiet voice of Yahweh.

Picturing the shallow trench in which he had buried Abel, Cain wasn't certain how to answer. Where *was* Abel, really? He clearly did not inhabit his body any longer. So where was he?

"I don't know." He resisted the conviction he felt. "Am I my brother's keeper?"

"Cain, what have you done?" the voice demanded.

He couldn't answer God. A pain grew in his heart.

"Listen!" God said. "Your brother's blood is crying to me from the ground, seeking justice."

Cain listened. He couldn't shake the image of Abel's splattered blood, his misshapen face, and his wounded head. He had covered Abel's blood with dirt, but God still saw it and heard it crying. He could bury Abel's body, but he couldn't hide what he'd done.

Would Abel's blood ever cease crying out? Would it haunt him all his days?

"Now you are cursed—hemmed in, rendered powerless, condemned." Yahweh's voice sounded grief-stricken. "From the fertile soil you are driven out—the soil that opened its mouth to soak up your brother's blood, which poured out because of your own hand."

Cain's parents had told him that God had cursed the serpent and He had cursed the ground because of their sin, but He had not cursed them. But God now cursed him. Obviously, he belonged to the serpent—an evil one.

"When you cultivate the earth," God said, "it will no longer produce its crops for you. You will be homeless, a fugitive—a restless wanderer on the earth, lamenting what you've done."

It was as if he'd been punched in the chest; the impact dropped him to his knees.

Cain loved tilling the earth. He was gifted to do it. Cultivating the soil filled him with joy. It now wouldn't produce fruit for him! Now he must wander—he couldn't go home!

Lilith! Would he ever see her again?

Huddled naked before God, he buried his face in the dust and sobbed out his confession.

"My guilt is more than I can bear. My wickedness overwhelms me; I killed my own brother!" Here he paused, struck dumb as Abel's dead face filled his mind. "My punishment is more than I can endure. You're driving me from the land. I won't be able to find you!" The agony of that reality crushed him. "I'll be hidden from your presence, beyond restoration ... alone! Abel was better than me, and I took him from them. If my family finds me, they'll kill me."

"Not so!" Yahweh said. "I will show you mercy. If anyone kills you, they will suffer my vengeance seven times over. I will mark you so no one will attack you."

A blazing white figure appeared, his radiance blinding Cain. Stricken with terror, Cain collapsed onto his face. If he could have dug a hole in which to hide himself, he would have. The searing pure holiness of Yahweh smote his heart with conviction. He was sore afraid.

God's hand tenderly lifted Cain's face from the dust, the palm caressing his chin. Cain's eyes stared wide at the brilliant light emanating from Yahweh, seeing only radiance. God's finger traced upon Cain's forehead. Gently, God whispered into Cain's dumbstruck mind:

"A broken and contrite heart I do not despise. Repent. Turn to me."

Cain couldn't respond. Unable to move, unable to think, he collapsed again, naked, into the dust—a broken man. His sin had destroyed everything. The only hope was the healing of Yahweh, and he wouldn't be able to find Him.

His own hard heart had done it.

All day long, heedless of time, Cain lay sprawled beside the river, consumed with his crushing loss, his culpability, his words, and his actions. Nothing could be done about it now.

As the sun set, he still lay stretched out naked on the ground, his face buried in the dust.

All was lost.

CHAPTER 17

ACROSS THE COMPOUND, ADAM LOOKED at Eve and Lilith as they went about their various duties. With eyes tight and brows furrowed into worried frowns, they often scanned the horizon and double-checked the direction Abel had gone. They appeared as concerned as he.

Casually, so as not to cause alarm, Adam motioned for them to meet him in their sleeping chamber. They stepped out of the sunlight into the peaceful room. The matting was drawn, casting stripes of sunlight on the floor and walls as it filtered through the spaces in the weaving.

"Let's go find them," Adam said. "My chest feels tight with fear."

Eve and Lilith nodded. Something was wrong.

"We should look first at the river," Lilith said.

Eve arranged for some of the older siblings to feed and play with the younger ones, as this was a holy feast day. The three of them would look together.

Cain and Abel were not by the river; perhaps they had gone to one of the fields. But which one? Trying to keep a check on his racing mind, Adam searched with Eve and Lilith. They spent the entire afternoon going from field to field then back home to see if the two had returned, and then back out again. Over and over, they repeated these steps, covering every possible location.

Late in the afternoon, as they walked through yet another field, they noticed the dirt looked odd in one corner. It had been scraped and smoothed, some of it pushed to one side forming a slight mound. There was some sort of moisture in one spot, almost dry, but wetter than the nearby soil. What had happened here?

Adam's chest constricted with dread; quickly, he looked to Eve. The same emotion showed on her face. He considered sending Lilith back to the compound with Eve while he investigated. But Lilith was a step ahead of him. She strode to the mound and kicked away the dirt at one end.

Dirt-encrusted toes popped out of the ground.

Lilith screamed.

Eve threw herself down, clawing aside the dirt. Wailing, she unearthed the legs of one of their sons. *Oh God! Which one?* Incredulous, they all gaped at one another.

Then they frantically dug together. Eventually, enough dirt had been scooped away that they could grasp the body and tug it free. It was stiffened like a piece of wood. Though the face was caked with blood and mud, it was clearly Abel—his hair curled dark-brown, not obsidian and smooth like Cain's. One side of Abel's head had been smashed in, the eye socket filled with thick mud. His lips were blue.

Cain had done this to Abel.

Stroking his muddy hair, Eve cradled his misshapen head against her chest, weeping all the while. Rocking him, she kissed his face and wiped his burial dirt over her face and into her hair. Appalled at finding his beloved son's body looking like this, Adam collapsed. Clutching his head, he curled into a tight ball, trying to block out the awful fact.

This was his fault! He had eaten the forbidden fruit. Death had come. It had taken his son. One of their own children was returning to the dust before they themselves.

Of dust they were made, and to dust they would return.

Adam couldn't bear this! Abel was no more.

****

Lilith ran away from the sight of her dear dead brother in the ground, away from her parents' torrent of grief. When they had first unearthed Abel's feet, she had been relieved that neither ankle wore the woven leather. But the fact that Cain was not in the hole meant he had done this! This was almost worse! He had committed an atrocity. Revulsion clenched her gut.

How could he kill Abel?!

What would she do if she saw him now? Would she run screaming? Could she ever trust him again? Lilith raced to the top of the hill behind the compound. There was an open place, a rocky ledge that jutted out there. Surveying as far as her eyes could see, she perched on the edge.

"Cain!" she cried out. "What have you done?"

Searching the horizon, she wept. Though she was now afraid of him, the terror of losing him overwhelmed her. In spite of what he'd done, she couldn't bear the loss of him.

"Cain! Come back to me! Cain!"

This last repetition of his name crescendoed into a high wailing scream. Birds in the nearby trees burst forth from the branches, soaring away over the cliff. Watching them go, she shielded her eyes, wishing she had their power of flight so she could search the distant forest.

Where was he? Desperately, she scanned the surrounding landscape.

Maybe if she stood here and screamed, he would return. She had to find him. She had to ascertain that he was alive and not a corpse like Abel, dead somewhere. The thought of Cain looking like Abel did, stiffened and pale and lifeless, made her frantic.

Eventually, her parents tried to remove her from the ledge, but she wouldn't leave. She stayed there screaming Cain's name for the rest of the day and into the night, until she lost her voice. She had not found him; he had not returned.

Hopelessness beat her down. Guided by the firelight in the distance, she stumbled home. As she drew near, she saw the entire family somberly staring into the dying embers. Many wept. From their postures and expressions, they obviously knew the horrific news.

Flinching and timid, Lilith crept out of the darkness like a frightened animal.

Her body hurt; she was bloodied. Distracted by her grief, she had torn at her face and arms with her fingernails, frustrated that she couldn't scream loud enough for Cain to hear her and return. She was terrified that he was mangled like Abel.

When her mother saw her, she ran across the clearing and embraced her, holding her up in her grief. They felt the loss with a physical pain none of the others experienced. Mother had borne Lilith's two brothers within her own body; Lilith was one flesh with one of them.

No one knew this but her, which made it worse.

She and Cain had not stood before everyone as man and wife. No one knew their bond of attachment had been made; it was a secret, an unshared blessing, now an uncertainty. Would he ever come back to her? Was he lost forever? It now hurt that they had pledged secretly. She needed everyone to know so they could support her in her loss.

Someone whispered that they should find Cain and kill him. Shrieking and tearing at the threatening voice, she lost control, turning into a wild thing, crying and screaming Cain's name in her hoarse, broken voice. Some of her siblings restrained her; others shoved and argued.

"You can't kill him!" she cried. "How are two dead brothers better than one? Cain has to be alive somewhere! Cain, come back to me!"

"Listen!" said the quiet voice of Yahweh.

Lilith quieted. They all stood completely still, the mere sound of God's voice bringing some peace into the dismal and terrifying situation.

"Cain has killed Abel. I have driven him from the land to wander on the earth. He must lament what he has done. The ground will not yield its fruit to him any longer. He will be a restless wanderer. He is broken; he must mourn. If any of you kill Cain, you will suffer my vengeance seven times over. He is under my protection; I have placed my mark upon him."

Lilith did not need to defend Cain—God Himself would do it. But the rest was bad news, horrifying news—news that destroyed your life and changed the rest of your days.

Stock-still, all waited, longing for Yahweh to say more. But He didn't speak again. Gradually the tension drained from each one, and they crumbled into their former grief-stricken postures.

Lilith's heart broke for Cain. She could not comfort him in his mourning; she could not soothe him with her presence. He was all alone, weeping and mourning his actions.

Would she ever see him again?

Silently, Lilith left the family circle, holding out her hand to stop those who tried to follow her. In the darkness, she stumbled to her room, heaped her things on her leather covering, drew together the corners, and hauled everything to Cain's room.

In the middle of the room, she dropped the bundle. She rolled back the matting on the ceiling—she had to see the stars. If she gazed on them as he did, from where he slept outside somewhere, if he could sleep at all—maybe he would know she was thinking of him.

Beside her possessions, she slumped to the floor. The moonlight fell on Cain's sharpened shaving tool. Her heart wrenched. She recalled each part of his face, the scent of his breath, the feel of his freshly shaven skin on her fingertips. She grasped the tool and sniffed his blood on the edge. Carefully she licked it off, tasting him. How could she live without him?

Grasping handfuls of her hair, she severed each tress with the sharp edge. Pulling each shorter hank of hair straight out from her head, she scraped the stone along her scalp, shaving her hair off at the base. Accidently, she nicked herself, mingling her blood with his. The pain cut sharp—excruciating! *Ah. Relief.* Purposefully, she slashed her arms, careful not to cut the bracelet. She kissed the leather he had braided so delicately.

Maybe the throbbing wounds would lessen the agony in her

heart.

Wrapping her bleeding arms about her body, she tried to hold herself together. He was lost to her! How could she bear it! Rocking back and forth, she keened a song of lament, croaking it out with her broken voice. The words worked their away around to the love song she had sung to him two days ago. She altered the words.

"I was Cain's, and he was mine.
I delighted in the strength of his arms
Holding my body against his.
I cherished his kisses.
He was like sweet perfume to me,
Resting between my breasts.
He was like a palm tree, laden with dates.
I sat in his shade and ate the fruit.
It was sweet to my taste.
I was my beloved's, and he was mine."

Crawling across the floor, she approached his bedding. Pressing her face to his coverlet, she inhaled deeply. It still held his scent. Gently, she lay herself down, as if embracing a sacred thing, breathing in his fragrance, willing the covering to be him. Arms spread wide, she vowed:

"Cain, I am now bone of your bones and flesh of your flesh. You are my husband, and I am your wife. We are one flesh."

Lilith was afraid she had lost her mind.

****

Unseen, Cain watched Lilith from the roof, peering through a corner of the ceiling matting. He didn't want her to know he was there. He was too ashamed. His actions were abhorrent; his face was now marred.

Her screaming had carried over the hilltops. At sunset, he had tracked her voice and had hidden at the cliff's base, peeking up at her. As she returned home, he had trailed her in the darkness. He had heard Yahweh's words and had crept along behind her as she moved her things to his room.

Death would have been more merciful than beholding the aftermath. When she disfigured her beautiful body and sheared her hair, he wished he were dead. Then he wouldn't have had to witness it. When she wailed the melody she had sung to him, his heart broke. When she spread herself out on his bed and he could not lay with her, he knew he would not survive being driven from her love. Her repetition of the vows destroyed him; he could barely breathe.

Slowly lowering himself from the roof, he climbed down the back wall, carefully feeling for each toehold. When he reached the ground, he pressed against the stone wall, mutely sobbing his inconsolable grief. Arms outstretched, he hugged the wall, embracing her through the stones.

This was as close as he could get to holding Lilith.

If he wandered for a very long time or never returned at all, perhaps she would forget him and find happiness again. She did not deserve a husband like him—a murderer, an evil one, one cursed like the serpent. God had rejected him, had taken everything from him.

But his punishment was just; he had taken Abel's life.

Cain knew he was getting exactly what he deserved.

CHAPTER 18

LILITH AWAKENED THE NEXT MORNING—bald, blood smeared, and alone in Cain's bed. Tempted to make his room into a shrine, she burrowed down into his bed, gazing at his possessions, inhaling his masculine scent. But she wanted to integrate herself into his room, as she would have integrated herself into his life tomorrow, on the day they were to have married.

Thus, she rose and got to work, intending to spend the day in solitude. Today Lilith couldn't bear anyone else's grief. It would pull her back into the black hole.

Crafting a place for her gifts, Cain had constructed stone shelves into his walls. Next to these, side by side and year by year, she arranged the ones he had given her, having brought them last night. Together, these now decorated the shelves. Remembering each gift exchange, she studied the progression of their artistry, smiling at the memories. They had grown in skill.

He had kept some of Abel's gifts. These she placed with theirs, admiring Abel's unique handiwork, gone forever. Tears slid slowly down her cheeks all the while.

Lilith smoothed Cain's leather covering over the grass bedding. It still smelled like him. She pondered how to preserve his scent. Maybe if she bundled up the covering, the inner parts of the bundle would retain the heady aroma of his skin. She would try this. Carefully, she folded it and then spread her own leather covering over his bed. The leather pillow filled with soft downy seeds still retained his fragrance, though she had wept on it and kissed it throughout the night. She would sleep on it, inhaling the perfume of him until the scent faded.

After she had arranged the room, she lay on the floor, arms outstretched, gazing at the sky through the rolled-back matting. Recalling every day since Cain had revealed his desire to have her as his wife, she lingered over each interaction, word, and expression, losing herself in her recollections. She fixed these beautiful memories in her mind, bypassing only two, saving them for later. Every day until he returned, she would exist solely in this world of remembrance.

This was how she would survive. It would be as if he had never left.

When she had mused her way to reflections on their last interaction down by the river, she sat up. Peeking out the door and finding no one outside, she left the room. Someone had removed her severed hair from the dust. Careful to avoid everyone, she sneaked to Cain's bathing place.

Hiding in the tall grasses, Lilith evoked the memory of Cain watching her in the river. Recalling his blushing embarrassment, she closed her eyes and sang to him again. It made her cry. Only one remained. She stored away this one to contemplate later. When she had calmed herself, she removed her garment and slipped into the water.

Wounds covered her upper body—her head, her face, her arms. Gingerly fingering the strange stubble on her head, she dipped into the shallows. Holding her breath, she gently rubbed her scalp. Her head felt exposed and cold and raw. Surfacing, she cautiously worked her fingers over her face and arms, careful of her injuries; then she immersed herself again. Injuries of her own making covered her body. She kissed the leather bracelet as she washed around it.

Once she was clean, she lay on the bank to dry, savoring

the most precious memory of all—the final one. She recalled the details of making love to Cain out in the meadow. This reminiscence was so fresh and painful that it bent her double, racking her with sobs. Huddled on the ground, she wept a long while.

Determining to be strong, she focused on what she had to do next. She sat up.

Blood and dirt from Abel's body and grave had embedded in her garment, the blood from her wounds smeared with his. She beat the garment against a rock. Then she scrubbed it, dunking the bloody places into the water and then wringing it out thoroughly. Only parts were wet, so she put it on. Now she was ready to face her family.

It was midafternoon on the holy day of rest—the day before she and Cain were to have married. Resolutely, she marched toward the center of the compound. As she approached, their quiet, saddened voices murmured more distinctly.

When she entered the family circle, her brothers and sisters stared at her, speechless at her appearance. They gaped at her. Having seen her reflection, she knew her bald head caused her eyes to appear larger, more stark and staring.

The nicked places on her scalp hadn't yet scabbed. Her head looked oddly naked, and it was shaved unevenly. Scratch marks just scabbing covered her face and arms. The gashes she had cut with Cain's stone striped her lower arms. Some cut deep. These still seeped.

Her parents wept. She held up her hand to stop them. Their grief would make her crumble when coupled with her own.

"I want everyone to know where I truly stand with Cain, and what I intend to do until he returns." Her voice sounded odd. It scratched hoarse and croaky. "Two days ago, Cain and I made our vows privately in the woods. We were united as man and wife; we're now one flesh. I will be looking for my husband each day."

One of her sisters, Mara, hissed an animalistic term at her. It was merely a word they all used, but when Lilith met Mara's eyes and saw her look of condemnation, the word now held an entirely different meaning. Shame flushed Lilith's cheeks. She would have to ignore this.

Determined, she continued. She had wanted to do this with Cain by her side.

"Since Cain and I can't make our vows tomorrow, I'm repeating the vow I made to him: I am bone of Cain's bones and flesh of Cain's flesh. He is my husband, and I am his wife. We are one flesh. He made his vow to me."

That said, ignoring their response and forcing herself not to care, Lilith turned and walked toward the rock ledge. Fixating on Cain's return, she would call for him again, pleading with him to return. That was the important thing, not what anyone else thought.

Maybe he was out there in the woods feeling alone and rejected, forsaken by the Creator and by his own family. She would make certain he knew she loved him if he was anywhere within earshot. She determined to do this every day until he heard her voice and they were reunited.

Stepping out onto the cliff, she scanned the area, searching through the trees below.

"Cain, I love you! Cain, where are you? Cain, come back to me! Cain!"

Since her voice was still hoarse, it didn't carry far. But she yelled with the same intensity. Each time she called his name it broke her heart again. She wept, her aching loneliness growing increasingly acute. Her calling became hysterical screaming.

Lilith felt her sanity slipping away.

****

Back at the compound, Adam circled among his family, listening to their discussions.

Some found Lilith's devotion to Cain acceptable. They regarded their vows in the woods as legitimate, since they had already been betrothed and Lilith had made it public. This group was comprised of many of the older children. They didn't know the details of the conflict between Cain and Abel, but after a lifetime of loving Cain, they knew his temper could get the better of him. But never like this before.

All week they had witnessed Cain's sarcasm, his temper, and his unwillingness to forgive. Most of them had experienced that firsthand at some point. They also knew this was not the way Cain normally treated them. When he lost his temper, he eventually came around, apologizing for his hot words and hurtful actions. His temper only showed itself on occasion. This week had been one of those occasions.

Cain had gone over the edge.

They knew Abel probably had been innocent of any serious offense, even though he had sought forgiveness from Cain repeatedly this last week. That had been Abel's way. He had always apologized first. As the kindest and humblest among them, he had always been quick to recognize when he had hurt another or had caused the situation to escalate.

They didn't excuse what Cain had done; but, after time had passed, they wanted him back so they could all be reconciled. They didn't want to lose both of their oldest brothers in one day.

Adam found that others, especially the children who were more attached to Abel, didn't feel Cain should ever be allowed to return. They didn't understand Lilith's devotion to him or the marriage that had occurred, if it was a marriage at all. In their minds, it was all wrong.

Some felt outright hostility about Cain and Lilith's deliberate flouting of all that he, as their father, had ever said to them about marriage and how it should occur. This group included Mara, who with a wordplay had created a derogatory name and had aimed it at Lilith. These children thought Cain should be put to death in the same manner, so he would know how Abel had felt. Only God's edict stopped them from hunting Cain down and killing him too.

Adam's stubborn inability to comprehend God's plan for the children to marry one another had affected this group adversely.

He was grieved it had taken him so long to see clearly. He should have listened to Eve. It hurt him that his fathering had caused damage.

He called the family together and stood to speak.

"We don't want our family to be divided. We want you to love each other. I don't know if God will allow Cain to return, but if He does, we must pray about what to do. No one has ever sinned like this, but we've all sinned in one way or another. This is my fault." Here Adam composed himself. "I deliberately disobeyed God and ate the fruit from The Tree of the Knowledge of Good and Evil, bringing sin and death on us. Now one son is dead." Overcome by the thought, his voice cracked. "Another son is banished, and one daughter may never recover."

Directly across from him sat Eve. He stared at her. Then he looked around the circle.

"In the meantime, God told us not to harm Cain. Killing Cain will not bring back Abel; it will only give you two dead brothers." Here Adam fixed his eyes on those who had voiced their desire for vengeance. "Let's respect Lilith's wishes. Be kind. They were publicly betrothed. Though they erred, I recognize Lilith's commitment to Cain, as does your mother."

Eve nodded her affirmation. He knew she blamed herself, as he also wanted to take the blame. But from over a century of loving her, he knew how self-blame always damaged her. Since she had been deceived by the serpent and had then tempted him to eat the fruit, Eve had periodic bouts of despair. Her hopelessness was especially dark when trials reminded them of sin's horror. It had come into the world because they had disobeyed God. And, now death, separation, grieving, and loss of sanity of their children had visited them. Her reaction would be worse. Adam determined to encourage and restore her, if he could.

Lilith's shrill keening echoed in the distance, growing in hysteria. Adam didn't know how long he could endure this. It made him feel as if he too teetered on the edge of madness. He was tempted to run out to the cliff to wail with her. Then he remembered one more thing.

"If any of you want to be married, there will be no delay. You can say your vows quickly and begin your lives together as husband and wife. We shouldn't have delayed Cain and Lilith. If we hadn't, we could have avoided this conflict between Cain and Abel. It was my fault. I made them wait because of my inability to recognize what your mother had seen for years."

He looked directly at Eve. These words were for her alone. "My love, I'm so sorry."

CHAPTER 19

UNABLE TO SLEEP, CAIN SPENT the night at the base of the cliff, pressed against the stones for warmth. Forgoing sleep, he stared at the stars all night, keeping his eyes wide as he battled thoughts of Abel and of Lilith.

For the rest of his life he would regret what he had done.

In the rapidly approaching dawn, Cain rose. Should he try to get one more glimpse of Lilith? No. He couldn't bear it. Seeing her again, especially since he would want to hold her and comfort her in her grief, would make it impossible for him to leave.

But he had to leave. Yahweh had banished him; he could feel God drawing him away.

This force couldn't be resisted. It felt like a cord that bound him, like a harness they put on the donkey and the ox to guide them. The tugging overpowered his desire for one last look at Lilith and wrenched him away from home right now.

Besides, what if she looked at him with horror and revulsion? What if she ran away in fear? His heart broke when he thought of that, but he knew it was a possibility.

If he were Lilith, he would be afraid.

Turning from the cliff face, he walked toward the rising sun, off into the wilderness away from the Tigris. On and on, he walked. The day grew warm then hot. Salty sweat now irritated his eyes. Thirst dried his mouth. In the exploratory trips he had taken in the past, he had always returned home by dark. Then he had carried water in a small clay jar secured to his side. Perhaps he would die out here, parched and desiccated.

Eventually, he reached unfamiliar territory. Forest continued unabated, but increasing hills and cliffs presented challenges. Since he hadn't turned around when the sun reached its zenith, by the end of the day he would be twice as far from home as he had ever been. With no purpose other than wandering and no pressure to return to his work, Cain set his mind free.

He came from a large family; there was hardly ever any hush of quietness. But now he had entered a world of stillness. He hadn't realized silence could be so encompassing. In fact, he felt oddly detached from his body. The silence expanded and enlarged the world of thought inside his head. As he walked, he answered his own internal questions.

He wondered whether he would forget how to speak, if he never again had any person with which to converse. That was a possibility. Would he forget to care for his body if he existed so wholly inside his own head? He might. Was this to be his permanent condition? Was he going to exist in this land of wandering all his days? He did not know.

This first day, most of his internal conversation consisted of asking himself how he had allowed the situation to spiral completely out of control, destroying everything. What had he done? What should he have done?

He had tried so hard to do what was right and had failed at every turn. He realized that he did not have the ability to do what was right. It was not in him.

He truly did belong to the serpent. He was evil.

But what did it mean that he was evil? Was he doomed to be only evil for all the rest of his days? If that was the case, why had God warned him of the evil lurking to destroy him? Did the fact that he hadn't done what was right, hadn't resisted that evil, mean that he could now only ever do evil all the rest of his days?

If that was so, why did he feel remorse?

He was not who he had thought he was. His actions had proved it. So, who was he? As this man, how would he live?

As darkness fell, he discovered a small babbling brook. Beside it grew a few recognizable plants. Parched and famished, he threw himself on the ground, scooping handfuls of water to slake his thirst. Then he sat by the brook and ate the green, leafy vegetation and edible berries.

Pitch black fell rapidly in the woods; deep gloom engulfed him. He had no fire, just the moonlight that barely shone through the openings between the trees. Small animals scampered nearby, their night eyes reflecting.

He'd never been afraid of the dark before, but he felt as though something frightening watched him, seeking his harm. Wrapping his arms about himself, he positioned his back against a large rock by the brook. It felt safer, and the rock still held warmth from the sun.

Facing the darkness, he shoved aside the dread and tried to sleep; but, as on the night before, each time he closed his eyes there was Abel. Recalling the last kiss before he covered him with dirt, Cain tasted the mingled blood and gritty soil. Bile rose up in his throat, and he wept.

Uncomfortably, he twisted his body into a different position.

Trying to avoid thinking of Abel, Cain's mind drifted to Lilith. He wanted her so badly! He had left a significant portion of himself behind. He should have been at home preparing for the celebration of their marriage tomorrow. Saying their vows before their family would have made it a true and recognized fact. They then would have lived together as man and wife.

What was she doing now that there would be no celebration? How was their lovemaking in the woods now hurting her when there would be no public proclamation or commitment?

Abel felt no more pain. He had departed. But Lilith was living with the horror of what Cain had done to their brother. She was probably embarrassed, angry, and hurt. Could she still love him? If so, she was hurting, suffering as was he.

Then a new horror hit Cain. What if she bore a child, and he was not there to father it? What if he had abandoned not only her, but his own offspring? Staring into the darkness, he fought the desire to shriek and howl with this new agony, clenching his teeth together to hold in the scream.

He told himself over and over to think of nothing, think of nothing, think of nothing …

That was not possible.

Day after crushing day he tortured himself with remembrance and recrimination; night after night he suffered, assaulted by recollections that made him sick, horrified, or heartbroken. Though filled with regret, there was nothing he could do to make reparations.

The situation was hopeless.

He had gone out from Yahweh's presence.

He could not be restored.

Seeking relief, Cain ate a large quantity of hemp. It only intensified the agony, turning him into a paranoid and frightened animal, tearing through the woods, waiting anxiously for his impending death, his heart clutching in his chest. After that, he didn't ingest any of the herbs he knew might soothe him. Nothing eased his pain.

One day, he stood at the top of a large cliff out somewhere in the wilderness, contemplating throwing himself off. He clutched the edge with his toes and leaned forward, feeling God's invisible harness pulling taut against his forward motion.

God would not let him die. Even this mercy was denied him.

But, with no family, no hope, and no will to live, Cain was a walking dead man.

CHAPTER 20

A YEAR HAD PASSED. CAIN didn't know why Yahweh was allowing him to return, but He was. However, Cain knew he wasn't done wandering—the process of self-reflection and mourning had just begun. The entire year had been spent within his own mind, mulling over his failings.

A first for him, he now saw himself clearly. His flaws were an inherent part of who he was, and no matter how hard he tried, he would continue to fail in some way. This he knew. There was nothing he could do about any of it, other than to grieve.

He also knew he was not the one chosen to crush the serpent's head. He was not perfect. No man was. It would take a perfect man to defeat the evil one.

Now the stars were again aligned for the time of the offerings. One year after the fateful day, the tug of the invisible cord loosened, allowing him to return; but he knew it would pull him back out into the wilderness again. He was certain.

If he stayed, it would only be a short time until he failed miserably again, wounding them all. The evil and weakness within himself was an intrinsic part of his nature. It was who he was. If he was alone in the wilderness, at least he couldn't hurt anyone but himself.

What would he find? Would they all be broken because of

what he'd done—strife and conflict, fighting and vengeance destroying the family? Would his parents have recovered? Would any of them even want to look on his face?

What if everyone was terrified of him? What if they loathed his presence?

****

As he drank from a pool of water, he scrutinized the fine black curves and strokes on his forehead. The mark was supposed to remind them that God would bring vengeance on any who killed him. Maybe they wouldn't care and would kill him anyway. It would be good to die.

However, above all he feared the condition in which he would find Lilith. Was her mind broken? As he traversed the journey's final paces, he mulled over these ruminations.

It was the morning of the sacrifice, the newly full moon having risen last night. His family would be in the field making their offerings of thanksgiving right now. When he thought of it, his heart clutched. He recalled the fateful day, now reliving it on familiar ground. Once more, he saw where it had occurred. He would soon behold the faces of the loved ones he had wronged. Abel's body was here, moldering under the dirt.

Suddenly, he felt sick.

Falling to his hands and knees, Cain retched up the contents of his stomach, staying there until he could think of being home without feeling nauseated. When he rose, he shook violently.

He headed toward the cliff face. This was where Lilith had screamed his name. Maybe he would find her there, so he could watch her unobserved, absorbing what his eyes beheld. That would be preferable—much better than coming upon her suddenly and unawares. He didn't want to stumble upon any other members of the family or walk into the family circle, surprising them all. He couldn't bear the looks of horror and disgust they would bestow upon him.

The cliff came into view. His desire had been granted. A lone figure perched on the edge, surveying the wilderness. It was she! A melody wafted toward him on the breeze. Brokenly, she crooned the love song she had sung him. His heart lurched.

Cain stayed hidden in the trees. A soft halo of curls now encircled her head, as it had when she was a small child. Her longest hair barely grazed her shoulders. She was much thinner; she hadn't been eating. Edging closer, Cain moved quietly through the forest until he stood at the base of the cliff. From behind a tree, he peered up at her.

When he examined her from this proximity, his heart grieved. Lifeless and sunken, her eyes seemed not to see what was before her. Moving her hands feebly through the air, she mumbled, seeming to communicate with things that dwelt only in her mind. Maybe she thought she spoke to him. Dark circles purpled the skin under her eyes. The bones at the base of her neck protruded.

Softly, she called his name, her voice stripped of all hope, as if he stood right before her refusing to respond, as if she despaired of ever receiving an answer.

Ah. No. I've destroyed her.

Against the bark of the nearest tree, he muffled the moan. It was as bad as he had feared. Her heart and her mind were broken. This was why God had sent him back, to put some hope and some life back into Lilith. In spite of what he'd done, she needed him. They were one flesh.

Gazing up at her, he stepped from behind the trees, cautiously approaching the base of the cliff, a mere four body-lengths below where she stood. When he stood near the cliff wall, he looked up. He didn't want to frighten her or wound her mind in any way, so he decided to wait until she called again. Then he would answer.

Would she be afraid of him? Would she run?

"Cain!" she muttered. "Cain, why don't you come? I call. Don't you love me anymore?"

The pain of these words caused his throat to ache with emotion. Fighting for control, he swallowed hard. He needed to articulate; he wanted her to understand his words.

"Lilith, I'm here." His voice thick, he pressed down a sob. "I've come back to you."

His voice shook; it didn't sound right to his ears. For the past year, he had spoken to no one but himself—only crying, lamenting, chastising, and arguing. Startled, Lilith peered into the woods. Shielding her eyes from the sun, she rose, trying to find him.

"Was that really Cain?" she said softly. "Did he really answer or is this another cruel imagination of my broken heart?" She sighed. "It's never really Cain."

"Lilith," he spoke more solidly. "I'm here at your feet."

Slowly, she looked down, and their eyes met. Stretching as far as he was able, he reached up to her. On the cliff's edge, she threw herself to the ground, straining toward his fingertips.

"Are you real?" she asked.

"I am."

"You look different."

"So do you."

Cain hadn't thought about his own appearance for a year.

A full black beard covered much of his face and neck. His hair was long, bound by the leather in which she had wrapped his gift. Without the straining labor of working the land, he was gaunt. A wanderer, he was now lean, much as Abel had been as a tender of sheep. God's symbol marked his forehead. His leather bracelet was secured around his wrist.

"You've moved the bracelet. In my mind, it's always on your ankle. You're real!"

"Yes, dearest." His voice cracked; he pulled it together. "I'm real. Are you alone?"

"Yes."

"Can I come up to you?"

"Oh! Please, come!"

"Stay there," he urged her.

Not wanting to encounter anyone else, Cain ran through the woods. It was early morning, so the family would still be occupied with the offering. Dodging trees and bushes, he ran up the hill to the far edge of the cliff. When the cliff's edge was low enough, he leapt, grabbed the rocky ledge, and hoisted himself over it.

Lilith hurtled toward him. Smashing into one another, they embraced. Weeping, they exclaimed over the changes they felt with their hands and beheld with their eyes. Every body part their mouths encountered, they kissed—cheeks, eyes, hands, hair.

He touched her again! Relief that Lilith wasn't afraid of him washed through Cain.

Lilith pressed her lips to his forehead, lamenting the need for the mark. He grieved as he examined how her beautiful gray eyes sank back into her skull. Caressing each of her wounds and scars with his lips, his heart agonized over what he'd done to her. Then he pulled her tightly against himself, holding her in firm embrace, never wanting to let her go.

He felt whole again.

Locked in each other's arms, neither of them ever intended to release the other.

"Lilith, I have so much to say. I need to beg your forgiveness."

She looked at him solemnly. He continued, "I destroyed everything. I killed our brother, wounded our family, and hurt you. I did everything wrong. I didn't realize then how flawed I am. I failed. I should have guarded you from my lust. Did you bear a child?"

"No, but I wish I had. It would have been a living reminder of you."

"I know you've had to endure criticism from some of our siblings. If you had given birth, their judgment would have been severe."

Lilith stroked his hair to calm him. "I wanted you as much as you wanted me. It was my fault too."

"I'm not much of a man if I can't even protect you from myself. I should have denied my need for your body until I'd secured you as my wife. I didn't make your heart my priority. I was selfish. I didn't even prepare a home for us. My focus was in the wrong place. I didn't love you as I should have. I left you vulnerable and unprotected. You've suffered for it, haven't you?"

She nodded; there were tears in her eyes.

"I should have insisted that we say our vows immediately. We'd waited for decades. That week proved too much. I wasn't thinking of you; I wasn't thinking like a husband. I was thinking like a son. You should have come first. I should have done what was right for you, even if Father wanted to have a celebration."

As he made his confession, she gazed soberly into his eyes. She must have realized that he was correct, because she made no objection. He pressed on, needing to say it all.

"I didn't listen to your admonitions to reconcile with Abel. If I had, none of this would have happened. Instead, I sinned against God, and I hurt all of us. Mostly, I hurt you. This is the time we should cleave to one another, but I'm now forced to abandon you when you need me most. Dearest one ..." He paused to kiss the slashed scars on her arms. "... can you ever forgive me for what I've done? Can you forgive me for ruining everything?"

With warm hands, she cupped his face. "I forgave you the instant I realized I was more terrified of losing you than I was of what you had done. When I found Abel's body—"

In shock, Cain choked, interrupting her words. He couldn't bear to look at her. He covered his face, attempting to eradicate the image her words conjured, lamenting that she had seen it.

"You found his body? You? I'm so ashamed. I didn't want you to see what I'd done. How could I have killed our brother? I'm an evil person, a wicked man. I'm so sorry."

****

Lilith pried his hands from his face. Studying his haunted eyes, she discerned the heartfelt regret he had suffered this year, the mental wounds inflicted by that pain, the suffering endured, the tortuous sleepless nights, and the long wandering days. Gently, she kissed his mouth.

"Cain, I love you. Even though what I saw terrified me, I was even more frightened of losing you. I found out this year that I can't live without you. Look at me."

His eyes acknowledged that she was correct. She couldn't.

Laying his head on her shoulder, he wept. She soothed him, stroking his head, holding him close, whispering words of comfort.

"Lily." He pressed his face to her neck. "I can't stay."

She inhaled sharply, grasping him more tightly to herself. "No! Why?"

"I hope you can understand this." He wiped his nose and looked into her eyes. "It hardly makes sense to even me. When I was banished, I thought I had left God's presence. But now, as I say this to you, I know that's impossible. You can't leave God's presence. Even though I have no fellowship with Him, I know He's there. He watches me. He pulls me along. There's no other way to explain it. He's led me in the wilderness, like we lead the donkey or the ox. I felt Him pull me away the day after I killed Abel. I realized He was leading me when every evening I happened to stop beside water that I could drink and food that I could eat. Then the next day He would pull me away, with the same result each night. He even saved my life when I tried to kill myself."

"No!" Lilith shuddered. "Say you won't do that! Say it!"

"I won't kill myself." He caressed her cheek. "Talking to you has given me hope. I've spent my days evaluating my life. But I'm not done. God led me back here, but I have more wandering until I'm healed. He's using my journey to work on my heart. When I saw you, I knew He had brought me back because you needed me. I'm your husband; you're part of my body. Just as you gave me hope, He sent me back to give you hope."

Nodding, she cradled his face again, staring hard at him. For the first time in a year, hope glimmered in her heart. "I need to hope. Tell me what you have to say."

"Know that I'm alive and that I love you. Start to live again. What you've been doing is destroying you. Can you trust God to take care of me and to bring me back if He thinks it's best? Can you stop what you've been doing—sitting here every day, calling for me, and breaking your heart over me? Please. It hurts me to know you're in this condition while I can't be here. It hurts to know I've done this to you. Can you start living again for me?"

Carefully considering all he had said, she looked at him solemnly. The mental picture of Cain on a leash with God leading him eased her mind somehow. He hadn't come back to her because he couldn't, any more than one of the animals could resist going where they led them. If his head had been free of the harness, he would have come to her.

In the same way, when God knew that Cain was a necessity to her, He had brought him. Today she had needed him. Her mind had teetered on the edge of cracking. This anniversary had pushed her to the brink. She might not have ever regained her sanity. She had lived this entire year in her imaginary world, seeing only the Cain of her memory.

Could she now trust God to lead him away and to bring him back when he was restored?

She could. Certainty and hope cleared her mind. .

"I can let you go," she said. "I will trust God. He brought you back to me today. He'll bring you back again."

"When He allows me to return, if He allows me to return, can I say my vow to you in front of everyone and take you away as my wife?"

"Yes. I want to be your wife."

****

Cain stared at her, probing her eyes, pleased by what he saw. Sane hazel-gray eyes met his gaze, frenzy and confusion lifted. Then, the sound of voices calling to Lilith reached their ears. Heartbroken, Cain panicked. Their time together was over. He had to go. How could he leave her so soon? The leash had tightened. It pulled him to his feet and out of her arms.

She followed along beside him. "Can I come with you now?"

"I have to go alone. He hasn't released me."

Crying, they clutched each other, walking together until he motioned for her to return.

"I love you, Lily. I'll always love you. Live. Take care of yourself for me."

"And you for me. I love you so dearly. I'll be waiting here for you."

Fastening his eyes upon her face, he walked backward as long as he was able, stumbling over unseen objects in his path. Fading from view, Lilith stood still, mournfully watching him disappear. And then, she was gone.

Cain turned away, lowered his head, and ran.

CHAPTER 21

EVE HAD SENT THE OTHER children back home when she didn't find Lilith sitting in her usual spot. For some time, she had been haunted by the apprehension that her daughter would fling herself headfirst off the cliff today. Cain's sin had destroyed Lilith and the rest of the family. Was another death to be added to their losses? Were they to have this horror too?

Stepping slowly to the edge, Eve peeked over.

Nothing.

Lilith was not shattered at the base. Relieved, Eve exhaled.

While Adam had made the traditional offering, she had stood silent and prayerless. As soon as he finished, she had walked away, coming to seek her girl, afraid of what she would find. As Eve combed the forest floor below, she considered all that had befallen them.

Division had arisen between those who thought Cain should never be readmitted to the family and those who thought he should be allowed back in, if he was repentant. When Cain was finished wandering, the larger group of her older children wanted him back. Abel had been their brother; but Cain was their brother too, and the driving force of creativity and innovation.

Together with Lilith, Yonas, and Abel, Cain's inspiration had sparked inventions that eased their lives. The best domestic ideas budded in these four minds. Now one was broken, one was reeling, one was dead, and the most creative was banished.

The older children realized the centrality of Cain's role. They missed him and hoped he could come back. They had loved Abel and knew Cain was terribly wrong to kill him, but they were willing to forgive. Yonas, who had loved Abel so dearly, remained particularly adamant. He insisted they follow Abel's example.

The group that never wanted to readmit Cain, who actually wished to end his life—nine of her children of marriageable age—always liked things done the same way. In this, they were like Adam; but unlike him, they hadn't yet learned to flex. Instead, they were becoming rigid traditionalists—stiff, harsh, and inflexible. They were especially hard on Lilith, calling her names, mocking her pain, and shunning her.

Consumed with their resentment, none of these nine had married, even though Cain and Lilith's relationship had motivated eighteen of the children to wed. Nine marriage alliances had been formed this year, with seven of the girls now expecting children. Two grandchildren had already been born. In the middle of death and destruction, life had reasserted itself, each of these events salving the wounds of the previous year. The blessing of these grandchildren brought comfort and joy to Eve's heart, almost as if she'd borne the infants herself.

The newly married focused on their love for each other and their delight in their new children or the approaching births. As a result, their wounds had largely healed. This overflow of life and love prompted them to respond magnanimously to the idea of forgiving Cain. They saw Lilith before them; they wanted to be kind.

Lilith. Eve sighed. Given her broken state, she could be anywhere. With toes curled over the cliff's edge, Eve shielded her eyes, probing deeper into the shadows of the forest.

Lilith lived in a world of her own imagination, a reality that existed in a time prior to Abel's death and Cain's departure. With the vision of Cain in her head, she stared off into a world that inhabited her mind. Lilith's behavior broke their hearts, banding them together to keep her alive. They made sure she ate, tried to ease her to sleep each night—*if* she would let them into Cain's room—guarded her from falling into the fire or into the water, and watched her as she went through her daily rituals of remembrance, lost in another time. Now Lilith was gone.

Eyeing the horizon, Eve thought she detected movement far in the distance; but something flashed at the corner of her eye. She turned. Lilith ran toward her along the cliff.

She was crying. That wasn't unusual. But her eyes had life in them; they focused on Eve and really saw her. Lilith was in her body, her mind clearly attached to it, not with Cain far away. She hurried toward Eve and hugged her.

"I just saw Cain," Lilith said.

Doubtfully, Eve considered her. This had happened before. Lilith thought she had seen Cain, but it had been her own mind stretching and warping against the bounds of reason.

"I know," Lilith said. "You doubt me. I really saw him this time. The Creator brought him to comfort me."

"Go on."

"Mother, he looked so different! He's thin, since he doesn't guide the plow. He's spent the entire year walking wherever God takes him, evaluating his life, and contemplating his mistakes. He apologized for everything. His beard is full and thick. His hair is long. He wears it tied back."

"The mark?"

"In the middle of his forehead is a symbol. It's hard to describe. I think I can draw it." Lilith picked up a small stone and etched on the rocky ledge, explaining as she drew. "It was exotic and fine, drawn in thin black lines. It looks like this."

$$יְהֹוָה$$

Eve studied the unusual markings carefully. She had no idea what it meant. Obviously it meant something to the Creator.

"Why did he come back?" Eve asked.

"God brought him because he was necessary. My mind was barely able to discern reality anymore. I needed Cain today. He asked me to start living again. He has to wander until God allows him to return. He begged me not to make his wandering harder by destroying my mind. He wants me to trust that God will bring him back if I need him."

"Has he forgiven himself?"

"No. I don't think he ever will. Over and over, he told me how flawed he is, how evil, how grieved that he had killed Abel. He asked for my forgiveness for pledging alone in the woods. His eyes looked wounded; I could tell he had suffered deeply." Here Lilith cried softly. "He still suffers."

"Why didn't he come to the compound to see everyone else?"

"God wouldn't allow him. When we heard your voices, it was as if he had a cord on him, and it yanked him away. He described it as being led like a donkey or an ox by a lead rope or a harness. The Creator takes him where He wants him to go."

Eve sighed. Weary, she lowered herself to the warm rock ledge. "Sit down, daughter." Eve patted the ledge. "I have something to tell you."

Lilith sat. Eve pondered where to start. The beginning seemed best.

"For five to six months after I tempted your father to eat the fruit in the Garden, I couldn't talk to the Creator because I was so ashamed of my actions. Imagine loving Cain with no sin, no selfishness, no discord—only bliss and tranquility and selfless love. That was what your father and I had in the Garden. But because I tempted him, he ate the fruit, and we lost it all. Our natures changed immediately. We realized we were naked. We hadn't known it before; we'd felt no shame or embarrassment. Our first argument occurred as we ran to make coverings for ourselves before we hid from the Creator. Do you understand?"

Lilith nodded. "Yes, but I can't imagine it."

"It was so long ago, but I'll never forget the reality of living in that state. God was near us every moment. We basked in His love. But then, we destroyed it all. Until I felt Cain move within me, I thought Yahweh had rejected me forever. He felt far away. When I knew I was bearing Cain, I understood that God still loved me. He had begun his work to bring the one who will crush the serpent's head. I thought it would be Cain—if not Cain, then certainly Abel. I idolized them in my anticipation of this act I thought one of them would perform, trusting in their abilities instead of God's. I had no idea they would end up this way—one dead, the other banished."

"No one did. Who could predict such a thing?" Lilith exclaimed. "It escalated so quickly."

"It did. This is a test. Do we still believe Yahweh's words that He'll send one to crush the serpent's head? He promised He would. I was wrong about who it would be, exactly as your father was wrong about how you children were to obtain your mates. Just because we were wrong doesn't mean God's promise has failed. It simply means we didn't understand His plan or how He intends to fulfill it. Maybe we still don't comprehend it."

"I don't understand how it will happen," Lilith said. "I've never even seen the serpent."

"It was more than a creature. The animal was indwelt by evil, but God was more powerful. The serpent cringed as God spoke. Yahweh told us He'll send one to destroy this evil one, and He will—in His time, not what we imagine to be the right time. Our only hope has ever been to believe that God's words are true, regardless of what we think or feel, or what we see that looks contrary to their fulfillment. He's also told us that Cain is broken. You've seen evidence of his contrition. God has put a mark of protection on him. God doesn't cast out those who are broken and contrite. He didn't cast your father and me away from His presence, merely out of the Garden. He still loved us. Even though Cain is wandering, his life is in God's hands. Neither you nor I can guide or protect him. God still loves him, and God will protect him. You must turn now, daughter, and try to live as if you trust God to do what's best for Cain, whether you see it with your eyes or not."

Lilith had remained focused the entire time, sanely

considering Eve's words.

"I will, Mother," Lilith said. "Will you help me when I get discouraged? I don't know how long he'll be gone."

"Yes, I'll help you. Will you help me, daughter, when you see me saddened by the destruction and division that have resulted from Cain's sin? My heart is embittered; I'm angry at Yahweh. I must always remind myself that my sin destroyed our family first, before Cain had even been born. I don't think I'll ever forgive myself."

"I'll help you, Mother. If you still can't forgive yourself, do you think Cain ever will?"

"No. Some things you regret all your days. Your father regrets eating the fruit. I regret tempting him. Cain will always regret killing Abel."

****

Once he could no longer see Lilith, Cain sprinted away, focusing on speed. It felt as if Yahweh pulled him away with a strong hand, as if He discerned how desperate Cain felt. If he didn't fly away, he would thrash and fight and claw to get back to her.

As he ran, tears streaked his cheekbones. Going back had ripped open all the wounds. Her promise to care for herself and to live again eased his mind at least.

God now dragged him in a new direction, bearing toward the pole star, the axis around which the sky rotated. Cain ran north as far as he could, finally walking when he could run no longer. He spent the entire day pondering Lilith's appearance, her words, and her promises.

Cain hoped and prayed—yes, prayed—that God would heal her. Could he talk to God? Could he pray?

Since their conversation on the bank of the river when he had tried to wash Abel's blood and gore off his body, Cain hadn't spoken to God. He had memorized Yahweh's words of judgment from that day, continually repeating them to himself, meditating on them even. They were seared into his heart and mind, condemning his motives and his actions. The last year had been spent lashing himself with God's words.

Cain didn't think God wanted to talk to him. God had issued what Cain had thought was the final verdict on his life. Unworthy and unloved, he had left God's presence.

But, as he had spoken to Lilith, a revelation had come—for a while he had known it was impossible to leave God's presence. Speaking to Lilith always helped him clarify his thoughts and feelings. It had helped him realize what he really felt about this year of banishment.

Cain didn't feel angry at God any longer; he was only angry at himself. Cain thought he might be ready to speak to the Creator again. He hoped God would hear him. He focused his thoughts toward Yahweh:

Oh God! Please heal Lilith! It hurt to see her in such agony of mind. Please! Please, God, don't let my actions cause her such pain. I'm so sorry I hurt her. Please help her!

Cain grieved for the woundedness he had seen in Lilith's eyes. He wanted God to protect her. But Cain knew he was evil; he knew he deserved any penalty God inflicted upon him.

CHAPTER 22

RACING ALONG THE TIGRIS, CAIN sprinted north, urgent to travel as far from home as possible. Out of the corner of his eye, he glimpsed the cherubim adjusting their positions, keeping him always before them. Suddenly, the unseen cord yanked him toward the river. He dug in his heels, but slipped down the embankment, getting his feet wet.

Then Yahweh dragged him into the water.

Cain knew how to swim, so he propelled himself across the river. But his mind screamed with objection—*I can't go there!* This was forbidden. Death waited on the other side. Why was God doing this to him? Perhaps this was the moment of his death. Having restored Lilith, maybe his purpose for living was complete.

When he reached the other side, he crawled onto the riverbank with trepidation. Countless times he had sat on the bank opposite the cherubim, astonished by their appearance, frightened by their quick and watchful eyes. How would it feel when they killed him? Would it occur quickly and painlessly, or the other more dreadful way, like he had killed Abel?

Afraid to look up, he stayed on his hands and knees until he caught his breath, postponing the inevitable. Then, slowly, he raised his head.

Unhurried and deliberate, the cherubim retreated before him, backing into the woods with all their eyes fastened upon him, stern in their assessment. Their massive wings whipped the foliage; Cain's eyes watered in the blast. Shielding his eyes from their radiance, he followed them. Soon they were far ahead, a shimmering vision in the distance, the setting sun blazing behind them.

His parents' journey away from the center of the Garden had required one long night of walking, the Creator's force propelling them at great speed as they barely skimmed the earth's surface. Cain walked all day. For some reason, God was allowing him to see this. His parents couldn't come in, but obviously he could.

Leaving the Garden was their banishment; this was his.

The quantity and variety of fruit trees and edible plants amazed him. As he walked, he picked and ate. No one had tilled the earth, yet food had sprung from the soil; but weeds had also encroached. Even Eden had been polluted by sin. Weeds, thistles, and thorns filled the place, choking out food-producing plants—all effects of his parents' actions and God's resulting curse on the earth. This made life hard, food difficult to obtain, requiring their blood and sweat.

There were many animals he'd never seen before, exotic creatures, large and small. Birdsong and scampering creatures captured his attention. With racing heart, he glanced about, trying not to miss anything. Strange animals spotted him and came near to investigate. Aloof and cautious, they shied away if he stepped toward them. From his father's descriptions, he knew the names of some. Others, he had spotted from across the river when they came to drink.

These creatures weren't domesticated like the animals at home. Neither were they friendly, as Father had recounted from their time in Eden. The fall had changed everything. These animals studied him with piercing gaze, startled and wary, then they ran away.

As nightfall descended, he settled down against a large boulder, doubting sleep would come. The cherubim halted in the distance, as if waiting for him.

As he watched the Garden grow black, it occurred to him that he might discover the serpent in The Tree of the Knowledge of Good and Evil, if he was allowed to travel that far. He dreaded seeing it. Somehow it embodied evil, having tempted his mother, and through her, his father, to give up all of this for some sort of knowledge it had promised.

What the serpent had done was so horrific that God had made a promise to crush its head, using a member of their human family at some point in the future. Cain knew he wasn't here to do that; he was an imperfect man, and, therefore, unqualified. More likely, the serpent would crush him.

He wasn't sure if he believed God's promise; it seemed a mysterious and impossible thing. Yet his parents had told them that God had said it. And now God had proven Himself to Cain in ways he never could have imagined before he began his banishment.

Miraculously, he was still alive, for one thing. Now he understood what kind of a man he really was. Finally, he had clarity about his failings, something he had been unable to see or comprehend for the first one hundred twenty-one years of his life.

In the darkness, he prayed again for Lilith. Then he prayed for healing for his parents and all his siblings. He told God how sorry he was for his many mistakes, enumerating them one by one to Yahweh. He hoped God heard him; he didn't deserve for God to answer. At last, he slept.

****

Cain journeyed for a week. Each day the cherubim progressed before him, their many eyes fixed on him at all times. Never before had he felt so scrutinized, but he realized he had been. All alone in the wilderness, God's eye had been upon him. Each night God had brought him to rest by water and food, and each day God had led him. He had even taken him back to Lilith.

Though Cain had *felt* abandoned, he had not been. This was a lie. God was always near.

This truth dawned on him more fully each day. As he journeyed one day, Cain remembered a long-ago conversation with Abel. Once again, Cain had gotten into trouble for being impulsive and doing something he shouldn't. Abel had warned him of the possible consequences, but he hadn't listened. After being chastised by their father, Cain had asked Abel how he always managed to be so good.

Abel had chuckled softly, shaking his head. "There's nothing good in me," he had said. "I can't be good in my own strength; even my motives are flawed. I have to cry out to God for help. He's always there. If I just go ahead on my own, I sin and get into trouble. I'm exactly like you."

It had seemed preposterous at the time but now made perfect sense: recognize you were incapable and then, aware of God's presence, cry out, asking God to help you.

To do this, you had to be mindful of God's watching eye. Not to cry out was to ignore the all-seeing God, the One who saw all your errors that no one else witnessed. To pretend those faults didn't exist, to ignore them and refuse to deal with them, was to forget that God saw everything.

Before he had killed his brother, Cain had not perceived his flaws. He had thought he was fine, even telling Abel that he didn't need his prayers. Cain had drawn from a well of strength he had thought he possessed, but which was an illusion. Ignoring and violating his conscience at every turn, he had always ended up making mistakes, hurting others, and hurting himself.

It was arrogant of him to think he could be good simply by willing it, living entirely unconscious of God's presence and his need for God's help. Cain now realized that God had not rejected him but had been patiently waiting for him to humble himself.

He was thoroughly observed, both internally and externally.

Yet, for some reason, he felt accepted and cherished. He didn't understand this. Could he cry out to Yahweh for help? Did God want to help him?

Would the Creator help one who had hurt everyone he loved?

Looking up from his musings, Cain discovered that the cherubim had stopped, each taking their position on opposite sides of a dazzling and enormous tree with golden shimmering leaves and bright golden fruit. Their flaming sword was raised high, pointed directly at him.

This must be The Tree of Life.

The thought of death terrified him—it was unknown and final. Abel was now dead. This fact chilled Cain's bones, sickened his stomach, and caused his heart to hammer. If the cherubim hadn't been there, he would have eaten the fruit from The Tree of Life, so he never had to die.

Beside it was The Tree of the Knowledge of Good and Evil, the fateful tree. It had the dark green leaves and the crimson fruit his parents had described, but no serpent. Knowing what Cain now knew about himself, he realized he would have eaten the forbidden fruit exactly as his parents had. He used to feel prideful toward them about their mistake, but now he did not. At least they hadn't killed anyone, least of all someone they loved.

He wondered if he would ever experience God's forgiveness as his parents had.

The rest of the day, he sat and contemplated the two trees. As the sun set, he lay on the ground, eyes fixed upon them. Again he prayed for everyone he loved, then described, lamented, and apologized for his sins once more before falling asleep.

Cain now realized God heard him, though he didn't deserve for God to answer.

****

This became the pattern of Cain's days. Each day the Creator led him to a new part of the Garden where he explored and contemplated. All the stories his parents had told him were true. Everything was exactly as they had described—a bit more overgrown with vegetation now, including the widespread weeds; but all was precisely as they had spoken.

Every night he prayed for Lilith and the rest of his family; then he wept and lamented his sins, telling it all to God, begging His forgiveness. While he explored the Garden, the realization of his powerlessness continued to grow as he mourned over all the mistakes of his life.

He remembered how he had felt when he first was led by Yahweh out into the wilderness. God had seemed distant and unapproachable. But now that Cain had acknowledged all his errors and had humbled himself, he grasped how intimate and personal God's leading had been.

God had crafted it specifically to break down his prideful heart. It had been for the purpose of making him into a new man—one who knew he was capable of committing any atrocity and so, as a result, who cried out to God for help.

As he hiked through the Garden each day and carried on this conversation in his head, Cain now recalled Yahweh's words of love and mercy—an offer to help. Cain had arrogantly pushed them aside. Then, powerless, he had toppled over the edge.

Why didn't I listen?!

Why hadn't he recognized that God had rejected his offering precisely so he could see himself clearly? His mind had been blinded by arrogance. But now, he understood.

Just as God had offered help to turn him in a new direction and to prevent him from killing Abel, so now God extended forgiveness in spite of the demands of Abel's blood. God tugged at his heart. But how could Cain receive this mercy?

He was so unworthy. His heart grieved as he considered it.

****

One day Cain came upon a mother that had died giving birth—some type of unfamiliar animal with short tan hair covered with dark, variegated stripes. He didn't know the name his father had given it. The infant's hips protruded partly from her body, stuck during the birthing.

Death's cold fingers extended into the Garden, as well as

outside of it.

Cain's clothes had been shredded in his wandering. In his mind, he had concocted better garments, hoping to make these one day. When he found the two newly dead animals, he knew the time had come. Spending the day preparing a stone knife, starting a fire, opening the bodies, removing the hides, and crafting from their bones and internal organs the remaining tools he would need, his creative faculties burst to the fore, energizing him.

As he worked, he whistled and hummed. He loved to work with leather. He could now meet his need for better clothing— God had provided. As he applied his mind to this artistic project he loved, his chest filled with inner warmth; frequently, he smiled.

When evening approached, his heart overflowed with praise to the Creator. Impulsively, he gathered stones and prepared to present the flesh and fatty portions to Yahweh, as an offering of thanksgiving. Compared to the last sacrifice he had made, this one felt different. This offering came from a truly broken heart, bursting forth with genuine gratitude to God.

As he held out the burning branch to light it, he had a moment of fear. Would God again reject his offering? Would he be reprimanded? If this happened, he would be devastated. His hand trembled as he held the fire to the offering. But it burst into flame.

"I accept your offering, Cain," God spoke quietly, in almost a whisper. Cain couldn't quite discern if he heard the Creator's voice audibly or in his heart. "You have offered it from a broken and contrite heart; you have given me the first fruits of your labors—the best you have to offer."

At last, brokenness and contrition had penetrated his hardened state. Cain's heart now pleased the Creator, his God. He collapsed to his knees before the blazing offering, covering his face as he wept. This was what Abel had done on that terrible day. Now Cain understood why.

Like Abel, he was unworthy, evil, filled with sin; yet God

loved him and accepted what he offered anyway. Forgiveness had been extended to him.

Until darkness fell and the starry canopy spread out above him, he wept on his face before Yahweh. Finally, the certainty of the Creator's presence filled him with peace.

A turning point had been reached; Cain now headed in a new direction.

CHAPTER 23

SHRIEKING, SATAN ROCKETED INTO THE heavens. God had wrenched Cain from his grasp. Earlier he had lost Lilith. Cain's return and her mother's encouragement had repaired her mind and turned her heart toward God. Seething wrath propelled Satan's flight. In an instant, he hovered in deep space, far from the human scene below. He needed distance.

Why had he been unable to destroy Cain? What was it about God's love and mercy that drew the humans? How did Yahweh win them? With their sinful natures, Satan had assumed the humans were all his. He hated being wrong. He had assigned his best princes to torment Cain. He had overseen the strategy. Satan let loose one final scream. It shook the stars.

Aggravated, he returned to the earth. His princes would be called to account.

Landing nearby, Satan screeched at the cherubim and all the rest of the elect angels who now encircled and enveloped Cain, readied in defensive posture. Then their attention fastened upon Satan. All of them stood poised, ready to jump into any fray he instigated.

But everything seemed to be going against him. He restrained himself.

"Samyaza! Azazel!" Satan glared at his demonic generals.

"Call your cohorts!"

Quickly they stood arrayed before him, all scorched in like manner as he from their joint ejection from Heaven. They all hated the human creatures who had taken first place in God's affection, though He had created the angels first. Each face twisted in hatred and frustration.

Seizing Samyaza, Satan yanked him close. Terror showed in the general's eyes, which he quickly veiled. Amused, Satan observed his attempt to appear unruffled and in control.

"You will pay for this," Satan bellowed. "How did you let him escape? How?"

"I'm sorry, my lord." Samyaza groveled. "I destroyed his self-worth. I insinuated these thoughts as if they were his own: 'God doesn't love me. I can never be restored. There's no point to my life. I should just die.' I robbed him of all joy. I confused his ideas. He lost himself."

"How did this fail?"

"It was the opportunity to work with leather again. The mere idea of it gave him pleasure. The spark of creativity flared—in that, they are like God. It reminded him of who he was. It gave him hope. And also, my lord, you know that the Spirit of God was there speaking to him too."

"I don't want to hear it!" Satan shoved Samyaza away. "I'll deal with you later."

Overpowering their schemes, God the Spirit always drew the children of Adam and Eve. Day in and day out, with gentle wooing, reasoning, and pleading, God had whispered to Cain. And, for some indiscernible reason, he had responded.

Satan couldn't comprehend why this drew the humans to God. It mystified him. As a fallen angel, he was fixed in rebellion. He could never repent, nor would he want to. How could they?

Clearly, this was the way Yahweh had designed them. He wanted them to be His.

"Your efforts failed." Satan fixed his gaze once more upon his generals. "Now, what can we do to destroy Cain's new belief? Better yet, how can we take his life?"

"We don't have permission," Azazel whimpered.

"I don't care!" Satan turned to glare at the nearby elect angels. "Let *them* try to stop us!"

The fallen generals moved about uneasily, each studying their opponents. The cherubim and the heavenly angels outnumbered them, and they all stood fierce and readied in battle posture.

"We can manufacture false devotion," Azazel suggested in obsequious tones, "filling Cain's embittered siblings with self-righteousness and nudging them to act as if on God's behalf."

"Yes." Samyaza nodded, along with the rest. "If we steer the siblings onto the wrong path, and they think they're doing good as they go the way we lead them, we can entrap them. Vengeance is a black hole. It will destroy those who seek it and eradicate Cain as well."

"Let's not forget Lilith." Azazel's eyes gleamed with menace.

Smirking, they all studied one another. Satan guffawed, his mind intrigued by these ideas.

He shoved aside the fact that he couldn't negate God's sovereignty. God would work all for good in the lives of the humans He loved. And, one day, God would call him to account for every harmful act he committed. Still, he and the other fallen ones would bruise, maim, and harm.

Together, they plotted a new strategy, and Satan dispensed his princes to carry it out.

CHAPTER 24

DAY AFTER DAY, AS CAIN labored over his new clothing, he found himself talking to Yahweh. He kept up a running conversation. Sometimes he conversed with God quietly, within his own head; other times, Cain spoke out loud. He discussed the puzzle in the leather, often receiving answers immediately after he queried, the solution now obvious. He talked about the questions and uncertainties he had about belief. He recounted all the ways God had led him.

Sometimes he cried about Lilith as he worked, remembering the last thing he had made—the bracelet he had given her. Pausing to kiss his bracelet, imagining it was her instead, he grieved his many failings in pursuit of her and the damage he had caused. He told it all to the Creator.

Other times, he cried over Abel, or his parents, or his other siblings. Often, he listed again and wept over his litany of sins. He followed whatever path his heart took as he talked to God.

He was no longer alone inside his head.

From the small infant animal he crafted a covering for his loins so he could remove his old garment and work more freely. This leather was softer and more pliable; it didn't bind as the sheepskin had. He called this new garment a "loincloth." Then he designed coverings to be laced up each entire leg. If he didn't want to wear the leggings, he could wear only the loincloth.

Next, Cain constructed a loose-fitting shirt made to lace up the middle. It covered his torso and hung down to mid-thigh, extending down each arm, shielding the place on his shoulders where the sun tended to burn his skin. He also created coverings for his feet. They wrapped around the entire foot, lacing across the instep. Running and walking about the Garden, he tested them. It was easier to walk in this type of foot covering; his feet were protected.

These clothes were comfortable to work and travel in. They were much lighter and cooler than the sheepskin. He had spent many weeks on this project, and it had been a joy. As he created these garments, he had felt whole again, contented for the first time in a long while.

Maybe this could be his new occupation, since he could no longer till the earth. He would trust the Creator to feed him, as he had during his wandering. Perhaps, in exchange for food the others grew, he could produce leather garments and jewelry. His days would be happy, especially if Lilith labored beside him.

Now that he could move about more freely and was covered more adequately, Cain began other projects. Wearing only his loincloth, he carried his stone knife into the damp cave behind the waterfall to pry and carve away as much of the gold and precious stones as he could remove.

He placed these into the carrying sacks he had made from his old sheepskin garment. The gold and stones dazzled. He imagined how Lilith's eyes would light up if he gave her a bracelet with these set on it. He would experiment, because the properties of each type of stone varied. For now, he gathered as much as he could carry with him.

Sampling from trees and plants, he tasted and enjoyed the varieties of food. He dried seeds from the ones he hoped the family would cultivate outside the Garden. Since he could no longer plow the land, he wouldn't be able to plant these. He hoped his hands hadn't tainted them, preventing them from sprouting.

The accumulation of seeds took many days. He could only eat so much in a given day then the seeds had to dry thoroughly before he stored them. When he had collected an adequate number of seeds from a plant, he carefully wrapped that kind together in a leaf.

Cain then let the leaves containing the seeds dry, each wrapped around a different type. This would make the planting and harvesting more efficient. He wanted an adequate number of seeds from each type of plant, so gathering them took many months.

As he worked on these things, all tasks he enjoyed, he became increasingly cognizant of Yahweh's love for him. He knew God heard him and answered his prayers. He was completely unworthy; it wasn't because of anything he had done that God answered. It was because of the inherent nature of God's own character that He loved and cared for someone like him.

Cain also became aware that within his own heart an intense love for Yahweh had been growing in reciprocation for the love and mercy God had shown him.

All he had seen here had proven that not only were his parents' words true, but also that the nature of the Creator God was true and faithful and loving.

Cain felt restored.

****

Two years had passed since Cain had entered the Garden of Eden; his projects were complete. As he sat for one last time, contemplating the two trees in the middle of the Garden and the mighty cherubim guarding The Tree of Life, he thought about his time here. Many significant events had occurred to prepare him to be reunited with his family. The most momentous was that he had been reconciled to the Creator.

After these three years of wandering, he now knew how completely he had always misunderstood himself and why his failings had always frustrated him, leaving him feeling insecure and defeated. He did not have it within himself to avoid sinning. No person did. Only a perfect man could defeat the serpent. He was not the one.

He could do nothing to earn God's favor. All he had to do was walk with God like an ox on a harness lead, following the Creator's direction and crying out to Him for help when he lost his way or couldn't take the next step. God was near.

Additionally, he had to humbly accept Yahweh's help when it was offered—to listen to God's quiet inner urging in his heart and to embrace His enablement to obey. That was all.

It was ridiculously easy, but it was only spiritually discerned. It had taken the destruction of all he had previously been and the loss of all he had previously had to realize this simple truth.

His pride no longer stood in the way.

Cain now understood that if God could do this work within his formerly hardened heart, then Yahweh could certainly fulfill His promise to one day crush the head of the serpent. He would bring a perfect man to do it, and the serpent's head would be crushed. Then sin and death would no longer reign, the earth would be restored, and Abel's blood would no longer have to cry out.

Cain now believed Yahweh's promise. He had faith.

His heart now humbled, Cain knew it was time to go. He no longer had to be dragged along to follow God's leading. He now loved God with all his heart, communicated with Him, and strove to discern the steps God would have him take.

And now, Cain wanted to take them; he wanted to follow. Much had changed.

In the sheepskin bags, Cain had packed all the things he had collected—the specially wrapped seeds, the leather gifts he had made for his family, and the gold and jewels from the cave. He now began his long hike out of the Garden.

God had given him a vision for the future. It involved a city, and it involved Lilith.

Soon he could return for her.

CHAPTER 25

CAIN SAT CROSS-LEGGED BY THE Tigris, binding his possessions together with hemp cords. Once secured, he tied them firmly to the small floating raft he had built. He removed all his newly made garments and fastened them on top. With a long leather cord, he attached the raft to his body, tying it firmly about his waist.

Shoving off from the bank, he asked God for help and swam for the other shore. Fighting against the current to go northward made a difficult swim. As he crawled out of the water, he thanked God for getting him safely across the river. Then, breathing heavily, he collapsed on the bank before hauling the small raft onto the shore and assessing his goods.

Some of the bundles had gotten wet, so he took everything apart and laid it all in the sun. Then he spread himself out in the warm sunlight to dry his body and to recover.

As he rested, he envisioned the home he was to build. It would be here, east of Eden, about a day's journey toward the pole star from the home compound. Trying to ascertain how far north he was right now, he surveyed the riverbank. He had come out of the Tigris much farther north from where the cherubim used to watch them as they moved along this opposite bank.

When he had first crossed the river to enter the Garden,

he had run along this bank for quite a distance, the two angels following him silently along the opposite shore as they awaited his crossing. However, he needed to go even farther north. He was still within a day's walk from home, which meant anyone could come upon him as he labored.

He needed to get the wall up before that happened.

Before he had left Eden, as Cain had contemplated what he would need to build into his city, a wall kept appearing before his mind's eye. Why would he need to build a wall? They had no wall around the family compound. Trying to discern why the wall appeared in his thoughts, he had turned the question over in his mind, asking the Creator.

One night while praying, the answer had come. Stunned at the realization, he had sat up. The wall needed to be built because of what he had done to Abel. Some of his siblings now hated him and wanted to kill him. God had given him the idea to defend his life, to prevent the necessity of bringing vengeance on any who killed him, and to forestall any more bloodshed.

While filled with gratitude to God for this new idea, Cain's heart had been grieved, nevertheless. With his act of violence, he had truly changed the world. But it was not in the way his parents had always assumed he would.

He had not crushed the serpent's head; he had invited the serpent in. It had only been crouching at the door. Now it was in the house, tearing and destroying the family.

As he now sat on the riverbank, his body drying as he recalled that night of realization, Cain again felt remorse. The effects and consequences of his sin, now unleashed upon humanity, would hurt and destroy humankind as long as they remained on the earth. His name would forever be spoken with derision and disdain because of what he'd done to Abel.

Once more, he begged Yahweh for forgiveness. Then he took action. He checked his possessions to see if all had dried. They had. He dressed, repacked everything, bound it in the leather carrying bags, and strapped them onto his back. Squatting by the river, he disassembled the raft and cast it off into the woods and into the water to eliminate any evidence of his location. Then he ran north.

If a wall was necessary for his protection, he needed to move a safer distance from the home compound. He needed to build a place of safety—a city of refuge.

As he ran, he considered how to build it. He needed many rocks and clay for mortar, like they had used to erect their sleeping chambers at home. Wood bound together with leather or strong hemp cord for a door in a gateway would be required— hanging woven hemp was now inadequate. He wasn't sure who would live in this city. Lilith and he wouldn't need much room. But the vision in his head included many people. A "city" was a place where more than one family dwelt together. Would some of their siblings join them? Apparently.

By midafternoon it seemed he was about a day's journey from the family compound, though it was hard to assess, since he had never been this far north. He kept alert for a good location. Soon he discovered a large brook that fed into the river. The brook snaked off into the woods. He headed east, following it farther into the wilderness.

Near sunset, he came upon a stony area near a cliff. The brook wound along its base. There was clay where the brook curved. Edible plants flourished on both sides of the brook— God's provision. Flowers bloomed; bees zipped by—a source of honey. There were many rocks here and a clearing along the base of the cliff, slightly elevated from the riverbank. Part of the cliff dipped back, forming a canyon away from the brook. The floor of the canyon was stone.

Assessing the cliff, he realized he didn't know how to think defensively. There had been no need before his act of violence. Where would be the best place to build his home? He had to imagine the strategy someone might use if they planned to attack him. This hurt his heart, because it forced him to recall his preparation for harming Abel.

Building this place of refuge would be more difficult than Cain had imagined. Not physically—he had expected it to be taxing and had looked forward to the hard labor; he loved challenging work. But this would be taxing mentally and spiritually. He needed to think like he had when he had been consumed with wrath and intent on hurting his brother; he had to reenter the mind of a murderer. Because Cain didn't want to recall it, he begged God for help.

Erecting the city at the base of the cliff would be most convenient. But he wondered if the top of the cliff would be a better location. If he built at the base, could someone scale down the cliff and get inside the wall? Yes, that could happen. If he built at the top, could access to the water supply be cut off by those outside? Yes, that could also occur.

Developing strategies to defend himself from his own brothers and sisters was something he had never had to consider in the past. He wasn't sure what to do. So, since it was now dusk, he decided to camp at the base. He would settle in for the night and tomorrow would survey the location more carefully.

He built no fire.

When he considered the need for this city of refuge, he felt exposed. He prayed for Yahweh to protect his life and to help him be courageous. He didn't want to be consumed with fear. Snug against the cliff wall, he eventually fell asleep.

****

Sometime in the middle of the night, Cain woke with a start and jerked upright. Drenched in a cold sweat and the ubiquitous night mist, his teeth chattered as he shivered.

He had had a nightmare about Lilith. Some of their siblings had been trying to kill her. For safekeeping, Cain had hemmed her inside a stone cave behind a wall. Trying to get around him to hurt Lilith, his vengeful brothers and sisters had swarmed toward him, their faces twisted with rage. They had overwhelmed him; he couldn't fight them all.

The horror of it had awakened him.

Cain wept over how he had changed the human race—the

family of which he was a part, who would now reproduce and fill the earth and fight each other until God himself would have to put an end to it. The cold terror of it filled his mind. He had changed everything.

There was no defense that someone, eventually, couldn't break through, killing everyone a man loved and cherished. Appalled, Cain sat with his arms wrapped around his knees, staring into the darkness for the rest of the night. As the sun rose, he was resigned. There was no perfect defense; he would have to trust in God.

Yahweh would be his refuge.

To stop an attack's forward movement, he would prepare a wall. On that wall he would carve the symbol that was on his forehead. Reminding them of God's promise to avenge him, the symbol might give the attackers pause. Then, once halted in their rush of rage, whoever attacked would be stalled long enough to reconsider. Perhaps they could even be reasoned with.

The wall would make a barrier that would force them to contemplate their actions—time to talk, time to reevaluate. And nothing else.

If he perished, he perished. It was all in God's hands.

That determined, he surveyed the cliff, discussing his plan with Yahweh. He placed every idea for the location and method of building before God and listened in his heart to the response. Finally, he felt peace about how he should proceed. He didn't feel the lead holding him back; his conscience felt clean.

He would build at the cliff's base. There the small canyon of rock formed a sheltered area.

Sheer rock rose on three sides. How high? He reckoned at least eight body-lengths, maybe ten. If he built a wall across the open side that faced the brook, behind that wall, within this canyon, homes could be built. For defense, everyone who chose to live in the city could retreat behind the wall.

If many people lived in his city, there was room to expand. By moving the defensive wall closer to the brook, farther out of the narrow canyon, the living area behind the wall could be enlarged. The brook was shallow here; they could plant crops on the opposite shore where a broad and flat area of ground lay.

Decision made, Cain stripped to his loincloth and got to work. The sooner the wall and a home were built, the sooner he could retrieve Lilith. He could now anticipate this event. The wandering was over; he was building a home.

It would soon be time to retrieve his bride.

Cain worked with purpose. Whistling and singing, he hauled large stones for building the wall, fashioned stone tools to cut down trees, and kneaded the clay to the right consistency. His step was light. Happy to his very core, he felt weightless. He loved to create things he had imagined in his mind. It filled him with satisfaction to watch the city take shape around him. Yahweh blessed his work, and Cain talked to Him over every detail.

Of course, it took longer than Cain had hoped.

Now that he knew he would soon regain Lilith, an inner urgency that hadn't existed before fueled his efforts. He yearned for her. He grew anxious about her. The remembrance of the nightmare haunted him. Keeping focused on the task the Creator had set before him, he prayed for her safety continually, reminding himself of God's care for them both. If he didn't, he couldn't sleep at night.

Cain built the wall and the house simultaneously. Starting with the wall, as he waited for the clay between each course of rocks to dry, he turned to work on the house. Several days were required for the clay mortar to dry. Rotating from one task to the other, he toiled from sunrise to sunset, the wall and the house rising level by level, evidence of his labors.

When Cain could no longer reach the top of the wall, he formed a ramp utilizing two logs lying side by side. Using this, he rolled the next course of stones up to the top. Holding each in place with a third log that he wedged into the soft earth, he climbed onto a stump that he dragged along the wall. From there, he carefully positioned the stone tightly against the rock it abutted and smoothed the clay he had laid prior.

To make the gate, Cain had chiseled a crevice into the cliff wall and had inserted one end of the large piece of timber he had hewn for the lintel. The other end of the timber lay across the top of the wall, overlaid and packed in with clay to hold it in place. On top of this timber, he had laid this last course of rocks. Into the center of this gateway, he had carved the symbol of the mark.

He wanted the rock wall to tower higher, but that would require his brothers' assistance. As he placed the last stone, his work on the wall was complete. To survey his efforts, he stepped through the gate, strode across the clearing, splashed through the brook, and turned.

The stone wall extended all the way across the narrow canyon. To make the gateway less noticeable, he had located it against the cliff's sheer side, not in the center of the wall. If he merely glanced at this area, the wall was barely perceptible, because it was made from the surrounding stones. It blended in. Cain was pleased.

Behind the stone wall, the home was constructed against the cliff's base. At the back of the narrow canyon, he had discovered a crack that formed a tiny cave. He erected their home in front of it, utilizing the fissure for storage. If he had to defend Lilith and their children, he would hide them in here. He remembered the dream. But he tried to be practical, not fearful. As he worked, it provided a dry sleeping place, a relief after years of waking damp from the night mist.

He built a home with two rooms—a large general room and a room for sleeping. For now, nothing covered the ceilings or inside doorways. Once the walls were up, he left the cave to sleep in the house so he could view the stars. They reminded him of Lilith and of God's watchful eye.

It was difficult not to think about lying with Lilith in this house. Sometimes he meditated on intimacy with her, and his sleep was fitful all night. With a pounding heart, he stared up at the brilliant display of starlight, praying for patience.

In front of the house, he erected a wood-and-mud walled

area for their private use. He experimented with mud stones—
"bricks," he called them, which he fashioned from clay and dried
in the sun. Of these, he built the walled enclosure, smoothing
the outside with more wet clay. To gain entrance to the house,
he walked through this walled, enclosed space.

Lilith and he would work outside in this area. When others
moved to their city, the two of them would have privacy as they
worked behind their brick wall. It would function as an outdoor
room, giving them one additional living and working space.

He hoped they filled the entire place with children.

Now that he had laid the last course of stones across the
wall, he fashioned the main gate of strong timber. He worked on
it while each brick layer of the enclosure dried. When the gate
was finished, and he had discerned how to attach it to the wall
so it could open and shut, he invented a mechanism that secured
it from the inside, barring outsiders.

He then worked on the final details of the house, finishing
the high brick wall that enclosed their working area and building
into it a narrow gate that could be fixed firmly from the inside,
obstructing the entrance. He constructed a front door, also
securing it from inside. Security was essential—he hoped he'd
thought of everything.

Then he cleared out his tools, moving them into the enclosed
work area. In the front room, he placed the seeds so they would
remain dry. In the cave, he stored the gold and precious stones.

Bringing in an armload of long, reedy grass, he spread
it on the sleeping chamber floor. Repeatedly, he returned to
the brook for more. When he arrived with Lilith for their first
night, the grass for their bedding would be dry. He would only
need to gather it and pack it into the bedframe in the corner.
Momentarily, he lost himself in the thought.

His city wasn't complete, but the wall and his own home
seemed to be ready enough—secure and protective. To finish the
city, more of their siblings needed to come and live with them.
They could all work on it together. Whether or not they ever
came, this would be a comfortable home.

As he lay down to spend his last night on the outer room floor, he considered each detail, making certain everything was adequately prepared. Could he actually, finally, go and retrieve Lilith? He brought all the details before Yahweh and felt released to bring Lilith home.

Overjoyed, he spent considerable time in thanksgiving and praise to God for preserving him alive through these nearly five years. He was now ready to return.

Cain placed his plans before God. He would leave at sunrise. Arriving at the compound after dark, he would assess the situation, unseen, evaluating from the cover of darkness. The following sunrise, he would walk into their morning gathering and claim his wife—glorious thought! They would leave immediately so they could be back inside the wall before they slept that night.

That was the plan. Filled with anticipation, he couldn't sleep.

CHAPTER 26

SOON AFTER SUNSET, CAIN ARRIVED near the compound. Happily, he had built his city at exactly the distance he had hoped. Blazing at dusk, the home fire burned. At nightfall, he slipped up to the family gathering. Hoping to determine how to approach them in the morning, he crept through the vegetation and stretched flat under one of the bushes, searching first for Lilith.

There she is!

He gasped. He had forgotten how exquisitely beautiful she was! His memory didn't do her justice. He yearned to go and claim her as his bride this moment.

She leaned against Mother, helping care for the littlest children. Lilith appeared healthy and well—much better than when he had last seen her. Her hair cascaded to her waist. Reflecting the firelight, her eyes shone clear. She was still too slender.

Relieved, he reminded himself to breathe.

Lilith engaged in conversation with their mother. He scrutinized their faces. Lilith looked sad, sighing frequently. He detected no bitterness, merely pining. He again grieved the consequences of his sin and how it had hurt her. *How much she has suffered!* With Yahweh's help, he would be an attentive husband, healing her heart with love.

His mother still grieved for Abel—it showed clearly on her face. Bitterness was evident. Mother didn't hold or nurse an infant; she had borne no more children. Judith still appeared to be the youngest at nearly six years of age. *Something isn't right.*

He begged God's forgiveness for what he had done to his mother's heart.

Shifting his eyes around the fireside, he observed that the dynamics of the family had altered. They seemed to be divided into groups that had not existed before.

Couple after couple of his siblings huddled together—nine marriage alliances. Their children clustered about them; some of his sisters nursed infants. How many children had been born? He counted twenty, at least! Making it impossible to tell which children belonged to which parents, the children moved constantly and intermingled.

Across the fire perched nine of his adult siblings who appeared to be unmarried. Sternly, with heads held high, they studied their married siblings. An attitude of condemnation pervaded this group. Cain continued to study the family, trying to interpret body language and figure out the factions. No longer was the family a mix of adults and children playing, chatting, and laughing. There was a palpable tension.

Father sat midway around the circle from Mother, rather than beside her. *They always sat together,* Cain remembered. Now he noticed they barely looked at each other. Father often gazed on Mother with wistful longing; there was some alteration in their relationship that Cain had never witnessed before. Had he placed a wedge between them?

Eventually, the fire died to embers. One by one, family members rose and departed. The married siblings headed in various directions. They seemed to have erected their own homes. He watched Lilith separate from Mother and the smallest children. She walked toward his old chamber. How tempted he was to join her there!

But he had come to restore Lilith's honor before them, to

restore Lilith's honor to herself—to prove that she was a prize worth obtaining correctly. He would honor marriage as God had designed it; he would be above reproach in the family's eyes.

A secret marriage, which wasn't really a marriage at all, was not good enough for her. In view of them all, he would pledge to her. He beseeched Yahweh for strength.

Cain watched his mother walk toward the parental bedroom nearest the fire. His father followed. They didn't touch each other. Cain prayed for a strategy.

Quietly, he slinked back through the woods, far away from the fire, circling the compound. He sneaked across the field where he had broken Abel's nose; then he crept slowly down the hill, arriving behind his parents' sleeping chamber. Inside their voices murmured.

Pleading gently with his mother, his father's voice rumbled low and patient. Mother's voice sounded hard, insistent, and determined. They argued. Cain didn't want to hear their words; not only was this private, but he feared it had something to do with him. He was almost certain of it.

Scooting back up the hill, far enough away that he couldn't discern their words, he quickly prayed. He felt as if God urged him to remain where he was. His legs twitched restlessly, but he stayed. Drawing in a slow breath, he fixed his eyes on the stars, waiting to see God's plan.

Eventually, his father ducked out and trudged up the hill, almost within reach. *Thank you, God!* With head down, Father passed, unaware that Cain watched. When his father reached the field, he paced back and forth. Silently, Cain stole up the hill.

Begging and pleading with God about something, Father uttered hushed prayers. He mentioned Mother's name. Back and forth, Father paced, resolution obviously evading him. Finally, he dropped down in the field, his head on his knees.

After a moment of hesitation, Cain moved forward uncertainly. *God, help me!*

"Father," he whispered.

His father raised his head, peering into the darkness. "Who's there?"

"It's Cain."

"Son!" Rising quickly, Father held out his arms.

Cain hadn't expected this. He had anticipated harsh condemnation, maybe a cool yet cordial greeting, but certainly not warmth and eagerness to see him. A sob built in his chest as he rushed into his father's welcoming arms. Cain poured out his tear-soaked confession.

"Father, I was wrong. I've hurt all of you. I'm so grieved! I failed you as a son. Everything I did was flawed—the way I treated Abel, how I pursued Lilith, my actions as your firstborn. I allowed my anger to defeat me, and I killed my best friend, my dearest brother, your own son. Can you find it in your heart to forgive me?"

Father squeezed him, burying his head on Cain's shoulder. Cain stood stunned for a moment and then hugged his father with the same force. Leaving his hands on Cain's shoulders, his father stepped back and stared into his eyes.

"Son, I disobeyed God, bringing sin and death on us all. I can and I have forgiven you."

"But you didn't kill anyone you love," Cain said, tears now flowing.

"No," Father said, "I killed every single person I love."

Cain paused. He hadn't thought of that. "But you didn't understand the consequences."

"Neither did you. None of us comprehend the consequences of sin until we commit it."

"That's true." Cain hadn't considered this either. Had his father always been this wise? Then he remembered his errand. "I've come for Lilith. I need your assistance."

"You can't stay?" His father's voice was crisp. "You'll be in danger in the wilderness again."

"No, Father. Yahweh allowed me to build Lilith a home, a safe place where we can live and have a family."

"Yahweh? Are you speaking to Him then?" His father chuckled gently.

In the darkness, Cain smiled. "At first I thought I'd left His presence. I spent the first year torn by grief and regret. Then I realized God was near. I started praying for all of you. I didn't know if He would answer, since I'm so sinful. I finally grasped that He heard me and He wanted me to hear Him. I grew to love Him. I now talk to Him about my thoughts, my desires, my fears, my mistakes. He urged me to build a home for Lilith, to come for her, and to talk to you first."

"Your journey back to Yahweh sounds much like mine, son." He paused a moment and sighed. "You're going to have opposition."

"To taking her?"

"Yes. You have brothers and sisters who disdain you for Abel's death. They want you punished equally and will seek vengeance. They might pursue you. I'll be unable to stop them."

"Yahweh helped me to build defensively. He will protect me as He protected you, Father."

"You really have been listening to God." His father paused. "How do you want to do this?"

"At dawn, I'll enter the family circle and ask everyone for forgiveness. Then I'll make my vow to Lilith. I want to help heal the shame she surely felt about our secret marriage. We'll need to leave immediately."

"No time for a celebration?"

"No, Father. We'll travel all day to return home. I want to arrive there by nightfall."

"You're determined, my son?"

"Yes."

"Alright. Your confession might soften the hearts of those who oppose you." Father peered at Cain's forehead, rubbing his thumb across it. "I can't see the mark clearly by the moonlight. Maybe it will remind them that in attacking you, they fight against God."

"God is merciful to defend me. When He rebuked me I thought I could never be near Him again. But He has welcomed me into His presence. "

"He is a God who forgives," his father said. "I know this too."

"I was allowed to enter the Garden. I beheld all you had seen. God showed me that He's faithful to His promises. I trust Him, and I now believe He will send one to crush the serpent's head. But it won't be me. It will take a perfect man, not one flawed like myself."

"A perfect man? That makes sense. We'll watch what God does."

"Yes." Cain paused. "How is Mother?"

"Your mother struggles. Once more, she's angry at herself for tempting me to eat the forbidden fruit, angry at me for eating it, and angry at God. She misses Abel and resents you for killing him. She doesn't want any more children—her children have broken her heart, she says. There's a great barrier between us. I can't get through to her. It's been very difficult."

"I'm sorry, Father. This is my fault. What can I do?"

"Pray. Yahweh must turn her heart toward Him."

"I will."

Cain considered what he had done to his mother and grew discouraged. Then he realized how exhausted he was. He had much to do tomorrow.

"I didn't sleep at all last night. I was so excited to come home. I'm going to sleep by the cliff where Lilith used to cry for me. She stopped, didn't she?" Cain looked at his father for confirmation and received it. "Good. I'll see you at dawn."

****

Cain woke at the first singing of the birds and watched the darkness slowly lose its grip on the earth. Listening to the birdsong, so overjoyed at the first faint hue of light appearing on the horizon, he felt as elated as they. Today he would truly make Lilith his wife!

Before coming, he had trimmed his beard and cut his hair. Now he combed it carefully before binding it with leather, painstaking about his appearance for the first time in years. With trembling hands, he straightened his garments and fastened the coverings onto his feet.

He was ready.

Walking back through the woods, he considered his plans. His palms sweated, and his heart thudded in his chest. Turning his thoughts toward Yahweh, he discussed all the details with Him. Acknowledging his fears and anxieties to God, he begged for courage and wisdom.

Cain stepped out of the woods. Treading carefully, he avoided the growing crops where he and his father had conferred last night. Before him protruded the outcropping of rock behind his parents' chamber; soon he would see the entire family gathered below, eating their morning meal. As he moved toward them, he heard murmuring and laughter.

Trembling, he paused. His heart pounded. Even his breathing shook. He inhaled deeply and pled for Yahweh's help. Then Cain stepped into view.

It took a moment for anyone to spot him. Father detected him first and smiled his encouragement—he appeared to have been watching. Nearby Lilith worked. She noticed their father smiling, followed his sightline toward the hillside, and turned. She caught sight of him.

"Cain!" With arms thrown wide, she ran to him. "Cain, you've come home!"

When he beheld her exuberant greeting, he thought his heart might burst right out of his chest. It had been nearly four years. He hadn't known whether her commitment remained strong; he had feared her ardor had cooled. Now he had no such fear. All doubt removed, Cain grabbed her up. Lilith clasped his waist. Neither released the other. He was home.

Finally, he let go, feasting his eyes on her face. Clear gray eyes filled with joy met his. He saw no shadow of sorrow or wounds to her mind. His assessment had been correct.

Behind her, he detected a tumult of activity. Reluctantly, he took his eyes off hers. With his arm around Lilith's shoulders, he faced the family.

Some ran toward them with arms wide; others approached hesitantly, though still welcoming. A smaller group stood with arms folded, not moving at all. Mother walked slowly toward them. Cain met her eyes and mouthed to her that he was sorry. She looked at the ground.

Holding up his hand, he signified his desire to speak. He hoped they would listen.

"I beg for your forgiveness. I'll understand if you can never give it. For the rest of my life, I'll regret killing Abel. I loved him; he was my closest friend. Our quarrel was my fault; he was innocent. God kept me alive, listened to my grief, and changed my heart. I'm a different man. I'm sorry I didn't pledge to Lilith publicly before I took her as my own. That's not how it's to be done. I set a terrible example as the firstborn. Please don't do likewise. I know I hurt her."

Here he stared down into her eyes.

Then he knelt before her, entwining her in his arms, hoping, imploring.

"Dearest Lilith, will you forgive me for all I've done to you— for securing our marriage in secret and bringing you shame, for killing our brother and having to leave you, for not focusing on your radiant person as I pursued you? Can you possibly agree to come and live with me as my wife? Do you trust me enough to allow me to be your husband?"

Gazing down, Lilith embraced him. "Yes. I've always loved you."

Closing his eyes, he clutched her near, pressing his head to her abdomen. *At last!* Inhaling her fragrance, he held her tight. Then, he looked up into her eyes.

"Say the vow," she whispered.

What?! Right now?

Looking at him with conviction, she nodded, pleading with her eyes.

"Lilith," his voice rang loud and clear, "you are bone of my bones and flesh of my flesh. I am your husband, and you are my wife. We are one flesh."

"Cain, I am bone of your bones and flesh of your flesh. I am your wife, and you are my husband. We are one flesh."

Their proclamation and pledge were now public. There was no more hiding; there were no more secrets. They were secured to one another for life, not only before God, but also before the world.

Filled with gratitude, Cain rose and cupped Lilith's lovely face. He would thank God for her every day. He placed a long, slow kiss on her willing lips.

This had all happened so unexpectedly that everyone stood speechless before them.

Then a voice sounded from the back of the family crowd. "You can't take her."

Everyone looked around to see who had spoken. It was Shafir. Cain and Shafir had never been close; Shafir had tended sheep with Abel. He was a little more than sixty years of age, barely an adult. Was this the leader of the opposition?

"Yes, he can," said Akiva at the same time as Father.

Hesed stepped over to stand with Akiva.

Cain kept his eyes focused on Shafir. "What would you have me do?"

"Leave." Shafir's eyes pierced cold.

Shoulder to shoulder, Efrat and Joda stepped up next to Shafir. One of the ten older brothers, Joda had always been attached to Abel. He was a quiet man, and Abel's gentle manner had always agreed with him better than Cain's impulsive personality. It had been so since his birth. Efrat was another of the younger brothers who had shepherded with Abel.

So this was how it was. Those who had helped Abel or been close to him in friendship now banded together against Cain. This was what he had witnessed around the fire last night. They also had remained unmarried, he had noticed.

"I'm leaving immediately," Cain said, "but I'm taking my wife."

As he spoke, all his siblings shifted into position on their chosen sides. Those who stood with him outnumbered those

against him, at least two to one. This surprised him. He had
expected the numbers to go the opposite way. Silently, he
thanked Yahweh and begged Him for wisdom.

"You can't take Lilith," Shafir said.

"Yes, he can!" Lilith now interjected her own opinion into
the conversation. "He's my husband, and I'm his wife."

Cain released Lilith and tread slowly down the hill. Lilith
followed right behind him; she gripped the back of his garment.
Shafir's eyes widened with fear. As Cain approached, he took a
small step backward. Since Cain had actually killed Abel, they all
probably had no idea what he would do in this situation. Would
he lose his mind and try to kill them all?

Cain knew exactly what to do; he had absolute confidence
that this was right. Kneeling before Shafir, he turned his palms
up in an attitude of supplication and bowed his head.

"Shafir, I've wronged you terribly by killing a brother you
loved and admired. My life should be forfeited. I don't know
why the Creator spared me. You may kill me if you'd like, since
I killed Abel. It would be just."

Absolute silence.

Then Lilith reacted. Bounding to protect him, she shielded
him with her body. Quickly, Cain lifted his head, lest he need to
protect her. She stared at their younger brother.

"No!" Her voice was hard and determined. "No! You may
not, Shafir!"

Flinching from her words, Shafir blinked.

"Killing Cain will not bring back Abel," she said. "It will only
make two dead brothers. You will bereave me of my husband
whom I just got back, like one from the dead. No!"

Still facing Shafir, she stepped back beside Cain, grasped his
head, and pointed at the mark.

"Look! Shafir! Efrat! Joda!" She made eye contact with each
one and with those who stood behind them in solidarity. "See
the mark God Himself placed on Cain. Yahweh Himself will
avenge Cain's death sevenfold. Do you want to go against God?"

Hoping the kindness and empathy he felt were apparent,

Cain stared up at Shafir. He knew how Shafir felt. He didn't blame him or the others.

All of them focused on his forehead. None had seen the mark until today. It couldn't be disputed. There it was—the reminder that God Himself was his avenger. Efrat looked away first, then Joda, then the others behind them. Finally Shafir looked down.

"We won't go against God," Shafir said quietly.

Cain stayed on his knees. "I pray that you'll forgive me. I don't want my sin to remain between us. I don't understand why God left me alive either. I deserve to die for what I did."

Those in opposition studied Cain's face then quickly looked away, agreeing with his assessment. Now their father stepped forward.

"Lilith," Father said, "go now and gather your things so you can leave immediately. You have a long journey before you."

****

Lilith released Cain, grabbed her mother's hand, and raced to pack her possessions. The day had arrived! When she had awakened, it had felt no different than any other day. Yet here it was! Her mother ran beside her, grasping Lilith's hand. This would be a difficult parting.

Once in Cain's old room, they placed her goods in the middle of the leather bed covering. One of the younger sisters arrived with three sheepskin bags Cain had sent for bundling her belongings. Silently, they worked side by side.

Finally, Lilith spoke. "Mother, I'll miss you every day."

"And I, you, my Lily."

"Please soften your heart toward Cain, Mother. You saw what happened. He's different."

"I witnessed it." Tears slid down her mother's cheeks. "I need to pray about what happened today. After what I saw, I trust him to take care of you."

"I've always trusted him. I was only frightened right after we found Abel's body."

"I'll pray for you every day, daughter."

Their work complete, each rose and hugged the other tightly. After the confrontation that had occurred, the departure would be quick.

"I hope to lay my eyes upon you again one day," Mother said.

"As do I." Anticipation swelled in Lilith; her affection turned away from home and toward Cain. "Let's go!"

Heading back, her mother carried one sheepskin bag and Lilith the other two, the entirety of her life compressed into three bundles. When they stepped into the clearing, Lilith searched for Cain, finding him in conversation with Father and a tightly clustered group of her brothers.

The mere sight of him gladdened her heart!

All his words and actions revealed a humbler Cain strengthened by trial. He seemed unknown and alien, yet in other ways familiar. With his shiny black hair long and bound, his beard full and trimmed, and his uniquely fashioned clothing of some mysterious leather, he appeared exotic. His muscles bulged again, as when he had tilled the earth; so he had been engaged in some type of physical work. What was it? She couldn't imagine.

In the past, he never would have handled a conflict like this. Then he would have shredded Shafir with sarcasm, bumping him with his chest out, perhaps shoving Shafir to intimidate him. He would have said something biting and belittling, but very witty; and they all would have laughed, making Shafir look and feel like a fool. Then Cain never would have knelt before anyone and apologized, as he had done repeatedly since arriving.

He was an enigma, and she was blessed with the privilege of delving into the depths and acquainting herself with this new man he had become. With all her heart, she cherished this challenge. She was eager to begin her new life.

Cain glanced up and caught her eye. He smiled widely, moving away from their father and brothers. Her heart swelled with happiness as she looked at him. Taking the heavier bundles, he shouldered them, adjusting the bags on his back. Having left her the lightest bundle, he helped her position her arms through the straps.

One of their little sisters ran to them with food packed for the journey. Both smiled down at her, and she blushed and backed away.

****

Eve watched, her heart battered with yet another change—children coming, children leaving. She hung back from the group, observing all. But now, Cain turned toward her.

"Mother, I know I've disappointed you in every way. You expected Abel or me to crush the serpent's head. Please forgive me for everything I've done. I hope you can soften your heart toward me. I love you and don't want bitterness between us."

Must my bitterness show so plainly on my face?

Longing to forgive him, Eve studied Cain's eyes. She didn't want to be angry anymore.

God help me.

"I'll try," she answered quietly.

Welcoming her to embrace him, he opened wide his arms. Hesitantly, she stepped in, and he hugged her gently, kissing the top of her head. Then he released her and looked kindly into her eyes. Her own eyes felt tight and hard in comparison.

Turning away, Cain seized Lilith's hand and hugged Adam exuberantly with his other arm. As they moved through the crowd of family, Cain patted some on the shoulder or embraced them as they crowded close. Then Cain and Lilith climbed the hill. At the crest, they both turned to wave. Then they walked away, disappearing over the top of the hill.

Eve expected it to be the last time she ever saw them. Her heart ached in her chest. How she wished she'd been able to forgive her son!

CHAPTER 27

LILITH HEEDED CAIN'S QUIET VOICE. With alert eyes, he strode confidently across the field, his body straight and true. All the while, he spoke softly, his lips barely moving. No eyewitness would discern his speaking. This was not the way home, he informed her; but, he intended to make it appear as if it were. This would lengthen their journey. All day Hesed, Akiva, Azriel, and their father would watch Efrat, Shafir, Joda, and the others, so they would not be followed.

Once they were in the woods, Cain stopped and turned to Lilith.

"Dearest," he said quietly, "we have to run. There's a long journey before us. We won't arrive home until after nightfall, and we have to start by running while we're fresh."

Home! The word sang in her mind.

As he talked, he removed a small bundle from a pouch secured to his waistband. Kneeling before her, he lifted her feet, one by one, and strapped on coverings similar to his own. Then he stood and secured her bundle to her body.

Admiring his handiwork, she studied her feet. "Thank you, Cain."

Glancing up, he met her eyes and gave her a smile as he prepared her pack. Grasping a thin strap that was secured to the bottom, he brought it around her waist and knotted it, binding the pack so the bundle wouldn't bounce as she ran. He did the same with the two bundles he carried. Then he squared his shoulders and looked up at her.

"Ready?"

"I've been ready for decades." Lilith took off, sprinting east.

Behind her, Cain chuckled. He soon caught up. "Pace yourself. It will be a long day."

Now Cain took the lead, and together they settled into a rhythm. Aiming for speed, they kept their breathing measured, so were unable to speak. After passing through the woods, they skirted the cliff. For a while, Cain continued toward the rising sun before gradually angling the pole star's direction. They traveled slightly more northward for a great distance; but these sites were familiar to her. They were still within a half-day's journey of the compound.

Eventually, Cain veered toward the Tigris and by mid-morning they spotted the river.

Cain ran to the water's edge, stopped, and turned to Lilith. Both breathed heavily.

"Let me remove your bundle."

She nodded. He tugged at the knot near her waist.

"Let's rest while we drink and eat."

Lilith was glad he'd stopped. Without a word, she allowed him to tend to her pack before she lay down to drink. After removing his, he dropped down beside her. Both drank deeply.

When the river water filled and sloshed in their bellies, she retrieved bread from his pack, took out enough for them both, and handed it across to him. After tearing off what he wanted, Cain passed her portion back to her. They finally caught their breath.

"I'm sorry I had to lengthen our journey," he said. "Father and the others know how to find us if necessary. I told them the directions to our home."

"Our home! I love the way that sounds. Tell me about it."

"I've spent nearly two years building a home that can be

defended. Yahweh prepared me to expect opposition. I built a stone wall across one side, and there are sheer cliffs around the other three. Inside the wall there's a large open area, so others can live with us. Against the cliff wall, I built our house. I hope you like it."

"Describe it so I can try to imagine it as we run."

"It has two rooms and is built in front of a cave, giving us an extra hidden room in the back. To walk in the front door, you enter through an enclosure that provides a private place to work while we sit outside. This enclosure is surrounded by a wall with a gate in it."

"What's a gate?"

"It's made of wood for covering and closing a doorway. We still have much to do. We need to make coverings for the ceilings and the inside doorways, plus all we need for our household."

"Good!" She smiled at him. "I can work with you."

He told her about a brook and fields and clay at the base of the cliff; he explained that he had laid long grass out to dry in the sleeping chamber to prepare for their return. They would sleep together in comfort tonight. As he spoke, they finished eating and stood, repositioning their bundles upon their backs. When he told her about the work he had done to prepare their sleeping chamber, she smiled at him, raising one eyebrow.

Then she shot off down the riverbank, yelling to him over her shoulder, "Let's go!"

Again she heard him laugh. Then he followed her.

Gradually, she slowed her tempo to his. For a large portion of the remaining morning, he kept a steady pace; but then he slowed to a walk. She was certain he could tell she had grown weary. They walked hard and fast, pausing for the midday meal and the evening meal. As they walked they discussed all that had happened during their nearly five-year separation.

Lilith was amazed at Cain's stories from inside the Garden. His visit there explained the disappearance of the cherubim. Cain had actually seen everything their parents had described to them so frequently—the two important trees, the abundant food, the herds of animals. He had made his clothing from two of them. No wonder he looked exotic!

She was excited that he had gathered seeds. She would plant them, and they would sample the many foods their parents had eaten. The gold and the multicolored rocks from the cave sounded intriguing. What could they make from them? How would it be done? This sparked her interest and creativity, as did the way he had fashioned his garments. She couldn't wait to learn. When they came upon an animal that had recently died, they would make new clothing for her.

His description of his spiritual journey engrossed her. She cried as he detailed his brokenness over what he had done. His grief over his wounding of her melded with his mourning over Abel. He told her about beginning to speak to Yahweh by praying for her, hoping that God would hear him and heal her. They wept as he detailed his longing for her, his regret, his yearning for Abel, and his recollections of the murder. He was still astonished that God had kept him alive, restored him, and made His holy presence known, even leading him.

Cain reiterated his mistakes, his unworthiness, his many flaws, and his shortcomings.

He had never talked like this before. He had always worn a façade of self-assurance, when underneath he had felt insecure and miserable about falling short of pleasing God and their parents. His misery was palpable over failing to become her husband in an honorable way.

Cain asked about her life while he was gone. She shuddered to think of the first year—he had seen the evidence. As she described that year, he stopped to hug her tightly. He was glad she had quit her daily review of their interactions and thanked her for taking care of herself after he left.

Hands now linked, they continued their walk northward.

The loneliness of the last several years had drained her. She chronicled her agony: missing him all day, longing, crying, and praying for him in the night, begging God to keep him alive and to bring him back to her. She had felt as if her life had been interrupted, as if she were stagnant, always waiting, looking, and listening for him, all the while trying not to lose her mind again.

She described the painful jealousy she had battled when their siblings married and bore children together. That was supposed to be them—Cain and Lilith—loving each other, holding hands by the fire, smiling into each other's eyes, making love in the night.

Her spiritual journey had involved learning to yield to God's plan and timing. She could do nothing to bring Cain back, nothing to keep him safe; so she had to trust God to return him when the time was right according to His providence.

She had fought with God, yelled at Him, gone through periods when she wouldn't speak to Him. She had tried to bend God to her will. Eventually she had let go, allowing the situation be what God wanted, trusting Him completely, loving Him no matter what happened. Still, she had felt sad. She missed Cain; she yearned for him.

Listening thoughtfully to all she had to say, Cain nodded and asked occasional questions. Their talking and fast-paced walking moved them rapidly through the day. At sunset, they came to a brook. Cain forked to follow it upstream.

"Arriving at the brook surprised me," he said. "The day goes much faster when it's shared with another person. I've been alone with Yahweh for so long that I've forgotten the dynamics of having another person present."

She didn't understand him—she couldn't relate to this experience; so she simply looked at him, waiting for him to continue.

"I have to learn how to interact with God and with you. How can I converse with one without neglecting the other? I've only been able to talk to the Creator as we ran, when you and I were unable to speak. I'm used to communicating only with Yahweh all day long."

As he spoke these last words, his voice quaked and his eyes teared up. Wanting to understand what he was feeling, she studied his reaction. He looked at the ground.

"Yahweh, my God, I feel as if I've barely spoken to You today. I love You. I've missed talking with You, but my heart is filled with joy that Lilith is with me. You've given her back to me! Thank You for this gift! How can it be that You would show such kindness to me, a sinner who killed his own brother and hurt the woman he loves?" He choked up as he said this. "I don't deserve Your kindness," he whispered, "yet You give it freely. Thank You. Help me love Lilith well. I'm nervous about what happens next. You know how I've longed for her. But I don't want my love for her to take Your place in my heart, as before. Help me find the balance of loving both Lilith and You, and loving you both the way I should."

Silently, Lilith listened. It had surprised her when he spoke aloud to God with her present. He talked so candidly, even expressing his love, as if he and Yahweh were dear and intimate friends. His love for God encompassed every aspect of his life. This drew her heart both to God and to him. Desiring to share this experience, she decided to talk to God openly too.

"Thank You, Yahweh," she prayed, "for bringing Cain home to me. I'm so happy to be his wife at last! Thank You for this beautiful, exhausting day. Help me to be the kind of wife he needs, to learn the rhythm of his life, to discover what he knows about You. Let me love him in the way he needs to be loved."

As she finished praying, Cain pulled her closer by their linked hands and kissed her gently on the forehead. Then he led her up the brook. Dusk deepened rapidly. Bats swooped. The flowing water gurgled around a bend. Here a cliff fell away, cleaving a canyon back in the darkness. Cain turned away from the water, walking toward the blackness formed by the cliff.

Out ahead of them the moon rose. When higher in the sky, its light would illuminate all. Fortunately, it was a full moon. Cain walked into the shadowed pitch by a sheer rock wall. The moon's light didn't reach into this crevice. She could barely see.

Bending down, he grasped a heavy rock, grunting with the effort. This rock buttressed something made of wood; she placed her hand on it—logs bound together tightly by cords of hemp. Cain moved the large rock aside. When he did, the bound logs moved away from her. He stepped through the opening, pulling her after him. Then he raised something heavy, which he slid into the cliff wall, securing the gap. In the gloom of nightfall she couldn't tell what he was doing, but she was intrigued. He had designed all of this!

"This is the stone wall that encloses the city," he said. "That was the gate."

An enormous cliff loomed ahead. Lacing his fingers through hers, he escorted her in. Lilith tipped her head back, viewing the top. Blocked from view now, the moon rose out there on the horizon. Faintly, its soft light outlined the clifftop. They traversed the canyon—the farther in, the blacker it grew. She peered ahead. The darkness obscured their home.

"Unfortunately, I can't start a fire tonight." His voice echoed off the canyon walls. "When the moon rises higher, we'll be able to see."

He stopped beside something solid. She touched it. Parts of it were smooth, like hardened pottery or dried mud; parts were made of wood. He moved another wooden object—a gate, he had called these—and he stepped through an opening, drawing her in.

"Now we're inside the enclosure in front of our house."

Cain turned and removed her pack then he lifted off his own. Her back and shoulders ached. Sensing her need, he rubbed her shoulders, easing the knots in her muscles. She relaxed into the warmth of his strong hands.

"Ah ... thank you."

"We can go down to the brook and bathe, if you'd like." His voice was low. "Or we can prepare our bedding and sleep. I know you're tired."

So it was up to her. Patiently, he allowed her to choose whatever made her feel most comfortable. Still massaging her shoulders, he awaited her response. She considered.

"I'm overwhelmed, Cain. There are so many new experiences!

I can't wait until the sun comes up so I can grasp all you've done here. I'm nervous about ..." She swallowed hard. "... about lying with you. You're so different in many ways, yet the same in others. I'm a little frightened."

"Hmm." He grew silent, pondering. "How about if we prepare the bedding then bathe in the brook? By then the moon will be higher. Then, if you're tired, we'll simply sleep. We have tomorrow and the next day and the next. There's no rush, Lilith. How does that sound?"

"Yes. Let's do all that."

"Alright. Come in."

Taking her hand, he shoved away a wooden slab and entered the black hole. *Another gate?* They passed through a large room; she could discern its size, because there was no ceiling covering. There would be plenty of room for their household activities. Straight through the room was another black doorway, probably their sleeping room. Releasing her, he stooped.

"Remember," he said over his shoulder, "I spread the grass on the floor, so it would dry. I'm gathering it into the bedframe built in the corner."

"That sounds convenient."

She was impressed. The grass wouldn't spread out across the floor, but would stay under their bedding. The grass rustled, and its fresh aroma filled the space.

"We'll see," he said. "I haven't slept in the bed yet. I was waiting for you."

The thought of him sleeping on the floor until her arrival touched her heart. She smiled. "I don't feel like I'm much help."

"That's fine. I know where everything is. I've worked on this for so long that I know the dimensions by touch." He moved by her to return to the blackened front room. His voice traveled farther away. "I'm going back out to get our packs. We need the bedding."

Outside in the enclosure, she heard him lift the packs; then his footfalls returned. As she listened to his steps padding closer, she realized they stood on smooth, warm stone. It still held the heat of the day.

"Here they are." He dropped the packs. They brushed the stone and softly settled. "Where is the bedding?"

"I put one of the leather coverings in the top of the lighter pack." She heard him open it; his shape squatted. "But the pillows will have no downy seeds in them, and the other covering is wrapped around objects to guard them from breaking. Can we do with just one?"

"Yes, I have a small one of my own laid ready ... here." He groped in the darkness for his covering. "We'll have to lie closely to one another."

 She wasn't sure how to respond.

"As long as that's alright with you," he said, after a long pause.

Lilith laughed. The fact that there was any question about her wanting to lie closely to him relieved the tension of the moment. They had touched each other all her life; they had already made love. There were nearly five years of separation now between them, making them awkward when they would have formerly been completely at ease.

"That will be fine, Cain." She caressed his beard in the darkness. "I'm having a difficult time adjusting to your presence, but it's becoming easier. Let's take off our clothes and wash in the brook. That should help."

He chuckled. With a whoosh of breeze, he cast her leather covering over the dried grass and tossed his covering over it. The grass fragrance filled her nose. Then he removed his clothing.

As the moon rose, the room grew less dim. It was not overhead yet, still needing to clear the cliff's full height before it shone into their home; but she detected glimmers of his body as they undressed. Soon he wore only a small garment that covered his loins, and she was completely undressed. He removed his loin covering and unbound his hair. Though she could barely detect his body in the darkness, it was strange to stand beside him, completely naked.

"Come, dearest Lily," he said.

Taking her hand, he led her through their home, into the enclosed area, and out the small gate. As they walked across the canyon opening, the line of moonlight lay sharp across the ground ahead, marking where the moon had risen far enough that the cliff cast no shadow.

They stepped out of the darkness into the soft light of the full moon, and he was no longer unfamiliar. She had seen this body before. A surge of emotion welled up within her chest, overwhelming her with the love she felt for him. It was he! No longer did he seem like an exotic stranger who had come for her and brought her far from home.

He guided her along the cliff wall to the gate they had first entered. Opening it, he piloted her through then he released her and sprinted for the water.

The soft glow of the moonlight illuminated him dashing across the clearing outside the wall. The light cast by the moon colored him all white and silvery. Cain laughed as he ran, the joyful sound pealing off all the rock walls. Lilith smiled. Then she ran after him.

Already he waded up to his thighs in the brook, so she stepped into the cool, dark water to join him. They looked into one another's eyes, hooded in the ethereal light. Then their gaze slowly lingered over the beauty of the other's moonlit body.

Grasping his waist, she drew him close. He cupped her face and kissed her tenderly. Then both dipped into the water. She ran her fingers through his wet hair, smoothing its unfamiliar length. He scrubbed her back, rubbing her shoulders until the knots relaxed. Then, hugging her tightly into the curve of his body, he kissed his way down her neck and across her shoulders.

The touch of his cool, wet mouth on her warm skin demolished the remaining barriers.

"Take me back," she whispered. "I want to lie with you and awaken in your arms."

He scooped her up and carried her. With her arms clutched about his neck, they kissed desperately all the way—across the clearing, through the gate, across the canyon opening, through the enclosure, across the front room, and into their sleeping chamber.

At last! Thank you, God!

Embracing her in his strong arms, Cain crawled across their bed and laid them both down. In the soft moonlight, he made love to her. Now united in the eyes of God, before the world, and in the hearts of one another, they spent much of the night rediscovering, remembering, and learning anew. The comfort of the other's body brought tears and joyful laughter.

Then, wrapped in one another's arms, they slept more soundly than they had in years.

CHAPTER 28

SHINING HIGH IN THE SKY, the sun beamed through the open ceiling, awakening Cain when it struck his face. He opened his bleary eyes. He lay tangled with Lilith in the leather covering, their bodies intertwined. Completely relaxed and blissfully aware of the tranquility in which they existed on this morning, he didn't move.

He breathed in the fragrance of her body. Still and serene, his head cradled on her belly, he encased Lilith in his arms. As she stroked his head, he listened to her heartbeat. This was what they hadn't experienced yet—the morning after they had vowed to each other and awakened together in the same bed as man and wife.

It was idyllic and peaceful—this was how married life was supposed to begin.

Against Lilith's soft abdomen, Cain whispered a prayer of thanks to Yahweh.

"Cain," Lilith murmured.

"Yes," he said softly.

"I didn't know you were awake until I felt your lips move."

"I'm awake. I was thanking God for you." He kissed the spot against which he had just offered his prayer.

"I don't think I've ever been happier in my life."

"That's what I just told Yahweh."

Cain kissed his way up from her belly and drank his fill of her again. Then, safe in her arms, he lay with his head against her shoulder, stroking the softness of her outer thigh. Savoring the pleasure of belonging to one another, they stayed in bed all morning, completely at ease, feasting on the sight and the comforting touch of the other's body.

****

The sun was at its apex when Lilith's curiosity prodded her. She wanted to see it all.

"Show me everything." She pushed herself up from Cain's bare chest.

"Gladly!"

Smiling, Cain offered his hand. Clasping it, she trailed him into the dark cave behind their room. The floor cooled her bare feet. He hoisted the bag of gold and jeweled stones from Eden and unfastened the top. She peered in but perceived nothing in the dim light. Beaming with anticipation, he carried it out into the sunlight that streamed through their bed chamber's ceiling.

"Oh!" she gasped when he dumped the contents onto their bed.

The hues of the stones and the softness of the gold fascinated her. The stones reflected subtle colored light. Lilith pressed her fingernails into the gold then bit it; both left an indentation.

"This is something to puzzle over, isn't it?" she said. "They're so beautiful, especially the gold. Each has a different texture and hardness."

"Yes, I've been perplexed. I know they can be used for adornment, but I can't imagine a method. If we can discern how to craft these, we can make some striking objects."

"What fun!"

"I know." He grinned at her.

He returned the mysterious objects to the cave then conducted her out through their sleeping chamber. She noticed the rafters in both rooms.

"How did you cleave the wood like that? At home you always used small trees."

"I looked for a sharp-edged rock, honed the edge with a whetstone I had found earlier, and bound it to the straightest and strongest hardwood branch I could find. Using that as a tool, I cut down live trees and split them in half along the grain. I call it an 'ax.'"

After hearing his description and examining these tools he had stored in the enclosure in front of their house, she decided this was why his muscles had grown so strong. The largest ax was heavy; swinging it would be difficult. With it, he had cleaved trees in two.

Leaning close, she examined the grain of the smooth wood he had hewn for the front door. Pressing her nose against it, she inhaled the wood's clean scent. The insides of trees smelled so fresh and alive! Back and forth she flitted, into the house and out, examining the different types of wood and the way he had split each piece, positioning it to serve a specific purpose.

All was stunning!

He had sized both rooms perfectly. Into the stone walls he had constructed stone shelves, using wider, flatter stones where he wanted a shelf to jut out a little further. To display a pattern of color in the wall, he had selected and positioned the stones following a plan. Artfully designed for usefulness, it pleased the eye.

In one corner he had organized the dried leaf packets of seeds from the Garden. She lifted each packet, smelled the seeds inside, and peeked in, carefully examining them. While she investigated, he described each plant and the taste each created on the tongue, talking on and on about his time in the Garden. She hung on every word. He hoped he hadn't ruined the seeds by touching them. Stopping his description, he prayed, thanking God for whatever result he gave.

Leaving the inside uncluttered, the enclosed area in front was a convenient place to store tools. She went back out and scrutinized again all the assorted axes. He explained why he needed many different sizes. Then she studied the other tools— the stone knives, the chisels, the scrapers and needles made of bone, the strips of thinly cut leather for lacing, the dried animal gut, and the bladders he used for hauling water. Some of the flat handmade stones—"bricks," he called them—lay stacked in the corner. Cain explained how he molded and used these. Hefting them to test their weight, she examined them carefully.

Turning, she appraised the front of their home. How well it blended with the face of the cliff wall behind it! She poked at the clay mortar he had layered between the stones, prodding the dried clay encasing the enclosure's walls as well. Exerting extra care, he had kneaded the clay thoroughly. It had dried smooth to the touch and pleasing to the eye—a masterful job!

As she studied each detail, she praised his efforts, exclaiming over his creativity, expressing amazement at his inventions. Thanking her humbly, he smiled, giving credit to God for the idea and the strength to carry it out. But she could tell her praise gratified him.

When she had investigated everything, she threw her arms around him, thanking him profusely, kissing the calluses his work had formed, inspecting the wounds he had incurred in the labor, and pressing her lips to those as well. She told him it was the best gift he had ever given her. As she said this, she raised her arm with the bracelet.

"I kissed this every day you were gone, glad I had a small piece of you reflected in the creativity and design and careful labor. But this! You spent so much time; you took such care; you pondered each detail! It all shows you made it especially for me. You captured what I would love, what you knew would make my heart sing as my eye fell upon it. Your love for me shows in every single thing you've done."

As she spoke this praise, his eyes looked hungrily at her, as if he received good news from far away, as if, desperate with thirst, she had brought him drink.

"I wanted you to know how precious you are to me," he said

softly. "I didn't even think to build you a home before. Abel reminded me. I wanted to redeem my previous neglect."

"I see your love in every beam and stone."

At that, he scooped her up and carried her back to their bed again. Their love spilled over, mending their hearts. The sun moved across the sky; the moving shadows cast by the rafters marked the passage of time. They lost themselves in one another.

When hunger drove them from their bed, it was long past midday.

Telling her the name of each article of his clothing, Cain pulled his shirt over Lilith's head so she didn't have to wear the cumbersome sheepskin. It fell below her knees. Dressing himself, he laced on his loincloth and leggings and stood before her, shirtless.

She hadn't realized his hips showed entirely when he was clad like this. The gap between the leggings and the waistband of the loincloth revealed a tantalizing glimpse of his skin. The shirt was long, so this skin couldn't normally be seen—but she had his shirt on now.

****

They left in search of food; there was none in the house. They would forage by the river. Cain grabbed one of the empty leather bags to carry their finds. Hand in hand, they crossed the open area between their home and the stone wall. By light of day, Lilith gaped at the size of the opening for the city. Many families could dwell here, if any of their siblings came. Surveying the entire area laid out for the city, she slowly rotated, amazed.

"I hope no one comes for a long time," she said.

"But they will come."

"How do you know?"

"It was part of the vision God put in my head. It's a city of refuge, a safe place. When I killed Abel I brought violence into the world. There needs to be a place to flee for safety."

Recalling her terror when she discovered Abel's body, she

considered his words. She turned back to look at Cain. There was no fear now. Her love for him had driven it away.

"What are you thinking?" he asked quietly.

"I was remembering—I'm not saying this to hurt you; please don't be hurt—I was reflecting on finding Abel's body. I was afraid of you."

With pain in his eyes, he nodded that he understood.

Throwing her arms around him, she gazed into his face. "But, Cain, love won. My love for you drove away the fear."

"Because I was gone."

"What do you mean?"

"Because I left, love had time to win. What if I had remained? What if I hadn't been driven away? Shafir, Efrat, and the rest would have killed me. Love wouldn't have had time."

"Hesed and Akiva would have gone after Shafir and Efrat. It would have escalated."

She shuddered at the thought. It could easily have happened. God in his mercy had banished Cain. When viewed in this light, she now understood it was best that God had done so.

"That's the purpose of a city of refuge," Cain said, "to give love time."

"Time to heal the hurting, to stop the vengeance."

"Time to let love win."

They stared into one another's eyes. They now lived in a world where violence would threaten again, one brother against another. But they were doing something to give time for healing, time for love to win, halting the escalation of death and brutality.

"What a wonderful plan!" Lilith whispered, amazed.

"It was God's idea. He inspired me to construct the city; He kept bringing it to mind in the Garden. When I left there I knew I was to build it. The wall was a picture in my mind. I engraved the mark above the gate. Come on. I'll show you."

As they walked hand in hand toward the gate, though Lilith loved the idea of allowing time for healing, still she hoped no one came for a great while. Not only because, if anyone came, it would mean more bloodshed had occurred, or would be occurring, but because she needed this privacy with him. They had been apart for so long. These last two days with Cain had been the happiest of her life.

In daylight, she could now see the gate's mechanism. Last night, unseen in the darkness, he had shoved a bar across the gate and into a crevice carved into the stone. This secured it, so no one outside could open it. Today, she scrutinized the gate's construction and positioning between the stone wall and the cliff. The wall's height amazed her! The top towered above Cain's head; she couldn't reach it with her fingertips, even standing on her toes.

"How did you do this?" She gaped at him. What other ideas did he carry around in his head?

He explained the process of making the wall and the gateway.

"It's a miracle you weren't injured," she said.

"God protected me. No stone fell."

"I'm glad!"

She threw her arms around him and squeezed him tightly. With their arms about one another, they passed through the gate. Cain turned her around and pointed to the symbol. There it was above the gate, exactly as it was written so finely on his forehead.

יְהוָה

With his own hand, he had carved it into the wood. On his forehead it was outlandish with its fine black lines; above the gate it was strong and masterfully engraved.

With both her hands, she pulled his head to her lips and kissed the mark.

****

Relieved to see Lilith now completely comfortable in his presence again, Cain sighed with contentment. She had regained her exuberance and spontaneity, showing no evidence of the internal wounds he had witnessed a year after he had killed Abel. She was no longer uneasy, as she had been last night. Her reactions to his creations, her loving heart, and her gestures of spontaneous affection had always been the qualities that had drawn him to her. Yesterday she had been reserved and uncertain, not quite herself; today she was herself again.

Smiling, Cain pointed toward the brook.

"Ah!" She laughed. "Now I can see it."

Shielding her eyes from the afternoon sun, Lilith surveyed everything that was so familiar to him. He tried to see it with her eyes. The sandy beach stretched along the brook. Red dirt lay between the sand and the stone wall. On the other side of the brook grew many edible plants. Suddenly, her stomach rumbled with hunger.

"I wondered when you'd get hungry." Cain kissed her head. "I can hear your stomach."

Smiling, Lilith kept her eyes on the field, peering closely as she pointed. "Is that grain?"

"Yes."

"Good! We can grind it, and I can make us some bread. It looks nearly ripe. We can harvest soon. What else is there?"

"Mostly legumes and greens, a few squash." He pointed out the location of each. "Back in the woods, there are grapes and a few fruit-bearing trees ... olives, peaches, and cherries. God provided for us."

"Wonderful! How deep is the brook?"

"To my waist in the middle, but upstream it's shallow."

Taking Lilith's hand, he guided her up the shore where the brook widened and swept around the curve of the cliff. Here, it only reached her knees, his calves. They splashed up onto the opposite shore and foraged in the field together.

Eating from the various plants, they picked their way across the field and through the trees, gathering enough food for the next several days. They placed the heavier items on the bottom of the sack and the lighter food on top. When it was full, they headed back, crossing the water. Lilith turned and raised one eyebrow at Cain, flashing him a mischievous grin.

"Race you back." Off she dashed toward the wall.

Amused, he tucked the pack against his side, positioning it so their gathered food wouldn't bruise. Then he ran after her, catching her right inside the enclosure. Cain thrust open the front door and they tumbled in, both dropping the provisions they carried.

He made love to her on the cool stone floor of the front room.

She was right. It was a good thing no one else lived here yet. They couldn't do these things if they were surrounded by watching people. The seclusion was a blessing, a gift from God. Cain too hoped no one came to their city for a long time.

But he knew they would come.

CHAPTER 29

AFTER MAKING LOVE LATE INTO each night, Cain and Lilith slept until the bright sunlight awakened them. Then, rising together, they worked and created, laughing and talking through each day. Lilith's mere presence soothed like salve to a wound. Cain needed her like he needed food and water. Days passed and no one came, much to his relief.

Sitting under the shady trees by the brook, they spent days weaving the long reedy grasses into coverings for the ceilings. Next, they dug clay from the base of the cliff and kneaded it to make cups and bowls. These fulfilled their most immediate needs.

Cain lamented that Yonas wasn't with them—he was the best potter in the family. Yonas had invented a way to form pots on a flat stone positioned between his legs. Sitting on the ground, he pushed the stone with one of his feet, turning it as he shaped earthenware with his hands.

In the shade near the clay deposit, Cain and Lilith tried to construct a potter's wheel like Yonas's. Here they argued for the first time since reuniting, disagreeing about how the wheel should be positioned to allow it to turn. Cain had helped Yonas design it. He felt certain he remembered the particulars. Securing the large, flat stone between his feet, he bent over it, chiseling a hole into the underside.

"No." Lilith snatched the stone away. "That isn't how it was done."

Biting back a retort, Cain leaned back, experiencing the first irritation he'd had with her for many years. *How should I react?* The anger that simmered in his heart terrified him. He was still the same man. He purposed to keep his mouth shut.

Yahweh, calm my heart.

As she fumbled with the stone, he studied her. Her tenacity had enabled her to survive his absence. He thanked God for it, even though it now provoked him. Then he worked his way down the list of her character traits, praising God for each one.

All was still. She was staring at him.

"I'm sorry," she said. "You helped Yonas create this, didn't you?"

"I did."

"You're a changed man. If I hadn't already seen the other evidence, I've seen it now. You didn't snatch the rock back or chide me or belittle my efforts."

"But I wanted to."

"Nevertheless, you didn't." Sheepish, she handed him the stone.

He didn't want her to feel embarrassed that her attempt had failed. "Everything you just tried, Yonas and I did as well. You were on the right course."

She smiled at him and sat back to watch.

The rest of the afternoon he chiseled and measured and worked over the stone. Helping to steady it, she sat beside him. Occasionally, she caressed his head or cheek or shoulder. Her nearness filled him with contentment. He hadn't lashed out at her—a cause for rejoicing.

When the wheel was readied, they spent many weeks creating pots and jars and platters. Taking turns, each bent over the wheel. Lilith thought her pottery inferior to his, but it wasn't. Pleased with her work, he detailed its merits. Reassured, she smiled at him. Together, they etched patterns into the earthenware, engrossed in their discussion of design and technique.

The week before his conflict with Abel, a discovery had been made. While preparing a meal, their mother had turned quickly, accidentally knocking one of the nearby pots into the fire. The pot had shattered, and they had watched the broken clay fragments glow red in the flames.

Early the next morning, they had met to dig out the pieces before the day's fire was kindled. Squatting together in the ashes, they had removed the broken shards. They found these stronger and less likely to shatter than the rest of the pottery. Now, they wanted to duplicate that result.

First, they gathered stones and constructed a large stone pit against the cliff wall by the clay deposits. They built the firepit with stone shelves along the inside. Onto these shelves they positioned all the clay vessels they had made, careful that none touched the others. Then they gathered a large quantity of firewood and built an enormous fire in the pit.

After it had burned down to embers, their glowing red earthenware slowly cooled as the fire turned to ash. The next day, when all was completely cool, they removed the pottery and were pleased with the results. They would continue to refine this process.

In the house, they organized the shelves, arranging all the objects Lilith had brought from home. They laughed together at some of the gifts they had made when they were young, remembering the occasions of their gift exchanges. It delighted Cain to see the items—the gifts Lilith had given him were precious, and there were some objects Abel had constructed as well. Each item held a remembrance of him. He cherished these.

Periodically, they puzzled together over the gold and precious stones and tried various methods of working with them. But they could make no headway.

They altered Lilith's sheepskin garment. Cain soaked the hide in the brook then softened it with animal fat and ashes—smelly work—before stripping off the wool, roots and all. This they washed, dried, and spun into fine fibers as they had done with Abel at home so long ago. Soon they had produced a ball of spun wool yarn. They would experiment with uses for it.

They had no disagreement, more evidence of change.

Cain recut the leather and sewed Lilith's new garment to fit her body, leaving hers fuller so there would be room when she bore a child. Enabling her to unlace and nurse a baby at her breast, he cut it deeply in the front. They hoped to have children soon.

Contentedly, they moved from project to project, completing everything together, talking over their work and adding details to their summaries of their lives during their absence. It was a time of healing and peace. They made love anytime and anywhere they desired.

****

Cain chose a rich, fertile-looking area on the brook's other side for planting some of the seeds from the Garden. He planned the work. Lilith would sow only a small area, in case the first planting failed. This would be the best strategy. Around the edges of the field and along the brook, she would plant the seeds for the fruit trees.

While she turned the soil with the light tool he had made for her, Cain squatted under a nearby tree. As he watched from the hillside's gentle slope, he chewed his thumb. But he couldn't stay still. Repeatedly, he jumped up, pacing back and forth before forcing himself to stop. It was impossible. He wanted to prepare the soil. He was the one with the expertise, and he was stronger. But he had to stay completely away from what she was doing, lest he taint it.

Yahweh had told him the earth would not yield its crops for him any longer.

That remembrance crushed him. The entire time she worked, Cain begged God to cause the seeds to grow. He confessed to God again his grief over killing Abel and spilling his blood on the earth. He knew he deserved this punishment. But Cain's heart felt crushed and destroyed as he watched Lilith work.

Finally, Cain sprang to his feet and stumbled downstream, remembering Yahweh's words: *When you cultivate the earth, it will no longer produce its crops for you. You will be homeless, a fugitive—a restless wanderer on the earth, lamenting what you've done.*

Recalling what he had done to receive this penalty hurt him.

Into his mind burst Abel's misshapen face and crushed head—*Oh God!*

If he could only relive that day and leave Abel alive! He could still hear Abel's voice begging him to stop. These memories had left a permanent gash in Cain's mind. The horror ripped the wound open anew, sickening him. Cain vomited on the ground.

How could I have killed my own brother? What a worthless man I am!

Devastated, his mind and heart rent and torn, he lay sobbing into the dust. He had never considered that watching Lilith plant the crops would bring it all back.

****

Lilith concentrated on digging. When she glanced up, Cain no longer paced on the hill. Silent, she stood and listened. From downstream she heard a soft sound, then coughing followed by muffled crying. She dropped the tool and ran. As she raced through the trees, Cain's broken weeping grew louder. She found him in the dirt.

Deep sobs shook his entire body. "Why did I do it? Why?"

Throwing herself upon him, Lilith draped her body over him. "Beloved, shhhhh." She stroked his head and patted his back. "Cain, I love you, shhhhhh; don't grieve so, dearest."

Kissing his head and his back repeatedly, she attempted to comfort him, to no avail. He continued to weep, and she continued to clutch him. This had probably been how he had spent his first years after Abel's death, alone then, with no embrace. Nothing could be done other than to grip him in her arms. He was correct—it couldn't be undone.

Eventually, he sat back on his heels, peering at her from swollen and hopeless eyes, his face streaked with mud. He wiped his nose on the back of his hand. He was broken.

What could she say to him? Kneeling before him, she encased him in her arms. Resting his chin on her shoulder, his arms hung heavily at his sides. He collapsed upon her.

Then Lilith prayed, "God of the universe, Yahweh, the One who redeems, please, heal my husband's heart. You've heard him cry for five years; you know he's broken and contrite. You've kept him alive. You've given him creativity and allowed him to build us a home. You've brought him joy in our unity as man and wife. Now, our God, please heal him. Please! We have no hope but You! You're the healer of hearts, the restorer of souls. You're sending one to destroy the evil one, so we know You're merciful. Please, let love heal Cain."

For a long while, Lilith grasped him, rocking back and forth. Then she rose and extended her hand. Cain took it, his head down. Despondent and shattered, he stood.

"Why do you love me?" he whispered. "I don't understand it. You've suffered so much because of what I've done."

"I love you because you're you. My love for you grows every day."

Head bowed, he allowed her to lead him. She guided him back to the curve of the brook, undressed them both, and ushered him into the shallow waters where she bathed him. He was lost in himself, overcome by recollections. Mutely, he permitted her care, silent in his grief.

Washing off the mud and the vomit, she sat with him in the shallows, her legs wrapped around his waist. Cradling his head against her shoulder, she washed his body, tenderly caressing him, cooing sounds of comfort, soothing his pain with her love. He permitted her ministrations.

When he was clean, she led him home. She brought him into the house and took him to bed.

Using her own body, she salved his wounded heart.

CHAPTER 30

THE NEXT MORNING WHEN LILITH opened her eyes, the desperate lovemaking that had occurred late into the night filled her mind. Whispering prayers against her skin, Cain had wept over her. Broken before God, he had taken consolation in her body.

Comforting him all she could, Lilith had kissed and caressed, adding her prayers to his, pleading with God to heal his heart. Once more, she now silently beseeched Yahweh to do this work of love, to bring healing to her beloved.

With his body pressed against hers, Cain slept on his stomach this morning. His skin warmed hers. On her outstretched arm, his head rested, his arm thrown across her abdomen. Face turned away, his cheek lay heavily against her shoulder. She didn't want to wake him—he was spent.

So, she lay still, reviewing all the days since their vows. Starting at the beginning, she recalled looking up the hill to see him gazing down at her, exotic and beautiful, come to claim her as his wife. How many days had passed since he had come for her? She had lost count.

Lilith reviewed the phases of the moon, recounting each waxing and waning. According to the moonlight that had shone down upon them in the darkness, she remembered which projects they had completed. These tasks marked the days.

Their lovemaking was passionate and exuberant when they were thrilled with the creativity of a project. It was gentle and prolonged when they were satisfied and content. It was desperate and needy when they were wounded. Based on these recollections, she counted four full moons since their first night together. They had been married for over four months.

Why had she not bled? When was the last time?

In her ecstasy of experiencing and loving this new and humble Cain, she had completely forgotten the monthly bleeding. She had last bled a week or two before he had returned for her.

Why hadn't she bled each month? Was she with child?

She remembered the signs her mother always exhibited—the vomiting in particular. But Lilith felt fine—strong, happy, content. She had never experienced a day of nausea or weakness.

Concentrating on her lower abdomen, Lilith attempted to detect movement. Nothing. Lifting her head slightly, she peered at her body. Her breasts had enlarged, and a hard, round lump bulged barely above her pelvic bone. She smothered a giggle. She was with child!

Now that she paused in her obsession with Cain's every look, every word, every revealed thought, and every touch, she felt absolute certainty. Why hadn't she noticed sooner? She had been so enthralled with him that she hadn't recognized the changes within her own body.

Cain now stirred, turning to face her. Gently, she kissed the mark on his forehead and smoothed back his hair. With heavy, sleepy eyes, he gazed at her.

"I love you," he whispered.

"I love you too, beloved one."

****

Cain looked into Lilith's eyes, silently thanking Yahweh for the marvelous gift of his wife. Her love healed his heart and made him whole. She was his treasure; he delighted in everything about her, both her strengths and her weaknesses. God was so good to him!

He didn't deserve such mercy.

Filled with some sort of inner delight, Lilith stared back at him. She looked more fully awake than he, bursting with some secret. She must have awakened early, lying still so he could sleep.

"You look happy." Cain kissed her shoulder.

"I am. You've sown a seed that has grown."

"What do you mean?"

"God has allowed your seed to produce something wonderful."

Propping himself on his elbow, he eyed her. What did she mean about the seeds from the Garden? Her expression mystified him.

"I don't understand you, Lilith."

"You've sown your seed, and it's growing."

"When? Where?"

"You've sown your seed in me. I'm now bearing your child."

Stunned, he stared down at her. *A child? Incredible!*

"I'm with child," she said again. "We'll have a baby in about six months."

Astonished, Cain pressed his forehead to hers. "Thank you, God!"

Teardrops slid down his cheeks, melding with Lilith's. She kissed his eyelids. His heart welled over with this evidence of God's forgiveness.

"My God," he prayed, "how can it be? You're merciful to one who has taken the life of another. You're granting a new life to even me."

"Who cares if the soil won't yield its fruit?" Lilith pressed her lips to his cheek. "My body will yield its fruit to you. Your seed grows in me. God has blessed the sowing of the most significant seed of all."

"You're right. Though I don't deserve it, Yahweh has blessed me. The yield of this seed is a far greater blessing than the seed that grows in the earth."

He drew her into his arms and kissed her. She was now even more precious. "We need to prepare. What must we do?"

"We'll need some soft leather for wrapping him."

"Let's pray for God to provide an animal. Yahweh, please hear us."

"Yes. We'll gather soft downy seeds from the river grasses to absorb his waste. Mother always swaddled the down against the baby's body with bands of leather. Do you remember?"

"I do." He chuckled at the fond memory. "I was amazed by the pile of seeds you girls accumulated while we tilled the soil."

She smiled. "I'll weave a basket so we can carry him around, unless you have an idea."

"I defer the weaving to you. You're better than I."

"Can you create some way for me to hold him against my body while I move about? A soft leather pack of some sort, like the packs you made for our backs. I want to hold him against my chest, so I can use my hands."

"Hmm," he said slowly, his mind already engaged. This would be fun, a challenge. "That's a good idea, Lily."

Through their tears, they smiled. The knowledge of this gift changed everything.

The coming of this child healed Cain's heart; it was living evidence of Yahweh's love and forgiveness. God had answered before they had even prayed. They hadn't known it until today.

****

Exuberant, they threw themselves into preparing for the coming child. It was a miracle! For years they had longed for their own family, and now it was finally happening!

Cain studied Lilith's belly every day, observing the subtle changes as the baby grew in size and strength. He loved the feel of her round abdomen between his two hands. Soon he could detect their child kicking vigorously within her. Lilith ripened before his very eyes. Her beautiful roundness represented the ultimate act of creativity—the making of a human life in secret, hidden from their eyes. The Creator labored mysteriously inside Lilith's body.

The exquisite wholeness of the spherical form captured Cain's artistic eye. He now noticed it everywhere in God's creation—the blue sky-bowl above them; the bright sun as it traveled across the sky's arch and the pale moon as it waned and waxed again; the colorful ripening fruit; the plumpness of Lilith's growing breasts; the curve of her smooth belly; the fullness of her cheeks as she glowed now with impending motherhood.

From all angles, he studied these changes in her body, using wide strokes to etch similar forms onto the cliff walls. She was lovely, her body magnificent. It held in its fullness a treasure from God. Cain sang praises to God as he went about his work.

> *"I will give thanks to God,*
> *Creator of the universe,*
> *Maker and giver of all life.*
> *His praise will be in my mouth forever and ever.*
> *He has shown his love and kindness to me,*
> *To even me—an undeserving sinner!*
> *He is good, and his love endures forever."*

****

Lilith rejoiced to see Cain's heart heal. God used the salve of her body in love and the fruit of that love—the coming child—to complete the healing. She knew he felt whole again. His step was light, his smile ready, his spirit uplifted; his creativity burst out everywhere. Not only did he adorn the walls and sing to the Creator, but he serenaded her. As they labored side by side, he sang soft and low, as if someone were near and he intended the words for her ear alone:

> *"My beloved was like a fragrant flower,*
> *A blossom opened to me.*

Her nectar flowed gently over my lips and teeth.
She now yields beautiful fruit;
Her breasts will sustain our child.
Let my left arm be under her head;
Let my right hand embrace her.
Let me delight in her always.
She has awakened my passion."

Whenever he sang like this, irresistible love for Cain welled up within Lilith's chest, washing over her. While he serenaded, he gazed upon her with passionate, loving eyes. Usually, by the end of the song, she rose, took his hand, and led him into the house to lie with him.

The beauty of his words coupled with the splendor of his heart and his eyes produced a combination she couldn't resist. She welcomed his right hand to embrace her, his left hand to be under her head. As if she were a sacred vessel, he made love to her gently and tenderly.

Within her body, she held the treasure of his child.

****

As they worked companionably, Cain's contentment increased. At their shared full moon, they paused to celebrate his one hundred twenty-fifth year on the earth and Lilith's ninety-fifth, rejoicing in God's goodness and mercy. The following day they returned to their labors, tackling the new garden. Before Lilith grew uncomfortable and large, they had to accomplish this task.

As Cain watched from the hillside, Lilith turned the soil. This time he felt peaceful. He had sown his own seed, and God had given life. Elated with the fruitful seed he had planted in Lilith's womb, he let go. Lilith could cultivate the soil and spread Eden's seed here by the brook. He was untroubled.

Calling down periodic guidance, Cain instructed her to stop frequently to rest her back. He advised her to sow each type together in its own section. From these plantings they would gather more seeds for bigger crops. Confidently, Lilith drilled the seeds down into the rich, dark soil. Near the brook she buried the seeds he had gathered from the fruit trees and the grapes.

Smiling as he watched her, Cain was pleased and peaceful.

God provided an animal. A female deer died near the field. After offering her flesh in thanksgiving, they tanned the leather, producing enough for many items. The bones and internal organs they put to good use. They cut and prepared a soft covering for the baby and bands for swaddling. Then, intrigued and excited with this imaginative project, Cain experimented with ideas for bundling the baby against Lilith's chest. Willingly, she allowed him to secure objects to her, adjusting and readjusting. She laughed at the odd "infants" he attached to her.

They had a creative idea for using the spun woolen fibers from Lilith's old sheepskin. In dye made from a woodland plant, they soaked the fibers, producing a dark blue color in the wool. Using the same method they had employed for weaving the ceiling's reed matting, they wove the threads together. As they fumbled with their fingers to complete this task, Cain had an idea. He would build a "loom," a small wooden frame on which to wind the woolen threads. This would secure the strands as they wove in the threads from the other direction.

It took Cain several days to construct the frame. When it was finished, they unraveled their previous work and started again, this time using the wooden loom. It performed well, holding everything in place.

With their heads pressed together, they worked as one. The sight of Lilith's honey-golden head bent so closely, united with him in concentration, made Cain smile. With her fingertips, she pressed the fibers tightly together as he wove them one over the other.

There was barely enough wool to complete a square of blue for wrapping their baby. With the last bit of yarn, Cain threaded the bone needle and went around the edges, binding the woven threads. Lilith removed it from the loom. Each held it up to their cheeks, savoring the warmth and softness. This "cloth," a covering of something other than leather—was a new creation. They both smiled. Their baby would have a woolen blanket and a leather one as well.

Standing, they stretched their aching backs and necks. Knowing the weight of the baby strained her body, Cain rubbed Lilith's shoulders and lower back.

"Come on." He scooped her up. "Let's soak in the brook."

Laughing and animated, she twined her arms about his neck.

"Cain, the blanket is blue like your eyes, like the sky in the evening. The baby will be adorable in it. Our son's eyes will be blue like yours."

"I favor gray eyes." He grinned at her. "Our daughter's eyes will be gray."

"He'll be a merging of us, like all of us are mixed parts of Mother and Father."

"Hopefully, we'll have many children and countless combinations. I'll rejoice over whomever God gives us."

"As will I," she agreed.

At the brook, they stripped and waded into the deep water. Lilith encircled Cain's neck with her arms, and he drew her close, so her belly pressed against his. The baby kicked him. He smiled at this intimacy, this greeting from within. Relaxing as they floated with the current, they drifted, enjoying the water's cooling sensation as it flowed over their skin.

When the sun neared the horizon, they scrubbed their hair and skin then sat on the beach to dry. As twilight fell, they dressed. Returning inside the wall, Cain latched the gate carefully. Hand in hand, they strolled to their house. He rekindled the fire in the brick-and-stone pit they had constructed in one corner of the enclosure.

Their small garden now produced vegetables Lilith was sampling for the first time. Cain enjoyed sharing these foods from Eden with her, watching her delighted expression as she took her first bite. They would eat some of the produce picked earlier in the day, coupled with some of the foodstuffs stored in the cave.

The sky grew dark. They leaned against one another, savoring the aroma of food sizzling on the rock in the embers. While they waited, they ate some fresh root vegetables.

"These are delicious," she said. "What are they?"

"I'm certain they're what Father called 'beets.' They grew thickly in Eden. The roots, stems, and leaves are all good. Here, try the leaf." He held it out to her.

As she chewed, her eyes revealed her enjoyment. "The color is striking! We should use it for dye next time we have wool. I'm glad you brought these seeds."

At that moment, they heard a noise that caused them to sit still—a shout echoed.

Halted in mid-motion, in mid-chew, in mid-comment, they stared into each other's eyes. Cain's chest tightened with fear. His heart raced. He remembered the dream of hiding Lilith in the cave and fighting to protect her. Strength and courage coursed through his body.

He would kill again, if necessary, to keep her and the coming baby safe. His conscience did not trouble him—somehow he knew protecting her would be acceptable.

"Cain!" shouted a voice, far away in the night.

They made no answer.

Who was it?

CHAPTER 31

WITH POUNDING HEART, CAIN STARED into Lilith's eyes, waiting to hear the startling call again. Had it actually occurred? Maybe they had imagined it.

"Cain!" the voice in the darkness shouted once more. "It's Akiva."

And it was. Lilith nodded—they both recognized Akiva's voice. What did this mean? Trying to discern what to do, Cain kept his eyes fixed on hers. Who was with Akiva? What would occur? Why had he come?

"I knew others would arrive," Cain said quietly. "Lily, our time alone is over."

Hungrily, she looked back at him. The seclusion of these past seven months had ended; the joy of complete abandon in each other, the precious intimacy—all gone. He saw her distress.

"I built our home knowing this day would come. Within the thick stone walls, we'll always have privacy. That's why I built this enclosure. We can even work together, alone behind our gate. I'll guard our time. I promise you."

Silently, she nodded, speech seeming to have been knocked out of her. They both rose. Pressing against him, she squeezed him to herself, holding him tightly.

"Stay here." Cain ducked to capture Lilith's eyes; she met his gaze. "Bar the enclosure gate behind me. Go into the house and bar the door. If you hear any conflict, hide in the cave until you hear Akiva's voice or mine. Otherwise, do not come out. Wait there; then escape to home and Father. Do you understand?"

****

Stunned, Lilith couldn't speak. Were the others here to kill him? She wanted to bear their baby into Cain's waiting hands. How could she endure being bereft of him? She stumbled woodenly toward the enclosure gate, nodding to him that she understood.

As he moved to go, he pulled her into his arms again.

"Lily, our lives are in God's hands. He will care for us. He's faithful. Don't fear, beloved."

Still unable to speak, she met his eyes.

He released her and seized a burning brand from the fire. Gazing at her once more, he caressed her cheek and dashed out through the gate into the night.

Clumsily, she barred the entrance behind him and lurched inside, in shock, the food abandoned. Barricading the house door, she retreated to their bedroom where she paced up and down, praying. Until this moment, she hadn't grasped that not only was the city constructed like a citadel—a place of safety, refuge, and defense—but their house was built like a fortress.

He had thought of everything.

She knew he would say the information was a gift from God. Realizing all that could occur now, she had to agree. Their lives were indeed in God's hands.

****

Cain raced toward the gate. What would he find? He was prepared to protect Lilith and their coming baby with his life, if need be. He begged Yahweh to give him wisdom and to keep him alive for Lilith and the child's sake. But he didn't know what

God had in mind.

My God! Guide and help me!

An idea came to mind. Cain did not open the gate, but stood inside it, leaving it barred. He held the firebrand aloft to light Akiva's way.

"Akiva," Cain called, "bear toward the light."

"Coming!"

Barely breathing, Cain pressed silently against the gate, straining to gather information. He heard Akiva and many others approach, but they spoke quietly, simple warnings to watch out for that rock or this branch. Finally, they breathed and moved on the gate's opposite side.

"Cain," Akiva said, "are you on the other side of these rocks?"

"Yes, brother. Is it safe for me to let you in? Are you being pursued?"

"We are. But I hope we have most of a day's advantage over them."

"So they won't arrive until tomorrow?"

"That's my hope."

Sliding the strong beam out of the rock crevice, Cain unbarred the gate and pulled it open. Stepping through, he held the brand high and embraced Akiva. Then he looked to see who had come. When he saw the crowd, he knew these were the city's first occupants.

Akiva had brought his family—Ariel, who was clearly with child, and their two small children. With him was Yonas, whose pottery skills they had recently longed for. Yonas had his arm around Raphaela, who cradled a sleeping infant. A small son clutched Yonas's knee. Behind these stood Hesed and Nissa, and after them, Azriel and Elkana, each couple clutching two children. Both Nissa and Elkana were also with child.

The light from the firebrand burned dim, so Cain couldn't discern the rest, but they were a crowd. Young Jeriel, Zuriel, and Gilam shouldered to the front, embracing him. As they stood arrayed before him grinning, he detected they had started the slow growth to manhood.

Love for his family warmed him. The trip was long and grueling, yet they had brought all their goods and their families. They had come to his defense. God was so good to him! Gratitude filled his heart, bringing tears to his eyes as he stepped back to welcome them in.

Holding the firebrand high, he greeted each one as they passed, returning hugs with his free arm, speaking his and God's blessing upon them all, and thanking each profusely. Once they were all within the city, he secured the gate then turned to face the group.

"Stay here. I must get Lilith. She'll be worried. I hid her away, not knowing what we faced. We'll get everyone settled for the night."

Cain handed the brand of fire to Akiva and pounded toward home, guided through the darkness by the hearth fire's glow. Standing outside the gate of the enclosure, he called, "Lilith! It's me! Our siblings have arrived to defend us. Come out, dearest!"

Surprising him with her rapidity, Lilith burst through the gate. Clearly she had heard his approach and had been poised for whatever action was required. She raced past him into the night. Turning on his heel, he followed, catching her as they neared the group.

Lilith embraced and welcomed each sister. She exclaimed over their children, commented on their expanding bellies, and accepted their congratulations on the coming child. Turning to hug each brother, she extended her gracious hospitality to the entire group, teasing Jeriel, Zuriel, and Gilam about their new height as she peered at their chins to detect if any whiskers sprouted yet.

Kissing, hugging, and exclaiming over each one, she made her way through the group. Cain followed, hugging them all again. Laughing, she informed Yonas of how badly they had needed him recently, urging him not to inspect her pottery too closely. When everyone had been greeted, Cain spoke again.

"We're so glad to see you!" Cain choked with emotion and paused to regain his composure. "We've missed you all, as is probably apparent." Everyone chuckled as they exchanged looks of familial love and friendship. "We must discuss the threat that provoked this trip, but let's settle the children first. Behind this wall is a large area with plenty of room for each family, or we can all squeeze into our home. It's built against the stone walls of the cliff. There are two large rooms and a cave at your disposal until we get other lodgings prepared."

Each couple spoke quietly together, quickly reaching a consensus. It was obvious they had discussed this on the way. Akiva acted as spokesman again.

"We'd all like to sleep outside, beside your home, but not in it. You're still newly married. We all remember ..." Everyone laughed, Cain the loudest. How well their siblings knew them. "We'll pitch our shelters against the cliff walls and encamp near your home."

"We have a fire going, as you can see." Cain pointed toward their house in the distance. "And we have plenty of food and water. Let's get everyone settled."

Shelters were erected, abutting their home, three couples on each side. Altogether, thirty family members had joined them, counting the unborn children. Even though Cain and Lilith invited them in, the younger boys settled against the stone walls of the house, insisting they wanted to sleep outside again, not within. It was obvious they had been instructed on the way.

****

It almost felt like a celebration to Lilith—they all talked, laughed, and shared what had transpired since they'd last seen each other. Some had only given Cain a quick greeting when he had returned for her, so there were many years to discuss.

Hungry and thirsty, the children grumbled—some crying, all tired—making it difficult to calm them for the night. Mothers scurried about feeding and tending to them. Lilith helped where she could. The older children remembered her and allowed her to stroke their heads, soothing them to sleep on their leather pallets.

While mothers quieted fussy children, fathers organized possessions and talked furtively together, probably discussing ominous facts. Just outside the ring of light from the torches and fireside, Lilith spotted Cain directing and conferring with different ones as they moved about. Eventually the small children slept; and, though they tried their hardest to stay alert, even Jeriel, Zuriel, and Gilam slumbered, snug against the warm stone walls.

The fourteen adults gathered within the enclosure. Behind the wood-and-brick wall, sounds muffled, and they spoke softly, preventing any children from overhearing. In a semicircle, they bunched close to the fire. Lilith passed around the food. Cain opened the discussion.

"What happened?"

"Efrat and Shafir seek revenge," Akiva said. "They believe your life must pay for Abel's."

"Don't Yahweh's word and his mark mean anything to them?" Lilith asked.

"They seem not to care."

Cain stared at her. What they had hoped would never occur was now, in fact, upon them.

"What have they done?" Cain asked. "How did you learn of this?"

"You know how absorbed I am in my work." Yonas met their eyes; they nodded. "Everyone forgets I'm there. I focus on the pottery, seeming not to listen. About two months ago they spoke of a plan to find where you'd gone. Keeping my eyes on the clay, I acted as if I hadn't heard."

"Then Yonas told Father," Raphaela added.

Yonas continued, "Father kept Jeriel, Zuriel, Gilam, Koren, and several others rotating, keeping a watch on them."

"But we made a false trail." Cain stared at him. "I took Lilith far to the east before heading north. How could they have found us?"

"Careful searching. First one went out, then another,

traveling a day's journey in every direction then returning in the night. Each time they varied their course slightly, working out from home like the spokes of a spider's web. They always made an excuse for their absence and only made two trips each a week. Eventually, one of them stumbled upon your location when they detected your fire far in the distance."

"How long ago?" Lilith asked.

"Seven days."

She looked at Cain. "That was the evening we fired the last pieces of pottery."

Cain nodded then met Yonas's inquisitive eyes. "We've made an oven for firing pottery using intense heat to harden and strengthen the pieces." Yonas's eyes showed he was intrigued. "It's down by the brook, so the water would have reflected the light."

"Apparently," Lilith said, "we chose a bad night to fire it."

Akiva took up the tale. "Koren trailed Shafir that night—he was the one who found you. Koren tracked him back home then went immediately to Father."

"Father informed us." Hesed looked at the others; all nodded. "We kept rotating watches on them day and night. We overheard their plans, and when they intended to leave—the full moon that marks Abel's birth."

"So, we openly organized a friendly visit." Akiva snorted. "You should have seen their faces. All of us said we missed you and were eager to see you. We packed everything, so it was obvious we planned to stay a while. We hoped it would prevent an attack."

"The full moon is tomorrow," Cain said. "That would put them here tomorrow night, if they follow their original plan. Or they could have attempted to get here before you."

"That's why we were so glad to hear your voice. We had no way of knowing. We couldn't travel very fast due to the children and our wives who are with child. We left the family compound in the middle of the night."

"They might have given up the plan then," Lilith said.

"Perhaps."

Uncertain, they all looked at each other. No one was sure what to do next; they hadn't had to plan for anything like this before. Lilith watched Cain; she knew he had already considered this. He would have formulated ideas. Lost in thought or praying, probably both, he stared at the ground. When he looked up, he met her eyes then addressed the group.

"When the Creator gave me the idea to build this city of refuge, I knew it was for protecting life and stopping the escalation of violence. As I tried to think defensively, I realized there was no way to stop someone bent on killing me. No defense was foolproof; each strategy could be breached. Heartbroken about it, I prayed most of the night. When I did sleep, I had a nightmare about Lilith. We were attacked, and I couldn't protect her. The wall around this city only slows an assault, giving time for the attacker's anger to cool. Perhaps love and reason can then prevail. God preserves life. It's in His hands. He's the only true refuge. While we consider a plan, we can't be fearful—me in particular. They're after me, not the rest of you. I won't allow any of you to give your life or be harmed for me."

When he said that, Lilith's heart clutched; her lower lip began to tremble.

She knew what he intended to do. If others were endangered, he would walk out there and offer his life to Shafir and Efrat again. And they would kill him. She would lose her husband. As their baby emerged from her womb, Cain would not be there to catch and hold him.

Their child would have no father.

Crossing her arms over her raised knees, she dropped her head to hide her face. Lilith didn't want anyone, particularly Cain, to see her fear.

CHAPTER 32

NO ONE KNEW WHEN THEIR embittered brothers would arrive to exact revenge. Someone needed to watch in the night. Since the long journey had exhausted the travelers, Cain volunteered. After all, they sought to harm him, not the others. He had slept well the night before and had performed no taxing physical labor today. He knew he could remain alert. They all agreed.

He stood to take his place out in the darkness.

"I'll come with you," Lilith whispered as she rose.

"Absolutely not."

With terror-stricken eyes, she stared up at him, reluctant and unwilling.

Sympathizing with the agony she felt, he looked into her eyes. He had watched her face—she knew what he planned. There was no need to speak of it. This was the inevitable consequence of crossing the threshold and inviting in the sin that had been crouching there. He had brought hatred, violence, and murder into the world. He should watch. This was the fruit of his sin. He wouldn't allow anyone else to be killed because of him.

"Lilith, no. Having you safely within our home will ease my mind. If you were exposed out there in the night, I would fear for you. Then I couldn't think clearly. I need to focus and listen."

She started to interrupt—he saw the objection in her eyes, but he held up his hand.

"You're carrying our child; you must care for yourself. You'll have much work tomorrow helping our sisters. Please, dearest. Please, go to bed. For me. And please sleep. I'll stay inside the wall tonight."

****

Lilith held onto him with her eyes. She couldn't do it. It was impossible. His reasoning was sound, but she couldn't part from him now that she knew he would die. She dreaded the coming wrenching separation, this time with no hope of him ever returning.

Cain pressed his forehead to hers, speaking for her ears only. "I won't die tonight, Lily. I'll shout if I hear anything. I won't do what I have to do without telling you goodbye."

As he whispered, she clutched him to herself. The baby kicked, and Cain swallowed hard. He didn't want to leave their baby without a father either. Lilith sighed. Rather than making this more difficult, she would make it easier for him, strengthening him.

"I'll do as you say, husband. You're right. I'll take care of myself for the baby, for myself, and for you." Pulling his head down, she pressed her lips to the mark. "This is the first night I'll sleep without you since you made me your wife."

It was a long night.

****

A bleary-eyed Cain greeted his brothers at first light. While their families slept, they huddled together within the enclosure, quietly discussing their strategy. They determined Cain should not leave the city; he had to remain behind the walls. Cain suggested they post someone to watch on the cliff above them. They agreed. He reminded them all that their best defense was their ability to reason with their brothers, to remind them of Yahweh's words, and to urge them not to escalate the violence.

Cain intended to ask their forgiveness again. Shafir, Efrat, and the others were still wounded by what he had done to Abel. Cain didn't tell the brothers now gathered around him that he would offer up his life, if the situation warranted it. He wanted to bring this hostility to an end—he would not allow his sin to bring any more death to the family.

Akiva left to take the first watch on the cliff as Cain headed inside to catch some sleep. Testing the door, he found it unbarred. He entered and secured the door behind him; then he padded softly toward their dark bedroom. The reed matting lay spread over the rafters, and the sun lay low on the horizon. All was silent and dim.

Quietly, Cain undressed and slid into bed. Leaning close to peer into Lilith's face, he found her eyes wide open. She had been watching him.

"Lily," he said softly, pressing his lips to her forehead.

"I missed you all night."

"As I missed you. Did you sleep?"

"Yes, finally. It took me a long while. I had to pray. I worried about you."

"I was fine. It was a quiet night. Nothing happened."

"What did you do while I was in here longing for you?"

"I walked back and forth along the wall, listening in the night, praying for God's help, asking for protection. Though the moon was full, my ears were probably my best defense."

"So, they didn't come?"

"No. Not yet."

"What will we do?"

"Akiva is taking the first watch on the top of the cliff. They'll wait to regain the surprise."

"So what will happen while we wait?"

"We'll get everyone settled in. It could be a while."

They looked into each other's eyes, assessing all that could mean.

Then Cain turned Lilith, so he could hold her close without her growing belly between them. He nuzzled behind her ear, down the back of her neck, and across her bare shoulders. He needed her body. The thought of dying and leaving her hurt him; it made him desperate and hopeless. But he had to do what was right. He couldn't allow any more killing. Cain asked Yahweh for strength then pushed the pain out of his mind, focusing on their lovemaking.

Afterward they slept, Lily cradled in his arms.

****

The bright light of late morning and the squabbling of small children awakened them—the small voices outside momentarily confused Lilith. Sitting up, she recalled the events of the night. Cain smiled up at her from the bed; the small amount of sleep had refreshed him. She had regained what she had lost in the night worrying over him. They rose.

Cain fondled her wrist. "I want to dress you."

She let him. Holding her head between his hands, he caressed her forehead with his lips. As he slipped her garment over her head, she breathed deeply, savoring the warm morning scent of his bare skin. He laced the front, tying it at her neck—no longer did she cinch it at the waist. Smiling into her eyes, he pressed his lips first to hers and then to her abdomen, briefly embracing her. With the wooden comb Abel had made so long ago, he smoothed her tangles then plaited her hair into one thick braid. Bringing it to his lips, he kissed the curls that escaped the end.

As he performed this intimacy, she stood in silence, watching him with sad eyes, studying everything he did, memorizing his expression and the feel of his hands.

When he finished, she clothed him. With tender, painstaking care, she covered his nakedness. She felt his eyes upon her, as she had gazed upon him. Meeting them, she smiled.

"I'm cutting your hair." She stepped to the shelf on the wall.

With one motion, he swept back the ceiling matting, enabling her to see. Then, awaiting her, he sat cross-legged on the floor. She knelt before him, stone shaving tool in hand.

"Are you taking it all off?" he asked.

"No, just trimming. I haven't shaved you since that day by the river. Remember?"

"I'll never forget it." He tipped his head; she grasped his beard, pulling it taut to sever.

"Nor I." She tilted his head, cutting the other side of his beard; then she paused to look into his eyes. "I couldn't resist you. I still can't."

"I've never been able to resist you." He chuckled. "I still can't believe it took me so long to realize we should be man and wife."

Having severed the extra length, she now trimmed his beard neatly, working her way around.

"We didn't know. It wasn't what we expected."

"No, it wasn't. You've made me the happiest man alive, Lily."

"I feel the same about you." She kissed his mouth. "Turn around; I'm cutting the rest too."

Using Abel's comb, she smoothed his hair and grasped it into one bunch. With the sharp tool, she sawed across the hank of hair, cutting it to his shoulders. Holding the hand's breadth of hair, she rose and tucked it into a woven basket on the shelf, saving this remembrance of him. Cain watched her, his eyes resigned yet determined. Their eyes met. He knew.

She decided to care for his body like this every day until he lay down his life. Then she would know she had sent him out, his body loved and cared for and cherished. With his eyes he made the same resolution; he would take his leave of her each day this way as well.

Standing, he faced her. Silently, they gazed into each other's eyes, focused on the other. Cain pressed his forehead to hers. Then he turned, and she bound his hair.

Finally, clasping hands, they walked out together to face the day.

****

Stepping into the enclosure, they found some of their siblings. Despite the circumstances, their presence healed Cain like medicinal balm. He was within his own family again. All greeted them warmly, offering the last of the bread they had brought from home. One of their sisters ground grain from their storage jar, preparing to bake more; another ladled out water for them. As Cain and Lilith ate and drank, Yonas and Hesed enlarged their discussion to them.

"How is Akiva?" Cain asked.

"Good. He's seen nothing," Hesed said. "Shortly before you came out, Jeriel returned to tell us. The three boys are ranging out from the cliff, exploring all directions to discover something before Akiva can see it."

"That sounds like a good plan."

"We think this should be our daily strategy," Yonas said. "What's your opinion?"

"Excellent." Cain looked at Lilith, and she nodded.

Yonas caught Lilith's eye, smiling at her. "Dear sister, your pottery is lovely. You didn't need to warn me not to inspect it. I'm curious to see this firing technique."

"Cain needs to stay behind the wall," Hesed said.

Lilith nodded, fixing her eyes on Cain's. "I'll have to show you alone then. Though I hate to do it without my beloved; most of the best ideas were his."

Hesed and Yonas grinned at Lilith's endearment for him. Cain joined their smiling.

"When peace returns we'll go out and inspect it," Yonas said. "For now, we husbands feel protective. We want our wives and children to remain behind the wall."

"Though they only want me, I agree." Cain looked at Lilith. "I want to protect you too. We don't know what they'll do. Rage is unpredictable; I should know."

"We also think we should prepare for a long stay," Hesed said.

"I built this city with that in mind," said Cain.

"Then we'll build homes of our own and enlarge your fields."

"That's what we hoped you would do. Can Father and Mother spare you?"

Hesed nodded. "We discussed it before we left. Because you'd already told Father about the city, he had decided this was best before we even approached him. He's been considering what's happening at home. He intends to send some of the younger ones down, removing them from the bitterness and hatred our brothers and sisters encourage."

How ironic. As Cain considered this, it seemed entirely unnatural.

He had murdered Abel—the kindest, gentlest brother any of them would ever have. Yet he was now considered the good example. The ones who had banded together in their bitterness over what he had done to Abel—former friends, admirers, and imitators of him—had become the ones filled with rage and bitterness, the bad examples.

God's ways were mysterious. It was unfathomable.

Everyone had fallen silent. Cain studied their faces. They awaited his response.

"I don't deserve to be the good example," Cain said quietly. "I'm not. I'm a murderer."

"But you've repented, and you've changed, dear one," Lilith said.

"Still, I carry around in me the ability to sin. Constantly, I battle my will, my impulsive nature, my temper, my selfishness. I have to cry out to God every day, every moment."

"We all do. The point is, you battle, you cry out. They don't. They've yielded to sin and bitterness. You've been crushed and destroyed by it. You've turned from it. Now you're a humble man."

Cain swallowed hard and looked around at them. "I'm not worthy for you to think well of me. I sin every day. You know how fatally I'm flawed. Don't look up to me. Please."

In their eyes, he saw their kind and understanding assessments, but he didn't want praise for his humility.

Accepting praise for humility destroys that very fragile state of actually being humble. For him, equilibrium required a constant realization of his inabilities. Existing in humbleness was necessary to maintain fellowship with Yahweh, to discern His voice directing him, guiding him, and convicting him. This, he was determined to hold on to.

"We're all flawed, Cain." Yonas flung his arm about his shoulder. "The only hope any of us have is to grasp that fact and live like we know it."

Cain looked intently at Yonas, found the camaraderie of a fellow repentant sinner in his kind eyes, and relaxed. All was well. They all knew him too well to idolize him.

He smiled. "How should we build your homes then?"

Returning his smile, everyone relaxed and sat back, contributing their ideas and suggestions. Some of the others had wandered into the enclosure during this exchange, and they offered input regarding their wishes. The women offered their opinions, telling their husbands what they desired and dreamed for their homes. They planned how to divide the heavy physical labor.

Excitement grew. They would build this city, all of them living together. It would be a place of reconciliation and humility.

****

Lilith strategized with the other women. First, they needed to stop the children's crying and fussiness. This required organizing them into some semblance of normality. If they fed them at the expected times and established the naptimes and routines the children had enjoyed before undertaking this long journey, the young ones would soon adapt to the new norm.

Hastening this, Lilith helped arrange each family's chosen area, bringing required household items. She and Cain had made an abundance. They had so enjoyed experimenting with firing the earthenware that they had continued to produce bowls, jars, lamps, basins, and cups, even after they had all they needed.

Apparently, the most recent firing had been their undoing.

All the women began weaving ceiling matting—a big project. For now, this would provide shade for their outside dwellings and covering from the nightly mist. As they wove, their husbands gathered rocks and clay and formed the bricks to construct their homes.

All day everyone worked, poised for action; but nothing happened.

The work of this day became the routine. Every day their tension and anxiety eased. Maybe their brothers' plan for vengeance had been thwarted by Father, or maybe rejected, now that so many of them stood with Cain.

Life reasserted itself.

And still, nothing happened.

****

In the darkness of the moonless night, Shafir and Efrat lay with their heads together on the top of the cliff. Down below, multiple fires burned, scattered within the walled city. Far away, their brother stood as watchman on the opposite edge of the canyon.

They had sneaked out onto the cliff each night, easily detecting the one guard silhouetted against the sky, especially when the moon shone. They moved only when he did.

They had become intimately acquainted with the habits and patterns of the city being erected far below them. The voices of their brothers and sisters carried easily in the night, their plans for each coming day forecast every evening, wafting up to them in the night air.

Shafir and Efrat's plan for killing Cain had been formulated.

Now all they needed was the opportunity.

They were patient. They would wait for it.

CHAPTER 33

SATAN WAS DISGUSTED BY ALL the humility and brotherly love displayed in the city. He hovered with the other fallen angels over Shafir and Efrat, fueling their hatred. The canyon that held Cain's city brimmed with blazing elect angels poised for combat, their expressions fierce.

God knew all. He protected His own. He had sent guardians. As always, Satan and his forces were outnumbered two to one. It had been this way since the rebellion.

Meanwhile, up here on the ledge, the fallen ones destroyed where they had been invited—in the angry, embittered hearts of these two young men. These, they swayed and nudged toward hatred and revenge. Their machinations successful, they scoffed at how easily these two had been toppled. Pride and bitterness made effective tools for destroying relationships and lives.

Since the fall from grace, Satan and his allies had constantly plotted against Adam and Eve, who had become more resistant to temptation. Their children, however, were much easier marks, vulnerable, crumbling to the same temptations their parents had at first and learning their sin habits. All Satan and his cohorts did was prod. They would do the same with the next generation.

Now that Satan had witnessed how sinfulness grew and

multiplied, he plotted his strategy, assigning one of his generals to each of Adam and Eve's offspring. These and their cohorts would torment each family tree from generation to generation. Samyaza he left to torture Cain.

In using Shafir and Efrat to kill Cain, Satan and his forces would wound and bruise many—the onlookers, Lilith, the fatherless child, the murderers themselves—producing more hatred, vengeance, and destroyed relationships. A cycle of violence would perpetuate.

Perhaps this would snuff out the head-crusher and end Yahweh's plan.

Cain no longer seemed likely. If not him, who?

CHAPTER 34

CAIN TOOK PLEASURE IN WORKING with his brothers again. Nearly three months had passed since they had arrived from the home compound. Spaced evenly around the canyon, new homes now stood, making ten homes in the city. Each couple had guided their own construction. One house had been built for unmarried men and another for unmarried women, with an additional house for new arrivals. Their brothers and sisters said more would come.

This was what God had prepared Cain to expect.

Often, he glimpsed Lilith working with their sisters. He missed the camaraderie they had enjoyed before their siblings' arrival. They still experienced that within their own home, when the cares of coordinating the efforts of so many people didn't press upon them.

Perhaps things would now slow down. This morning, the top course of stone had been mortared into the last house; now it only needed to dry. Their siblings organized to move their possessions. As Cain looked about the city, it reminded him of an anthill and the swarm of activity when the hill was disturbed. All around him, families relocated.

Many of the children fussed about this latest change. The process of settling in the children began anew. They had become accustomed to sleeping outside under the matted reed coverings, mingling together, running throughout the city, and playing in one mass while their parents worked together. Chaos and liberty had reigned. Now they had to learn to sleep inside with their own families, their lives ordered by their own mother's and father's direction.

As he watched his brothers and sisters cope with their children, Cain smiled. Soon he would be a father. He prayed God would allow him to raise their child. He wanted to live.

Oh God, please make it so!

They now hauled the matted reed coverings to the ceilings of the new homes. Each home had a front and a back room; each had been erected to ease future expansion. If they all bore the same number of children as their parents, they would fill the city.

The sun approached its zenith—time for the midday meal. Work slowed in anticipation of food and a break. Cain secured the woven ceiling covering over Akiva and Ariel's bedroom, patted his brother on the shoulder, and headed home.

"Cain!" shouted a young male voice from outside the wall.

This was a shock! Shielding their eyes, everyone looked at the watchman on the canyon rim.

Hesed waved back. "It's Koren."

The voice yelled back, "Hesed!"

Directing Koren, Hesed pointed toward the gate. Everyone hurried there. This arrival didn't bode well. It concerned Cain. Who had traveled in this group? He was startled that one so young had come alone or had led an expedition. Koren had barely reached manhood.

Cain threw wide the gate. A group of smiling young faces greeted him.

Welcoming them warmly, he embraced each one as they passed through. Glad to see them, he handed them on to Lilith, who now stood beside him. They had all grown tall since Cain had been banished! He had missed them!

"Koren! Danika! So good to see you," Lilith said. "Who's with you?"

She leaned around him. Behind these two stood three of
their younger brothers and three sisters. Everyone was under the
age of fifty-five, the oldest barely adults. The boys' beards were
thin or nonexistent, their muscles lean. The girls were young,
barely women; Cain wasn't certain if they could bear children
yet. Shocked, Lilith stared back at him, raising her eyebrows.

"Father sent us all down together." Koren exuded excitement.
Clearly, this had been a grand adventure for him. "Danika and I
were married only three days ago. We left the day after we were
wed. Since I'm the oldest, Father put me in charge."

With gusto, Koren seized Danika, bestowing a wet and
passionate kiss upon her. She kissed him back then stood
giggling and blushing.

Rolling his eyes, Etan plodded through the gate after them.
"And that's why the trip took two days. I don't ever want to see
anyone kiss again. All the kissing and cooing slowed us down.
We had to stop and camp on the way. Please, please, tell me I
don't have to live anywhere near a newly married couple. Oh,
sorry. I forgot that included you two. Whoa! Lilith! Look at you!"

Etan gaped at her enormous belly—the child was due any
day.

"We can arrange that, Etan." Cain chuckled.

"Thanks be to God!" Scanning his new surroundings, Etan
trudged into the city.

Amused, Cain grinned at Lilith then he sorted through the
rest as they entered. They ranged in age from Koren, who was
fifty-five, to Etan and his twin Etana, who were barely forty and
still growing. His smile faded. What had prompted their parents
to send youngsters?

Used to caring for their younger siblings, the others gathered
them up to get settled.

Cain transferred Danika's bundle to his back, draped his arm
across Koren's shoulder, and guided him toward the extra house.
It had been constructed next to theirs, built specifically for this
type of situation. Smaller and simpler than the rest, it had only

one large room. The doorway opened by the canyon wall, giving more privacy and an area for reflection. When more houses were built, they would relocate Koren and Danika, leaving this one always open for new arrivals. Cain wanted newcomers housed next to him and Lilith, especially if they were fugitives.

****

With her arm around Danika's waist, Lilith followed Cain and Koren at a slower pace. The pregnancy had loosened her joints; she waddled, and her belly stuck out hugely. She listened to her younger sister gush about Koren's proposal, their love, their wedding day, and the difficulty of making the journey so soon after becoming man and wife.

Their union hadn't surprised Lilith. Danika had been born two and a half years after Koren, and they had always been inseparable. Their relationship was much like hers and Cain's in its intensity. Still, there was so much they needed to learn. They were so young! Cain was much older than she. They had been mature adults when they married. Lilith was glad the young couple would be housed nearby so they could oversee them.

At the temporary house, Cain guided them to the secluded entry. The private house was perfect for the newly married. He helped Koren carry in their things; Lilith followed.

Cain stood in the room's center. "Here's where you'll live until we can build you a home."

"This is perfect!" Koren looked around at the four walls.

The ceiling matting was already up and rolled back, allowing in plenty of light. A woven door hanging had been drawn back from the doorway.

"We'll soon be adding a wooden door for more privacy. Lilith and I live right there." Cain stepped to the doorway and pointed across to their home. "We have anything you might need. Come over and eat with us. We need to talk. We'll expect you shortly."

Cain took Lilith's hand, and they went ahead to prepare the meal.

"This is a surprise." Cain glanced at her as they walked away.

"I know. Something must be wrong. They're all too young. Father and Mother normally want ones this age near them for firm guidance."

"That's what troubles me. I think something terrible must have happened."

"So do I."

Upon the stone hearth, Lilith spread the food she had prepared. Squatting down, she organized the meal. It was difficult to lower her body.

Cain squatted beside her. "Lily." She met his eyes. "Sit down and rest your back. I can arrange the food."

Gratefully, Lilith complied, easing herself against the wall near the hearth. She watched him while he worked. Deep in thought, he worked silently. At last, he turned to look at her.

"Can you imagine if we'd married when you were Danika's age, just barely done growing?"

"You would have been about eighty then. That was when you built your bedchamber far away from where Mother and Father slept. I never asked you why you did that."

"I was a man. I didn't realize it at the time, but I was ready to be your husband. Occasionally I could hear Mother and Father in the night, and it disturbed me. It gave me troubled dreams. I had a hard time controlling my thoughts when I was that age. You were newly grown, shaped like a woman—so beautiful! In the darkness of my room I did things I shouldn't have done as I thought about your body. I didn't know I could have you for my wife, remember?"

Lilith sighed. "I wish we'd known then. If we'd married forty some years ago, we'd have a house full of children by now."

"Hopefully, we will soon."

They stared at one another. With the current events unfolding, they both knew this was not likely. Lilith knew Cain was as desperate as she to have more time.

"Yahweh, our God, please make it so," he whispered.

A rap sounded at the enclosure gate.

More unspoken prayers showing in his eyes, Cain gazed at her. Speaking from the hearth, he kept his eyes on hers as he invited them in. Koren and Danika shyly poked their heads in.

Smiling, Cain turned toward them. "Come in!"

"I can't get up, now that I'm down." Lilith scooted to make room. "Cain is finishing the food preparation. Join us."

"When is your baby due?" Danika asked.

"Any day. It's been ten months since we married; the child was conceived shortly afterward."

"What a gift! You both waited so long."

"Yes," Lilith said at the same time as Cain.

Their eyes caught and held. Lilith hoped and prayed their time together wasn't ending soon. The same prayer gleamed in Cain's eyes. He broke their gaze and fixed his eyes on Koren.

****

Cain had to know the facts. "So, tell us. Why has Father sent you younger ones up here?"

Koren sighed then launched into his tale. "You already know Niran, Aviv, Lavan, and their families stayed to assist Father, though they all wanted to join you. They hoped they could help him keep an eye on us younger ones, preventing the others from influencing us. However, it grew more difficult. Some were swayed. When Joda left and didn't return, Father decided Danika and I should go ahead and marry, so we could bring those near our age here to warn you. Efrat and Shafir have been gone for months. Joda's departure can only mean they intend to harm you."

Considering all this, Cain kept his eyes on the fire, processing the specifics. Finally, he looked at Koren again. "You don't mention Mother."

Koren slowly exhaled a puff of air. "Mother is consumed with bitterness; she hasn't recovered. There's some strain between her and Father. They sleep separately."

Stunned, Cain gaped at Lilith. This grieved him. He

remembered his father's pacing in the field and what he had said about their mother not wanting any more children. In his joy over bringing Lilith home, he'd forgotten. He offered a quick prayer for his mother, asking God's forgiveness again for what he'd done to her heart.

Lilith looked grim. "Has she allied with Shafir and Efrat?"

"No," Koren said. "Not at all. But she's bitter. Cain, I'm sorry to say it. She doesn't desire your death. That's not it. She just can't seem to forgive you. And there's some other issue that Father and Mother argue over privately; they take care that we don't hear their words."

Grief-stricken, Cain stared into the flames. His actions had harmed his parents' marriage. The ramifications of Abel's murder ransacked wide and deep. The human family would never recover from the carnage. This news devastated him. Cain's throat ached with the agony of it; he hoped he could speak clearly. He needed more information.

"So." He swallowed hard and fixed his eyes on Koren's. "They still think my life should be forfeited because I killed Abel?"

"Yes."

"In spite of what Yahweh said?"

"Yes."

"How long ago did Joda leave?"

"Five days now. We married two days after."

"I'm sorry the solitude of your first days had to be disrupted on my account."

"How have you borne the lack of privacy?" Lilith said.

Danika and Koren looked long into each other's eyes before Danika spoke. "We decided that if you two could survive what you've had to suffer, Yahweh would surely help us through the minor inconvenience of a few days' travel."

Koren grinned, and said, "Besides, hurrying our wedding has been its own consolation. There are advantages, you know." He aimed his smile at Danika, who reddened.

"Yes." Cain looked at Lilith. "I know."

****

The food was ready. Cain gestured for Koren and Danika to go first. Lilith kept her eyes on him, knowing the anguish he must be feeling at this news. Danika now asked questions about their house. With a small smile, Cain rose to lift Lilith.

"Thank you." She kissed the hand that raised her. "It's so difficult to move about."

Her side hurt. One part of the baby always poked her there, making a little lump near her now-stretched belly button—a tiny bump in her otherwise smooth belly. To ease the pain, she pressed on the lump; it felt like a sharp little heel. The infant pushed against her hand.

To study this little lump, Cain often sat before her naked body—his seat against her crossed legs, his legs bent up over hers. He would put pressure on the bump then watch it reappear as the baby popped its little heel back out. Smiling widely, he would envelop her in his arms, bending to kiss the little lump. With his mouth against her skin, he would admonish their unborn child in gentle and affectionate tones, affirming his love but insisting the baby quit poking his mother.

With this bad news that had just arrived, reflecting on this intimacy now hurt Lilith as she pressed against the baby's heel. Her heart ached. She wanted their child to know and be loved by his father. She didn't want her baby to be bereft of the passionate love of this man.

Before she could stop it, a tear slid down her cheek.

"Are you alright, Lilith?" he asked. "Are you in pain?"

"No, I'm fine." Quickly, she wiped the tear away, unaware that he'd been watching. She needed to be brave for him. "Let's show Danika and Koren our home."

Koren exclaimed over Cain's creativity. The shelf design and the bedframe impressed him. He puzzled over the hewn rafters and doors. He enumerated the stone floor's virtues. The structural plan to remove wall portions for later expansion he considered ingenious. He intended to build these ideas into their home.

Lilith showed Danika the baby items they had readied. Danika was fascinated by the woven blue blanket. Wondering how they had done it, she peered at their weaving, asking about the process and the dye in the wool.

After they'd seen everything, Lilith noticed Cain eyeing her face.

"Lily, will you lie down? I'll clean up. Danika and Koren will go now so you can rest." He looked hard at Koren.

"Yes, we need to go." Koren clasped Danika's hand and headed for the door. "It's time to organize our house. Thank you for the meal and your company."

Cain led Lilith to bed. Easing her down, he sat beside her, stroking her head. "Lilith, are you sure you're fine?"

"I'm just ready to have this baby. Bearing children makes women weepy. You know this."

"Roll onto your side. I'll rub your back as you go to sleep."

She complied. His hands and his softly sung melody lulled her to sleep.

CHAPTER 35

LILITH WOKE, STRETCHED, AND WENT to seek Cain. Weariness weighed her down, but walking felt good. When she approached Yonas and Raphaela's home, she detected Cain's voice in the work area near the gate. Yonas had chosen the home nearest the clay deposits and the pottery oven. It would be easier to transport unfired pottery if he only had to carry it a short distance.

Rounding the house corner, Lilith discovered Yonas and Cain covered in clay up to their elbows. Wearing only his loincloth, Cain kneaded the thick red earth. Yonas bent over his wheel, producing vessel after vessel. Several already sat in the sun to dry. Raphaela etched lifelike designs into the sides of the drying earthenware, adding her imaginative touch.

"Lilith!" Cain smiled warmly. "How are you feeling?"

"The sleep did me good, beloved. But my back is so uncomfortable today."

Raphaela looked up, carefully studying her face. Lilith shook her head, aware of her sister's assumption that labor was near. Raphaela glanced at Yonas.

"Sister," Yonas said, "sit against the house, rest your back, and watch us work."

"I'll sit. My back would hurt too much to bend over a wheel

today."

Yonas nudged his small son, who hurried into the house and returned with a vessel of cool water for her to drink. Thanking him, she kissed his little head and smiled at Raphaela.

"So, brother," she said to Yonas, "you couldn't wait to get busy, now that you've barely moved into your home."

"These new arrivals and all of us finally settling inspired me." He grinned at her.

"We hope to fire them tomorrow evening or the next," Cain said. "It's hot today; these should dry adequately by then."

Full of anticipation, she looked at him. "Can we go out to watch?"

Cain's forehead creased. "I'd better stay inside the wall, but I don't see why you can't go out for a while. You love firing pottery. A brief time can't make a difference; the cliff wall is on one side, the water on the other—no one can surprise us."

Lilith smiled. Stepping outside the wall would be a blessing. She leaned her head back against the cool stone of Yonas and Raphaela's home. They had built the workspace on the side of the morning sun; so now, in late afternoon, it was shaded. Lilith loved watching them work with the clay. It was something she herself relished.

Today she was simply too tired. All the frenzied activity of the last few days had taxed her. Periodically, Cain glanced up at her, his brow furrowed. She knew her fatigue concerned him.

Laughing easily, Yonas and Cain bantered as they worked, switching jobs occasionally, so Cain could rest his arms from the more difficult job of kneading. Cain felt his pottery was inferior to Yonas's, but only the two of them could see it. To everyone else, all the pieces appeared equally beautiful. Lilith knew her work was merely adequate compared to theirs.

She loved to watch Cain make pottery. His long, supple fingers cupped the red earthen lump as it rose between his hands. Carefully, he smoothed the perceived irregularities, focusing entirely on the task. He studied the pot, tilting his head slightly as he pondered what it needed. His eyes had an absorbed, introspective depth, as if he were thinking with his hands, his whole body flowing into his palms and fingertips. This was how he looked at her when they made love.

She adored him; she could watch him forever. How she would miss him! A tear slipped down her cheek. Before he could see it, she wiped it away.

As sunset neared, Cain and Yonas rose to wash. Yonas went out to bathe in the brook, bringing back a large vessel of water for Cain. Splashing and scrubbing, Cain removed all the clay from his upper body and his legs.

When he finished, Lilith gathered his garments, folding them over her arm. Linking hands, they walked home, Cain's body and loincloth drying in the remaining rays of sunlight.

****

When they arrived home, Cain barred the enclosure gate. He had told Yonas the information Koren had brought, asking him to inform the others and giving input about security measures they might want to take. Yonas had realized Lilith was near delivery and understood that Cain wanted solitude with her with no intrusion. Perhaps the baby would even be born this night.

Cain now faced Lilith. He had watched her all day—she couldn't hide her heart from him; she never could.

"We'll be undisturbed. I've made arrangements for no one to bother us." He caressed her soft cheek, tucking a curl behind her ear. "Please tell me why you've been crying."

"You saw me?"

"Of course."

"I can't tell you."

"Yes, you can—you must. We're one flesh. I want to share all your heartaches."

"But I don't want to hurt you."

"Am I lacking in some way as a husband? Am I sinning against you?"

"No! No! You're a wonderful husband! It's not that."

"Then what?"

Silently, Lilith stood before him, hanging her head. She sighed.

"The threat has arrived." Her voice was low. "I know they're out there waiting to kill you. You'll sacrifice your life to spare the others. I can't bear to lose you."

Cain cupped her cheeks and lifted her face. He needed her to look into his eyes. "I can't let anyone else die because of me."

"But I can't bear to lose you. I want our baby to have a father. I want our child to know your love. I don't know if I can survive losing you again."

"What would you have me do?"

"I don't know." She trembled with agitation. "I know you have to do what's right. But I still can't bear it. There's no solution." She dropped her voice as if fearing eavesdroppers. "I would choose to save your life over any other person in this city."

"But, Lilith, my conscience can't bear the thought of anyone else dying because of me. How many of our parents' children will I take from them? How many will I cause them to lose?"

"And can your conscience bear me, your own wife, being robbed of your presence?"

These words hurt him. The pain of the coming separation weighed on him. It was unbearable. He agonized over the inner conflict she had forced him to reveal.

"No," he said. "My conscience can't bear that either."

"Then why?"

"Because you wouldn't be dead. Anyone who gave up his life to protect me would be."

"But it will kill me if I lose you."

"No, Lilith. No, it won't. You didn't die before. You're strong. You would survive for the sake of our child."

Closing her eyes, she sank to the ground. Tears wet her cheeks, dropping onto the mound of her round belly. He sat in front of her, encasing her in his arms.

"You're right," she whispered.

"I know." He leaned his forehead against hers.

"There's nothing else you can do, is there?"

"No."

So this was why she had cried. He had felt like weeping himself, but had drawn strength by crying out to God for help. Now he prayed for them both.

"Yahweh, God who loves us, help us face whatever You have planned, whatever You choose to unfold as our brothers come to attack. Protect us. Our hope is in You. You're the avenger of my life. Care for my Lily if I must die. Strengthen her. Allow me to live if it's Your plan. I don't want to leave her or my child. I want to live."

His voice broke as he uttered these last words, his tears joining hers, falling onto her round abdomen full of their baby.

****

The next morning, they woke in each other's arms; Lilith had not given birth.

Several times in the night, she had awakened and had relieved herself in the flat clay pot designed for this purpose. Cain would hand it out to someone to dump in the designated area. After each awakening, though her womb had contracted, she had settled again into his arms. He had drawn her close, kissing her head and murmuring his love; then they had slept once more.

Holding her close, he now kissed her shoulder, stroking his fingertips lightly across her belly.

"I fully expected you to give birth last night."

"As did I. We've been given another day, it seems. Will you make love to me?"

She felt his face move against her shoulder. His beard tickled her; he was smiling.

"I'm always happy to comply with that request."

Gently, he united his body with hers, murmuring endearments as he kissed her neck and shoulders. She needed his closeness. If they killed him today, this would be the last time. Somehow, she had to bear the thought. Who knew what this day might hold? Their lovemaking caused her womb to cramp. Perhaps this would hasten the birth.

****

By late afternoon, Yonas and Cain decided the pottery could be fired. Gathering Gilam and some of the others boys to help, Yonas began carrying the pottery out to the oven. Cain remained inside the wall. Sitting on the ground, he held a piece of dried gut stretched taut, carefully sliding it under each pot to loosen it from the ground where it had hardened.

Lilith asked to help Yonas position the first pots. The younger boys ran outside, searched the area, and returned. All was safe. Cain saw no reason Lilith couldn't enjoy these few moments before her confinement with a newborn. The early signs of childbirth were apparent. The contracting of her womb had continued all day, gradually increasing in strength and frequency.

Cain's eyes followed her as she waddled by, her feet splayed. "See you shortly, beloved."

Looking back over her shoulder, her eyes twinkled at him. He smiled.

For some reason his heart clutched in his chest—something wasn't right. Not wanting to react out of insecurity or lack of trust, he pressed the fear down. Surely he could give Lilith this brief moment to place the pottery in the oven, since she loved it so much. He didn't want to overreact when everyone said all was well. He didn't want to give way to an irrational fear.

Looking down, he continued to work, all the while begging Yahweh to help him.

But now, from the other side of the wall, he heard a commotion—scuffling, a struggle, the tinkling of pottery breaking.

Then Lilith screamed.

Cain leapt up and sprinted for the gate.

From the outside, Shafir yelled, "Cain! I'll slit your wife's throat if you don't come out."

Knocking the restraining hands away, Cain ignored all the voices saying surely Shafir wouldn't kill his own sister. There was no hesitation; there was no decision to be made.

Yanking the gate toward himself, he knocked aside everyone who tried to stop him, punching someone in the jaw. He wasn't sure who he had hit. Bursting through the opening, he raced hard around the cliff toward the clay deposit and the oven. What he saw as he rounded the corner took his breath away but didn't slow his forward motion.

Shafir was dripping wet. He clutched Lilith to his chest, holding a stone knife to her throat. Efrat, also wet, wrenched her arm, his knife poised over her abdomen. Back and forth he flashed the knife between her and the cliff wall. There, Yonas and Gilam flattened themselves against the stones, surrounded by shattered pottery.

A drenched Joda was positioned to fend off attackers.

Lilith's eyes bore into Cain's. She was clearly terrified, but she held utterly still. It had never occurred to them that he might have to offer his life for her and their child. He should have listened to the cautionary fear that had gripped his heart; he now realized it had been the voice of God. As he raced toward them, he silently begged Yahweh's forgiveness.

"Take me!" Cain cried. "Let her go!"

Feet pounded behind him. His brothers raced with him toward the attackers.

Near his shoulder, Akiva shouted, "How do we know you'll release her if you get Cain?!"

"How do *we* know you'll give us Cain if we release Lilith?" Joda countered.

As Cain drew closer, he detected a bead of blood on Lilith's neck where the knife pressed. The blood trickled slowly down. When he saw this, he collapsed to his knees, his hands up, imploring. He couldn't escape if he was in this position. Surely they would see this, and he could gain their trust. Akiva stopped behind him.

"I'm giving myself up to you." Cain stretched out flat on the ground. "Look! I can't run. Now let her go! Please. She's with child. Don't harm her!" He was desperate. He couldn't let them hurt her. Without any regret, he would die for her. "Take my life for hers."

Planting his chin in the clay so he could see her, he lay prone on the red earth.

Joda took a step toward him. His feet loomed before Cain's face. He couldn't see what Joda was doing; he stood too close. But Lilith saw, and her eyes grew large. At the sight of Joda's actions, she struggled. Shafir hissed a warning, and she inhaled sharply. More blood trickled down her neck.

"Kill me! Do it!" Cain demanded, his eyes fixed on Lilith. "Let her go! Don't harm her!"

"We'll let Lilith go," Joda said. "We only demand your life in exchange for Abel's."

"Lily, I love you." The ache in Cain's throat made it almost impossible to speak. "I regret every way I ever hurt you." He stared hard at her, yearning for more time.

She sobbed out her love for him. He grieved that she had to watch his death. This was the nightmare she had hoped she would never have to face. It would occur right before her eyes.

His breaths came shallow and fast. His lower jaw trembled. Waiting ... Waiting ... The sound of his own heartbeat pounded in his ears. He forced himself to lie still. He had to save her.

Joda adjusted his feet, spreading them. His body twisted as he raised something. Unable to see it, Cain assumed it was a heavy rock. Swallowing hard, he braced himself for the crushing blow. He deserved this. He'd done this very thing to Abel.

"No!" Lilith closed her eyes and screamed, high-pitched, hysterical. "No!"

Then something heavy landed, making a soft, squashing thud. It had sounded like that when he hit Abel's head. But Cain was fine. What had happened? Simultaneously, running feet pushed off the ground by his face. Koren hurtled through the air; then one of Joda's feet kicked Cain in the face, blocking his view. Thuds, grunts, gasps, blows.

"Cain, get up!" Akiva shouted.

Thrusting himself up from the ground, Cain charged toward Lilith. She was now held only by Shafir. Efrat lay unconscious and bleeding on the ground, his head crushed by a large stone that lay nearby. Koren had driven his shoulder into Shafir's side, knocking him lose from Lilith. Just as Lilith was about to fall, Cain caught her and cradled her in his arms. She fainted.

Lilith's water had broken; the front of her garment was soaked. Onto Cain's supporting arm, the wetness still leaked. Safe in her belly, the baby kicked against his chest as he held her tightly. The kick was strong and vigorous, just like all the baby's previous movements had been.

Both Lilith and the child were fine. Though there was a lot of blood, the cut on her neck wasn't deep; but it would leave a scar like the marks on her arms—another scar on Lilith because of him. Other than that, once the wound was cleansed and bdellium applied, Lilith would be fine.

Relieved, Cain smiled and exhaled, thanking God for their survival.

Looking around now, Cain saw Joda pinned by Hesed and Akiva. A large stone club rolled loose from his hands. A shout sounded above his head. He peered up at the watchman. Solemn-faced, Azriel waved. He had dropped the rock right onto Efrat, hitting him on the head and setting off these events. Cain nodded his thanks then he looked down at his wife.

"Lily," Cain said quietly. "Lilith ... dearest."

She stirred. Her eyes fluttered.

"Lilith ... beloved ... Lily."

Disoriented and frightened, she blinked her eyes. She gaped at him as if she thought he was not real. Cautiously, she touched his head, turning it so she could see both sides.

"Joda raised a horrible club." She sucked a sob back in. "I closed my eyes. I couldn't bear to see you die. I heard the stone hit your head. I heard it!"

"It was Efrat's head. Azriel dropped a rock on him."

"It sounded awful! I couldn't bear it. I thought it was the sound of you dying. I screamed, trying to drown out the sound. But I couldn't. I kept hearing it in my head. How can you be alive and unharmed?"

"Somehow, Akiva and Hesed pinned Joda to the ground just as Azriel dropped the rock. I didn't see it. Koren knocked Shafir lose from you. They're holding him now."

Lilith now clutched her abdomen. Her hand encountered the wetness. Gingerly, she touched first one place then the other. Fearfully, she stared hard at him, afraid to look.

"The baby's fine." He kissed her forehead. "He just kicked me. But, dearest, the water has leaked out. The baby will be born soon."

"You're not dead!" She sobbed. "You can father our child! I won't have to live without you. God is so good to us!"

Then she cried. Lilith clutched his neck and wept hysterical sobs—months' worth of weeping.

****

Cain carried Lilith home. As they entered the city gate, their sisters waiting there offered help with the delivery. He thanked them, saying he would call out if he needed them, but informing them that Lilith had, all along, wanted only him.

CHAPTER 36

AS CAIN STRODE HOME, GRATITUDE overwhelmed him. He was glad to be alive. Bending to kiss Lilith's forehead as he walked, Cain soothed her, but she cried all the way. Gently, he laid Lilith down on the bed. Standing up, he raked back the ceiling covering. The light would fade fast. He needed to examine her body and clean her wounds before evening. He squatted to look at her.

Her eyes met his. "First the baby."

Palpating her abdomen, he pressed where they thought the baby's head lodged. Everything felt as it should; the baby kicked him. The little bump where the heel poked against Lilith's side still protruded. Cain pressed against the lump, pushing it back in. It reappeared as the baby kicked and pushed its little heel back against Lilith's side. Cain smiled.

He looked up at Lilith. She smiled through her tears.

"See," he said, "all is well. Let me check where you'll birth him."

She lay back, and he examined her gently.

"No bleeding. Does the cramping of your womb continue?"

"It seems to have stopped."

"That happens to the animals when they're frightened. I was watching you all day. You seemed to be in the early part of childbirth. Let's clean your wounds."

She nodded.

A large jar of water stood in the corner. Each morning one of their kind siblings filled it after they emerged from their home, since they couldn't leave the city. Cain dumped some of this water into a basin. He would cleanse the wound using some of the soft downy seeds they had gathered for the baby. She started to rise.

"Stay where you are. It will be easier to clean your neck if you're lying down."

Carefully, he trickled water over the wound, catching the excess with the down. With this damp fluff, he dabbed the dried blood. Several times, he drizzled clean water over the wound, cleansing it. This rinsing process washed the blood and clay from his hands. He wiped his beard as well. He had buried his chin in the clay to be able to see her.

With beautiful gray eyes fixed on his face, she lay motionless, allowing him to minister comfort. As he worked, he felt her adoring eyes gazing at him.

Smiling at her, he retrieved the small jar of paste made from bdellium sap and pressed olive oil. They had made this recently, like their mother always did; but they hadn't needed it yet. Taking a small amount, he smoothed it along the wound, careful not to cause further injury.

"I still can't believe you're alive and the baby is unharmed," she whispered.

With tender eyes, he glanced at her. "I'm alive." He smiled. "Now, I want to wash you."

She couldn't bring forth the child in this state of heightened anxiety. He needed to calm her.

After helping her to stand, he removed her bloody clothing, discovering another wound. Attempting to soothe her with his touch, he bathed her, using care around this additional injury.

"Talk to me," he urged. This would ease her mind.

Tears welled up in her eyes. "It's too awful."

"Tell me."

"Since everyone arrived, I've been dreading your death. I didn't think you'd have to offer your life for me." She buried her face against his chest. He kissed the top of her head. "I should have stayed in the city. I shouldn't have gone out with Yonas."

"Why do you say that? Did you feel something was wrong?"

"Yes, but I ignored it. I thought it was just fear of being outside the city after so long."

"I felt the same thing," he said, "but I pushed my fear away."

"Yahweh warned us, and we didn't listen."

"Our God, please forgive us for not heeding Your voice. Thank You for sparing us."

Seemingly taken with Yahweh's mercy, she was silent. Waiting, Cain watched her. Soon she spoke of the horrifying confrontation. He comforted her. At his urging she talked through each terror. Telling the tale would put it behind her. At last, she reached the conclusion.

"It's over," Cain said. "We're alive. All is well. Don't allow the memories to fill your mind. You told it all to me; now put it out of your mind. Do you want me to sing to you?"

She nodded emphatically.

Cradling her in his arms, he wrapped her in the leather coverlet. She snuggled into the curve of his body. Singing softly, he caressed her pregnant abdomen. Finally, she slept.

Rolling away, he stripped to his loincloth and padded out into dusky nightfall. He had to prepare. Opening the gate, he discovered food and a jar of water; he carried these in. Hastily, he ate. He stoked the fire, checking if they had plenty of firewood. They did. He scrubbed the blood from their clothing and spread it out to dry.

Finally, he gathered the birthing items: their sharpest knife, hemp to tie the cord, herbs for drying it, and the tiny lamp with the precious olive oil. They would need this if the baby was born in the night. When he had everything, he carried it in, moving silently. Tiptoeing into the cave, he found the herbs that would ease Lilith's pain if the birth was difficult. He positioned everything near the bed.

Then he curled up on the warm stone floor, determined to catch some sleep. He didn't want to wake her by crawling across the crackling grass bedding. With no idea how long she would sleep, or what would be required when she awakened, he needed to rest while he could.

****

The moon shone through the ceiling when Lilith gasped and moaned in her sleep. Cain bolted up. High in the sky the moon sailed, and the stone floor cooled his skin. It had to be near the middle of the night. Quietly he rose, stretching his back and rubbing the sore place from the odd position he'd slept in. He passed noiselessly out to the enclosure, added a log to the embers, and pushed one of the clay jars near the fire to warm the water. Then he returned to watch her.

Periodically, Lilith moaned in her sleep, turning as if she were uncomfortable. Then she became still and slept soundly again. This happened several times. Her labor seemed to have begun anew. Certain she would awaken him when it became painful enough to require his assistance, he propped himself against the wall and closed his eyes. Perhaps he could sleep.

****

The sound of her cry startled him. Cain jerked awake and crawled across to the bed. Bleary-eyed, he could barely detect her by the light of the moon—it was much lower in the sky now. Her skin flashed pale. Moaning, she was on her hands and knees, rocking back and forth. Uncertain what she needed from him, he caressed her head. Soon she sat back on her heels.

"I was trying not to wake you," she said. "I'm sorry I cried out."

"Dearest, I was sitting there so I could help you."

"I know, but I wanted you to get some sleep."

He kissed her forehead. "Thank you. How are you?"

"First babies take a long time. But the pain is already more than I can bear. I didn't mean to cry out. My back hurts."

"Let me rub it." He applied pressure low on her back.

"Ah, that's perfect. Press harder. Oh!"

The groan seemed to be punched out of her mouth by her body. Moaning through her teeth, she rocked, crying out about halfway through. Cain's stomach clenched. Seeing her in travail was more difficult than he'd expected.

When the pain ended, she stayed there. "Can you press even harder?"

"I was afraid I'd hurt you. Why are you rocking like that?"

"I don't know. It seems to ease what's going on inside me. It makes the pain bearable."

"When I helped Abel with the lambing, the ewes always knew the best position for giving birth. You're probably doing the same."

"Cain, I'm afraid. This reminds me of Ariel's first birthing. The baby emerged faceup. The delivery was difficult, the pain excruciating. Akiva wore himself out kneading her lower back with his fist. She bled and screamed most of the night. Her recovery was slow."

Hearing this terrified Cain.

"Mother says your back hurts more if the baby isn't facedown."

Cain didn't like the sound of this. Maybe he should call out for one of their sisters. He begged God to be merciful, to ease her pain. He hadn't expected this. Yes, the oxen lowed and the sheep bleated piteously. He'd heard their mother crying. But this was his beloved wife.

They spent the remainder of the night attempting to bring forth their child. Lilith suffered and wept; he rubbed her back until he thought he could rub no longer. Though she apologized each time, she sometimes screamed with pain. She refused to allow him to call for their sisters.

Gradually, she quit communicating, becoming totally absorbed with her internal sensations. Between the labor pains, she collapsed against him, immediately falling asleep. Cain reacted to her moods and sounds and cries, trying to help her, feeling as if he failed. It was like a dance.

As early morning light filtered into the room, he suggested she rise and walk, hoping it might improve the situation. As he helped her up, something happened. She clutched her lower abdomen and stared into his eyes as if she saw right through him.

Lips pursed, she gaped at her belly, astounded. Then she squatted, beginning to push and strain, crying out with each effort. This startled him. He had thought they were far from the birth, yet here she was bearing down. He wasn't sure what to do.

She gasped for breath. "Cain! The baby's coming!"

He dropped to the floor, primed to catch the new infant. Lily squatted between his legs.

When the pain ended, she eased herself onto the floor, her knees drawn up, resting. Finally, she focused on his face. "When I stood, the baby turned. It shouldn't take long now."

"Is this where you want me?"

"Yes, I can hug you. It feels good to push; it's a relief." She sighed.

Brushing her hair back, he noticed her dry lips and grabbed the water jar. When he put it to her lips, she gulped it down. Then something seized within her, and she shoved the jar away.

"Pull me up!"

Letting lose a guttural scream with each effort, she bore down. Closing his eyes, he concentrated on what he felt with his hands. Their baby! The infant's head eased into his palms a little more with each push. When the pain weakened, she remained squatting before him.

"I can't move." She draped her arms around his neck. "I'm just going to lean against you."

Engrossed in her work, she still travailed; but he had touched their child!

"He's coming, Lilith! The baby has hair. His head retreats between your pushes."

"How much can you feel?"

Grinning, he held up his hand to show her. She twisted her head to peek.

"Good. He'll be out soon." She exhaled slowly. "Thank God."

Pressing down his excitement, he kissed her head. "Rest."

She complied, laying her cheek against his neck. But soon, Lilith rocked onto her heels, seized her knees, and bore down again. Several times they repeated this pushing and this resting, and then, at last, the little one's head slid out entirely into Cain's waiting hands. He felt the tiny face. The half-born infant gasped and sputtered. Quickly, before Cain even had time to feel for the cord, the baby's head turned, and its body slithered out.

Lilith sat back. Smiling widely, Cain held the newborn up to her. It was a man-child.

Examining his miniscule perfection, they gazed at him. His knees were drawn up tight against his body. He grimaced and frowned. Cain thought his heart would burst with the love that washed over him. He saw the same look on Lilith's face. It was a miracle! Was it possible to love another person this much? It was different than the love he felt for her. This was a united love, a bond of passionate protectiveness, such camaraderie of adoration and joy!

Carefully, Lilith lifted the wet, squirming baby from his cupped hands. When the infant touched her warm skin, he searched with open mouth. Scooting closer, Cain engulfed them both in an embrace as Lilith moved the baby's mouth to her breast. Their son latched on and began to suckle, staring up at his mother with dark infant eyes.

His head was covered with thick black hair. Lilith bent to kiss his little head then she gazed at their son. After regarding him for a while, she beamed at Cain, adoration for them both shining out of her eyes. Cain didn't know if he could hold this much love in his heart! He leaned his head against hers, looking down at their boy, drawing near the two people he loved most on the earth.

"Thank You, Yahweh," he whispered. "Thank You for this

entirely undeserved gift. You've given me a wife I adore and a beautiful son. You're so good to me! I don't deserve Your love."

Tears ran down his face. He should be dead, but instead here he was, the father of an infant son, holding the woman he had always loved. He couldn't comprehend it.

Lilith nuzzled her cheek against his then turned to kiss him.

"Thank you for a fine son," he whispered against her face.

Gently, she smiled back in reply. Then, overcome with love, both of them studied their baby, laughing softly together at each adorable thing he did, his little sounds, his greedy assault on Lilith's breast, his steady gaze into their eyes. They were entranced.

"What's his name, beloved?" Lilith asked.

"Enoch—the one who follows, the firstborn's firstborn, the initiator. He begins our family."

"Enoch," she whispered, gazing into the baby's dark eyes, "I love you." Then she looked back up at Cain. "Will he be the one to crush the serpent's head?"

"It will take a perfect man; only time will tell."

****

After Cain had cleaned their room, he refilled the bedframe with the fresh dried grass they had stored in the cave. Then he tucked Lilith back into bed with Enoch. She looked weary.

As Enoch's eyes blinked and slowly closed, so did Lilith's. At last both slept soundly. Cain watched them as they relaxed together, growing sleepier by the moment. He adored them; he couldn't take his eyes off them. He felt completely contented.

Thank you, kind and merciful God!

Realizing he was exhausted as well, he slid into bed beside Lilith, enfolding them both, cradling them under his arm. Soon all three slept.

CHAPTER 37

THE FULL FORCE OF THE sun at its zenith woke Cain, shining into his eyes. Carefully, he stood and quietly pulled the reed matting back across the ceiling, dimming the room. Lilith still slept, as did little Enoch, breathing rapid and uneven baby breaths, eyelids fluttering. Perhaps he dreamt of being born. Keeping his eyes on them, Cain dressed. They looked beautiful!

Silently, he slipped out of the peaceful room and left the house, gathering jars that needed to be refilled and empty bags to bring back food. He wanted to announce his firstborn son's birth.

As he headed toward the gate, he spied Danika and Koren by their doorway, leaning against the cliff wall eating their meal. They both smiled at him. Lest their voices should carry and wake Lilith and the baby, Cain walked toward them before speaking in hushed tones.

"We have a son—Enoch."

"Thanks be to God!" they both whispered. Then they turned to smile at each other because they'd said exactly the same thing. Danika giggled.

"We heard Lilith's screams," Koren said. "It sounded grim."

"We prayed for you both during the night," Danika added.

"It was painful for Lilith. Apparently, the baby was positioned badly—Lilith thought perhaps faceup, rather than facedown. Early this morning, he turned. Then the birth came quickly."

"Are they sleeping?" Danika asked.

"Yes. I just woke. I'm going for food and water. Koren, thank you for saving my wife and son. I'll always be grateful to you."

"You would've done the same. You laid down your life for her."

"Still, you're a good brother to me to do what you did."

"God helped me—it was the right choice. Do you need help hauling water?"

"Yes. I need to get enough to bathe Lilith. Can you show me what part of the brook is being used for bathing? I haven't been outside to wash since everyone arrived about three months ago. I want to immerse myself in the brook—it will be a blessing!"

Koren rose to help Cain.

"I'll prepare some food and sit it by your hearth," Danika said.

Cain thanked her; then he and Koren headed for the city gate, pausing at each house or workspace to announce Enoch's safe delivery. Cain received hearty congratulations and prayers of God's blessing. Though the birth had been difficult, he assured them Lilith was fine. During the night, her cries had echoed off the canyon walls, heard by all.

It was agreed that in the evening they would meet to discuss what to do about Shafir and Joda, who were bound in the back room of the unmarried men's house. Efrat lay, barely alive, in Azriel's home, being cared for by Elkana.

When Cain arrived at Azriel's home, he stepped in to observe Efrat. Cain didn't expect him to survive; his head wound was severe. Azriel stepped outside with him.

"I'm grieved my action is going to take Efrat's life," Azriel said, "but I saw no other option to save your life and Lilith's and the baby's. I wasn't trying to hit his head."

"I understand, brother. You didn't kill him in anger; you were acting to defend."

"Still, it's grievous."

Cain nodded. More than anyone else, he knew this to be true.

Koren and Cain left the city and waded across the brook at the shallow place. They went upstream and around the bend, to the area now designated for bathing. Carefully, they examined where they believed Efrat, Shafir, and Joda must have crossed.

On the opposite side was an impossibly narrow ledge that ran along the base of the cliff, right above the surface of the water. The water ran deep there; but they could have pulled themselves out of the water and perched on the ledge, waiting until they could ease their way along it. From there, they could jump out near the pottery oven. This was surely what they had done.

Cain and Koren stripped and swam across to examine the ledge and the water's depth. The current was strong against the cliff as the water swept around the bend; it would have been a difficult feat to accomplish. Koren grasped the rock ledge and, with much effort, hoisted himself out; then, slowly and cautiously, he stood and edged toward the clay deposits by the oven.

"I'm sure this is how they did it," Koren said.

"Yes, we should have been more thorough in our defensive plans."

Koren dove back in, and they swam the short distance to the other side of the brook.

Being underwater again felt refreshing, but Cain wanted to hasten back to Lilith. After leaving the water, he grew impatient and slipped his garments onto his still damp body.

"I need to return, Koren. I miss my family. I could hardly take my eyes off them."

Koren smiled. "I hope Danika and I are parents before the year is out. Let me pat dry. I'll go with you to gather food. Akiva and Hesed showed me the crops from the Garden. They've enlarged the fields and replanted a bigger area."

Walking up the slope toward the field, Cain was gratified to check the garden with his own eyes. Everything flourished. The young fruit trees they had planted nearby looked healthy and strong. He inspected the areas that had been reseeded. He and Lilith had eaten this food during their three-month confinement; but he hadn't been able to behold how well the crops grew. It filled his heart with joy. His hands hadn't tainted the seeds. Lilith would be delighted with the vegetables that had ripened. He gathered her favorites. He smiled. All was well.

At the brook they refilled the water jars, and Koren helped Cain haul it all home. Quietly, they sat everything inside the enclosure near Danika's food offering on the hearth. As Koren departed, he patted Cain on the shoulder and winked.

Noiselessly, Cain entered the house and padded to the bedroom. As he drew nearer, Lilith's soft singing floated toward him. Now he hurried. Too much time had passed. Little Enoch nursed and slept once more. He wished he'd arrived sooner, while his son was still awake.

"Cain," Lilith said gently, smiling up at him as he entered.

"I've brought fresh water and food. I tried to move quickly, but everyone wanted to give their blessings and learn how you are—everyone knew your labor was difficult. I looked in on Efrat. Koren and I examined how they came around the cliff."

"Can we not talk about the attack?"

"Alright, let's focus on Enoch and taking care of you." He squatted to kiss her then nuzzled the baby's head, asleep at her breast. "It's nearly midafternoon. You must be famished."

"I am!"

"We gathered some of the Eden food. I'll bring it in to you."

Before serving the meal, he refilled the water jar in their bedroom so water would be handy for Lilith. Then he pushed the other jarful near to the fire, warming it for her bath. He prepared beets, greens, legumes, and other foods she enjoyed. Danika had made some bread, which he included on the woven grass platter as well.

Lilith smiled up at him when he carried it in. His heart filled with happiness.

While they ate, little Enoch slept on the bed between them, breathing rapid breaths and sighing as he dreamt. His little eyes often fluttered open and then closed again. The aroma of his new body wafted up from the bed. Cain inhaled Enoch's sweet fragrance and gazed at him. Caressing Enoch's delicate skin, he was overcome with happiness and gratitude.

"Lily, I'd like to name the city after Enoch. He's given me hope for the future—he's evidence of God's blessing. Do you think the others would mind?"

"It's a wonderful idea. You can suggest it and see what everyone says."

"They're all coming here tonight to discuss what to do with our brothers."

"Cain, I don't want to think about this."

"We'll talk about it out in the enclosure; but our voices might carry. If we shut the door at the front, you should be spared."

"I want to forget it and lie in here with my baby, enjoying peace and tranquility. I trust you to make the best decision."

"Everyone will want to see him."

"That would be wonderful. Just take everyone outside again to talk about it. Please, Cain."

"Of course. I want you to have whatever you need."

After they ate, Cain helped her to bathe then reapplied bdellium balm to her wounds. She slipped her garment over her head, because everyone would come in to see the baby. They exchanged the soiled down she sat upon for fresh; he tossed the soiled down into the fire.

Enoch woke again and Cain picked him up, happy to unswaddle the bindings that held the soft dried grass seeds against his body and exchange them for fresh ones. He re-wrapped Enoch in the woolen blanket and handed him across to Lilith. As the eldest brother in a large family, he had done these tasks countless times in his one hundred twenty-five years.

Testing whether they had constructed her garment adequately for nursing, Lilith pressed Enoch to her breast. It worked admirably. She smiled up at Cain then scooted down to sleep again. She looked weary. Now that the trauma of uncertainty was over, the assault conquered, him alive, and the baby delivered, she said she wanted to sleep for days. Overwhelmed with love and the desire to protect, Cain listened, catching the note of relief in her voice.

Sitting with his back against the wall, he watched them drift off to sleep, pondering what to do with the attackers who had threatened the lives of the people dearest to him. Part of him wanted to exact the very revenge they had sought. Yet Lilith and Enoch were unharmed. Part of him recognized God's mercy. He had actually taken Abel's life, yet God had spared his.

Cain spent the rest of the afternoon in prayer, keeping his eyes fixed on Lilith and Enoch as he talked to God. As the afternoon light began to fade, he felt he had the answer; but he wanted to discuss his views with the others.

Enoch stirred, whimpering slightly with each inhalation. Carefully, Cain slid him away from Lilith. Perhaps she could sleep. Grabbing more downy seeds, Cain took his son out to the front room to change the soiled down for fresh. After rewrapping Enoch, he carried him outside. Sitting against the stone wall of the house, he held Enoch before him, gazing into his dark eyes.

What did God have planned for his son? Would he be a humble man? Would he need to be broken down by his own failings as he had been? Would Enoch crush the serpent's head, or did he have another destiny?

As the two of them regarded each other seriously, Cain was so engrossed in his thoughts, prayers, and musings over Enoch, that he was startled when someone rapped at the gate.

"Cain!" His father's voice—what a surprise! Cain hadn't noted any commotion or sound of voices approaching his home. "Cain, may I enter?"

"Father! Wait a moment."

Cain cradled Enoch and drew back the wooden bolt. The gate swung open, revealing the familiar face. A spasm of love shook him—he had missed his father.

****

There beamed the familiar face of Adam's oldest son, kinder now, wisdom chiseled by pain into his handsome features, purpled shadows of sleeplessness under his blue eyes—hooded in shadow in the afternoon light. A tiny newborn with a full head of black hair snuggled against his shoulder. Smiling widely at Cain, Adam threw his arms around both of them.

"Son, I'm relieved to find you alive! Overjoyed to find you're the father of a son! The others tell me his name is Enoch."

"I'm glad to see your face, Father."

"After sending Koren I had no peace. We came to see if you were attacked. We suspected you would be. Niran, Lavan, and Aviv are with me. We didn't know if you'd need help. I've heard what's happened. How's Lilith?"

"It was horrible for her, but she doesn't want to talk about it. She just wants Enoch and peace. Her labor was difficult, partly because of the baby's positioning, partly because of the fear. She was in early labor when they seized her."

"And how are you, son?"

"Father, I understand their desire for revenge. I don't know how you've forgiven me for taking the life of your son. I'd kill anyone with my bare hands who tried to take the life of mine. But I'm a murderer myself; I must show them mercy."

"I thought you'd feel that way. We'll discuss this together. Now, let me see my grandson."

Enoch was now awake. His eyes were dark, impossible to tell what color they would be. Adam remembered how surprised he and Eve had been by Cain's blue eyes, since theirs were dark. Could eyes be the color of the sky, they had wondered? The baby rooted against Cain's chest, searching for his next meal.

Cain laughed softly. "I have nothing for you, my son."

Tenderly, he kissed Enoch's little head before handing the baby across to him. Adam was pleased that his son was a warm and affectionate father—more evidence of the inner healing. He took Enoch and gazed into his eyes, feeling the familiar pull of protective love and devotion that each new baby brought. He looked up at Cain and smiled.

"A fine son! I see you in him."

"Unfortunately."

"No, son. It will be fortunate for Enoch if he's like you. He'll be a blessing to all those around him."

Their eyes locked. Adam meant this with all his heart; Cain was now a better man than he had ever been. With his free arm, he pulled his son toward him, embracing him tightly. Adam held Cain on one side and Enoch on the other, overwhelmed with gratefulness to God.

"Thank you, Father," Cain said. "I regret what it took to humble me."

"God is merciful to us. He knows we're weak."

"Yes."

"Cain," Lilith called from inside. "Beloved, who has come? Where's Enoch?"

Cain turned away and wiped his eyes, beckoning for Adam to follow him into the house. Little Enoch was, by now, whimpering with hunger.

"Dearest, it's our father. He's come to make sure we're alright."

In the fading light, Adam admired the work Cain had done on the house, carefully holding his now wailing grandson. When they entered the bedroom, he knelt to embrace his daughter with his free arm then handed her the crying newborn.

"He's all changed and dry, dearest," Cain informed her.

Lilith brought Enoch to her breast. After calming down enough to realize where he was, he greedily latched on, nursing contentedly and soon falling asleep. Adam chuckled—how often he had witnessed this scene. Glowing with new motherhood, Lilith smiled up at them. The bittersweet longing he always felt for Eve pressed on his heart—he missed this intimacy with his wife, the repetition of this very event. Would they ever reconcile?

Leaving him to converse with Lilith, Cain hurried back out to gather some food for them, mentioning over his shoulder that the others would be arriving after the evening meal. Adam was careful not to discuss the tragic events of the previous day as he talked quietly with his daughter. He only imparted news of the welfare of each person at home. He did mention that three of her brothers had accompanied him.

Soon Cain returned with a platter of food and a small oil lamp, lit and shedding soft light. They all sat on the bed and ate, catching up on family news.

Adam was glad he'd made the trip.

****

As Cain finished eating with Father and Lilith, many voices approached the house. Enoch had finished nursing, so Cain lifted his son from Lilith's arms to change and rewrap him. Everyone would want to pass the baby around. As he cared for the baby, Lilith smoothed her hair and laced up her garment. Then Cain handed Enoch back, leaving her sitting, beautifully arranged in bed with their new baby, eager to greet their siblings.

He hurried to the gate. Everyone had come bearing small gifts and their own softly glowing lamps. Cain welcomed them. Soon forty-two family members gathered in their bedroom, beholding the newest addition and offering their blessings. The brothers congratulated them; the sisters sympathized with Lilith's difficult labor. All offered love and kindness. Welcoming aunts and uncles passed Enoch around, holding him down for cousins to kiss. Everyone admired him. He slept through it all, completely relaxed, his delicate eyelids fluttering as he dreamt.

Cain kept an eye on Lilith. When she looked fatigued, he suggested everyone move out to the enclosure. He took Enoch from the last adoring aunt and handed him back to Lily, bending to kiss her head as he did. Then he turned, arms spread wide, attempting to gently and graciously herd his father, his siblings, and all their children out through the door.

Soon only a few of the sisters lingered with Lilith, including Nissa and Ariel. From Lilith's expression, Cain could tell she welcomed this chance to talk about her difficult labor. They were already engrossed in the details. Storing up knowledge for future reference, Danika sat silently against the wall, somberly listening.

Once everyone else was outside, Cain shut the door—now for the conference.

The other married sisters who hadn't stayed with Lilith took all the children to their homes to put them to bed. The rest remained. They had important decisions to make.

Azriel informed them that Efrat had died immediately before they came. He and Elkana had washed and prepared his body. Azriel wept as he told them. Though he had dropped the rock on Efrat to defend Cain, he had still taken his life. He was grieved.

Cain and their father embraced him. Cain determined to spend much time with Azriel in the coming weeks and months, comforting and consoling him. They all lamented the fact that Efrat's desire for revenge had led to this result. Father was especially broken—he had lost another son.

They decided to bury Efrat in the morning. Cain expressed what he had earlier told their father: Though his family had been attacked, he felt he had to offer mercy. Regardless of their intentions, no one other than Efrat had died. Cain urged banishment as the consequence. He explained how his time of wandering had been used by God to bring him to repentance and humility. After Efrat's burial, Cain felt Joda and Shafir should be sent away.

Some raised their voices in opposition. All their objections began with "What if," but Cain reminded them that the things they suggested had not happened. God had prevented it. Others expressed fear for their safety now. Cain reminded them that their lives were always in God's hands. They could do their best to protect and defend, but the outcome depended upon Yahweh.

By the end of the discussion, all were in agreement.

CHAPTER 38

SATAN HAD TRIUMPHED AT LAST. He had entrapped one. When he had witnessed Abel's welcome into Heaven, he had wondered if he was only able to wound and maim the humans during their earthly lives. Now Satan knew their deaths could bring everlasting separation from God.

Efrat had resisted his conscience and God's Spirit, and here he was, writhing in the heat, his spirit dying eternally. Wounding them on earth was delightful. But this! This was far more destructive!

"Come!" he ordered his demonic ranks. "Assemble!"

Quickly they all appeared.

In this dark and desolate place, devoid of all beauty and all sensory stimulation, Efrat's spirit decayed, his mind reeled, and his hope extinguished. The demons surrounded him, jeering as they mocked. Savoring their triumph, they ignored this example of their own coming doom.

"You're never getting out of here," Azazel hissed.

"You'll suffer agony forever!" Samyaza taunted. "It will never end."

Efrat shuddered from each verbal barrage, cringing as he flinched away.

As Satan regarded Efrat's tears, confusion, and pain, he

laughed at the irony. Though Efrat had been one of Abel's young disciples, he hadn't lived like Abel. He had died with a hard heart—angry at God's injustice regarding Cain, judging God, intent on murder.

Doubting God's promise, he had been far from him, his heart unbelieving and faithless.

Efrat did not love Yahweh with all his heart. He never had. He loved himself.

These were the necessary ingredients, the missing clues to the enigma. Now Satan knew. Though Yahweh kept other significant facts hidden from him, Satan could now devise strategies:

Snare them in their own lusts, thus destroying their lives and their hopes.

Lie about God, so they disregard His promise and doubt His love, mercy, and justice.

Urge them to distrust God, so they take matters into their own hands.

Remind them constantly of their failures and inadequacies.

Assure them of their hopeless and worthless condition.

Satan was an excellent liar. This would be easy. Believing his lies, they would forget they were created in God's image. They would not comprehend that God cherished them. They would not believe this ridiculous head-crushing promise with its eternal saving offer of hope.

Apparently, this would be effective with some, but not all. Which ones was a matter of speculation. It was impossible to discern. If Satan took aim at each human, he could damage all and keep hold of some. If they died in this condition, some would suffer the same fate as he.

Head uncrushed, Satan determined to corrupt and destroy as many as possible. He was only beginning to fashion his designs for their wounding. The more sin in which they entangled themselves, surely, the more he could grasp.

He had to bruise the coming seed before it crushed him.

CHAPTER 39

EARLY THE NEXT DAY ADAM'S family gathered to bury Efrat's body. Lilith remained in bed with little Enoch, recovering as she was from childbirth. The younger boys had dug the grave at the first light of dawn. Somberly, Azriel, Akiva, Koren, and Cain carried Efrat's stiffened body on a leather covering held taut between them. Adam followed, mourning the death of another son.

Shafir and Joda followed behind him. They hadn't been able to look him in the eye when he had gone to speak to them. He knew they were frightened. They didn't know what to expect. Adam felt torn with emotion. He loved every one of them. They were his children; yet their sinful natures now provoked them to turn on one another.

No matter what happened, it hurt him. It hurt Eve too. He wished she were here.

There lay the fresh gaping hole in the red earth. They approached it, and Efrat was lowered in gently. All gathered around, solemnly peering down at his pale and lifeless body. Adam stepped up to the burial place, remembering the day they had uncovered Abel's body.

Falling to his knees, Adam wept. "Oh God! My heart is broken. I've lost another son. The sin I committed when I disobeyed you has wrecked it all. It has taken another one of my family, another one I love. Please forgive me. Have mercy on us all. We will all die. We have no hope but You. Please give us faith in Your promise. Give us hope. We commit Efrat's body to the ground, his spirit into Your hands. He is dust, and to dust he shall return, as we all will one day."

Adam scraped the soft red earth into the hole, weeping as he shoved it onto his son's body. He held up his hand to stop anyone from helping him with the task. He felt his own personal responsibility for yet another death, for another child returning to dust. Because he had disobeyed Yahweh, sin and death had come into the world, destroying them all.

****

As Cain listened to his father's words and observed him burying Efrat's body, he was overcome with grief. He remembered Abel's body when he had attempted to hide it. Efrat looked like Abel had—bluish lips and damaged head; but Efrat's body was stiffened and cool to the touch. It had been difficult for them to pick him up. It felt odd and unnatural.

Azriel had wept the entire time. Their father had said this was how Abel's body had looked when they found him. Horrifying! How could he have borne this if it had been his own son, his own Enoch grown to manhood, now dead? It seemed impossible. The agony crushed his chest.

And yet, his own father had lost two sons now, both in ways associated with his sin. Of course, his father said that he himself was ultimately responsible—he had disobeyed God. As a result, they were now all deformed by sin. It tore and ravaged them daily.

They would all die one day. Sin and death now reigned.

It seemed that once sin was let loose, once it had attacked and one had succumbed, it had the power to multiply and destroy. Sin had been crouching at the door, and Cain had invited it in and embraced it. Sin had had its way with him; Cain had given way.

His brokenness and repentance had brought healing in his own life, but his actions had multiplied sin on the earth. Now another one was dead, his own wife and child had been endangered, and Joda and Shafir stood before them ready to receive their punishment.

If ever there was a time to crush the serpent, wouldn't it be now? Now. Before more died. Before sin touched—*Oh God! Protect them!*—before sin touched his own little family again. How could he bear them ever to be hurt or taken from him?

He thought of Lilith tucked safely into their bed with little Enoch at her breast.

Cain felt fiercely protective and completely powerless.

In spite of his best efforts, they could be harmed. Their lives were not their own. He almost gave way to despair. Yet Cain reminded himself:

God is God. He loves and cares for us. Our lives are His. He knows His plan.

Yahweh had made the plan for their redemption even before Cain's parents had sinned. He would bring about the crushing of the serpent in His own time and in His own way.

Squeezing his eyes shut, Cain bowed his head, silently begging Yahweh for mercy, for His deliverance, for sin and death to end, for even Enoch or one of the others to be the one to crush the serpent's head. Mutely pleading with the Creator, Cain begged.

Then Cain yielded. Since God had already ordained the plan, He had surely ordained the timing. They would see God's deliverance at the appropriate time.

Efrat now buried, Father began to speak again. Cain stood beside him with his eyes clenched shut, listening to the verdict, tears slowly running down his cheeks.

"Shafir and Joda, the decision has been made concerning your punishment for the attack you made upon your brother and his family. Our family received God's direction not to take Cain's life. Yahweh Himself has shown Cain mercy. Cain has argued for you to be shown that same mercy. He has convinced us not to take your lives, urging us to banish you, because during his banishment, God made him into a new man. Cain wants this for you."

There was a long silence.

Cain opened his eyes. They all looked at him. Shamed by his clemency, Shafir and Joda peeked up at him from under their brows, heads ducked in embarrassment.

Cain needed to speak.

Grieved, he looked sadly at the two brothers before him. His heart ached for them. Terror showed clearly on their countenances. In spite of what their father had just said, they knew the decision was his, and they were afraid. They awaited his verdict.

Were they going into the grave like Efrat, their eyes asked? *Is this the moment we die?*

Cain spoke, his eyes on them, yearning for them to see the error of their ways.

"I forgive you. Go out and wander. Seek God through repentance. You will find him. When you've repented, come back and live in our city with us. God directed me to build it as a city of refuge for those suffering from the consequences of their own sins. Yahweh is merciful. He's willing to forgive one who is broken and contrite. I should know. I actually succeeded in killing the brother I attacked, yet God has shown me mercy and kindness. We all sin every day. Our only hope is our anticipation of the One who will put an end to all this suffering, death, and brokenness, the One who will crush the serpent's head. We all long for the day He comes."

Cain stepped over to his two brothers and embraced first Shafir and then Joda. Then he turned and walked through the gathered crowd of brothers and sisters and their families and headed down the hill to cross the brook.

Cain needed to go home.

His murder of Abel and its consequences would follow him all his days. As the founder of this city of refuge, he would have to deal with this type of conflict the rest of his life. It would always remind him of his own fallen state and how he had taken Abel's life.

It would be good for his soul to be humbled all his days—he would never forget his dependence on Yahweh. God's plan for him to build the city was not only for the benefit of others, but for his own welfare.

Cain crossed the brook and the flat area of land between the water and the wall. He burst through the gate and broke into a run, anxious to be within the four walls of his own home, holding his own dear family in his arms and gazing at their faces. He was no different than these men—his own brothers, who had attacked his family—and he knew it.

As Cain ran, he fixed his eyes on his own home and thanked God for His mercy.

ACKNOWLEDGMENTS

Dan and Elaine Viergever, for a lifetime of support. Thank you for allowing me to read novels even into the wee hours when I was a little girl. It's a blessing to have literary, education-minded parents. You've been my cheerleaders.

Jackie Garrett, for serving as my first editor. Thank you for all your encouragement as I've sought to get this story published. Your support made an enormous difference.

Janice Burton, for believing in me. You were the first publishing-industry writer, a "real" writer, to welcome me into the club. You called me an author. It meant the world to me!

Patricia Durgin, for preparing me and helping me to clarify and refine my message. I couldn't have gotten to this point without you!

REFUGE STUDY GUIDE

This study guide is designed to help you think about the Biblical truths embedded in *Refuge*. This is a novel that illustrates how spiritual battles are fought, lost, and won. It reveals Satan's tactics for attacking human beings. It also shows God's mercy for even our blatant sins.

Each study section has questions and scriptural passages for you to consider. This guide can be used for group discussion or for your own contemplation. Below are two ideas for your use.

How to use this study guide:

Work through each meditation and discussion section at your own pace. Two options:

When a portion of the story sparks your curiosity or prompts you to seek deeper answers, focus on the topics that address your questions. Pick and choose the areas where you want to go deeper.

The second option: Work straight through the guide as you march through the story. The guide follows the story, allowing you to pause and reflect before moving on.

Look for the obvious as you answer the questions. Each question aims at simple observation. What do you see? The answer is right there in the written text.

I hope this guide enriches the story by highlighting God's desire to restore and forgive. God's loving purpose is eternal. Satan desires to ensnare human beings in sin. His tactics remain the same, though they adjust to our culture and our time. Yet God's love trumps Satan's efforts.

Refuge **Study Guide Topics**

Satan's limitations

Jesus and Satan

Why do we need someone to destroy Satan?

Who was the Seed? How did God shape His lineage?

The Genesis 3:15 promise fulfilled in Christ

Marriage

What does it mean to become *one flesh*?

Cain's character and his mentions in the Bible

Lilith: the facts

Lilith: the legends

Lilith: Why use a name of myth and legend?

What do we know about Abel?

Cain's repentance

What was the mark?

What was the purpose of the city?

List of sources

Discussion Guide and Meditations about Satan:

First step: Reflection

The conversation between Satan and God in Chapter Five of *Refuge* is based on the book of Job, Chapters One and Two. This provides us with a Biblical model of Satan's limitations.

For now, simply think about these questions:
• How much power does Satan have?
• What actions can he take to impact the lives of people?
• How is he limited or constrained?
• How do we prepare for Satan's attacks and respond to them?
• What is the undergirding truth about God's intentions toward us?

Read and contemplate the following passages:
Job 1 and 2

1 Peter 5:6-11
Ephesians 6:10-18
Romans 8:26-39
Pause to think about this. The next step digs deeper.

Second step: Reflecting on Satan. Digging in.

What particularly does Satan do to gather information about specific people? In Chapter Two of *Refuge* we find Satan on a fact-finding mission, attempting to glean information about Cain. Throughout the story, we then see Satan adjusting his data and tactics. Take your time to work through these questions. They are demonstrated throughout *Refuge*.

Examine these verses to find the Biblical model. What do you think?

- In 1 Peter 5:8-9, Ephesians 6:11-12, Job 1:6-7, and Job 2:1-2, what does Satan do? Is he everywhere at once (omnipresent)? Or does he travel from place to place?
- In Job 1:8 and 2:3, who draws attention to Job in the conversation between God and Satan? Has Job done anything wrong, according to God? What kind of man does God Himself say Job is?
- Though we never learn God's reason for testing Job, his refining uncovered areas where he needed to grow in humility and trust. God had a good purpose in mind. Read Romans 8:26-39. What is God's purpose in any trial or test He allows to touch a believer's life? Can any type of trial separate us from the love of God?
- What do we see about Satan's desire to tempt us? In contrast to God's purpose to strengthen us through our trials, what is Satan's goal? What do Job 1:9-22, Job 2:4-7, Ephesians 6:10-18, 1 Timothy 4:1-5, and 1 Peter 5:8-9 tell us about Satan's aims?
- In Job 1:9-11 and 2:4-6, had Satan already spied out Job's weaknesses before God spoke about him? How do you know? What is the evidence?

- In 1 Peter 5:8-11, 1 Timothy 4:1-5, and Ephesians 6:10-18, how does Satan ascertain our weak spots? Does he already know them from previous attempts?
- How could Satan attack Job? Whose permission was required, according to Job 1:12 and Job 2:6? Who established the perimeters? How does this mesh with Romans 8:26-39?
- Consider the harm that befell Job and his family. Satan will be held accountable for harming them, even though it was allowed by God for a good purpose (see Revelation 20:10). In Job 1:13-19 and 2:7-10, what tools did Satan use to attack Job?
- How did Job respond in Job 1:20-22 and Job 2:10? For a deeper study, read Job's responses to his so-called friends' attempts to blame and/or comfort him. Their words became the next assault on Job, but God used the conversation to accomplish good.
- Based on the book of Job and on 1 Peter 5:6-11, 1 Timothy 4:3b-5 (more instructions are given throughout the letter), Ephesians 6:10-18, and 1 John 3:9-10, how should we respond to spiritual attack?
- To discover the outcome, read Job 38-42 for the end of Job's conversation with God.
- Why did Jesus, the Son of God, come into the world, according to 1 John 3:8?

Want more information?

Online source: *A Collision of Worlds: Evil Spirits Then and Now*. C. S. Lewis Institute:
http://www.cslewisinstitute.org/A_Collision_of_Worlds_page1
Bible Study: *LORD, Is It Warfare? Teach Me to Stand*, Kay Arthur, WaterBrook Press.

Discussion Guide and Meditations: Jesus and Satan

Read and contemplate these passages spoken by Jesus. Take your time.

Jesus's words and interactions about Satan:

Jesus's temptation by Satan: Matthew 4:1-11; Mark 1:12-13; Luke 4:1-13

Beelzebub (a name for Satan): Matthew 12:22-32; Mark 3:20-30; Luke 11:14-28

The sower: Matthew 13:1-23; Mark 4:1-20; Luke 8:4-15

The weeds: Matthew 13:24-30, 36-43

The sheep and the goats: Matthew 25:31-46

Jesus predicts His death: Matthew 16:21-23; Mark 8:31-33

Jesus's authority and what He allowed Satan to do: John 8:39-47; Luke 10:17-24; John 6:67-71; Luke 22:3-6, 31-34; John 13:1-30

Jesus heals a woman: Luke 13:10-17

What do you think?

- What key teachings contained in more than one of the gospels provide us with most of Jesus's words about Satan?
- What principles about Satan do we have straight from Jesus Christ—God in the flesh?
- How do Jesus's words guide our words and actions about Satan?
- What do we learn about Satan and how he works?
- How do these words help us to gain courage in the lifelong struggle against evil?

Meditations about the Seed—Jesus, the One who crushed the serpent's head: Why do we need Him?

First step: Reflection

What do you think? Take time to consider.

In the time period of *Refuge*, did Adam and Eve's family know who the serpent was?

Did they know who would crush Satan's head?

Read and contemplate these passages then answer the questions.

Genesis 3:1-19. The serpent is the embodiment of Satan. Notice the serpent's tactics. Review: Jesus told us of Satan's character as a liar in John 8:44. Read it again.

What is said about God's truthfulness in Hebrews 6:17-20 and Titus 1:1-3?

- Who can we believe, Satan or God?
- What did Satan try to get Adam and Eve to believe about God?
- In what ways does Satan continue to habitually insinuate or imply that God is a liar, when it is Satan himself who always lies?
- How does Satan still introduce these lies about God into hearts and minds when he tempts?
- How does Satan still tempt us to take matters into our own hands and to gain knowledge in a way that is contrary to what God desires for us?
- In what ways does Satan still try to get us to ignore our consciences and to determine what is right and what is wrong, contrary to our consciences and to God's words?

Read Genesis 3:8-24. What do we see about God's holiness, justice, and love?

- How do God's holiness and justice inspire worship? How does it relieve us that a holy God is just and will bring justice? How does it produce holy reverence and fear in us?

Read Exodus 34:4-7; Romans 1:18-20; 2:5-11.
- What is said about God's holiness, love, wrath, and justice?
- What about God's wrath and justice is a relief when we consider the evil and injustices in the world? What about God's wrath is terrifying when we consider our own failings?
- Why do we need someone to pay for our sins so we ourselves don't have to?

The next step digs deeper.

Second step of reflecting on the One: Why do we need him?

We will read and contemplate these passages:

Genesis 3:15. This is the promise that the Seed would triumph over Satan.

Romans 1:18-32. This shows how sin works and why we need Christ and the gospel.

Romans 3:10-20. This is the present reality in all our lives.

Romans 5:12-20. These are the effects of the actions of two men: Jesus Christ and Adam.

Revelation 12:7-12 and 20:7-10. Two passages that detail Satan's destruction and defeat.

What do you think?
- Read Genesis 3. When did God first promise Satan's destruction?
- Read Romans 5:12-20. When Adam (the "one man" who sinned) listened to Satan, disobeyed God, and ate the forbidden fruit, what was the result?
- How does that sin multiply within humanity? To what/ whom does God give us over? (Romans 1:18-32)

- Since sin has entered the world, in what state do we all find ourselves? (Romans 3:10-20)
- What did God promise to do about it? (Genesis 3:15)
- Read Romans 5:12-20 again. What resulted from Christ's death and resurrection?
- Read Revelation 12:7-12. Theologians differ over this event's timing. But, regardless of the timing, what happens to Satan ("the dragon" or "great serpent") in this passage? How is Christ victorious? Read Revelation 20:7-10. What is Satan's ultimate destination?
- How are we given salvation? (Romans 1:16-17) How must we live to be righteous?

Step Three: Digging deeper still.
Who crushed Satan's head?

Since before the beginning, God has overseen history. Adam and Eve's son Seth, who was born after Cain killed Abel, was chosen by God to be the progenitor of the family lineage through which God would bless the world with a Savior (Genesis 4:6; Luke 3:38). The Old Testament record focuses on Seth's family tree, tracing his descendants through Noah to Abraham, Isaac, Jacob (later renamed Israel), and Jacob's offspring through the generations. Abraham's family, the Jewish family, is the lineage of the Promised One, Jesus Christ.

God promised Abraham that the entire world would be blessed by His Seed, and that His spiritual descendants would be as vast as the stars (Genesis 12:1-3; 13:14-17; 15:4-6; 17:1-9; 21:1-7). God reaffirmed this covenant with Abraham's son Isaac and his grandson Jacob.

The book of Ruth, an Old Testament event in Jesus's lineage, held up Boaz as a model of the coming Seed, our Kinsman-Redeemer. In Jesus's lineage in Matthew 1:1-6, four women are included in what was usually an all-male list. Two are Gentiles (Rahab and Ruth, 1:5), and two are controversial (Tamar, 1:3, and the wife of Uriah, Bathsheba, 1:6). Additionally, Jesus's family tree was peopled with notorious sinners. In this way, God illustrated that the Seed was coming to redeem the sins of all kinds of people, regardless of gender, ethnicity, or sin history.

God promised Abraham's descendant King David that his offspring would reign forever (1 Samuel 16:1; 2 Samuel 7:8-17). All of the Old Testament points to God's love and mercy embodied in Jesus Christ the Redeemer and Coming King. With His sacrifice on the cross, Jesus fulfilled all the prophecies of His coming and blessed people from every nation. He destroyed the power of sin and death and brought all believers—Jews and Gentiles—back into God's family as in Eden. When He returns to reign, the restoration will be complete.

How are we made right with God through Jesus Christ?

• Read Genesis 15:1-6, Romans 4, and Hebrews 11:8-16.

Long after the flood and the tower of Babel, God appeared to Abraham (named Abram then). God led him to a new land and promised to bless him with a son who would father the lineage that would bless the world with a Savior. In these passages, why did God bless and fulfill His promise to Abraham, count him as righteous, and give him eternal life?

• Read Romans 1:16-17.

See the similarity between Romans 1:16-17 and Genesis 15:6. The message of the Old Testament and the New Testament is the same. Salvation has always been given as a result of faith in God's promise of the One who would defeat Satan—Jesus Christ.

Do you believe? Do you have faith in Jesus Christ as Savior?

• Read Job 19:25-27

Job was not in Christ's lineage. But his prophetic words in this Old Testament passage show that from ages past people knew in Whom to place their trust for redemption and salvation. On what future coming One did Job have his eyes fixed? On whom did he rely for eternal life?

• What do these passages and God's orchestration of human

history to bring a Savior into the world to redeem us tell us about God's love and eternal focused intentions?

The Genesis 3:15 promise fulfilled in Christ:

How did God fulfill His intention to redeem sinners and destroy Satan?

Read Matthew 1:1-16. This is the lineage of the Seed since Abraham. Read Galatians 3:5-14, 16. Notice the emphasis on faith and on the singular Seed or offspring—Jesus Christ.

Read John 1:1-34. Then answer the following questions.

- In John 1:1-18, what all is said about the Word—Jesus Christ? Whose Son is Jesus, the One and Only God, v. 14, 34? What is His task, v. 16-18, 29?

Read 2 Timothy 1:8-10
- What did our Savior Christ Jesus do? When was God's purpose to do this established?

Read Colossians 1:13-20 and consider these questions.
- When God rescues us from the dominion of darkness into Whose kingdom does He bring us?
- In Christ, what do we have, v. 14 and v. 20? How did He accomplish this?
- Look at verses 15-17. As the image of the invisible God, Who presided over creation and acted as Creator? Who is before all things? Who holds all things together?
- Read verses 18-20. Who is the head of the church? Who defeated death—the first to rise and never die again? How? What dwells in Christ?

Read Colossians 2:6-15
- By what are we taken captive, v. 8? On what do these empty delusions depend or rely?
- What dwells bodily in Christ, v. 9?
- Over what is Jesus head, v.10?
- What benefits does Christ's death on the cross give to you

by faith, v.11-14?
- How were the angelic powers and authorities disarmed or deprived of power, v. 15?

Read Romans 3:19-26 and consider this:
- Every person sins. All are in need of a Savior. We cannot earn our own redemption. That we are justified by His grace is a gift. How did God redeem us? How did Christ pay for our sins?

Read Romans 5:1-11
- How did God show love to us? At what time did Christ die—what was our condition?

Read Ephesians 1:3-14 and consider these questions in this order:
- Before the foundation of the world, Who chose people to be "in Christ" so we could be holy and blameless before Him, v. 3-4?
- Why did God predestine believers for adoption as His heirs (sons), v. 4-5? Through Whom was this accomplished, v. 5?
- According to God's purpose and glorious grace, His purpose was to bless us in Whom, v. 6?
- Through Whose blood are we redeemed and forgiven, v. 6-7?
- According to God's wisdom, insight, and purpose set forth in Christ, on whom does He lavish the riches of His grace as He restores in the fullness of time what was lost in Eden, v. 7-10?
- Having been predestined according to God's will, how do we come to salvation, v. 11-13?
- With Whom are believers sealed as a guarantee of our eternal inheritance, v. 13-14?

Consider God's eternal purpose to send a Redeemer and to restore the damage Satan provoked by tempting Adam and

Eve and then all of mankind. God's plan was in place before
time began. God's motive was love and compassion. Consider
the forethought and power of an omniscient and loving God
Who crafted history to bring this about, just so you and I could
become His.

Discussion Guide and Meditations about Marriage: God provided the model with Adam and Eve.

The first two chapters of Genesis tell the same story, but
Chapter Two gives more detail about the pinnacle events of Day
Six, the creation of humanity. Read the creation account in this
order:

Genesis 1:26-27
Genesis 2:5-23
Genesis 1:28-31
Moses's editorial comment: Genesis 2:24-25.

**What do you think? What principles can we see in
the Biblical model?**
- In bringing Eve to Adam and making her to be his wife,
  how did God create marriage?
- What vow and statement did Adam make to Eve?
- From this God-initiated model, what can we learn about
  the covenant of marriage, what two people comprise a God-
  ordained marriage, and how is marriage to take place?
- In *Refuge*, how did the characters attempt to follow this
  model? How should we?

What does Moses's editorial comment in Genesis 2:24
mean?

"According to the Bible marriage is a permanent, formal,
human relationship created by God between one man and one
woman. What Genesis 2:24 is telling us, among other things,
is that marriage is not just a man and a woman deciding to

be monogamous sexual partners. Instead, it is telling us that they made formal, legal promises to each other before God. Proverbs 2:17 describes this explicitly when, speaking of an unfaithful wife, it says that she 'has left the partner of her youth and ignored the covenant she made before God.' This is why a biblical definition of marriage calls marriage 'a formal human relationship.' Note that it is a 'formal human relationship.' That's important, too, because there are animals that mate for life, yet they are not married. Only humans were made in God's image and, as we saw, this is why humans have intelligence and free will. Although other animals may mate for life, they do not make formal legal relationships before God." [1]

Read the following passages about the marriage model:
Ephesians 5:22-33
Remember the Old Testament account on the book of Ruth.
Song of Solomon

What do you think?
- In marriage, what do we learn about the relationship between Christ and the church?
- What kind of experience does married love give us that models our relationship with the Creator of the universe, Christ Jesus?
- What type of language does married love provide that gives us vocabulary for the wooing and pursuing God does of our hearts?

Consider now the anthropological and theological implications:

"Secular anthropologists admit that marriage is universal in human societies, that it is different from monogamy (which they believe, based on their evolutionary assumptions, developed first, before marriage), and that it precedes recorded human

---

1   Brian Gordon Jones, Christian Faith & Modern Family (Brookpointe Ministries, 2013), pg. 2, 4.

history. However, they cannot explain these things. Why is it that marriage exists in every human society? Why, if some animals practice monogamy, would marriage be necessary for humans? Why did people make promises to each other in marriage before anyone started writing down human history and why do they keep doing that in every human culture? Secular scholars have no good answers to these questions. The Bible, however, tells us that marriage exists and is so universal because God created it. Again, Genesis 2:24 says, 'For this reason a man will leave his father and mother and be united to his wife, and they will become one flesh.' In Genesis 2:24, Moses gives us his conclusion to the story of the creation of Eve, and his conclusion is that marriage exists because God created humans. As the human author of Genesis, Moses is telling us where marriage originated and why it is such a dominant force in human societies. All human societies in every part of the world, in every historical time period, practice marriage. It transcends geographic, ethnic, racial, religious, and chronological boundaries. Why? Because God created it." [2]

- How does this evidence reinforce and prove God's creation of marriage?

---

[2]   Brian Gordon Jones, Christian Faith & Modern Family (Brookpointe Ministries, 2013), pg. 5.

Discussion: What does it mean to become *one flesh*?

God's purpose in creating marriage was for companionship, for the spread of godliness and stability, for populating the earth, and for subduing it. In creating Eve for Adam, giving them a blessing and instructions for living, and then mandating them to take dominion over the earth, God provided this model. In giving Adam a wife, rather than merely a friend, God created sex.

• The first sex occurred after the first vow. How does sex provide the "one-flesh" bond?
Read Genesis 2:24 again.
Read 1 Corinthians 6:15-20.
Read Christ's comments about Genesis 2:24 in Matthew 19:4-6.
• What are the reasons given for avoiding sex with someone who is not your spouse?
• What is the proper response to the temptation to immorality?
• When a married couple has sex, Who joins them together?

"When two people have sex, they become so closely joined emotionally and psychologically that they become united, almost as if they were one person. Sex seals the legal, covenant relationship of a husband and wife. It unites them mentally, emotionally, and spiritually in a way that no other human covenant can unite people. And this is why God created sex; he created a unique physical activity that would create a permanent psychological bond between them." [3]

---

3   Brian Gordon Jones, Christian Faith & Modern Family (Brookpointe Ministries, 2013), pg. 17.

Discussion Guide and Meditations about Cain:

Read and consider this narrative:

Genesis 4:1-17

This is the Biblical framework for *Refuge*. The fictional story was carefully crafted to conform to all of the elements of these real-life people and events while filling in the details with a story.

What do you think? Who was Cain? What kind of man was he? What can we learn from the Biblical record?

Read and consider the other Biblical references to Cain:

• 1 John 3:11-12

Why did Cain murder Abel according to this passage?

• Hebrews 11:4

Here we learn about Abel's offering. What do we see about Cain?

Read and consider these other passages related to Cain:

The following passages describe false teachers and people who turn from worshiping God and idolize their own desires. In Jude 1:11, Cain is compared to this type of person.

Jude 1:5-16

2 Peter 2 (a similar passage to Jude 1:5-16)

Romans 1:18-32

• As Cain is portrayed in *Refuge*, what qualities from these passages showed in his life?

• What type of man do you think Cain was? Does *Refuge* give an accurate portrayal?

• Cain presented an offering to God and followed an outward form of religion, yet his heart was not right with God. How is he like a person who attends church and claims to be a Christian while living a life of hypocrisy and hardheartedness?

• Is there hope for such a person? Can God show mercy?

Read and consider the following passage about Cain's descendants:

Genesis 4:17-24

What do you think?

What do we learn about Cain from his descendants?

• What kind of people were Cain's descendants?

• What were their gifts, skills, and aptitudes? From whom would they have inherited these?

• How did they gift mankind with their creativity?

• Cain introduced the sin of murder into humanity. What new sin did his descendant Lamech introduce? God gave Adam one wife. What did Cain's offspring Lamech do?

For any questions regarding the early events of mankind's history: http://www.answersingenesis.org/ and/or http://www.icr.org/

Discussion Guide and Meditations about Lilith

Consider this passage: The facts about Cain's wife

"And the LORD put a mark on Cain, lest any who found him should attack him. Then Cain went away from the presence of the Lord and settled in the land of Nod, east of Eden. Cain knew his wife, and she conceived and bore Enoch. When he built a city, he called the name of the city after the name of his son, Enoch." Genesis 4:15b-17 (ESV).

What do you think?

• When did the real-life Cain and his wife have their first child?

• What was the timing of Cain's marriage? How do we know?

• What might the birth of his firstborn tell us, considering that the prevention of conception and birth control did not exist at this point in human history?

Lilith's Name: The Legends

Moses recorded the first five books of the Bible—the Pentateuch—over two thousand years after creation. The Old Testament was inspired by the Holy Spirit; therefore, Genesis contains the factual and infallible account of the early history of mankind. There we have the facts. Genesis is the God-given account of the creation and these first events in our human history.

The Genesis 4:15-17 contains the only factual information we know about Cain's wife. We don't know her real name. The use of the name "Lilith" for Cain's wife is my nod to the wealth of mythology on the subject. "Lilith" is a Hebrew word with a history. It is used in Isaiah 34:14 and means "a night specter." It is not a person's name, but is a Hebrew word associated with a type of demon that inhabits the desert. What does such a name have to do with Cain's wife?

The first people were ancient Sumerians and Akkadians. Adam and Eve were not Jews. All humans are their descendants. They lived in Mesopotamia, also known as Sumer. The ancient Sumerian and Akkadian pre-Hebrew cultures were Adam and Eve's descendants to the tenth generation down to Noah, and they were Noah's descendants in Mesopotamia after the Flood. All people descended from Adam first and then from Noah. The Jewish people are the offspring of Abraham, the first man to be called a Hebrew. He lived near the Sumerian city of Ur.

Long before Moses recorded the opening pages of the Bible, these first people on the earth all shared a common history, language, and folklore based on oral tradition, including accounts of their shared experiences of creation, of the worldwide flood, and of the events immediately afterward. Because these events are humanity's common history, they were passed down verbally in the histories of ancient peoples all over the earth.

The Sumerian King List quite possibly detailed Cain's lineage. In their dialect the first king's name was Alulim, the first of eight (or ten, depending on the source) kings who lived incredibly long lives and ruled in a walled city in the days before "the Flood swept over" the land. The Sumerians and Akkadians had a myth about a female demon named Lilitu, a name similar to Lilith. The Epic of Gilgamesh, a Sumerian history legend, mentioned this female demon.

Over the centuries, these Sumerian legends were incorporated into ancient Jewish writings, such as the Babylonian Talmud. Here rabbis interpreted and commented on the Scriptures (including "lilith" from Isaiah 34:14). Just as commentators today offer their opinions on Scripture, so these rabbis offered theirs. These writings were not Scripture.

Though modern scholars argue over these sources, the fact remains that these murky legends were morphed into Jewish mythical folklore. Because these were only stories, of course the details varied, as is the case with all ancient mythology. These are not facts.

Since we do not know Cain's wife's name, I chose to use the name "Lilith" for two reasons:

1) The Hebrew word is used in the Old Testament in ways that prompted storytelling—ancient fiction that sprang from fear of the unknown demonic world.

2) These stories then became attached to Sumerian and Akkadian pre-Hebrew legends and myths associated with Cain's wife. These were then incorporated into Jewish stories.

For more information on Lilith visit the author's website:
http://showknowgrow.com/a-novel-journey-mythology-and-lilith/

Why use a name of myth and legend?
Refuge is a fictional retelling of a Biblical story, filling in the gaps with details that might have happened while adhering to the factual Biblical framework. In writing a story that is linked to a true Biblical account, it was imperative that I strive for accuracy. Since ancient legends were birthed around the Sumerian and

Akkadian campfires of Adam and Eve's descendants, I had to consider what non-recorded events or actions could have sparked a legend.

The storytelling of both friends and foes of Cain and his wife would have birthed the myths, and they would have been passed down generationally. As I studied, I began to imagine the type of real-life behavior a strong and misunderstood actual woman—Cain's wife—could have exhibited, leading her remembrance to be objectified, demonized, and mythologized. What kind of a woman would marry Cain and leave their family to live with him after he had killed their brother? What might motivate her? I attempted to build a strong female character who could have provoked a legend.

What do you think?

- Why would the wife of such a man spark speculation?
- What about the woman who would marry Cain might prompt curiosity? Is it the man himself? Or is it the question of what kind of woman would attach herself to him?
- What about Cain's wife and her actions, as I have portrayed her in *Refuge*, might be fodder for storytelling if this were an era of campfires and oral traditions?
- Were you inspired by Lilith's unwavering love for Cain? Or did her continual forgiveness of his violent flaws trouble you?
- What did you learn from Lilith?

More information, if you're interested:

A concise Bible-based source about this myth is contained in *Biblical Demonology* by Merrill F. Unger, Kregel, Grand Rapids, 1994.

Use online search engines to research Lilith and Jewish mythology.

Discussion Guide and Meditations about Abel:

Abel fills this novel, even though he dies early in the story. He is humble and self-effacing, trying to do what is best for everyone. Through no fault of his own, he is caught up in his older brother's rage spiral as Cain struggles with his conscience and with the unseen evil forces arrayed against him. Abel is the victim of Cain's approval-based religious efforts and failures. After his death, Abel's murder shapes Cain's repentance, his city, and his succeeding decisions.

What does the Bible say about Abel?

Though Abel was on history's stage for a shorter time than Cain and he left no descendants, Jesus spoke of him, and he appears in the Faith Hall of Fame of Hebrews 11. As the first victim of violence, his blood is used in a comparison to illustrate the redemptive value of Christ's blood.

Read and consider these passages:

Genesis 4:2-11, 25-26

Judgment on the hypocritical scribes and Pharisees: Matthew 23:29-36; Luke 11:47-51

Through his faith, Abel still speaks to us: Hebrews 11:4, 6

Hebrews 12:18-24

- What do we learn about the eternal value and example of a godly life?
- For what did Abel's blood cry out? What is the better word spoken by Christ's blood?
- What about Abel's actions and attitudes in *Refuge* inspired you? How do you feel he modeled righteousness in his life?

Meditations on Cain's repentance:

Read and consider this Biblical exchange between God and Cain:

"Cain spoke to Abel his brother. And when they were in the field, Cain rose up against his brother Abel and killed him. Then the Lord said to Cain, 'Where is Abel your brother?' He said, 'I do not know; am I my brother's keeper?' And the Lord said, 'What have you done? The voice of your brother's blood is crying to me from the ground. And now you are cursed from the ground, which has opened its mouth to receive your brother's blood from your hand. When you work the ground, it shall no longer yield to you its strength. You shall be a fugitive and a wanderer on the earth.' Cain said to the Lord, 'My punishment is greater than I can bear. *Behold, you have driven me today away from the ground, and from your face I shall be hidden. I shall be a fugitive and a wanderer on the earth, and whoever finds me will kill me.' Then the Lord said to him, 'Not so! If anyone kills Cain, vengeance shall be taken on him sevenfold.' And the Lord put a mark on Cain, lest any who found him should attack him. Then Cain went away from the presence of the Lord and settled in the land of Nod, east of Eden." (Genesis 4:8-16, ESV). [*4:13 Footnote: Or "My guilt is too great to bear"]

What do you think?
Did the real-life Cain repent?
What is the evidence for repentance?
What is the evidence against?
Is it possible to be forgiven for this type of sin?

Why Redeem Cain?
God is capable of redeeming anyone. He is willing. The One who would crush the serpent's head has come—Jesus Christ. Fulfilling all the prophesies from the very first one given in the Garden, God put on flesh, lived a perfect life, and died to redeem all who put their trust in Him alone. We're all sinners, just like

Cain. None of us can live a righteous life. Christ did it for us. His perfect life and His sacrifice on our behalf were accepted by God. He paid for our sins and rose from the dead to legally justify us in God's eyes, thus crushing Satan's head. In this tale, the One holding Abel in His arms in Heaven hinted at this.

As I researched theological material, I found that, though most Biblical scholars think Cain justified his sin rather than repented, they puzzled over God's response if that was the case. Enough scholars believed that Cain's words to God and God's response in Genesis 4:13-15 might indicate repentance and God's response to repentance that I felt I could pursue this in a fictional story. Most English versions translate Cain's words as "My punishment is more than I can bear!" or "My punishment is greater than I can bear!" However, the footnotes of the English Standard Version, Crossway Bibles, and the Amplified Bible, Zondervan, note that some ancient versions read: "My guilt is too great to bear!" or "My guilt is too great to be forgiven!"

"The fact that the Lord's response was one of mercy and protection suggests that the author understood Cain's words as those of a repentant sinner. By themselves Cain's words do not necessarily suggest repentance, but the Lord's response ('Very well; if anyone kills Cain, he will suffer vengeance seven times over,' NIV mg.) implies that Cain's words in v. 13 are words of repentance."[4]

Did Cain, in fact, actually repent? Only God knows. Not much literary space is given to Cain's life. As far as we are concerned, whether Cain repented or not is immaterial. It affected only him and his eternal destiny. The effect on humanity was the same. As with other notorious sinners who came later, his sin is held up as a deterrent, and God brought judgment because of it.

What played out in Cain's family is what we often see in families where a progenitor has committed a life-altering transgression, regardless of that ancestor's repentance. Sin

---

4   The Expositor's Bible Commentary, Twelve Volumes on Interactive CD-ROM, Frank E. Gaebelein, General Editor, Zondervan, 2006.

affects future generations. This is one reason God hates sin—it harms the children.

In *Refuge* we see the effects on Adam's family. Likewise, David's sons demonstrated hardening toward sin (2 Samuel 13-19, etc.), because of the adultery, murder, and other sins David had committed, though David repented (2 Samuel 12). Similarly, Manasseh's son Amon carried on the atrocities his father had implemented before his repentance, walking in all the previous idolatrous ways of his father, as if Manasseh had never repented (2 Chronicles 33).

Often, those who are most affected by a sin are the ones whose pain prompts them to seek vengeance, thus destroying their lives through bitterness and creating a sin paradigm in their own families. These are the dynamics I crafted into this fictional story with the siblings who were closest to Abel, and which I develop more fully in the tale that follows this one. In my opinion, the rapid spread of evil over the face of the earth was driven by this first murder, not only through Cain's descendants justifying sin, as we see in his family tree (Genesis 4:19-24), but by the way it affected all of Cain and Abel's siblings and their families, increasing violence through attempts at retribution. More families were corrupted by Cain's murder of Abel than just the direct descendants of Cain. If it had been otherwise, more than eight people would have gotten onto the ark and God would not have had to destroy the earth with a flood.

What do you think?

A story Jesus might tell:
Refuge is a tale of murder, revenge, and broken dreams: Can we ever find God if we kill someone we love and have to run? All of us face moments in our lives when we realize the damage our sins have done to ourselves and to others may not ever be repaired. Is God there?

My story illustrates the power of God's mercy. This is a redemption story. With fiction, a writer can produce a "good Samaritan" type story, one where the person we expect to be the bad guy is transformed to become the good guy. Jesus used this technique. It shocks and gets across a point we can't in any other way. God is able and wants to forgive any sin. He wants broken people to turn to Him. Staying true to every Biblical reference of Cain, I crafted my fictional story based on God's decision to grant him mercy.

What do you think?

- Does this story give you hope that you too can be forgiven? Can you also turn to God and receive forgiveness through belief in His Promised One, Jesus Christ?
- Do you have painful regret over something you have done that has damaged others?
- Can God forgive you? What do you think?
- What will God's forgiveness look like in your life? How will you respond?

The purpose of the mark and the city:

There is much curiosity about the mark God put on Cain. What was it? What did it look like? Literature portrays it in a variety of forms, usually as a festering, ugly scar. I aimed in a different direction. The mark in my story is the Tetragrammaton, the four-letter Hebrew representation of God's own name Yahweh: YHWH. In *Refuge*, God marks Cain with His own name in a written language not yet invented when these events occurred. This mark is a sign that Cain belongs to God and that God will draw him and transform his heart, giving him the necessary faith in the coming One who will crush the serpent's head. Salvation has always been by faith, and those who believe belong to God, marked with His name.

There is also a theological idea that the city itself might have been the mark. Later, in Jewish history, God established cities of refuge for protection from vengeance, allowing time for due process. This first city offered the same: protection, time, and lessening of bloodshed. Cain's city may have served as a foreshadowing or type of the coming Jewish cities of refuge.

Since there is no eyewitness account of Cain's mark, there will always be speculation.

Read and consider these two passages:

Genesis 4:15-18

Numbers 35:9-34

What do you think? How could the city be like a mark for protection?

These scriptures and sources were consulted:

The Holy Bible, translations: ESV, NIV, NASB, and Amplified. No Scripture text is quoted verbatim within the novel. Conversations are paraphrased. Passages consulted:

Genesis 4:2-17

Job 1, 2

Hebrews 11:4; 12:18-24

Matthew 23

Luke 11:47-51; 16:19-31

1 John 3:11-12, 15

Jude 4-11; 2 Peter 2

Psalm 32, 34, 51

Song of Songs 2:3

Lamentations 3:31-33

Answers in Genesis website:

http://www.answersingenesis.org/

Arnold, Clinton E. "A Collision of Worlds: Evil Spirits Then and Now," Knowing & Doing. C. S. Lewis Institute, Summer 2009.

Bauer, Susan Wise, The History of the Ancient World, W. W. Norton & Company, Inc., New York, NY, 2007.

Dickason, C. Fred. *Angels: Elect & Evil*. Moody Press, Chicago, IL, 1975, 1995.

ESV quote in this study guide: Scripture quotations marked (ESV) are from the ESV® Bible (The Holy Bible, English Standard Version®), copyright 2001 by Crossway Bibles, a publishing ministry of Good News Publishers.

First Book of Enoch, extra-biblical, pseudepigraphical Jewish literature.

Gaebelein, Frank E., Editor. *The Expositor's Bible Commentary*: Twelve-Volume Interactive CD-ROM. Zondervan, Grand Rapids, MI, 2006.

Hamilton, Victor P., Editor. *The New International Commentary on the Old Testament (NICOT), The Book of Genesis, Chapters 1 – 17*. William B. Eerdmans Publishing Company, Grand Rapids, MI, 1990.

Jones, Brian Gordon. *Christian Faith & Modern Family*. Brookpointe Ministries, 2013.

Lewis, C.S. *The Screwtape Letters*. Harper, San Francisco, 1996.

Lutzer, Erwin W. *The Serpent of Paradise*. Moody Publishers, Chicago, IL, 1996.

Unger, Merrill F. *Biblical Demonology*. Kregel Publications, Grand Rapids, MI, 1994.

Waltke, Bruce K. with Cathi J. Fredricks. *Genesis: A Commentary*. Zondervan, Grand Rapids, MI, 2001.

CPSIA information can be obtained at www.ICGtesting.com
Printed in the USA
BVOW09s0408250214

345874BV00002B/49/P